TO DEFY AN OATH

SARA SULTANE

To Defy an Oath

Library of Congress and Publisher's Cataloging-in-Publication data

Identifiers: LCCN: 2025907325 | ISBN: 979-8-9859902-6-3 (hardcover) | 979-8-9859902-7-0 (paperback) | 979-8-9859902-8-7 (ebook)

Subjects: LCSH Iranian Americans–Fiction. | Witches–Fiction. | Magic–Fiction. | Love stories. | Paranormal fiction. | Fantasy fiction. | BISAC FICTION / Fantasy / Romance | FICTION / Occult & Supernatural | FICTION / Romance / Multicultural & Interracial | FICTION / Romance / Paranormal / Witches| FICTION / Middle Eastern & Arab American | FICTION / Romance / Erotic

Classification: LCC PS3619.U4555 T6 2025 | DDC 813.6–dc23

For more information, visit:

www.sarasultane.com

Content Warnings

This book contains scenes of sexual assault and dubious consent, PTSD symptoms (including flashbacks and panic attacks), anxiety, murder, violence, blood, kidnapping, drowning, and misogyny.

Reader discretion is advised.

AUTHOR'S NOTE

Dear reader,

This book shows my love of food, traveling, languages, music, and different cultures. Some parts will make sense, others might not.

Throughout the book I have sprinkled songs that inspired specific scenes. I can only hope you will enjoy reading this book as much as I enjoyed writing it.

For those who are lost in dreams . . .

ONE

Maya

The world was beyond saving the day I set eyes on Adam. With him, it was instantaneous; there was an unshakable feeling that somehow we were destined to cross paths. He was as attracted to me as I was to him. Both of us involuntarily seeking something in the other. Adam was unable to help himself because his soul needed to unite with its other half. But I would be lying if I said there wasn't an uncontrollable pull to him.

Once, I thought he was the only person who could put my broken pieces together, the only one who could reach what was left of my true self. But truth be told, I had forgotten who I was—or perhaps I never knew. I was trying to force something that was never there to begin with until the rose-tinted glasses faded before my eyes.

After I lost my soul to him, something shifted, something I couldn't put my finger on. I thought I was being crazy, not feeling like I belonged with Adam or in that home. Yet I still clung to mere hope and fell deeper and deeper into the illusion of love. It turned out I couldn't trust my heart, that I could not grasp the true concept of love. I didn't think anything could come between us, but all it took was releasing a soul.

I thought I would feel something when I found out he was the last one I had to pursue. The one whose blood was the final task to fulfill the prophecy. I realized I wasn't myself anymore because I wasn't scared for him, wasn't even remorseful. Sure, it felt good to see him again, but Adam wasn't my missing piece—he had never been.

I was the one with the other half of his soul, the one carrying what he had been missing all his life. We were never meant to be. We were attracted to each other because of the soul that connected us, the soul that wanted wholeness, the sad reality of the twin flames.

After my death and rebirth, I spent a long time reading, evaluating, and deciding what my truth would be. I read up on prophecies, trying to decipher their meaning. Initially, they stated the same thing, that a Sāher would lose her soul and end the Dūshev legacy. One in particular said,

She who forcefully bears the soul of our enemy must release it to the thirteenth son on the thirty-third day of Nowruz with the blessing of Goddess Ishtar. She will sacrifice our blood and flesh to retrieve what is rightfully ours and bring order to nature.

I had no idea who or what I was dealing with. I was anticipating a battle, as I thought we would all be at war and that my family would kill Adam first because he was the thirteenth son.

The reality was neither the Sāhers nor the spirits cared what happened to Adam so long I was aligned with the prophecy. I wanted to believe in its greater good. Yet, there were days I couldn't tell up from down. Most days, I doubted if my thoughts were my own, while on other days, I didn't care.

In my search for the truth, I found vague descriptions of what a twin flame was, and for a time, I tried to make it fit. I had dreamed about it enough times to convince myself it was important, that Adam and I were twin flames, but his soul was never mine to keep. I was just a vessel of convenience. In the end, I couldn't do anything.

I didn't claim it was easy to turn my back on him and betray him like it did. He had never intentionally hurt me, and even when he had the chance to kill me, he didn't. I saw it in his eyes, understood how he felt, but the more time passed, the less I cared.

It was malicious of me to feed into the ruse of the twin flames, even more evil to sleep with him for one thing only. I only had one goal and didn't care how I succeeded. I needed Adam to trust me, to see someone he used to know, someone who loved him. With enough truth mixed into the lies, he was eating from my hand.

When I walked out of the cabin, I felt at my lowest. I had crossed the line and would live to regret it.

Regardless of the betrayal, I gave him enough of the truth to help him stay out of this suicide mission I was on. This wasn't an act of kindness. Blood was on my hands, blood I couldn't wash off no matter how hard I tried. Perhaps it was my way of repenting. After all, I killed two of his brothers. If I hadn't told him the whole ordeal, he might have tried to kill me and cause his own death.

Luckily, he stayed behind, probably still in shock and gutted. Eventually, he would come to understand nothing was left of the Maya he used to know, only fragments were left behind. I was like a shell, one so desperate to find my missing soul, knowing full well I had none. I was nothing—less than nothing, a marionette in the hands of my ancestors.

٢
TWO

Leyla

Cursed with infertility, I had no right to become the next *Kāheneh azam*, a high priestess. All I wanted was to teach my family the true path, to be the leading beacon for the next generation and make sure our daughters continued in our footsteps. So, I made a deal with the jinn.

My sister was pregnant with her first daughter when it happened. Her husband worked abroad, which helped tremendously. I had barely turned sixteen when my sister and I fled to a village, to hide from prying eyes. For us to be pregnant at the same time was a coincidence beyond my wildest imaginations. Claiming my daughter out of wedlock was impossible then.

It wasn't long before the midwife took notice, and despite her disapproval, she helped me deliver my angel Shirin. Regardless of her help, I wouldn't let my secret see the light of day. I made sure it was carried to the grave and not spread by the tongue of a common midwife. My sister never forgave me for the death of the midwife. But she took my Shirin in like she was her own, raised her, clothed her, fed her, and loved her.

My punishment was that I had no claim on Shirin. My daughter grew up in a happy home and decided it was all that mattered. At least I had a daughter with my blood running through her veins. Only when my sister died was I allowed to step in her place and become the High Priestess.

Having Shirin came with a cost, one offspring to fulfill the wish of the great Kāheneh azam, Parvaneh and to split the fabric of the universe. *A prophecy carved in flesh, a fate sealed in blood. A daughter long sought, a wish bestowed. A soul yet to be claimed, a death etched in sand. All falls to one who must see it to the end.*

I was young when I made that bargain, and I had no idea what I promised in turn for a daughter who secured my title.

Time ate at my patience and thinned my skin down to the bone. I could wait no longer. I let the jinn claim her soul before she was born and made sure everything aligned with the prophecy that I had set in motion.

My intentions were questionable, yes, but in the end, my path aligned with the greater good of all Sāhers. I acted on the High Priestess's command, making sure the Dūshevs never took another soul, never broke another home, never had powers that didn't belong to them. These powers belonged to Mother Nature, to the universe, not man. While we borrowed the gifts Earth granted us, they stole, and while we repaid mother Earth, they clawed and stole even more.

The Dūshevs had no redemption. Even if they never took another soul, their bloodline was impure. This was the doing of Fyodor Pavlenko, and all would pay the price.

I could have lived on without a daughter and let this prophecy befall another coven, but I was selfish and didn't believe another coven deserved the glory, or would have the resilience we did. In the end, it was an honor to fulfill a prophecy by Parvaneh. Death and pain followed, but we would be remembered in the books. Tales would be told about the priestess who led her coven to greatness, the priestess who devoted herself to the practice.

I would make sure the prophecy was fulfilled and that Maya's final act would be to drain the chalice of blood. They would all know what the Sāhers were made of.

٣

THREE

MAYA

In a justified turn of events, everything went to hell unexpectedly. Before this moment, I never questioned why all my poorly executed plans never got me in trouble, never questioned why everything seemed to go according to plan. Perhaps I expected it to because of a promised victory, a prophecy, or because I was the chosen one. I should've known better and been more cautious.

In the back seat of a vehicle, completely covered by fabric, I was lying on my side. My arms and legs were numb, like I hadn't moved for hours. I didn't know if this was reality or another illusion. The air I kept reusing for my shallow breath was heavy, like I was breathing inside a plastic bag. Then panic set in because I could barely move my limbs.

I'm in a body bag! Whoever put me here thinks I'm dead.

The last thing I could recall was leaving Adam in his cabin. I was putting on my clothes, picking up the jewelry I so theatrically got rid of, then kissed him goodbye one last time and walked out.

Did I ever make it to the rental?

Everything else was a hazy dream. I had a faint memory of sitting on the side of a deserted road drinking water and another of being helped into a bathroom by someone.

A bump in the road rattled me back to reality. Slipping in and out of consciousness, I was still inside the presumed body bag, taking humid, unsatisfying breaths. My arms and legs wouldn't take commands—they could've been amputated for all I knew. I wasn't bound, but my strength was limited, to say the least.

I tried to push away the fabric from my face, but every movement was a struggle. My jewelry and watch were gone. My head was pounding, my clothes drenched in sweat.

They couldn't have been Dūshevs. I would have known if they were—I would have felt it. They must have hired bounty hunters to get me—but how did they sneak up on me and knock me out like that?

I'm a Sāher, for God's sake, and not just a Sāher—the chosen one. I tried to focus on my breathing, searching within myself to find the source of my power and blow up this whole car if I had to.

I dove deep into my core but nothing. To my surprise, the well of my powers was drained. I was on my own and wholly defenseless, physically and mentally.

I had nothing, neither my own powers nor my ancestors'. They had taken all my jewelry, either because it was real gold and they were looking for profit or because they were given the task by the Dūshevs.

The latter was more probable because my worthless watch was gone, too. A tiny piece of Firuzeh would have been inside of it had they caught me a month ago. If I hadn't taken precautions, I wouldn't even be swinging in and out of consciousness but would probably be dead.

The last time Sepideh and I returned to Iran, I had this overwhelming feeling of being suffocated. Like I had foreseen something terrible was about to happen. If only I had been half as good at decoding my visions, I could have been more prepared.

Paranoia led me to the dentist in Iran. I paid good money to place the smallest stone from the watch into my wisdom tooth and covered it up like a cavity. It took a whole lot of convincing because the dentist couldn't fathom the idea of something so ridiculous. Reluctantly, he agreed, saying that the composite filling might not stick to the stone.

Without the Firuzeh pieces on my possession, every time I closed my eyes, all I saw was a void, an emptiness I couldn't explain. Whatever they had drugged me with worked well.

When I first parted with my jewelry in front of Adam, I wasn't sure if this tiny piece of Firuzeh would be enough to keep me alive. It was a huge gamble to make such a scene. I blacked out the moment I took them off. Maybe the same had happened this time because they were forced off me. It would explain why I was so drowsy. My body was still so weak I could barely move.

The car suddenly stopped, and two doors opened and closed, which made me realize I hadn't heard anyone speaking since I woke up.

Another door opened, and someone's hands yanked at my ankles. The cover was removed from my face like a weighted blanket. That's when I realized I wasn't in a body bag. I saw nothing but stars in the black sky.

Two male figures towered over me. I wanted to scream, to resist, but I had nothing left in me. They didn't look bothered or surprised that I was awake.

One was a tall, skinny guy with a pointed face that was scrunched up like he was uncomfortable, the other built like a Greek god.

"She's awake!" said the skinny one, covering my face before dragging me out of the vehicle.

I couldn't tell if they were Dūshev. If I could just touch one of them, I would know. Perhaps then, I could steal some power and have a fair chance. Though, if they were avoiding my touch, they probably knew who I was and what I could do. It also ruled out them being regular kidnappers.

The skinny guy carried me on his shoulder, and I had no energy to thrash against him.

"We're here, witch!" one said.

The climate was different. We couldn't possibly be in Europe anymore. It wasn't nearly as cold as it should have been.

A door creaked open, and we passed through them. A cold draft hit my body, and I started to shiver. My clothes were drenched in sweat, so this would probably make me sick.

They hauled me up a set of stairs, and when we finally stopped, one knocked on a door, which screeched open.

"They are waiting for you," a female voice crooned.

Panic set in because it finally dawned on me how much trouble I was in. The guy carrying me let go midair. I dropped to the floor, and the cover fell apart around me, revealing an opulent throne-like room of a castle. The gigantic space was only lit dimly by the candles along the casting shadows and reflections from the crystal chandelier. Long tables sat in the center, forming the three sides of a square. Half a dozen men were sat on one end farthest from us. There was so much to take in I almost felt dizzy. A weight bore down on my chest, like a heavy blanket.

"Please, make yourself comfortable," one said and looked away from me. "Zaki, remove the cover from her."

The fabric was pulled from under me, and I rolled on my stomach. It took me a good minute to get to a sitting position and look up.

These are definitely not human!

But I felt nothing, and that almost scared me more.

Once I had determined they were all Dūshev, it was easy to spot Adam's father. He was the one with the graying hair and crocket nose, sitting in the middle, next to his elder sons.

"How do we know it's her?" one asked, looking at the man I suspected to be Adam's father.

"Oh, it's definitely her."

His voice came from behind me, his footsteps deliberately slow.

I was too much in denial to turn, but before I could consider it, he gripped the hair on the back of my head, and I was hauled up in the air. A raspy scream escaped me as he pulled me closer to him, forcing me to look him in the eyes. Tears prickled my eyelids. I guess I had it coming.

"You could have had me," Adam sneered into my ear before dropping me.

I collapsed at his feet, utterly at his mercy.

Adam's father was mere steps away from us.

"Adam," he said and embraced him.

I'm so screwed.

If only I could've channeled my ancestors or produce power to defend myself. There were so many of them that all hope seemed lost. I had thought I could siphon power from one, but when Adam touched me, it hadn't worked. My powers were gone, and even teleporting didn't work.

Dragging myself backward, I tried to push closer to the open door since they were all consumed by victory, laughing and chatting as if I wasn't there.

Funny how I thought I stood a chance against so many of them.

"Oh, darling, you look pathetic. Surely, you must have considered something other than dragging yourself across the floor."

I could smell his cologne before he fully emerged behind me.

The chatter stopped.

"What the hell is he doing here?" Adam snapped.

"Aldridge has made amends. Everything he did was try to prevent the prophecy from unfolding. He was trying to kill her before it started. Your brother deserves a second chance, just like you," Adam's father said, looking at Adam. "We will persevere as long as we help one another."

Adam didn't seem thrilled but didn't say anything after that.

His father glanced at me again. "Until we figure out how to stop this prophecy, you are our guest—with restrictions, of course."

"You mean prisoner."

My voice came out like chalk against a blackboard. In the same breath, I was hauled fifteen feet in the air by an invisible force while my air was completely cut off. I wanted to squirm and gasp for air, but I couldn't move an inch.

"You will not talk back to me. Under my roof, you will speak when spoken to."

He let go, and I collapsed.

My right leg and kneecap took a severe hit against the marble. It hurt so much the pain went through my leg and up my spine.

Adam didn't flinch with all this violence committed against me—and why would he? Maybe I was looking at him, hoping to find someone I used to know, but he wasn't there—and maybe I deserved that. I gave him all the answers, everything he needed to know to stay alive and away from this war, and he still sold me to his father. I didn't want him to get hurt in the mix, only wanted him to survive.

Before I took his blood and rubbed it between my fingers, I made sure he understood that if he killed me, he would eventually die himself. My sparing him apparently meant nothing.

"Take her to the third floor."

A needle was jammed in my arm before I could register the Dūshev at my side.

۴

FOUR

ALDRIDGE

Something wasn't right. I couldn't quite put my finger on what it was. Of course she was the chosen one and would have different powers than the others in her coven, but there was something off about her. Perhaps it was that she was without a soul. My father was observing me himself. He demanded firsthand knowledge he couldn't get without torture—at least he was smart enough not to implement that interrogation technique. We weren't equipped to deal with the wrath of a thousand witches.

If my father could extract my knowledge and thoughts by force, he would have done so long ago.

I sat on a chair beside her bed and put my hand on her forehead. The moment I touched her, I was met with both darkness and relief. It was a bizarre sensation, molecules buzzing under my skin. She was such a powerful witch I felt like I was being drained.

I tried my best to filter through the darkness and fog, but she had been heavily drugged and hadn't woken up since being injected with the sedative.

"There is nothing for me to see," I told him.

"You barely gave it a shot."

"The dose you gave her was probably too high." I got up. "When it wears off, we can try again."

The drug was to suppress her powers, to keep her in a groggy state, to keep her in line. My father wasn't taking any chances. He wanted the stone before killing her. He wasn't pleased with my argument but relented. We tried again a couple of times the following days until we finally had a breakthrough. My father was there every time, and every day, I gave him descriptions of what I saw and how she pursued the prophecy. How she was beaten up by Idris, how she tricked Kristian, and how Adam was present in her life during those days.

"The girl and Adam, what has been exchanged between them?" my father asked, anger coating his words.

"Nothing in particular. He was trying to stop her, but he didn't know what she had planned," I answered truthfully.

Adam was in love with her, wanted to pull her out, not knowing how entangled she was. He wanted to run away and never look back—such delusional aspirations.

"Be honest with me instead of protecting your brother," my father commanded.

"You might have guessed that I'm not particularly thrilled with Adam. I'm not protecting him. He has always been oblivious to everything around him, and all he did was try to help her because he didn't know who she truly was."

My father listened, stroking his beard and staring out of the window. "He can't be alone with her," he whispered before looking back at me. "Find me the final piece." He ad'hāred out.

Out of curiosity, I went back into her mind, lurking in her dream world. Contrary to belief, I couldn't look through memories but could only be present in the dream world and, from there, lead in the direction I wanted to go. I could also create false visions, emotions, and sensations within the dreams, but that was a secret I kept to myself.

Most of the time, I was just an observer in a theater who played whatever dream she had. I could engage with her, but that required more from me than I was willing to give.

Most nights, her dreams were meaningless and abstract. She often dreamed of flying fast through the clouds or swimming in deep, dark oceans. Some of her dreams, I didn't disclose to my father—I didn't want to strip her bare for no reason. They were dreams of her family, of the time spent with her brother, and the guilt chafing her skin. She felt responsible for the boy when he failed his tests in school, as if she was supposed to be the one teaching and raising him.

I hated being in her head, hated that I had to do this for my father just to be in his good graces. Ev never faced punishments—the girls never did—but we were different. We were Dūshev. The more time I spent inside her head, the more it seemed she was a victim. From what I had gathered, this prophecy had chosen her rather than her dedicating her life to it.

What a life it must be.

One day, you meet someone you like, and the next, he takes your soul. Then your life turns upside down. From there on, all the Dūshevs she had met were either trying to hunt, harm, or kill her, including myself.

Would she have gone on this quest had I not scared her to death? I was one of the first few Dūshevs she met, and compared to Adam and Elias, I was the devil.

Of course she went running back into his arms, where she felt the safest, when there was nowhere else for her to hide.

I had a hand in this prophecy, whether I liked it or not. Even without the persistence of Dissie and her elaborate plan, I would have gone that far to get my soul back from Adam. I was desperate and relentless. Nothing could keep me from getting my soul back.

I left the girl in the maid's room and locked the door. Anyone could adʿhār in, and it made me uneasy to think about. If I tampered with the wards, my father would know because no one else had a witch for a mother. Of course, my father had no clue how much she had taught us. And I liked to keep it that way. The less he knew, the better.

Obviously, I couldn't keep all my secrets. He had his eyes on me the moment I was born without a soul.

A Dūshev without a soul was unheard of. In the beginning, he tried to give me multiple souls, only they wouldn't settle in my core. My mother told me he accused her of cheating—he thought I wasn't his until I started to look more like my brothers.

Later, I inherited the practice from my mother's side, and suddenly, my father was interested again.

I could walk in dreams at a very young age. When my father discovered this, he would ask me to go on these missions before I was old enough to understand what I was doing. I was merely happy to spend time with him because we rarely saw him when we were kids.

One time, he wanted information from a man he kept hostage, a murderer. His dreams were of his elaborate fantasies of dismembering women. I had walked into any child's worst nightmare, and I couldn't unsee it. As a six-year-old, I had a hard time distinguishing between the dream realm and reality.

When my mother found out what I was doing, I wasn't allowed to go with him again. No matter what I said, I couldn't convince her. I promised I would be good and wouldn't cry again, but she wouldn't budge. My father was only allowed to see us at her house from that day. Things changed when she passed.

I went looking for Edgar and found him with our father in his office. I had hoped to find him alone, but reporting to my father directly would please him more.

"What have you uncovered?" my father asked.

"Nothing useful. Her mind is a whirlwind of trauma, and there is a lot to dig through."

"Did you steer her in the right direction, like we discussed?"

"No matter what you have been told, she is a witch. If I force it, she might sense the intrusion and lock me out completely."

"Very well. We will continue tomorrow evening." He turned his attention to Edgar, dismissing me. "Perhaps you can oversee it from tomorrow."

Yes!

The idea was to get Edgar to oversee everything so my father would get off my back. He didn't quite trust me—not that I expected any less; it wasn't something to worry about.

Even when my father put a price on my head, he didn't put much effort into finding me. Yes, he had casually told my brothers to find me but hadn't bothered to burden

Everie with Dūshev matters. He knew I would occasionally see her. Still, he never questioned her, never stationed anyone near the house to see if I would show up.

Everie lived in our mother's house, and I even had a room there. He could easily have threatened me with her, but he didn't. The consequence was too great for him because he would lose her, and he wasn't willing to risk it. Ev was sacred to him, and I was grateful for that.

All his daughters were sacred, and he wouldn't let anyone come between his relationship with them. They were meant to be kept secret. The daughters weren't Dūshev and didn't possess the same powers as us, but they aged slowly like we did. They couldn't adhār, couldn't take souls, and had no control over the elements.

The few of my brothers who had a sister were instructed just as I had been to keep it secret. We weren't supposed to know about each other, but every once in a while, someone slipped and accidentally said something along the lines of *I'm meeting up with my sister.*

Perhaps my father thought the rivalry between his sons would trickle down and affect his daughters. That they would fight one another for his attention—which is why he devoted so much time to each of them.

He was genuinely invested in their lives, which wasn't something you could say about how he treated us. He was the only one to blame for his relationship with his sons, having created the environment for rank and rivalry.

We all fell victim to his schemes and manipulation. Edgar pulled me out of it. He wasn't much older than me but acted like the father none of us had. He knew how to handle my father, and in some twisted way, my father was the softest with him. He let Edgar take the lead in many situations, and he knew how much better we got along with Edgar. He didn't mind being the bad guy if the job was getting done—the job of taking souls.

My father had instilled in us from an early age that we were the backbone of humanity, that if we didn't take and give souls, society would collapse. We believed him because we had faith in him. Then Edgar became an elder, and little by little, he changed. It wasn't immediate, but we all noticed the change in our beloved brother. He was distant and spent more time with the elders than with us.

My father's demands grew with each passing day. If we weren't hunting souls, we were allowed to study or be a master for one of the younger ones. Many of us went to school and got one diploma after the other, but eventually, everyone fell into his claws and started taking souls. It wasn't the worst job, per se, but it was the most demanding. The masters weren't required to take as many souls as they were busy mentoring.

Other duties were positions you earned, not given. Only when we served him as soul takers could we request to be reassigned.

My father didn't want me to have other duties than taking souls. For years, he kept ignoring my requests, which made me question my father's methods. My mother's constant focus on the balance of nature kept looping in my head. Soul-taking was unnatural, which raised other ethical questions about our practice.

I confided in my sister, not without a vow, of course. We weren't allowed to tell them anything about the soul-taking. My father said it was for the best. When I told her, she broke out crying and demanded change.

I agreed to bring Edgar over, not knowing how he would react to what I had set in motion. The shock on Edgar's face was evident. He didn't say much but wanted time to think about it.

My sister, being stubborn, made him promise to return with a plan. She wasn't having it, and she believed in natural selection, which meant we ought to stay out of it.

Most of us knew of our wrongs. We saw the shells we left behind. Yet we were too cowardly to act on it, too scared to refuse our father.

That's when the resistance began. It all started with Ev and her determination. One after one, we initiated my brothers. The scheming began long before Edgar had told us the worst of it.

The first thing Ev focused on was making a potion that could mimic a soulless person. So, each case we hunted down was deemed fruitless. My father double-checked most cases and still couldn't figure out what he was doing wrong.

Of course it helped she was the greatest witch of her generation and thereafter. With my father's blood running in her veins and our mother's ancestry, Everie was no ordinary witch. Her mission was to bring an end to everything my father had built. She loved our father more than most of us, but she didn't believe he would change, so she took matters into her own hands.

Most of my brothers accepted this to be the right thing to do, but not everyone was as easily convinced. In fact, a few were just as dedicated as my father, and we almost blew it a couple of times.

Unfortunately, souls were still being taken at a rapid pace. In fact, more than ever in the past few decades. It wasn't until I stumbled upon the kidnappings and told Edgar about it that he came clean. Kidnappings occurred shortly after soul-taking for every child who hadn't received Ev's potion. Edgar knew of this but didn't want to add fuel to the fire, believing we were making progress, and didn't want Ev to know about it. This was my father's biggest scheme to date.

When Edgar became an elder, our father had bought a fully staffed medical clinic in Russia. According to Edgar, the facility harvested stem cells from patients for therapies like bone marrow transplants, cord blood banking, and regenerative medicine. After the clinic was sold, no public records existed of what was going on in there.

Only the elders were aware of my father's secret medical facility. It was a place where soulless boys were flown in on a private plane and escorted to the clinic in the dead of night. The facility was warded against adʿhāring and secured by military-style guards.

Edgar had found early studies about a boy whose soul had been taken. They had noticed a pattern in the aftermath, and my father discovered a way to use it to his advantage.

The trauma caused by the soul being forcefully removed caused the cells to mutate. The boys' appearances transformed, their skin smoother, and they became healthier than ever. Their vitality increased drastically.

It turned out my father was selling whatever was within their changed DNA as a treatment. The doctors would perform a biopsy, which involved taking a small solid core of bone marrow tissue. Then they isolated the cells from the tissue and sold the byproduct to a skincare company.

Since these kids were undergoing repeated and high-volume marrow extractions, they needed blood transfusions to stimulate marrow recovery. Unfortunately, the recovered marrow did not contain this magic element they needed. So, the soulless boys were used until they collapsed, and a new set would be admitted to the clinic.

The skincare company catered to the elite. They didn't ask any questions and were happily ignorant. Each treatment was the price of a small London townhouse.

Plenty of filthy rich people were more than happy to pay when they saw the results from the clinical trials. The once-off treatment restored vitality and appearance. A sixty-five-year-old could look like they were in their early thirties. For the wealthy, it was a small price to pay.

Stopping it required a lot of planning. Regrettably, I wasn't so patient. When I found the location, no thanks to Edgar, I was finally able to break in and let hell lose. My anger consumed me when I saw the state of some of those kids. I destroyed the place, which led to alarms going off.

This cost my father millions and millions of dollars. Of course my father found out. He didn't know my reasons, nor did he care. All he wanted was to make an example of me, which is why he put a bounty on me. Had he known that his rogue son was the root of the resistance, he would have had my head. He didn't acknowledge that I had found his secret facility, didn't even address why I was to be punished. He made sure I knew I wasn't welcome in his home unless I offered him my soul for a year as retribution. This was a technique he used on my brothers when we were younger. Only, back then, the punishment would last a day.

Even a day without a soul was unbearable, and to think he wanted me to willingly offer mine when I had only gotten mine after our mother passed.

I didn't want to jeopardize Ev and her relationship with him, so I didn't tell her and stopped visiting. The isolation was hard on me. I was drunk and careless the night I was found by Adam. I didn't have the slightest clue they were looking for me. Perhaps because I had tossed my phone into the river and never looked back. Edgar would have told me—many would, but they had no way of contacting me.

It was too late, and by then, Adam had disappeared. The following month, I was bedridden. You would think I was struck by lightning and had food poisoning at the same time.

When I finally regained my strength, I searched for Adam. I wanted revenge, and I didn't care who got hurt in the process. Of course, it didn't take me long to figure out where Adam was. I had never thought about his whereabouts up until that point.

Adam had been a Dūshev master and, apparently, was excellent at his job. Edgar told me he had a way with the younger generation. He had trained with a handful, with the latest one being Edgar's own son, Elias. I kept an eye on them. Even though I was feral, I was in a good enough headspace to know I didn't want to involve Elias into my mess.

Clearly, I hadn't been discreet enough, since Dissie found me. I was having breakfast at a quiet café when she approached me. At first glance, I had no idea what she was and, frankly, didn't care.

"I've been told you're looking for a soul," she said, pulling the chair out in front of me.

I arched a brow, focusing on not revealing myself. "You take a soul for me, and I will make sure you get access to Adam when it's done." I put down the teacup, indicating I was listening.

What was one insignificant human soul in comparison to mine? Dissie told me what I wanted to hear. She helped me plot against the one person who had stolen my whole sense of being. Her take on it was compelling, speaking to the anger brewing inside me.

Adam had been showing Maya interest, and if he cared for her as much as Dissie was claiming, her plan would work. All we needed was to divide Adam's attention. He couldn't protect her and fight me, too.

Of course, things didn't go as planned, and the further we got, the more of Dissie's scheming was revealed. She had a hidden agenda with Maya, so even though I agreed to take her soul, I wasn't planning on it. I wanted to scare her enough to lure out Adam, and I thought if I did so, I could best him. I had underestimated his abilities and the lack of my own. I was very powerful when I had my soul and had forgotten I was nothing without it.

Ever since I inherited my mother's soul, I had felt like an overflowing vessel, the result of a Dūshev father and a High Priestess mother. There was too much of the power, and it had made me arrogant. We were made of mind, body, and soul, and I had never put much thought into what our powers was attached to. It turned out most of it was connected to the soul.

FIVE

MAYA

I woke up lying on a bed in a small room. Streaks of sunlight were coming in through the linen curtains hanging over the barless window.

I could jump.

My sense of self felt closer to normal from the first time I woke up. My muscles were sorer, and I could barely muster enough energy to swing my feet down from the bed. No matter how much I massaged my temples, my head was pounding to the point where I thought I would throw up from the discomfort. Even though I wanted to open the window to let in fresh air, I couldn't make myself move.

"Good, you're awake."

The same woman from last night had silently walked into the room.

The door stood ajar.

I could run.

A Dūshev stepped in front of the door.

"Now, undress," she said and closed the door.

She wasn't scared of them and must have had some say with the Dūshev to smack the door in his face.

"I can't."

My voice came out like sand in a blender.

"You're either going to get up willingly and undress yourself, or they will hold you down while I undress you. Then you can be certain more eyes will be upon you."

I didn't refuse her because of modesty, as I had nothing to hide beneath my clothes. But the threat motivated me more than anything else, so I obliged.

She inspected me from top to bottom when I was completely naked, took my hand, and spun me around. After sliding on latex gloves, she ran her thumbs over my nails, checked my scalp and the insides of my mouth, ears, and nostrils.

I wouldn't know whether to laugh or cry if they truly believed I was hiding a weapon in my nostrils.

"Lie down." She gestured to the bed and took out a speculum.

"What!?"

She couldn't possibly mean that. This was a high-security-prison pat down.

It's fine. It's fine. I'm fine. At least it's a woman. At least they are not watching.

"Spread your legs."

I closed my eyes and did as I was told, gritting my teeth and breathing heavily through my nose.

"Get yourself washed up. I will leave you clean clothes and towels. By the time you're out, there will be a bowl of soup for you. You will eat that. Don't drink from the tap—you will get sick." She gathered her things into the basket she had brought with her and left folded towels and clothes on the bed.

"I'm not hungry."

"Stupid girl! Do you think they will poison you when they can just kill you?" she scoffed. "They use syringes for sedation."

I felt dumb for thinking this was some kind of medieval fairy tale, where they poisoned their enemy's food.

I got up from the bed to get cleaned up, as she had instructed. Not that it was the worst thing in the world—at least I had my own bathroom. When she left, she slammed the door and locked it behind her. I found a bar of soap, a loofah, a toothbrush, and toothpaste in the bathroom.

Wow, almost like a spa.

I stood under the hot shower for so long that my father would have shouted for me to get out if he was there, but he wasn't there—no one was. With no other options, I used a bar of soap to wash my hair and body. As the soapy water washed down my legs, I noticed two identical ornament-like tattoos that had appeared on the backs of my ankles.

Shit.

I had actually succeeded in my task. The prophecy was still on track. Not that any of it mattered. I was a prisoner without my powers or support system.

Sepideh would never find me, and as long as I was alive, she could do nothing but sit tight and wait for my return. Technically, they could keep me there fed and dressed for the next sixty years until I was too old to fight back or do anything substantial.

Somehow, being weak and powerless felt so real. For the first time in a year, I started to remember what it was like being human, what it was like being me again. There was a familiar feeling of being in my own skin, one I had forgotten existed since dying. For a second, I wondered if they tried to stop the prophecy by giving me a soul. I crossed that thought when I remembered how the father looked at me with contempt.

On the bed was the folded pile of clothes, socks, underwear, a pair of wide linen pants, and a matching tunic in neutral colors. I looked like a pilgrim.

I smelled the waft of the food, and I caved. I ate like I had been fasting. The soup was amazing. It felt like I was eating for the first time in ages. There was no way of knowing how long I had been unconscious. It also made me wonder why she hadn't done the body search while I was out. Did they really have that much common decency? For a prisoner, I wasn't treated poorly.

After eating, I dared to walk to the window and face reality—I had to see with my own eyes where I was and what it looked like. The moment I glanced outside, I was hit with a ton of emotions, making everything so much more real than I had anticipated. Deep down, I knew I was in Egypt—I just didn't know how fucked I was until I saw how far the desert was spanning.

You need to do something, need to form a plan.

Until I got my strength back, I needed to keep my head low and behave as docile as they wanted me to. As long as I didn't upset the father, I would be safe until I could escape. I needed Adam. I needed him to trust me again. Maybe then he would find it in himself to forgive and help me.

The lady—Nashir was her name—came back and escorted me out of my room. Dūshevs were everywhere in the halls. Even though I had no powers left, they had taken precautions, which was understandable. If I had my Firuzeh, I could probably take them all out or at least do some damage.

The mansion I was being kept in was spectacular. It had shiny marble floors and golden candle sconces on all the walls. The ceiling was all made of intricate wooden panels, with beautiful murals covering almost the entire hallway.

We walked into a giant ballroom where the walls were covered in what looked like real renaissance oil paintings in carved golden frames. A long table had been set, with dinner ready to be served.

A lot more Dūshevs were present this time. I would be lying to myself if I didn't gawk over how beautiful some of the Dūshevs were.

Get your head out of the gutter.

Their murmur muted as I was led past them. Nashir's hand firmly pressed on my back, leading me forward.

I didn't see Adam among them, but I caught Elias staring at me and when I looked at him, he glanced away. That almost broke my heart because I used to know this guy, lived with him for some time, and we were friendlyish. I had to remind myself that period of my life was over.

I continued walking toward an empty seat next to Adam's father.

Am I expected to sit there?

As I got closer, his father gestured to the vacant seat. Across from me was Seema's boyfriend—I remembered him from the visions, and I wondered if he could be an ally. Maybe he meant what he said to her. Perhaps he did love her enough to help me out. Or maybe he could at least tell Seema where I was. Would she care?

"Go on, Samuel," Adam's father said, looking at Seema's boyfriend.

Samuel, that's his name.

"From what I have gathered through my sources, there was only supposed to be one big stone, not four small ones," Samuel said.

Dammit, not an ally!

It triggered something within me.

"By 'sources,' you mean everything you got from fucking my cousin, right?" I said and regretted it immediately.

I was sure I would be punished for speaking without being spoken to again, but his father seemed amused.

Samuel didn't seem bothered.

"Five pieces," another guy said. "There are five pieces. The last one is missing."

How did he know? Was he one of the guys who had brought me here?

"Yes, Fidel, there are five pieces," Adam's father said. "Perhaps Maya can enlighten us. Where is the last piece?"

I couldn't stay silent for too long, or they would think I was making up a lie.

"I was unconscious, remember? Maybe those two morons lost it when they took me." I gestured toward Fidel, who was sitting next to the skinny guy.

Adam's father smiled and tilted his head. "Someone ought to cut that filthy tongue right out of your mouth."

"It would be my pleasure, Father."

Adam's voice came from behind me, and a second later, his hand found my throat. His grip was so hard I thought I would pass out. He hauled me up by the neck effortlessly and tossed me aside to take the seat next to his father.

"Your vision is clouded, Adam," the father said, looking at me. "I hope you didn't think you would dine with us tonight."

I glanced away.

Of course I didn't think that, but it didn't make it feel any less humiliating.

Air was sucked out of my lungs, and a searing burn flared in my temples. You would think acid was being poured right into my head. I could vaguely hear Adam's father speaking over my own screams until the pain subsided.

"Remember that you are at my father's mercy. If he wasn't here, you wouldn't be breathing," Adam said to me.

I was on my knees, blood dripping from my nose onto the marble tiles.

"Such dramatics, Adam. I didn't know you had it in you."

I didn't need to look up to recognize his accent. He had whispered enough times in my ear for it to be a permanent reminder of his manic behavior. I could only pray that I was never left alone with Aldridge.

"Take her back," the father said.

Two guys were instantly on each side of me.

Again, a needle was stuck in my upper arm.

SIX

Adam

Confessing my mistakes to my father didn't come without a cost. It was a spur-of-the-moment decision I have not regretted one bit. She was as heartless as they come, and I would never forgive her for using me like that.

I called my father the moment she left the cabin in Scotland. Turns out my brothers were already on the hunt for her in Glasgow. Fidel and Zaki arrived within a few seconds after we hung up. They grabbed her from behind and shot her with a strong sedative before she had the time to think to defend herself.

I watched them as they dragged her out of sight and didn't accompany them when they drove to the airport in the car she had rented. My father had arranged for a private plane out of the country.

With the right amount of money and connections, you could pay your way out of any situation. My father's name was good on both accounts.

Since she apparently was the chosen witch, her powers prevented the sedative from working properly. It was supposed to keep her sedated for at least a day, but they told me she woke up groggy and disoriented during the flight, asking for the bathroom. She could barely stand on her feet, so Zaki helped her up.

I must admit that the knowledge triggered me, but I suppressed the feeling.

They gave her a second injection on the plane, and she woke again when they were driving through the dunes. She had started throwing up, so they had to stop and clean up in the middle of the desert. They shot her with a third dose, even though they were instructed not to, which knocked her out until they arrived at the facilities. God knows how she was still alive.

I had conflicting feelings about what was being done to her and the way she was being handled. I felt terrible but also angry and hurt. I had to remind myself that she didn't love me.

This wasn't Maya—it couldn't have been her. It didn't matter how we treated her because her soul wasn't there anymore. Nothing was real about her. Their kind had bewitching powers beyond the ordinary, and it was up to us to control our desires. None of my feelings were real.

To my surprise, my father didn't condemn me for keeping her from his grasps all those months, though he had lied to me about her death. Of course, it wasn't something I addressed or he acknowledged. He was still disappointed in me, and I could tell he was going to be wary of me. I should have believed him when he warned me against her.

Maya's soul wasn't hers to keep, and it meant that it was never real between us. I was simply drawn to her by the force and tugging of my own soul. The signs were there from the start, but I was too ignorant to see them.

It looked like she was here, like she was really alive. I should have known solely from experience no one survived a soul-taking.

So many emotions ran through me, emotions I couldn't sort through. I hated her and still missed her when I looked into her eyes. When I forced myself to remember what she did, I wanted revenge.

I couldn't decide where to stand, but I would listen to my father because I was clearly unstable. I didn't admit to any of my emotions in front of him. I didn't want him to see that I wasn't in control of my feelings. I wanted him to believe in me, wanted him to have faith in me, to believe I would make things right.

My father had plans for her, plans he wouldn't share, at least not with me. He didn't trust me yet, which was understandable, but why he trusted Aldridge blindly was a mystery to me. What had Aldridge done to earn his trust after all the shit he put us through?

"Aldridge, I am aware it takes a toll on you to continuously do this, but these are some difficult times, and we all must carry our burden," my father said, which brought me back to present time.

He spoke in riddles again, not wanting us to know more than necessary.

"What is it that Aldridge is doing for us, exactly?" I asked.

He could strain himself to death, and it would be another Tuesday for me. I just needed to know what he helped my father with.

"If you had chosen to father a son, you could ask the comings and goings of your brothers," my father answered dismissively and looked back at Aldridge.

"Yes, Father," Aldridge said like the good dog he was and carried on as if I had never spoken. "I am doing so to the best of my abilities, but something is blocking me. I don't have full access. All I see is a haze. Usually, I can either follow their lead or instigate the direction."

"Have you had this issue before?"

"It's probably the *mosaken* doing a far better job than we intended it to," Edgar chipped in. "She is weak, so weak she can barely stand."

The sedative! What else are they doing to her?

"Fine." My father waved a hand. "There is no risk in removing the dosage from her food so long we keep the dose in her drinking water."

If things got out of hand, or if she appeared too strong, they would inject her with a high dosage and knock her out. After what she had done to the cabin, we weren't taking any risks, but I wasn't aware they were drugging her through the food, too.

That's when it finally clicked. They were experimenting on Maya, and they were doing it through Aldridge.

My father needed him and was using him. *Good!* He wasn't just favorited by default. Though I still didn't know what special abilities Aldridge had. He kept his powers to himself. Almost all of us played around our skills when we learned to control them, but Aldridge never did. He and Joseph were so reserved about their powers they never showed more than they had to.

Up until last year, we didn't know Joseph had so many tricks up his sleeves. I didn't think Aldridge had anything spectacular besides the ability to manipulate air. This conversation my father was having openly made me believe I had been led astray on purpose. What more could Aldridge be hiding and to what end? None of the elders could see that Aldridge was never really a part of this family.

Since childhood, he had been an outcast. Though a fast learner, he resisted the practice. He did everything to hide the fact that he was a skilled Dūshev.

I only figured it out because I kept an eye on him and put my nose where it didn't belong. One day, I caught him ad'hāring before he was supposed to know how to. He was in his first year yet in no way, shape, or form old enough to know how. That was probably why I was adamant about learning to ad'hār before I was taught properly by a master.

I never told anyone because I thought it was a clever way to stay ahead.

Ever since we were kids, I was in constant competition with Aldridge. In the beginning, I looked up to him, wanting to bond with him. He never took an interest in any of his brothers, wanted nothing to do with our family, and he kept to himself. He would disappear for days and then come back and repeat the circle.

Aldridge's childhood was different because he didn't lose his mother like the rest of us. She was the only woman who didn't die during childbirth. Since Aldridge lived with her for the first few years of his life, many of his ideologies and beliefs were different from ours. Of course, our father always visited them but never intended to maintain a relationship with Aldridge's mother since he expected her to pass at childbirth. I think that was what fucked Aldridge the most. That his mother was replaceable. None of us could relate because we had never met our mothers.

With a lot of pressure from our father, Aldridge completed every level of Dūshev training and disappeared shortly after. He would show up from time to time, fight with our father about not wanting to take souls, cause a lot of havoc in Egypt, then vanish again. A couple of years ago, my father told us Aldridge had become a liability. Apparently, he was taking and releasing souls as he saw fit, and that was the last straw for my father. Whoever found Aldridge first in the hunt was to take his Dūshev soul from him as a form of punishment. For us, that was the worst infliction our father could serve, the idea blasphemous on its own.

As Dūshevs, our souls were transferred to us from our mothers the day we were born, and usually, they never survived childbirth. The twins, Elias and Daniel, shared their mother's soul in a similar fashion to twin flames. And in Aldridge's case, he got his soul later in life, when his mother passed, which, funnily enough, was on my thirteenth birthday.

Perhaps that's when he started resenting me. Seeing me celebrating my birthday with our brothers on the day his mother died. Of course it was never our intention to hurt his feelings, but he couldn't expect me to pretend I didn't have a birthday because of his mother.

When my father announced the hunt for Aldridge, I wanted it to be me who found him. I had to prove I could finally win the last round, and I did. I had gotten stronger and more experienced, and when I found him, he was blindsided by my strength.

As for present day, I didn't know what kind of lies Aldridge had fed our father, but he was not there to be my father's new right hand. Since Zaki and Fidel had brought Maya here, my father had returned to his glory days. It was as if he had taken a sip from the fountain of youth and was aging backward. I assumed having the stones back where they always belonged helped. He seemed radiant, his power oozing from him.

"Fidel, we need to speak to your lady friend," my father said.

"But—"

My father put his hand up. "You will do as I say. She will be offered a room, or she can stay in yours if you prefer—but not to worry, she will be treated like a guest."

A guest. Like he had told Maya.

Fidel's eyes were back on his plate. He wasn't going to challenge a direct order.

"And, Adam, I expect your temper to be in check because I have a task for you."

"Yes, Father." I gave him a curt nod.

Lord knew what he wanted from me, but I would tear out my own kidney if it meant he would see me as an equal to the elders. I was on shaky ground with him, and I really wanted to change that.

V

SEVEN

Maya

I jerked awake and took a deep breath. Two days in a row, I had dreamed of Aldridge. This time he was my dentist asking me why I insisted on putting the Firuzeh in my tooth. The dream was abstract, where my brain tried to entertain me in my sleep. Yet it was so vivid I thought I could still smell the faint scent of his cologne when I woke up. It was my mind playing tricks on me because if they knew about the Firuzeh in my tooth, I would have been done for.

The sun was beaming, and the air was humid. Again, I was sweating through my clothes—or the clothes they had put me in. I had no idea how much time had passed since I was last awake. A bowl of chicken soup and a tall glass of water stood on the stand next to me.

I gulped down the soup from the side of the bowl, barely chewing on the pieces of shredded chicken.

It was actually delicious, even with the celery and carrots being so mushy. I was almost out of breath when I put down the empty bowl and leaned on the headboard. I couldn't believe what had become of me. I had to get out, even if it meant cutting the sheets into ribbons to make a rope and jumping out of the window. If I ever could escape, where could I go?

I opened the window. The desert heat slammed into my face the moment I put my head through it. I tried leaning further over the ledge, but my forehead instantly hit an invisible barrier that felt like hard air.

Fuck!

The place was warded with some strong magic. Out went any hope of escaping. I couldn't jump to my death even if I wanted to.

I sighed and closed the window again. There had to be a way out.

The thought crossed my mind again as I stood under the shower, dwelling on my own misery. I thought about ending it.

There were multiple ways it could be done. One: smash the mirror and cut an artery. Two: trigger a younger one to fight me until they beat me to death. Three: make a rope out of the sheets and hang myself. I couldn't see a way out, and after looking at that mirror hanging over the sink, I must admit it was tempting. The mirror was the easiest. It could be broken with the bedside table and voilà!

Dying was inevitable—I was living on borrowed time anyway. What difference would it make if I ended it myself before the Dūshevs claimed my life?

You must endure this pain. Stay strong. There is a way out.

"Maya," a soft whisper said from the room.

His voice was so small I thought I had imagined it.

I quickly jumped out of the shower and wrapped myself in a towel.

A soft knock sounded on the bathroom door.

"Maya," he said again.

I slowly opened the door. My heart was racing, not because I was practically naked—Adam had seen all of me—and many times at that—but because I was actually scared of him. I didn't know what to expect. Was I scared he would hurt me? Or was I afraid of what he would do to me while no one was watching?

Adam's eyes looked cautious, one hand in his pocket, the other slowly reaching. When he moved closer, I didn't dare move. One wrong step, and he would put me through that agonizing torment again.

He pulled me into an embrace and kissed the top of my head.

My breath hitched.

He drew back to look at me. "I don't have time to explain, but you will have to trust me on this and play along. I'll try to come back later tonight."

"Adam—" I tried to collect my thoughts, but he was gone before I had said the last syllable.

I couldn't believe it! It wasn't over. He hadn't given me up to his father. Something had gone wrong, and somehow, his brothers had found me.

I started sobbing.

So many thoughts ran through my head. I couldn't decide if I was relieved that I still had Adam on my side or if I was worried about how I would explain myself once this was all over.

Although I truly appreciated that he was helping me, I was worried he was doing it for the wrong reasons. If he was still in love with me or hopeful we would end up together, then I was going to disappoint him tremendously. If I would survive this, I would still have to fulfill the prophecy.

You must.

Whether I liked it or not, it had to be done.

It's your duty to fulfill the prophecy.

The sun went down, and the afternoon bled into the night. Only then did I realize that my room didn't have a lamp. There were two brass candle holders, candles in the drawers, but no matches anywhere. Even the bathroom didn't have a light. Only a tiny window where the moon could shine through.

I sat on the bed in darkness for what felt like hours until the door to my room was finally unlocked.

Nashir walked in and collected the empty bowl. "You haven't touched your water."

I looked at her, not understanding why she even cared to comment on that. "I would love a cup of tea."

She glared at me, scoffing, and had left before I could get on my knees and beg.

I would've literally killed for a cup of tea. Even boiling water would have been better than nothing. At least I could close my eyes and pretend it was tea.

More time passed, and the halls grew silent. I had searched in every nook and cranny of this room, and there was nothing remotely interesting to fidget with.

I was lying down, trying not to fall asleep, when I felt the energy shift in the room. I wasn't sure if it was a sign of my magic returning in small doses or if I was so bored out of my mind that I started making things up.

The moonlight was the only light source, which was enough since my eyes had adjusted to the darkness. I hauled myself to a sitting position and looked around, but the room was still empty. But then Adam materialized in front of me just when I was about to lie back down. A creepy sensation washed over me. Why did it feel like I was seeing him for the very first time?

"Are you okay?" He hesitantly reached for my face when I didn't answer. "Be strong, Maya, until I find a way out."

I let him pull me up to a standing position until our bodies were inches apart. His forehead touched mine, and he closed his eyes.

I exhaled a long, shaky breath. "What's going on, Adam. Why am I so weak?"

"They inject you with a sedative daily to keep you under control. They know how strong you can be. They know about the prophecy and the stones. They know everything."

His eyes found mine where I held his gaze. Something was off about him, like he was more exhausted than ever. He had changed, and this war had shaped him. He was trying so hard to be strong and maintain appearances in front of his family.

"Do you trust me?" Adam said and lifted my chin.

I did. He had my back, he always did, even when I didn't deserve it.

"Yes."

He kissed me, and I let him. Although I felt nothing, I let him believe there was more to us. With every breath, our kiss deepened, and I was more sure than ever that I was not in love with him anymore. I would be lying if I said I didn't miss the comfort I used to find in him. I didn't want him to hurt, but I couldn't deny that I was using him. *Whore.*

Adam had missed me, too. He wasn't letting himself hold back. His hands roamed over my body and mine his. I pulled the shirt over his head, and slowly, he peeled off my clothes. His mouth went from my lips to my ear.

"Try to keep it down," he said as he kissed me behind the ear and licked his way down to my breasts.

He hoisted me up, and I wrapped my legs around his waist. First, my back was against the wall, but then, in one stride, we were on the bed. His finger trailed my torso, counting every rib, going down to my thighs and lazily finding their way to my entrance.

"I would've had you kidnapped sooner if I knew how wet it would make you," he said as he pushed two fingers in.

A moan slipped out of me, and he immediately covered my mouth. His fingers jerked in and out of me before he took both my wrists, held them above my head, and pushed himself inside me in one hard thrust. My eyes watered while he continued without removing his hand from my mouth.

I tried to say "easy" against the palm of his hand, but it didn't register with him.

"Adam!" I said louder, still muffled by his hand.

At that, he removed his hand from my mouth and leaned down but didn't change his pace, his left cheek flush with mine.

"Where is the last piece, Maya?"

"What—"

"You're not wearing it, and it's definitely not inside you." I could feel his smile smearing across my face, scratching me with his stubble. "So, where is it? Where is the last piece of your precious stone?"

My vision blurred, and my throat dried up.

His grip tightened around my wrists above my head as he kept thrusting against my numb body. I couldn't move, couldn't fight it. My world crumbled. Everything around me crashed, and suddenly, I couldn't breathe. It wasn't Adam pulling the air out of my lungs but rather shame. My body was utterly still as he kept thrusting and thrusting even harder each time.

Instead of screaming, fighting, or even trying to push him off me, I lay still like a corpse. I couldn't do anything. I couldn't breathe, couldn't think, couldn't move. Everything was black until he spoke again.

"This is exactly what you did to me. Fuck and betray me." He finally released me, got up, and pulled his pants on. He teleported out of the room and left me covered in his grime.

I had never felt so dirty, used, and worthless in my entire life.

This is what you get for whoring your body out.

After what seemed an eternity, I mustered enough energy to get up from the bed. Shakily, I went to the bathroom. As his sperm ran down my thigh, I vomited into the toilet until I had nothing left inside me.

No matter how much I washed myself and how long I stayed under that scorching hot shower in the dark, I couldn't get his smell off of me. My skin was raw from the scrubbing, and I realized no amount of soap or water could make this feeling go away.

Whore. Whore. Whore.

I finally got out of the shower and dressed in my own dirty clothes, the clothes I had been kidnapped in and not the borrowed garments.

I couldn't sit anywhere. The room smelled like him, the bed sheets stained with his remnants, tainted. I had to get rid of everything he had touched.

All I wanted to do was burn the clothes, the sheets, and even the places his hands touched my skin. Instead, I took it all to the bathroom to wash them. I kept rubbing the sheets against each other, trying to erase what had happened. When I couldn't scrub anymore, I sat for at least an hour on the floor staring at the pile of wet fabric.

He made me worthless, made me truly hate him. *I hate him . . .* I told him everything, left him with clues, left him to free himself from his family, from the prophecy. *I didn't take away his choice.* Did he have the same desire to burn the whole world down, himself included?

I leaned against on the cold tiles and wrapped my arms around my knees. My clothes were soaked, but at least they were *my* clothes, not something they had given me, not something he had touched. My hair was wetting the back of my sweater, something that would have driven me mad before but seemed so trivial. *To hell with it all.* I would watch the world burn before me and still not move.[1]

The longer I stared at the pile of sheets, the more the fire I pictured felt real. I imagined the sheets to be soaked in gasoline so they would burn faster. Flames danced before my eyes, whooshing as they spread to the shower curtain. I convinced myself I could feel the heat reaching my cold, bare feet. Had I been myself, I would've had a meltdown

Gole Yakh – Kourosh Yaghmaei

from my soles touching the wet tiles, but I was too numb to care.

"What on earth—"

Hearing his voice shattered my reality. The fire before me vanished into thin air because it never was.

Aldridge was standing in the doorway of the bathroom. Smoke curled between us, a lot of it.

I couldn't help but scoff. My brain never let me down when it came to creativity. Obviously, there couldn't be a fire without fumes clouding the room. Perhaps my brain was protecting me once again, only letting Aldridge watch me through the smoke. So, he couldn't see the shame coating my skin.

What more could they take from me that I hadn't already lost? I had no soul, no dignity, and no will to live.

"Are you here to have your way with me, like your brother before you?" I asked.

His eyes narrowed and jaw clenched for the shortest second that I thought I imagined it.

He didn't care, none of them did.

"Who, Adam?" he whispered.

I looked back at the pile of sheets. Smoke was still rising from the ashes, covering every layer of the bathroom.

Did that really happen? Is it really burning?

Aldridge stepped into the bathroom and dragged me out, nearly yanking my arm off. He closed the door behind him softly and froze. Behind his eyes were a thousand emotions.

He rubbed his jaw, then frantically looked around the room until his gaze landed on the bedside table and widened. "Don't make a sound," he muttered and disappeared.

Before I could form a thought, he reappeared in the room with candlesticks and a matchbox. He shoved everything in a drawer and then took the two candle holders and went inside the bathroom with them. When he returned, he seemed more rigid than before.

"You brought the candles with you while taking a shower. After finishing, you forgot the lit candles inside the bathroom, and the curtain caught fire! You tried to put it out with whatever you could," he said, grabbing my shoulders and shaking me like I wasn't listening.

His touch sent a shock wave through me, his scent surrounding me like a fog. "Do you understand?"

His voice was so powerful but still a whisper.

Seeing the open drawer and candles, I realized he was helping me. My heart pounded.

"Do you understand, Maya?" he said again, my name on his deceiving tongue.

Careful, they're all the same.

"Yes."

"When I leave, you go and bang on that door and scream for help."

Why are you helping me. At what cost?

I nodded.

"If they find out you can produce fire, demon blood, they will double your dosage, so you better act your heart out." He took the glass of water from the stand and poured it out. "Our water is clean. Drink from the tap. You owe me!" He disappeared again.

At what cost!

His help wasn't without a price—probably a fool's bargain—but what choice did I have?

I went to the bathroom and opened the door. When the smoke slithered into the room, I screamed for help and shouted "Fire!" while pretending to put out a blaze.

It helped that I was breathing in the smoke and frantically coughing. Three men came in after the door unlocked.

"Adel, give her a shot and take her to my father. No need to wake *Jedo*."

Fear washed over me at what was next. If I acted on my impulses, they would call my bluff. So, I pretended to continue to cough and let them jam the needle into my arm.

EIGHT

ADAM

I had gone back home to catch up on work and maybe some writing.

My agent had tried booking me for several gigs that I either canceled or turned down. I had been too occupied and overwhelmed. I had asked for a break from performing, but I was still on a contract to finish the book. I never reviewed her edits, and because of my lack of commitment and communication, she dropped me. Granted, it was done in the nicest way possible. She told me to get my shit together and come back to her when I was ready again. Writing had been an outlet for me, somewhere I escaped to when I lost myself. With everything going on with my family, it had become another chore.

As I was writing a generic thank-you email to my agent, a message popped in from Herman, summoning my return to Egypt. I hadn't been back more than a couple of hours, and they were already on my ass.

Whispered gossip spread by midday, and I got sketchy glances my way.

Apparently, Maya's room had caught fire, and somehow, without being there, I was still the problem. Nothing had happened to her, but I would have lied if I said I hadn't wished the fire had taken her with it. It was a terrible thing to say, but I was sick of having to be reminded of what she was and what she had done to me.

She wouldn't pretend to be Maya and get away with it. I would never let anyone manipulate me and fill me with lies again. She was going to pay for what she took from me because I could hold a grudge like no one else, and I wasn't going to let this one go that easily.

We didn't know what caused the fire. My brothers had shot her with the sedative before asking her what had happened. The drug was a safety measure my father didn't take lightly—with good reason. She was the second strongest being under this roof, whether she knew this or not. My father didn't care what happened to her so long he got the last piece of stone. After, he would probably get rid of her, and I couldn't wait for that day to come.

I walked into my father's study where he, Edgar, and Herman were sitting. The two were my father's most trusted.

One day, things will change between us.

It was her fault I had lost my father's trust, and I had to rebuild my relationship with him like I was not a part of the family.

"Have you heard any word from Fidel?" my father asked Edgar.

"Yes, he will bring her in today."

"Father, I will find you the last piece, I promise," I said.

My father finally acknowledged my presence, his eyes burning with rage. "Do you think me an imbecile, boy! I granted you permission to access her room, and suddenly, a fire breaks."

It got so quiet you could hear a pin drop.

"That had nothing to do with me!"

I had asked him for permission, told him every detail of my plan to seduce the information out of her, and he had approved, even seemed proud. How could he blame me for what he deemed a good idea? Yes, I lost my temper and didn't get all the facts, but after me having told him everything, he still held me responsible.

"Don't insult my intelligence, Adam."

"You think I did that?"

My voice was rising.

He shot to his feet, jabbing a finger at me, his eyes blazing. "Not another word from you."

His voice thundered, rattling the air, and the ground beneath us trembled as if fearing his wrath.

I was in no position to argue. Too many times, I had chosen Maya before my family and did the opposite of what my father commanded. Had I not paid for it in other ways? He set me up to be Maya's last victim by making me the next in line for his throne. Did that even count? Was I still next in line? Could I pull rank?

Things were changing for the worse, and I was no longer the favored or the chosen son. He could just as easily rip my title from me and give it to one of my useless brothers. They were good for nothing, only warming the bench next to my father.

Fidel's girl arrived. I didn't see her, but Samuel did. He told me Fidel was keeping her close and seemed to genuinely care for her. Not that she was treated poorly. My father kept his promise. She was given a room of her own and a tray of food. My father told her she could ask for anything she needed, and Nashir would bring it to her.

The thing I had come to learn about my father was that he would let anyone live in peace if they didn't interfere with his plans. She was safe because my father found her useful, and whatever he promised Fidel could change if she did not deliver.

He had arranged a meeting with Fidel and his girl. And probably for the fright factor alone, he wanted us present. I believed he used the opportunity to read the room. Were it not for the private talk with my father after his scolding, I would have thought he was still angry with me and would exclude me from the meeting. I was given a task to keep an eye on her, to be alert, and not to underestimate her.

If I felt anything amiss or feared for our safety, I was allowed to use my powers on her. There were ways around any promise. He might have vowed to leave her unharmed, but I hadn't. I was his safety net, a precaution, which meant there was still hope.

I entered the evaluation room to find my father had arranged for the dining table to be moved in there. The table was full of sweets, Egyptian bread pudding, baklava, and other pastries. Teapots were steaming, sitting on top of candle warmers.

I was about to walk to the two empty seats next to my father when he caught my eye.

"Adam, your seat is next to Adel."

I wouldn't have cared if it wasn't Aldridge sitting on his left with another empty seat beside him. Why was he held in such high regard all of a sudden? What had he done for this family besides being a complete pain in the ass?

I couldn't keep dwelling on it because, suddenly, Fidel walked in with a beautiful dark-haired girl. Her limbs were long and elegant, hair sleek, eyes sharp like a fox. Her hand was in his, and her knuckles were white from gripping it so hard.

My father gestured them to the empty seats next to him.

Luckily, I was only five seats down, so I didn't miss anything. Not the fear in her eyes nor the hitch in her breath as she said "*Salam*" in a low voice.

My father smiled, a smile that didn't fool me. "What is your name, my dear?"

"Sepideh," she answered, meeting his eyes.

"Ah, beautiful. *Light of dawn*, perhaps you will be," my father said. He glanced at Nashir as she strode toward the table and poured Sepideh a cup of tea.

"You had questions for me," Sepideh said and dared to keep her head held high while clutching to Fidel.

"Yes." My father sipped from his tea and met her eyes.

"Know that my answers do not come for free."

Oh. The audacity of this witch.

"Your freedom and well-being are of no concern to me. I will grant you this because I love and trust my son. Not because I trust that you will tell me the truth but know that if you lie to me, both of you will vanish from the face of the earth," my father stated nonchalantly, as if he didn't just threaten to kill Fidel right in front of us.

Fidel's hand squeezed around hers for a second before letting go to sip from his tea.

"Long ago, a respected seer gave me a prophecy." My father looked from her to me for a moment. "On the last day of Pisces, he is truly born, his soul full but not wholly his. Hand in hand, they share a soul and carry the Feyrouz into darkness so grim that all shadows pale in her steps."

The last day of Pisces! There is no way . . .

I tried to put the pieces together. I was born on the last day of Pisces and was too late when I tried to give Maya her soul back. *Which meant . . .* she walked into the darkness and out of my life.

The only thing my father ever said to me as a child was that my soul was split in half. Why didn't he warn me with the same prophecy he feared so much? We could have prevented it. I could have stopped it.

"So, you see, my dear Sepideh, I need the last piece of Feyrouz to stop this prophecy. If not, so help me God, I will drag you and your entire bloodline with me to hell."

Sepideh gave him a feline smile. "Do you want to hear her prophecy word for word?"

Everyone waited in anticipation.

My father said nothing.

"She who forcefully bears the soul of our enemy must release it to the thirteenth son on the thirty-third day of

Nowruz with the blessing of Goddess Ishtar. She will sacrifice our blood and flesh to retrieve what is rightfully ours and bring order to nature . . . So, I'm asking you, *aghaye* Fyodor, who forced his"—she tipped her chin toward me—"soul upon Maya?"

Fidel must've told her. She couldn't have guessed that I was the thirteenth son.

"What the hell is going on!" I asked without thinking. "What do you mean forced?"

My father cut me a glare that chilled the entire room.

"Neither of us wants to sacrifice flesh and blood for prophecies written before time, so spare me your threats, sir. We both have the same agenda."

This girl was bold for speaking to my father this way in a room full of Dūshevs. My plan was to remain collected and neutralize her if necessary, yet my overwhelming sense of betrayal took over.

"Such a brave girl, you are. You will get your chance to prove yourself worthy tomorrow," my father said and gave Fidel a nod. He took Sepideh by the hand and led her out.

"Joseph, make sure to double the guards at the chambers."

Joseph nodded.

Then my father looked at Aldridge. "Stay behind."

Which meant the rest of us could fuck off. But I wasn't going to let that nugget of information drown in all the chaos. He split my soul and forced it on Maya, and I needed to know why or the hatred would grow and fester inside me.

"Father, can I have a word with you?" I looked at Aldridge. "Without an audience."

"Now is not the time."

Aldridge didn't make an effort to move, and neither did I. I wouldn't leave until he told the truth, but demanding it wouldn't work.

I sat next to Aldridge, facing my father. "Please."

A long moment of silence fell between us. I had to pretend Aldridge wasn't there, or I would lose my shit. Sometimes, you have to choose your battles.

My father finally relented. "You were the only one born on the last day of Pisces." He paused. "I thought I could redirect the prophecy by splitting your soul. I kept half of it far away from you so you couldn't share it with anyone, as the prophecy claimed you would. I thought I had been successful because, host after host, your soul was safe. Still, it became apparent that, no matter where I placed it, you would eventually end up nearby. Maya was the last host, and it was the first time you made contact.

"Fearing the outcome, I made all sorts of claims. I convinced myself that if I told you to make her a mother, I could reclaim our path, unaware of the true gravity of the prophecy," he breathed out and looked away. "Forgive me, son. I was trying to save us all from this prophecy."

"What . . ."

"It was your soul all along. Never hers to keep."

I leaned back in my chair, not knowing how to process this newfound knowledge. It changed everything.

"I'm sorry it brought you so much grief."

٩

NINE

Fyodor Pavlenko

To right the wrongs I had done, it was important to acknowledge all my mistakes—those made intentionally and those born of sheer impetuosity.

"We need to consider the facts to understand where we went wrong," Edgar said.

Always the one to soften the blows.

"No need to spare my feelings, son. I take responsibility for my actions, whether they were made with ill intent or not."

Knowing my strengths and weaknesses, I created the council to help with sounder judgments and more informed decisions. If they took the responsibility of fatherhood and accepted all the hardship that came with it, they were considered to sit in my council.

If I wanted to decipher the prophecy once and for all, I needed help.

"Then, you must share everything with us, Father. We cannot help you if we do not know what we are dealing with," Karam said.

"The prophecy was created by a demon blood witch. You have all heard stories in bits and pieces because I never considered the prophecy a threat. It took me far too long to understand the severity of her words. Too late, I have come to understand that demon blood witches are not to be messed with," I started, hoping my honestly would compel my sons to be just as transparent with me.

"It's no secret that we are drawn to these practitioners. It's the women all of you find yourself entangled with one way or another. We can't help but fall in love with them because there is no love like it. Nothing will compare, and nothing will ever fill the void they leave behind. It's a curse I have experienced firsthand. Long before any of you were born, I met the daughter of a demon blood High Priestess. She was a phenomenal witch for her age and was said to surpass her mother in ways never seen before. Parvaneh taught me everything I know about the craft. She taught me to draw energy from the elements, taught me to ground myself, and she helped me solidify my powers. She is the reason all of you have the skills you have today.

"When I first experimented with soul transfers, I didn't tell her. I wanted to perfect the skill, and I was eager to show her I could create balance in the universe, just like she had taught me. As you might have guessed, she disagreed with my methods. No matter how much I tried to convince her that this would help humanity, she wouldn't listen. Our beliefs and methods became a barrier between us and drove us apart. The last words she spoke to me were, *If you continue on this path, it will force your demise. On the last day of Pisces, he is truly born, his soul full but not wholly his. Hand in hand, they share a soul and carry the Feyrouz into darkness so grim that all shadows pale in her steps.* Of course, I didn't know it was a prophecy at the time and only realized her words might carry weight when Adam was born."

It was all I was willing to share, all they needed to know, to understand the gravity of the situation.

"And then you split Adam's soul in two," Herman stated.

I nodded.

"Father, forgive me if I'm being too forward, but did you run background checks on the people you used—I mean, how did you decide where to place the other half of Adam's soul?"

"My options were limited. Dūshev souls can only be carried by those with a magical lineage, whether it be Zoroastrian practices, Sufism, juju, voodoo, etc. Which is why I chose offspring of those who had stopped practicing, those who had forsaken their ways in favor of God or science. I had deemed it the safest option, but I was wrong. I should have known there was something wrong when I found the girl without a soul. It wasn't rare to find a practitioner without a soul—it was impossible."

"Help me understand why we can't kill her. Wouldn't that solve everything?" Herman asked.

"If we kill her, we might never know where she hid the last piece of the Feyrouz. Without it, I cannot guarantee that the prophecy will not prevail."

There was much more to it, but my boys needn't know all the foolishness of my past. The Sāhers had inherited the stones. They had been passed down through generations, but they had been stolen from me, from my chambers, many years ago.

I had them made for Parvaneh—a collection of jewelry embedded with both the most precious diamonds and the magical turquoise stones. They were her favorite.

The diamonds represented the strength of our love and the turquoise the fragility of my heart. The turquoise contained a piece of me, a piece of me only meant for Parvaneh.

"What is the correlation between the prophecy and the stone?" Edgar asked.

My clever boy.

"They carry the prophecy."

The one Maya broke into pieces was the one stone that I had made into a pendant for Parvaneh. She used to wear it around her neck, hanging from a long chain close to her heart. Without the Feyrooz, Maya would be aimless in the prophecy.

"I'm sure the girl can help us get it back," Edgar said.

١٠
TEN

Sepideh

When I first met Fidel, my main objective was to honor my duty, to make sure we were the generation to make the change and fulfill the prophecy. It was what I believed to be true, what I fought to achieve. I had been just as blind and devoted as Maya.

I had one goal and one goal only, to find out whether I was the chosen one. I convinced myself I didn't care about him, that I left my heart at home, that it was all for the greater good.

It was a clean breakup. Fidel didn't understand it, but he respected my decision and swore I would never hear from him again. I made him promise because I knew we could never be. When he left, I wanted to erase him from my memories, wanted to forget every whispered word and shared breath between us. I wanted to forget I ever laid eyes on him. Asking him to leave was the hardest thing I ever did, even though it took me years to admit it to myself. It was never my intention to fall in love with Fidel or to let him turn my life upside down.

Fidel only broke his promise and got in touch with me when he found out the truth about the prophecy and wanted to warn me. I hadn't meant to answer his call, but I couldn't resist it. To hear his voice, his plea to abandon the prophecy was like reopening a wound that had never fully healed. The cut was fresh, and my heart bled scarlet all over my draped veil.

Fyodor Pavlenko had a curse over his head since the dawn of time. The prophecy rang true, yes. What had started it was himself, messing with the wrong people, with the wrong coven, and most importantly, with the wrong High Priestess. Fortunately, for Fyodor, he had also learned everything he knew from said High Priestess.

His defenses were flawless. But even the most polished surface cracked over time, and the time had come for the Dūshevs to be dragged to hell for the mistakes of one man. Fyodor Pavlenko had kept his family safe behind wards and glamorous facades, successfully distancing them from the prophecy.

Everyone had failed to bring them down until the task had landed into the hands of Leyla. It could have been someone else's burden to carry or Leyla's alone, but her selfish desires cost her our entire family the coven. No, happy and healthy families only existed in fairytales. Our family used us, betrayed us, and sold our souls to the devil. The prophecy had not fallen upon all Sāhers.

Leyla made a bargain and paid the price with our blood. She manufactured different narratives and fed us lies and empty promises about a brighter future, pointing out how ignorant we were to believe everything she said.

Of course, it was too late when I found this out myself. We were all blindsided by Leyla and her schemes. I was never meant to be the one. None of us were. Leyla manipulated the coven into believing a Sāher would be born without a soul to fulfill a prophecy. However, in fact, Maya was always the chosen one, whose soul had been bartered with before her birth. And so it all began, our indoctrination.

The title of Kāheneye Azam fell on Leyla the day of my grandmother's passing. She became our High Priestess in every sense and swore a blood oath to protect the coven, to have our best interest. *It was all lies . . .* All she ever did was to uphold her end of a bargain, whatever that entailed. She was to see this prophecy through and wipe the Dūshevs from the face of the earth.

She was determined to succeed, regardless of who was in her way. She bent the rules, dabbled in forbidden magic, and tainted our entire coven and bloodline with her dirty hands. She fabricated prophecies within prophecies, altering time and space. She weaved stories, rewrote grimoires, and distorted Maya's reality. Everything around Maya was tailored to Leyla's liking.

That was the reason why Maya always ended on the "right" path, why she never seemed to veer off, why all her steps led her to Rome. Maya hadn't been trained properly and never learned to distinguish between visions, dreams, glamours, or even simple spells. She was learning, though, doubting herself, waking up to see glimpses of the truth.

I wanted to confide in Maya, tell her everything I knew, but she was in too deep. She was convinced of the prophecy. She believed she had no other choice but fulfilling a prophecy that restored the balance of nature. Thus, I had to stop her and had to turn on my family and everything I was brought up believing because it was all a lie.

ELEVEN

MAYA

No matter where I turned, beautiful colors flooded the sky above the desert. In the darker end was an immense depth, and in the pinks and violets, there were streaks of warm sunlight.

The shape of a man appeared next to me. I didn't look. I was too mesmerized to be bothered. Even in the heat of the desert, he smelled like a cold ocean breeze and musk.

"What are you thinking?" he said into the setting sun.

"I'm thinking I lost the ability to trust my own judgment."

The words tumbled out before I thought better of it. I turned away from the sunset, and his features came into view like déjà vu. Light danced in his amber eyes. I took in his face, the scars on his cheekbone and through his brow, the point of his glistening canines. *Who are you?* I couldn't put a name on him. When I blinked again, my eyes landed on the heavy dunes.

He glanced over the edge of the balcony and into the abyss. My eyes followed.

"If you fall, who will catch you? Who can you trust with your life?"

"Sepideh. I trust her with my life," I said without missing a beat, wondering how she was faring.

"Has she failed you?"

The question took me by surprise.

I turned and faced him again. "No, I failed her."

I failed all of them.

"Sometimes, the enemy is disguised as an ally, and the ally as the enemy."

"And what does that make you?"

He winked at me, a grin splayed on his face. "You tell me, bruja."

Aldridge! It finally clicked for me.

His skin was coated with ice, hiding his truth. All Aldridge did was tell me lies. I blinked once, twice, and when I blinked again, everything went dark. Stars filled my vision, and I fell through the skies with no end to the darkness, no bite in the wind, and no sound to my screams.

With a thud, I landed on a soft surface, and my vision cleared. I tried to move, but my hands and feet were bound. His weight shifted on me before our eyes met. I froze under him, and my breath caught in my throat.

I was drowning, cold, and couldn't move.

I can't breathe.

Adam's eyes were unmoving—dead, even—as they bore into mine. His movements were practiced, his pace rhythmical.

I lay there immobilized as he continued to take more than I offered. My hands were free yet unmoving.

I was forced to relive it, unable to make it stop, unable to tell him no because I consented to this. I deserved it, deserved to be punished.

He kept going, holding me down with no more than a stare. So, I closed my eyes and wished for death to claim me, for time to swallow me, for air to drown me . . .

I gasped awake, convinced I was drowning. *It was a dream!* All of it, just a dream.

It was unclear how long I had been asleep. I was back in the bedroom, a Dūshev towering over me with an empty glass.

Nashir walked in and took the glass while giving him a disapproving look.

"What! She was screaming, and I didn't want to listen to it," he explained.

My hands shook as I tried to wipe the water from my face. They both walked out and locked the door behind them. I took a survey of my surroundings. It didn't look like there had been a fire the night before. Not even the faint smell of smoke lingered. I must have dreamed it all! My reality was blurring into my dreams, and I couldn't trust my own judgment.

As I tried to get up from bed, I was surprised to feel the ache in my body. My muscles were sore and limbs stiff. Whether the retched feeling was an aftermath of the sedation or the nightmares, I didn't know. Some things were better left unsaid, unopened even. I would gain nothing from dwelling on the sourness coiling in my stomach. Things had to change. I had to change!

The Dūshevs were drugging me more frequently—I knew that much. They were either worried or unsure of what I was capable of. And if they believed I was powerful, perhaps it was time for me to believe in me, too. With my powers weakened, all I needed to do was find a way to restore them.

I forced my way into the bathroom and washed the sleep off of my face. The bathroom was clean. No sign of fire, nothing on the tiles, no residue on the shower curtain. The creases where it had been folded were still visible.

On the bedside table was a cold bowl of chicken soup. I guzzled it down before Nashir walked in again. She brought with her a tall glass of water and took the empty bowl.

"Drink." She handed me the glass. "You are dehydrated."

Just as she said it, the sentence looped in my head.

Our water is clean . . . Drink from the tap.

"I think I ate too fast. I'll throw up if I drink water now." I took the glass from her hand and placed it on the table next to me.

She didn't seem bothered by this and left me again. I poured the water down the drain and rinsed the cup. Perhaps if the sedative was in the water, I could rinse it from my system and regain some of my powers. Perhaps then, I would have a chance.

They were trying to smoke me out of my own head. I thought I didn't mind the waiting game, but then I felt myself losing sense of time and reality. Slowly but surely, anxiety crept up my sleeve and crawled its way through my veins. I was waiting for something dreadful, anticipating a bomb to set off.

Minutes became hours, and hours became days. The only positive thing was the change I felt in my body ever since I stopped drinking the water that was provided for me. With every passing minute, I was coming back to myself. The grogginess was gone, my energy was back up, and I could feel my powers buzzing under my skin.

Somehow, it felt different from before. The powers weren't coming from the Firuzeh or my ancestors. They were mine alone.

I had to collect my thoughts, be smart, and act accordingly if I wanted to get out of there alive. There were a lot of them and just one of me. I couldn't fight them all, even if I had all my powers restored.

Murmur and a loud thud sounded from the hall and brought me out of my trance. I bolted upright from the bed and took featherlight steps to the door to eavesdrop.

"I don't care if she dies of internal bleeding as long as she tells us where it is."

Internal bleeding? What were these Dūshevs going on about? I felt fine.

Their footsteps grew louder and louder.

"Leave her. It doesn't matter," one of them said.

Another thud sounded, and this one was too close to my door, so I hurried back to the bed and sat there in case they decided to pop in. Low and behold, shortly after, they did.

A younger Dūshev opened the door and stood there with a devilish grin. Probably because he saw the horror in my face. Not for the reason he probably thought, though.

I was starting to feel them again, feel their presence around me, their powers charging the air around them. It was the first time since I got here.

No rash decisions. No rash decisions. No rash decisions.

This Dūshev had limited powers, like a glass half full. He was probably fifteen years old and barely capable of using what he was blessed with.

I scanned him from top to bottom until my eyes landed on the second pair of feet lying on the floor, female and unconscious.

Am I about to be next?

"We thought you needed company," he said, not hiding the fact that he was enjoying dragging this out to see the fear spread through me like a tidal wave. He bent down and picked her up like a drunk girlfriend.

Her limbs were dangling, her fingernails bloodied and dirty. Her hair spilled across her bruised, swollen face.

I didn't recognize her until he stepped inside and let her fall onto the floor. The sound of her head hitting the hard marble floor sent electricity through me.

"Oh God! Sepideh!" I gasped, slamming my hand to my mouth as I rushed to her broken body.

This was all my fault. She was there because of me. I looked back up to see him pull an envelope from his pocket and throw it on the floor before he turned on his heel and left me with Sepideh.

"Sepideh, Sepideh, please!" I cupped the back of her head.

She wasn't fully unconscious. Her lashes parted slowly and closed a couple of times. It took every ounce of strength in me to carry her over to the bed.

"Maya," she whispered, barely audible.

I helped her to a sitting position, adjusted the pillow behind her back, and reached for the glass of water on the side table. But she shook her head when I shoved it up to her lips.

"I'm fine," she said and pushed my hand away.

Pay attention, Maya!

"You're absolutely not fine," I insisted, but she wouldn't drink. "What happened? How did they get you?"

"I'm not sure." She shifted and pressed the heel of her hands to her eyes. "Last thing I remember is leaving the hotel, and the next thing I know, I'm here. They have kept me in a room for days now and beating me up every chance they got because I couldn't tell them where the last piece of Firuzeh was."

Her lips were quivering, her eyes not meeting mine, and her hands clenched in fists, turning her knuckles white.

"Do you know anything about the others?"

She shook her head.

If they had found Sepideh, they could find all of them.

I let out a breath. "I'm so sorry. This is all my fault."

I should have been more careful, should have taken precautions.

She shook her head again. "I signed up for this. We all did. I'm just glad they left you unharmed." When she looked at me, the guilt drowned me. I was being kept here, fed and clothed, and although not free, I was arguably okay." She saw the shift in my face and quickly put a hand on my shoulder. "I promise you I'm fine. It's worth it, as long as you have the last piece." Desperation burned in her eyes.

I tore the envelope open, careful not to give away too much in my expression.

> Dearest Maya,
>
> As you might have guessed by now, we are locating all the Sāhers of your coven. One by one, we will break them, in spirit and other imaginative ways until we have what belongs to us. In my absence, please enjoy my hospitality.
>
> Fyodor Pavlenko

If it wasn't for Sepideh's bruised face in front of me, I would have thought he was bluffing.

"What does it say?" she asked.

I handed her the letter.

There was no reason for me to keep anything from her. In the end, I couldn't hide the fact that I had brought this upon us. Her face gave nothing away as she was reading. Not fear nor anger or disappointment she must have felt toward me.

I didn't have enough time to devise a good plan. Instead, I drew a deep breath before pushing her to think with me.

"I know it's a difficult ask, but I need you to focus. Try to remember as much as possible from when you arrived here. I'm assuming they took your Firuzeh from you, but did you see anything of significance when you arrived here? They must have cars here. Not all of them teleport yet, I'm sure of it. I remember something about—"

"No, I have my necklace." She pulled it out from under her shirt. "I don't think they can take it from us unless we're dead."

I would have kept rambling.

"They took mine," I said. "And if that was true, what's actually stopping them from killing us?"

It wasn't making any sense.

"I don't know what stopped them from killing me. Tactics, maybe, but they're not going to touch you because they need that last piece of Firuzeh. They probably took yours because they knew you could part from them."

Adam had seen me take them off and probably told them.

The Dūshevs had their own history with the Firuzeh, I had guessed as much. Besides that, I knew nothing of where the Firuzeh originated from or who it belonged to first. It could very well have been theirs from the beginning of time—no one knew. It clearly wasn't as connected to me as Leyla claimed. Otherwise, I wouldn't be alive.

The Firuzeh was a transmitter of sorts, and all that mattered was who was wielding the powers, not who rightfully owned it. The question was, did I really need it? Was I dependent on this last piece to channel my power, or could I get rid of it completely? Perhaps I didn't need the Firuzeh. Perhaps my powers would manifest without it. What if my powers had nothing to do with the Firuzeh?

"You know, you can take yours off, too, right? I think it was a precaution, in case we were being inconsistent in carrying the Firuzeh. But, clearly, it won't kill you," I said and gestured to myself. "As you see, I am very much alive. Not exactly thriving, though."

Her eyes widened. "So . . . you don't have it?"

Her voice came out raspy, and suddenly, her eyes were cloudy.

"Of course I have it," I whispered. "What I'm saying is you can part with it without dying."

"How have you managed to hide it from them? They must have searched you."

When I first broke the Firuzeh in pieces and had them made into jewelry, I didn't tell my cousins. Obviously, Sepideh knew, but she was out of the question, sworn to me with a blood oath. The blood oath didn't bind us or take away her free will. It was just a visual representation of what she had promised. She was marked with an X on her palm, and the scar would stay as long as she honored the oath and by extension, the prophecy. The moment she decided to break her oath, the scar would fade to nothing.

"Last time we went back, I made Reza fix it for me."

I didn't want to say dentist out loud because the walls had ears, and Sepideh knew that. Besides, Reza was a friend of the family, and just like Ashrafi, everybody knew him by name.

"Oh."

Sepideh said nothing else. Her eyes were hollow, and she was fidgeting, pulling off dead skin from her cuticles.

"You need to drink some water. When was the last time you ate or drank something?" I took the glass again and tried to hand it to her.

"No. I promise I'm fine," she declined again, putting her hand up, pushing the glass away from her face.

Fuck! I prayed the realization of my mistake didn't show on my face because there was no denying it.

Sepideh had broken the blood oath. In the time we had been apart, my cousin had made her decision and turned against me.

I took a deep breath and calmed myself. I had already confessed to having the Firuzeh.

You are no longer safe here.

Instead of insisting, I drained the glass, looking her in the eyes trying to find a clue, an answer. She didn't flinch, didn't look discomforted or remorseful.

"You know . . . I never asked you which one of them you dated?"

"What?" she asked and looked sincerely confused.

"Since all four of us had to sleep with a Dūshev to see whose soul would be taken," I reminded her.

"I've wanted to talk to you about that, actually. Yes, we all had to do that, but it was always your destiny to fulfill the prophecy, Maya. Leyla made it all up. Neither one of us had ever met a Dūshev, so we were instructed to find one and seduce him to see who would trigger the prophecy. We all tried and failed because it was always you and the thirteenth son. You never had to do anything to find him. He just fell onto your lap. You have been lied to. We all have."

It sounded like the truth, like she wanted to tell me more.

"But that doesn't answer my question. Who did you sleep with?"

Why was she avoiding my question?

"What do you mean? Are you questioning my loyalty?"

Her whole demeanor changed like she was offended.

Before I could take hold of her wrist and twist her palm upright to show her the disloyalty, Adam appeared in the room.

"Who brought her in here?" he said, sounding pissed, but his features neutralized fast, and I saw him stepping into character.

Within seconds, a plan formed in my head, and I, too, stepped into character. Two could play this game. Only flaw in his was he didn't know we were playing.

"Adam, please. You need to help her! I don't know who did this to her, but your brothers came in and just left her here—"

I would have continued in an endless stream had he not stopped me.

"Can you calm down for a second?" He pinched his brows.

I didn't pay attention to Sepideh. Whether she caught on or not, I didn't care. This was probably the only shot I would ever get.

"Please, Adam. I swear she has nothing to do with it," I said and stepped toward him until I was so close I could touch him. "She needs to see a doctor." I touched his sleeve, and luckily, he didn't shy away. "Please." I took his hand in mine.

I can do this. I felt his powers running through me. *This is it!*

"I couldn't have done it without you," I whispered when he finally looked at me.

I disappeared just before chaos erupted in his eyes.

١٢

TWELVE

Adam

It had been two weeks since I was last in Maya's room. I had left her somewhat disheveled, and I had to make it right. I had a plan, thought I could talk to her and perhaps convince her to trust me. All my plans went down the drain when I entered her room and saw her cousin lying in her bed, beaten and bruised. No one bothered to tell me they had moved her to Maya's room. Yet again, my brothers did as they pleased when my father left for Russia.

What was I supposed to think when she was so convincing? When she grasped my hand, I saw a glimmer of hope for redemption, but it faded as she pulled away and adʰāred before my eyes. It took me a moment to process what had just happened. They would blame me for it. My father was going to murder me. He trusted me with one task, and I fucked it up. If I went looking for her without notifying the others, he would assume I was a traitor and that I would let her escape—or worse, planned it.

The elders were there when father gave me one final chance to redeem myself. He told me I had one shot at getting Maya to tell me where the last piece was. I could have gotten it out of her if I had played my cards right, if I had been patient and more like myself, but anger and hate clouded my vision and my judgment.

The stinging corrosion of betrayal took charge of me. I fucked up immensely by letting my need for revenge steer me. I could have played nice and made her think I still believed in her, in us, and maybe I could have earned her trust. But no matter how hard I tried, I couldn't shake the thought of her deceit.

The only thing I could think of was how fucking convincing her tears were, the story she spun, and the sweet nothings she whispered in my ear before she revealed that it was all a lie wrapped and tied in a bow.

I told you, baby. This time, I came for you.

The sentence was going in a loop in my head. All I could think of was sweet revenge. I wanted her insides to churn and rot.

I wanted her to hurt so much she would break from within.

My father had been cautious with Maya. Torture was an option he had considered, but he worried that, even with sedatives, her ancestors' interference was unavoidable. They would give her access to their powers because the prophecy always came first. As long as she was left unharmed, her physical body belonged to us. He had plans with Fidel's girl, too. She was allowed to keep her necklace on the sole condition she help us in getting the last piece from Maya. Of course, she played us all and helped Maya instead.

I had no choice but to confess to my brothers exactly what happened. We couldn't avoid it, and denial only wasted precious time.

"Notify the elders that we are having an emergency meeting. You will not mention a word about what you just witnessed, or I will have your head. Is that clear!" Nashir gave a curt nod, already forming theories on me.

Nashir was swiftly out of sight and left me alone with the cousin who seemed just as stunned as I felt. She was standing, showing no sign of distress, even though her body and face looked wrecked. I walked closer to her and pulled air from her lungs, making her light-headed enough so she wouldn't dare scream and make a scene.

"You will tell me exactly what you did to help her escape and how you did it."

She took deeper breaths, so I eased on her. Beads of sweat formed on her upper lip.

"I had nothing to do with this. We were just talking and then you showed up," she panted.

"Then how the fuck did she just teleport before my eyes!" I shouted.

It was pointless to keep it quiet. She would lie to me regardless of what I did.

The fact that Maya escaped while my father was absent was the biggest catastrophe. We had her. She was right here, and we kept under strong wards and even heavily drugged. How could this happen? What had we missed?

If the witch didn't want to confess to me, she could explain it to my brothers, so I dragged her through the halls and into the evaluation room. What I wanted to do was drag her by the roots of her hair but instead took her from the crook of her elbow because she didn't resist or utter a word.

Her silence came with defiance, with superiority, thinking my brother's mercy would save her. Fidel could do a backflip, and it wouldn't change the verdict in my head. She was to blame, and no one could convince me otherwise.

I let her stand in the corner while we waited for my brothers to pop in one by one.

Everyone except my father and the younger ones had been called to the meeting.

Fidel walked in after Samuel and Zaki and sauntered directly toward the girl.

He didn't seem fazed about her appearance. If this was someone I loved, I would have been more concerned.

He just stood beside her, looking at me.

Until all the elders were present, no one said a word. Karam and Fazel were the last to arrive, giving the witch a suspicious glance before assuming their seats. As long as my father lived, I was still nothing to my brothers. It didn't matter I was the direct successor to him, as I had no authority and had to wait for the elders out of respect. Edgar, Herman, and Darius were the ones in charge when he wasn't around. The rest of them were Christmas ornaments, nice to have but not necessary.

"You called for a meeting," Edgar stated coldly.

He couldn't even be bothered to even glance at me.

"Yes. I called this meeting because Maya has escaped."

There was no reason to dance around it.

"Excuuuse me?" Karam rose from his seat.

If he was going for the threatening approach, it had the opposite effect. Herman put a hand on his arm, and he sat back down.

"How?" Edgar asked, his eyes boring into mine, waiting for me to slip and lie.

But I wasn't going to do that.

"I . . . I went to her room and found her cousin with her, looking like that." I nodded toward the witch. "Maya came up to me, begging me to help her cousin—"

"You did what!" Karam raised his voice again.

I was a bit taken aback, since Karam never interjected conversations.

"The important part is, she took my arm and disappeared. We have to—"

"Adam, why don't you clear the air and tell us what you were doing in her room in the first place?" Aldridge asked.

His presence alone gave me a headache. He wasn't even a part of the family a week ago.

"I don't need to explain myself to you! I already discussed this with the elders." I turned to Herman instead because if I kept looking at his smug face for one more minute, I would blow it to pieces. But I wouldn't let him get the best of me. So much had gone wrong for me. "We have to act fast. Father will be furious if we don't find her."

"Father will be furious with you, yes. You were given clear instructions, Adam, to stand back until further notice. If she is by foot, she will not get far in this desert," Edgar said, keeping his steady eyes locked on mine. "If she adhāred, using you as a power source, then there is no rush because she can be anywhere in the world, and so can we."

"You said I was allowed to try again!" I countered.

I wouldn't let him frame me for something I didn't do, and I had no idea this was a possibility. I had told them I had seen her adhār, had told them everything I had witnessed her doing. It wasn't my fault they hadn't taken better precautions.

"Yes, I approved of you talking to her, but you were under clear instructions to wait. Were you not?"

His voice was threatening and lethal. He had clearly forgotten my respect for him only went so far.

"I do not take orders from you, brother." I used the same monotone voice against him. "Besides, if that witch wasn't put into the same room as her cousin, she wouldn't have plotted with her and escaped. Who allowed that?" I peered at Fidel, who didn't acknowledge me.

"Were you successful?" Fidel asked the girl, taking her hand in his.

"I think I know where she might have gone," she said, barely above a whisper.

"Successful? Are you kidding. She is the reason Maya escaped. Probably with the help of the stone that you let her keep!" I burst out, unable to control my anger.

Fidel got up and matched my energy. He knocked over a chair and marched toward me. "Father put her on a task, and you fucking blew it!" he spat and shoved me. I stumbled backward. "You're a narcissistic prick, and you don't think about anything but yourself! If Father likes you, if you're his favorite son. This has been your fucking problem your whole life. Grow the fuck up and act like an adult. We are dealing with something bigger than your ego—and believe me, I know how big that is. But we can't follow along your stupid plans just because you want to be the hero."

When he finally stopped yelling, his chest was heaving.

I was too stunned to react, to say anything to my defense. Was that what they all thought of me?

I caught Fidel's girl moving. She unclasped her necklace, pulled the stone pendant out of the chain, and threw it in my direction. It nearly slipped out of my grasp.

"The stone is fake," she hissed. "There are a lot of rumors about whether or not we can part from the Firuzeh, but they are not true. The first time we do, it feels like the end of the world, but we don't actually need them to survive. We only use the Firuzeh to siphon the powers. Your father, on the other hand, really wants them for some reason. That's why I took mine off before coming here. It's my only insurance. So, no, Adam, I didn't help her escape."

"How did she do it, then?" I asked under my breath.

She used me, touched me, and exploited my powers.

"Before you came and ruined everything, she told me where the last piece is or alluded to it. I think it's embedded in one of her teeth. Even with the tiniest piece, she has endless resources of magic. She's not like the rest of us.

With or without her Firuzeh, she can do things we only dream of," she said, her eyes burning a hole through my skin. "It was your fault she escaped! You shouldn't have come. We had a plan."

"Don't you dare pin this on me, you wretched little bitch. It could have been any one of my brothers!"

"But it wasn't any of your brothers," Edgar said after letting her point her fingers at me in front of everyone. "It was you who went in there."

My mind was split down the middle. I was hurt, broken but also angry with myself, with them.

"Nonetheless, we must find her," Herman said, bringing me out of my misery.

"I can try with a tracking spell, but if she is protected, I won't be able to find her," the girl offered as if she belonged here.

Edgar nodded and looked at his watch. The elders discussed strategies on how we could search for her without spreading ourselves thin and risking security. Fidel led the girl out and didn't come back again.

I finally snapped out of my haze and reclaimed my power. I wouldn't let them get me, wouldn't let them bully me out of this family.

"I will go back home and see if she has shown up there, but she will most likely be in Iran," I said.

"You will do no such thing, Adam. We don't need more of your mess to clean up," Karam said.

I was just about to have a fit when Edgar stepped in front of me. "If you fail to follow these instructions, you will be considered a direct threat to the family and dealt with accordingly. Am I making myself clear?"

I took a deep breath and counted to three before speaking. "I want you to remember this day because it will haunt you for the rest of your life, brother." I looked away from Edgar and to the rest of them. "Now, if you will excuse me. I'm apparently off duty." I adhāred.

If I had stayed there one more second, I would have blown the lot of them to pieces. I wouldn't allow anyone to speak to me in such a demeaning way and not regret it, not even my brother. He would regret ever pulling rank on me. My father would be back soon enough, and they would all know their place. I wasn't made the successor and my father's first choice for no reason.

١٣

THIRTEEN

MAYA

My mother's place was the best option because both Mist Creek and Iran would be too obvious. My father's would be the first location Adam would look, even though I had told him how I removed their memories of me.

Of course, I couldn't go back there even if I wanted to. I was a complete stranger to him and my brother. Luckily, I once told Adam my mother lived in Portland in a stupid web of lies about my health. So, if he wanted to search for me, he would need to do some digging. My mom actually lived in Salt Lake City between Liberty and the Sugar House district. Her apartment complex was large, with a lot of residents. I hadn't visited her in ages, and the place hadn't changed much since I was last here.

When I appeared in the hallway in front of her door, no one was there to witness it. As I was approaching my mother's door, a woman's hoarse whisper sounded in my head. *Dried cranberries have sugar in them.* The voice seemingly came out of nowhere and scared the shit out of me. No one was in the hallway, so I figured the noise came from an apartment and proceeded to knock on her door.

My mother looked like she had swallowed chalk when she laid her eyes on me. She pulled me inside and into a tight hug, and when she withdrew, tears were streaming down her face.

"Please, *maman*, I don't have time. Any second now, they can come for me. I just need some money to get by with until I get my shit together."

I hated having to beg her for money.

Instead of being confused or asking questions, she hushed me and ushered me to her kitchen and into her pantry. She moved boxes of whole grain cereal and pulled two fully stuffed duffel bags out from the shelf. Within a minute, a jacket and a cap was handed to me. Then the lights were off, her coat and shoes on, and the door locked.

I followed her blindly, and without a word, she took me through the back stairs and down to the building's parking garage.

Then that voice came again, the same whispery one from upstairs. *They won't help. No one will help you now.*

Again, I tried to shake it off. I didn't have time for voices in my head or to question my mental health.

As far as I knew, my mother didn't have a car, but apparently, I was wrong. She unlocked the doors to a semi old silver no-name-brand car.

"Don't worry, it's not registered in my name," she clarified, as if she could see the anxiety plastered across my forehead.

While I got into the car, she was going around to every window and windshield, drawing on them with her finger. All this time, she had hidden our practices, kept me out, rejected me.

"What was that?" I asked, knowing I saw her drawing sigils on the windows.

She exhaled a long-held breath and looked up at the ceiling, tears lining her eyes. "*Khoda mano bebakhsh.*" She asked god for forgiveness for the heresy she just performed, then she recited a verse from the Quran, and when she finished, she looked at me. "I know what I'm doing is wrong, but I will not let the devil take my daughter again. There is a way out. *Khoda bozorge.* The moment they took you, I knew."

"How did you know?"

"*Yadet nare man madaram.*" She put her seatbelt on and backed the car out.

Don't forget I am a mother. Don't forget I am a mother. Don't forget I am a mother.

Her words went on a loop in my head until we were on the road, and she broke her silence.

She explained everything to me. Ever since I arrived in Iran for my grandmother's funeral and till this very moment, my mother had been trying to protect me, keep me far away from the prophecy and all the things our family wanted me to partake in.

My mother left us because she always knew this day would come. She believed if I hated her enough, I would stay away from her and her family in Iran. She hadn't expected Leyla and Shirin to pull a stunt like that right after the funeral. In fact, she thought they would respect the dead and at least wait forty days before they disgraced grandma's honor with their *jadugari*. Back then, she had no idea I had already slept with Adam and put the prophecy in motion. She begged Shirin and Leyla not to claim me, not to drag me into the Sāhers' claws. Not that it mattered—the reverse psychology Leyla pulled on me made me want it more.

It made me want to belong somewhere, be a part of something great. I just wanted to be wanted, to be important enough for someone. I wanted my existence to matter, to make a difference.

"As much as I prayed to God, I couldn't protect myself against the visions. I have been running from this fate for decades, but now is the time to run alongside the devil and try to redirect our path instead of pretending it doesn't exist."

She was having dreams about me, dreams of me being double-crossed, being forced into a castle, dreams of them torturing me, drowning until they got what they needed, and they finally killed me. These reoccurring dreams had been terrorizing her for months, the entire duration of my stay in Egypt. I had been in and out of consciousness too many times to truly grasp how long I had been imprisoned.

"I knew you would come, so I prepared for your arrival and our escape. I will do anything to save my children." She was looking ahead, not knowing how her words affected me.

She went on, telling me her reason for leaving my father. It was all for me, to keep me as far away from the Sāhers as possible. It wasn't because she didn't love us or that we weren't good enough for her. It wasn't even our western ways or lack of understanding of our culture and religion. The fact that she became religious had nothing to do with it. By moving away, she sacrificed the love of her life, sacrificed seeing her kids grow up.

She did it to keep me alive. Because of me, she left my brother, too. And for what? To what end?

I still did the exact opposite of what she had prayed for. I jeopardized my family, my brother's life, and put everyone at risk by giving in to my impulses. I ruined everything by being stubborn and rebellious.

Because of that, my brother and mother had a strained relationship, and my father had a midlife crisis and an affair with a much younger woman. My father was a fool, yes, but I almost couldn't blame him for sleeping with Dissie. She was ready to do anything to get me out of that house and into Adam's arms.

It was my fault.

A pit was growing in my stomach, a cavity so dark and rotten filled with all the terrible things I had said to my mother over the years.

She never stopped being my mother, never stopped protecting me, loving me, but I stopped being her daughter long ago. I visited her out of obligation when she moved out, but then my resentment grew. I became more and more distant until I forgot about her.

I opened up and told her everything that had happened to me, all the terrible things I had done, the blood on my hands, the Dūshevs that died because of me. I told her about the voices in my head, how I wasn't sure if I was losing my mind. Even tried to tell her what happened with Adam, but it took my breath away thinking about it.

You brought it upon yourself!

My vision blurred, and my body stiffened. I couldn't relive it, couldn't let the words repeat the scenes playing in my head.

Words had been spilling out of me like an avalanche for the past hour while my mother wrapped her warm fingers around my frozen fist. It helped calm my beating pulse and blurry vision. I had lost myself in the mix of it and was trying to make sense of all of it. Voicing my thoughts helped, and a weight lifted from my shoulders.

"I still haven't told you the worst part." I looked at her, seeing her one more time before telling her what I was sure would change her opinion on her daughter. "I left Sepideh there. On pure speculation that she was in tow with them."

My mother's head snapped to mine. "Did you tell her where you would go?" she demanded, the fear clear in her expression.

"No, I barely got ten minutes with her before Adam came into the room, and I decided to escape."

Her shoulders relaxed again. "You can't trust Sepideh or anyone else."

"I trusted her because she was sworn to me, blood sworn to help me."

"Perspectives change. What was once your reality might not stand true in the future."

Although my mother was prepared to take me in, I couldn't stay with her. They tracked me down once and could do it again. It would take time, but when they finally came looking for me in Salt Lake City, I wouldn't be there.

Only when they realize my mom won't be home to answer the door will it raise the red flags, I reassured myself.

Eventually, I would have to leave her. It gave me enough time to think of a plan. The true dilemma was not where I wanted to go but what my next step was. I needed my mother's help in figuring out everything about this prophecy and whether I had a choice in its course. All the information I had on our history was from my family, and maybe that wasn't the whole truth.

"No matter what I do, it feels like I'm just getting closer to fulfilling the prophecy. And we still have no idea what happens next." I pulled my knees to my chest. "Except that I'll die," I whispered mostly to myself.

Acknowledging the possibility made it easier to digest. So what if I died? I had caused so much pain. To my father and brother, before they forgot I existed. To my mother, who was always trying to keep me safe. And to Adam, whose heart I broke so severely it changed him as a person.

"Only if you fulfill the prophecy." She sighed and shook her head. "I am not meant to bury my daughter." She choked on the words. Transfixed by the road, she tightened her grip on the wheel. "You will survive this. We will find a way."

Despite my lingering fear, knowing my mother opposed the Sāhers and their claim on me eased the terror. She would do anything to help me.

١٤

FOURTEEN

ALDRIDGE

Sometimes, I wondered how I got away with the things I did. Either Edgar was doing the most behind the scenes, or I was born under a lucky star. How I planned to accomplish getting this girl out, I had no idea. I barely had to lift a finger. We did make sure she wasn't as drugged as my father intended, but for her to aḍhār out of there, I hadn't thought a possibility.

We needed the girl free and compliant because she was the only one who could bring us the grimoire, preferably before getting herself killed. It didn't take a genius to find everyone she had ever known and wait for her to show up.

When my father got the news, he was fuming. He had a plan set in motion within a couple of hours. Each of us got assigned a house to scout on. A crew was roaming around the houses in Iran. My father warned those in Iran to exercise extreme caution, as they might encounter experienced witches, not just someone like Maya.

The next best crew went to Mist Creek. I would bet my left arm Adam was there looking for her even though he wasn't asked or allowed on the task. He wanted to make things right and finally get father's approval.

I was sent to Salt Lake City with Skandar and Ethan. In front of Ethan, I had to at least fake some interest in finding her. Skandar knew, so we sent Ethan away and decided Skandar would stay near the apartment complex and wait for the mother to return while I went home. We would tell them I was searching in the homeless shelters in the area if anyone came around to ask questions.

I went back home because I was sure I had left her trainers in the boot of my car.

For the longest time, the road had been my home. Without my soul, I had grown accustomed to driving instead of using my powers unnecessarily. I lived in the car, and like the idiot I was, I had put off emptying the car after I stopped running from my father. The boot was filled to the brim with bags of clothes, shoes, empty boxes, old tools, and whatnot and would take an eternity to clean. Anything I needed was in that car.

"What are you looking for?"

Ev came out of nowhere.

I almost hit my head on the doorframe. "Why do you always sneak up on me? I'm looking for a pair of white trainers—whiteish. They were dirty."

"Oh. Who are we stalking?"

Her eyes glimmered with mischief. She always knew what I was up to. Being the High Priestess and greatest witch of her time provided an unfair advantage.

"The witch without a soul," I replied with a bit more confidence than I could afford.

"You're a fool if you think she will help you." Ev turned to leave.

Perhaps she was right. But I was hopeful, and I was counting on it to work. Never before had the possibility of retrieving the Grimoire of Harut and Marut felt so within reach. This opportunity was golden because not only did she meet all the requirements to pass the through the wards and portals, she was also soulless—in case Solomons curse was real. *No soul in this realm may lay a hand upon the Grimoire of Harut and Marut.*

Had I left her at my father's mercy—and by extension, ended the prophecy—I would have lost my only chance to end the practice of taking souls.

In exchange for her help, I would vow to keep her away from my family. It was a deal, a simple service trade. How I would hide her from my father for the rest of her life, I would worry about later. Ev would tell me it was a recipe for disaster. I happened to love disasters, to thrive in them. The real question was where she stood regarding the prophecy. Was she a prisoner of fate, bound against her will, or did she view it as a chance to honor her people? I needed to convince her, change her perspective, make her see things differently.

An hour after gutting my car, I eventually found the trainers. If the girl was smart, she would be warding against this, against me. I was betting on her not to, though. Betting on her to panic and make mistakes, which was why I had to act fast.

"Ev!" I shouted into the house when I didn't find her in the kitchen. "Ev, I need your help."

"It's always 'Ev, I need this,' 'Ev, I want that.' 'Ev, Ev, Ev.' How about you magic your ass to Oaxaca and bring me more cheese like I asked you to."

"I did. It's in the fridge. Now, come and help me, will you."

She sat on the chair with a sigh, her hand reaching out. "Let me have a look."

She grimaced when I handed her the shoes, then closed her eyes without further comment. Most practitioners would need to perform a full tracking spell, not my sister. No, she could see beyond the veil using far less resources.

After a moment of silence, she threw the shoes back at me and scoffed. "I thought you said she was a witch." She crossed the room and placed her palms against my temples.

Ev had countless gifts passed down from our mother. She was an acutely aware seer, connected to spirits and earth, conjuring images by touch. And the elements, they answered to her. I was grateful she couldn't also extract my thoughts because she already saw enough as it was.

When we were kids, she used to create images inside my head as if I was a blank canvas. She would make up teddy bears made of candy floss, rainbows made of cake, and once a horse that was chewing a huge pink bubble gum.

The horse with the gum became her favorite trick when I didn't listen to her. I would cry because I was scared of chewing gum.

When I got old enough and started dreamwalking, I would make the same horse chase her in her dreams. We used to get in so much trouble until we made a pact to never cross the line without permission.

Everie's touch on my temples conjured a vision of a flawless house, white picket fence, vibrant garden, and an old, unidentified car. In front was a *For Sale* sign.

Breaking and entering an empty house. What a bold move, bruja.

١٥

FIFTEEN

MAYA

We stayed at a house located two hours south of Salt Lake City. It was my mother's friend's place that sat empty. It had been on the market more than two years. Her friend had let her borrow it, as long as she cleaned and tidied up before the realtor came to do showings—which wasn't very often.

Very quickly, it became apparent to me why the house was still on the market. Echoes of screaming spirits filled the house. An infant was crying, a child wailing for help, a man begging god for forgiveness, and a woman shouting and cussing.

Something terrible had happened in this house, and the spirits had never left. My mom didn't seem too bothered by it when I told her. She relied on the protection of God and thought her prayers would keep the devil out, but I wasn't convinced.

All it would take for them to find us was a bit of detective work or beginner spells.

I need to remember to braid my hair.

I had purposely left my hair unbraided when I was in Egypt in hopes of being rescued. But since having been out, I had to protect myself, ward from them.

I wanted a way out of this prophecy—I truly did. Finding a solution meant leaving my mother. I was unstable and dangerous, and I had to leave.

Of course I didn't tell her that because she wouldn't let me out of sight if she knew. Knowing I was putting her in danger was gnawing at my guilt with every passing minute. We had been at the house for three nights, and I was still looking over my shoulder. My anxiety wouldn't subside until I was away from her, certain my presence no longer endangered her.

These past few days, I had worked so hard on regaining control and managing my powers. I just needed a bit of time to collect myself.

Ever since I escaped, I hadn't been myself. My magic was different. It acted on its own accord. I conjured fire, moved the wind, and I could have sworn I made the earth shake. I didn't have it under control, and I wondered if the Firuzeh was helping me with that, grounding my energy.

Without the entirety of the Firuzeh, I was on the verge of eruption.

My body was in fight-or-flight mode at all times. More than anything, I felt like the earth was draining me, pulling me backward, drowning me. The elements were reaching out to me, begging to be touched. The wind called my name, whispering revelations to me. Water blocked them out—blocked out everything, really. Only when I showered did my energy ease. The voices disappeared, and the images resurfaced.

I need to braid my hair.

"How long will you be? I need to go to the supermarket," my mom said, knocking on the bathroom door.

"Coming out now!" I said and turned off the water.

I had been standing under the scalding hot water longer than I had intended because it was so peacefully quiet. When I came out, she was on her way out with the keys in her hand.

"The realtor might come by today. Don't make a mess."

I wanted to argue and tell her I needed to make tea, but she didn't need to know that. I could make it and clean the kitchen before she got back.

I quickly patted myself dry with the towel and threw something on, so when the realtor came, I wouldn't have to change.

As I was brushing my hair, I realized I forgot to ask for a tub of curl cream or a leave-in. I could survive without it, but it would have been nice to get definition back in my curls. I went through her toiletries, but the only thing she had was makeup and moisturizers.

She hadn't left a phone for me, so I couldn't call her.

"Maybe there is almond or coconut oil in the kitchen," I said to myself.

I forgot what I had come for as I walked into the kitchen. On the kitchen island, she had left a pot of tea on a teapot warmer with a lit candle underneath. I poured myself a mug and let the heat burn my hands. The first sip was always the best, especially when it was so hot it hurt when it landed in the stomach.

The tea had made me so happy I could almost cry. I had to appreciate the small things, all the things I didn't have access to while I was locked up in that room. Just as I sat to finish my tea, a knock came from the front door.

I was living in a bubble and hadn't realized how fast life would throw me a curveball. Because when I opened the door, I was met with Aldridge's wolfish gaze. He was standing in the doorway, looking at me like he had won the lottery. Maybe he enjoyed a game of cat and mouse, toying with his prey before he clawed into it.

I had been exceptionally stupid. *You forgot to braid your hair.*

I knew better and had prepared for this exact moment. I sucked in a breath and couldn't seem to collect my thoughts.

When my mind thought my body was in danger, everything went cold, and time slowed. I wanted to learn to embrace the shivers down my back, to take a quick survey of my surroundings and act. Instead, I froze.

"I'm here to collect a debt, *bruja*," he said, grinning and stepping inside. By instinct, I reared back. "I hope you appreciate my efforts. I waited till mother dearest drove away before interrupting your day."

The wheels were spinning in my head. I could do something, could fight, but my powers were chaotic. Though I could teleport, that would leave him here, waiting for my mother to return.

Aldridge toured the house, first the living room, then the kitchen like a museum.

I followed him silently, hoping my mother was still at the store not coming back anytime soon.

She had been gone for a while, had she not? Fuck!

Aldridge took the mug of tea from the counter, drank from it, and grimaced a surprised look. "Oh, well, we must get going, darling. How long do you need to get ready?" he asked casually, as if it was always planned.

He wanted me to go with him, alive. The ball was in my court, and I could decide how I wanted this to play out.

Be smart!

With shaky hands, I wrote a note to my mother telling her I was leaving, that she had to forget ever having a daughter because I didn't want anything to do with her . . . That everything I told her was a lie, that I had used her for the greater good of the prophecy, and that nothing she ever did could make up for the lies she fed me.

She had to believe I hated her because I couldn't have her follow me. If they tracked down my parents, my father and brother wouldn't know a thing because they simply didn't remember I existed. Hopefully, they would think the spell had worked on my mother, too. Of course, by blood. She was still a Sāher, and a spell like that would never work on her or anyone with a magical bloodline. Luckily, I hadn't disclosed that tiny piece of information when I told Adam everything.

I left the note by the mirror and went to pick up things for myself. Even though we had stayed at this house for a couple of days, we were always ready to leave at any point. I took the packed bag from the bedroom, stole the emergency cash for good measure, and headed to the kitchen.

Aldridge's eyes were fixed on me as I poured the remaining tea from the pot into a large thermos. He didn't interfere with my doings but instead helped himself with the tea left in my mug. It was important to bring the tea with me. This could very well be my last cup of tea, and I was determined to enjoy it.

Priorities! You're such an idiot! You need to get out!

I wanted to tell him I was done and that we could go, but words wouldn't come out. I was afraid that if I spoke, a wall of time and space would collapse. So, I headed toward the door, and he followed, walking past me, his cologne trailing behind him, leading me to my death.

Aldridge hadn't come to hurt my mother. He was there for me and wanted something from me. He was the reason I stopped drinking their poison in Egypt. Yet seeing him in my space sent a panic through me, and I just wanted to get him as far away from the house as possible.

A beat-up car was parked in front of the house. The paint looked new and shiny, but the car itself was dented in more than one place. He got to the passenger door and opened it for me.

"Your highness," he said mockingly.

I rolled my eyes, climbing into his car. He slammed the door behind me, almost crushing my foot in the process.

Before I could buckle up, he sped off.

"Jesus, can you give me a minute!" I snapped.

"She speaks." He glanced over but made no attempt to slow down.

I kept the thermos with me but threw the bag over my shoulder and onto the back seats. Then I clicked in the seatbelt after pulling hard at it a couple of times. The farther we got from the house, the more I relaxed. The tension seemed to leave my body bit by bit. I stole a quick look at him before mustering the nerve to ask the dreaded question plaguing my thoughts since my escape. *At what cost?*

"What's the price for my freedom?"

"I reckon your freedom is priceless. Don't you agree?" His smile did not reach his eyes. "No need to be sulking, demon blood. We have things to do, places to be, and more things to do."

He spoke so nonchalantly as if our families weren't mortal enemies. I was going with him willingly, but there was still the element of threat to my family. We could act civil all he wanted, but I wouldn't entertain him and his sadistic attempt of being friendly.

The initial panic settled after we got on the highway, and I could finally breathe again. I flipped the lid open to my thermos and took a careful sip. It was still so hot it would be deemed undrinkable by most people. He glanced in my direction twice, wanting to say something but kept quiet.

"Where are we going?" I asked him instead.

"New Orleans." He reached his hand out to me. "Share your tea with me. I haven't had my morning coffee today."

I almost wanted to laugh. The idiot had been contemplating how to ask for tea. The same person toying with my freedom like a carrot on a stick.

Perhaps I had to play his game after all. I handed him the thermos as an offering, for information. "New Orleans! That's, what, a two-day trip?"

He shrugged and sipped a bit of my tea. "It's quite good. I like it." He took a big gulp before slamming the thermos back in my hand and putting his palm on his abdomen.

That feeling was very familiar. When it hurt so much, it felt like you were burning from the inside.

"That's what you get from gulping it down like you're late for school."

He snickered at that, showing off his fangs—not canines. No, those were perfectly sharpened fangs.

"Why are we not flying to New Orleans? Is that not in your budget? I mean, I could teleport if you let me try, but you would have to tell me how to navigate because I wouldn't know how to get there. I would love to get this gift exchange over with as fast as possible."

I wasn't trying to be sarcastic. It just sounded that way when I tried to be normal without smacking him across the face.

"We're not flying to New Orleans because we're avoiding law enforcement until we find a way out of this predicament, Ms. Fugitive." His eyes found mine for a second before he looked back at the road. "So, while you make yourself comfortable here, try making yourself as invisible as—d'you know what?" He took a more measured look at me. "A buzz cut would make you look less like you."

"That's not happening!"

I could glamour, but I didn't tell him that, in case I needed to escape him. He didn't press on the matter. He was probably trying to mess with me. I left out the part about how my hair was the most potent part of me, how it grounded my energy. The thought of cutting my hair felt so adverse.

"Wait, why are we avoiding law enforcement? I don't exist here. My family made sure of that. I have fake documents."

"And my father made sure you reappeared." He pulled out his phone, went on a website, then handed it to me.

"Interpol!"

They had my actual passport photo with my real name and surname. The only inaccurate information was nationality and place of birth, which they had conveniently changed to Iran because *with Iranian roots* didn't have the same ring to it. It had to be as foreign as possible to make them believe I was an enemy of the American people.

"Have you read this! 'Participation in the activity of an illegal armed formation. Organization of activity of a terrorist organization and participation in the activity of such organization'—is this a joke?"

"You must admit, he is thorough. Making you a top priority target," Aldridge said without a care in the world.

I didn't know why I thought I was free just because I got out. Most people didn't give Interpol a second thought, but he was right. I couldn't just hop on a plane. I thought escaping Egypt would release the pressure suffocating me. But even when I was with my mother, I was confined to the four walls, and this was no different. I was prison hopping.

Only upside was they probably couldn't track me while I was with Aldridge. Because if Aldridge was good at something, it was flying under the radar. Adam once told me how all his family was looking for him. *He still got caught.*

It was different being near a Dūshev again. Not that Aldridge felt like one—his energy didn't ooze out of him like the rest. Somehow, his powers were encased. His energy had the same bounce as someone veiling. Which reminded me of my unbraided hair. It had honestly slipped my mind. I couldn't do it in front of him because I would have to recite the enchantment out loud, and I didn't want him to know my secrets. I wasn't sure it would work if I did it in my head, but I still tried. I made a French braid with my damp hair and recited the words to myself.

By shadows cast and unseen ties, cloak me now from their prying eyes. Cloud my presence, make me unseen, keep me safe from any harm. Guardian mothers, silent and wise, wrap me in your darkest skies. As moonlight weaves its silver thread through my hair, protect me now from all despair.

A blanket of silence roofed us. With the braid, I was more at ease, even with Aldridge by my side. Looking out of the window, I drifted off without warning and fell asleep.

When I woke up again, it was dark, gray, and cloudy. I went into fight mode before I cleared my mind and grounded my energy. My body had somehow betrayed me by falling asleep under these circumstances. I was so exhausted I could easily fall asleep again. The car was parked outside a gas station, and when I looked over, I realized I was alone in the car.

I tilted my head back against the headrest, and my eyes closed again, not giving a damn what kind of hell he had gone to. *Be darak.*

I only woke up when Aldridge wrenched the car door open and jumped in.

He was completely oblivious that he scared the shit out of me, and I almost reacted on impulse.

For the past few days, I had slept with one eye open, and I don't know why it stopped. My magic had been on edge. It buzzed under my skin whenever something unexpected happened, begging to be let loose—to cause havoc at any uncertainty. I was still learning, still having difficulty working through my emotions and the fear that fueled that force.

I took a deep breath before asking, "What time is it?"

My voice came out raspy. Showing no sign of the explosion that was about to happen. I kicked my shoes off and pulled my knees to my chest. My neck hurt from sleeping in an awkward position, but I slept surprisingly well.

"Just past midnight. I got paninis. Bresaola or veggie?" He gestured for me to take the bag.

"What?" I muttered because I was still trying to process how I had slept for nine hours straight. "Did you drug me?"

"What? No, are you having a laugh?" He picked a sandwich and handed me a bag with three sandwiches, some oranges, water, and organic carrot juice.

"How was I gone for that long?"

"I don't bloody know. Is it the first time you fall asleep or something? Is the concept new to you?" His accent got thicker as he got more frustrated. "If I needed you drugged, I wouldn't have bothered with knocking on your front door." He struggled to unwrap his sandwich one-handed, nearly dropping it.

His knee was keeping the steering wheel in place because god forbid he stopped the car to eat or at the very least focused on the road instead of his next bite.

"Eat. We have an hour's drive left to the motel. There, you can stretch your legs or run away if you dare."

"Funny," I deadpanned and grabbed a sandwich from the bag.

I hadn't realized how hungry I was until I was halfway through. It was probably the best thing I had had in a long time. The combination of pickled red peppers, eggplant, and fresh mozzarella cheese drizzled with herb dressing was divine. It was so good it was starting to overwhelm me.

I wasn't sure I could contain my emotions, but I didn't want him to see I was having a mental breakdown over a sandwich. Suddenly, I wanted to sob so badly I simply couldn't finish eating. I wrapped it back up, drank half a bottle of water, and pushed the tears back. If Aldridge took notice of the shift in my mood or the fact that my knees were held tightly to my chest, he didn't comment.

An hour later, we pulled up to The Vidor Lodge on the side of the road.

Aldridge jumped out without a word and disappeared into the motel.

I wasn't sure if he actually meant it when he said I could go for a walk and stretch my legs. But he didn't leave the keys, so I could lock the car if I decided to go for a stroll.

What do I care about the car?

I didn't go anywhere, though. I was surprised by the level of confidence. He really didn't expect me to run away. Or perhaps it didn't matter to him if I did—he could probably find me just as easily. *I could try . . .*

My thought was cut short by Aldridge's return. He went to the back of the car and took something out of the trunk. Then he walked up to the passenger door behind me and took out my bag.

"What are you doing?" I asked when he slammed the door and opened mine right after.

"Unfortunately, this is the only place with vacancy, demon blood."

"I'll stay in the car."

I really didn't know what to do with myself, but one thing I knew was I didn't need to be glued to him to pay my debt.

"You will get shot out here, and I can't keep up both a ward on the car and the room." He patted the roof twice. "We're losing daylight, sweetheart."

There had been a protection ward on the car without me realizing it. I wish I knew his agenda because the façade he was putting on was creeping me out. While I aimed to destroy his father's legacy and his father aimed to kill us, Aldridge's mission was entirely different. While we were running around playing tag, he was playing chess and laughing to himself. He was answering to someone else, maybe someone with far more influence than any of us.

I slid my feet halfway in my shoes and hurried behind him. Sharing a room with him was much more than falling asleep in his car. Luckily, I had done just that and didn't need to get more sleep.

The motel was outdated, to say the least, and smelled like a common room for chain smokers. An old TV hung in the corner, blasting Fox News. The receptionist was an old wrinkly lady with the nametag *Margret*. She had long yellow teeth, red lips, silver hair twisted in a hair clip, and daisy studs. She turned down the volume before sliding a paper across the desk to Aldridge.

"Fill out the top half for me, boy," she said to him in the most condescending tone. Then she turned her attention to me behind her dirty glasses. "You Mexican?" she asked shamelessly.

I looked up at the TV, registering the words *ILLIGAL MIGRANTS* flashing red, then back at her.

"Worse. I'm Muslim," I said and smacked a hand on the desk. She flinched. Aldridge coughed, holding back his scoff. "Sorry. Thought I saw a roach." I smiled, giving it my best.

The hag probably thought Muslim was a country, a bad, bad place in the Middle East. She laughed nervously before taking the paper and handing Aldridge the key.

"If I get woken up because she calls the cops on you, I will murder you in your sleep," Aldridge said, leading me down the hall with old floral wallpaper, mustard-yellow carpet, and dust-covered lamps dangling from the smoke-infested ceiling.

He stopped in front of door 21J and fumbled with the key and its massive key chain until he managed to unlock the door. He gestured for me to go in first and walked in behind me. If someone had told me a year ago I would willingly go anywhere with Aldridge and sleep in the same room as him, I would have thought they had gone mad.

Twin beds. How decent of him.

He put his bag on the bed closest to the door and mine on the other, then went on his knees and stripped the sheets off.

What the fuck is he doing?

"Checking for bedbugs. You should do the same."

So, I did, even though I wasn't going to sleep in the bed, but even sitting on it would be bad.

Not long after, Aldridge was knocked out.

I could kill him . . . With what, bitch, your bare hands?

Of course, I did nothing. For hours, I was twisting and turning with nothing to entertain myself with. There was a TV in the room, but I doubted there was anything remotely interesting to watch.

I dozed off a couple of times and scolded myself for almost falling asleep. So, I went to the bathroom and splashed cold water on my face to wake me. When I lay back down, I didn't expect to sleep after the nine hours on the road. It felt like I was catching up on missed hours.

I didn't wake before a subtle rustling put my nerves on high alert and my eyes snapped open. In the pitch-black room, I made out a silhouette of a tall figure bending over at the end of Aldridge's bed.

My heart caught in my throat. In an instant, I was in fight-or-flight again, ready to use my powers.

I bolted upright, slamming my hand on the light switch. The brightness blinded me. My eyes adjusted, and I realized it was just Aldridge.

His head turned halfway, watching me warily through the corner of his eyes. Waiting for me to say something.

I was still drawing back my powers, focusing on not burning the place down. Everything under me shook, the lamps flickering, and a flowerless vase fell to the floor without shattering.

"Take deep breaths and hold them in."

Aldridge's voice was scarily calm. Calmer than I would have been if it were me standing there. I wasn't sure why, but I listened. I took deeper breaths each time and tried to hold them in. Gradually, my energy stabilized with my breathing.

"Keep going," he said as I pulled it all back and glanced at him.

"I'm—"

I pressed my palms against my eyes and rubbed them vigorously before removing the quilted duvet cover and swung my legs over the edge.

I ran into the bathroom, washed my face, and combed out the knots in my hair so I could do a proper protection spell. I whispered the incantation while making a French braid in my hair.

I looked at myself in the mirror and couldn't recognize the reflection. My eyes were red, as if I hadn't slept for ages. I washed my face again and still felt as exhausted as I looked.

"How can I still be so damn tired?!" I asked myself.

"You're recharging," Aldridge said from the bedroom.

I had closed the bathroom door and didn't think he could hear me.

What else had he heard?

I was ready to leave, standing by the door, wondering how I could utilize these powers. My volatile outburst was beyond my control, but perhaps I could learn to manage it without splitting the earth and burying myself in the rubble.

It was still at the crack of dawn when we left the motel. Margret wasn't there, only an elderly man who accepted the keys from Aldridge. He walked ahead of me, threw his bag in the trunk, and left it open for me. He was on his way to the front when I saw them in the trunk and froze in place. My grip loosened, and the bag slipped from my fingers. I reached in and took out my old sneakers.

"This . . . this is how you found me," I said and holding up the shoes.

Aldridge looked taken aback, like he had completely forgotten about them. He had used a tracking spell, one of the most effective ones. I could still have blocked it, had I braided my hair, and cast the incantation over myself. He had a witch on his side, someone helping him find me.

"All this time, you knew what was going to happen. From the very first time you kidnapped me, you knew where I would end up."

Why did I expect anything less from a Dūshev. Of course he knew.

"Far from it. Put your bag in the boot." When I didn't move, he closed the distance between us and took the bag, closing the lid behind him. "Get in the car, and I'll tell you what actually happened."

I did as I was told without a fight. Did I ever make my own decisions? Was I merely the result of the people around me? A product of my surroundings? Did I have any independent thoughts or opinions? Archived memories resurfaced one by one. All the steps that brought me here, to this moment. Why even bother when everything had been planned?

Let the current drag you under. It will soon end.

I had been completely numb until Aldridge broke the silence in the car.

"I took your shoes as a precaution in case I had to find you again. It was never about you when I first kidnapped you. Adam had my soul, and I wanted it back. My lead convinced me that you were my only way in. That Adam's attention would be split between the two of us, and I would have a better chance of getting my soul back. Of course the witch had a different agenda."

"The witch—" I turned to him, wide-eyed. "Dissie?"

I had completely forgotten how much of a part Dissie had played in all of this. She had her dirty little fingers in every aspect of my life. All the scheming she did and all the people she seduced to further her agenda.

"Yes." He scowled. "She tried convincing me it was in my best interest to take your soul. I had no interest in your soul. If I had the slightest inkling that the prophecy was linked to you, I—"

"You did try to take my soul!"

I remembered the first time I saw it happening, the smoke rising from Dissie's mouth in that dark alley near Hen & Co.

"And I saw you try taking her soul, too."

"I was never going to actually take her soul. I was just trying to put her in her place. And you . . . I wanted to scare you." He grinned with a glint in his eyes, like the trauma he caused meant nothing to me. "When I first came to Mist Creek, looking for my soul, I had no idea how I would handle Adam. The witch offered me a way in, and I took it. One day, we were having an argument about our loose terms, so I reminded her who she was dealing with. I tugged at her soul slightly. Nothing happened. She did eventually convince me that you mattered to him. And by taking you, it meant getting him, but Adam was stronger than I expected, and without my soul, I was so bloody powerless. When I tried to best him the second time and failed again, I fled for good."

He wasn't embarrassed about being weak or having to flee. His tone of voice was more matter-of-fact.

"That first time, when you almost broke my arm . . . You told me to stay out of the claws of Adam. Why? if you had no idea about the prophecy."

He was hiding something.

"I told you to stay away from him because people are better off without us regardless of the circumstances. Had I known you were carrying Adam's soul all along, I would have taken it and traded it for my own."

I scoffed, rolling my eyes. At least that was the truth. I couldn't actually blame him for being selfish.

"What do you know of the prophecy?" I asked, hoping he hadn't noticed how much information I was prying out of him.

His brows furrowed. The glint of the sun reflecting on an approaching car had caught his attention.

"I have gathered quite a lot of information on this prophecy and your role in it." He looked away from the road and studied me for a second. "How do you feel about being the one everyone either wants to protect or kill?"

Smart. Not giving me an answer. He thought I didn't see through it, then it dawned on me that no one else had bothered to ask me how I felt. I was either expected to fulfill it or hunted for it. I had detached from the life I had before because I knew I was never going to get that part of me back.

When I died that day, it wasn't a metaphorical death. My life would never be the same. I thought I didn't care what would become of me, if I lived or died. I pushed all thoughts, hopes, and dreams of the future away. Dreams I thought I didn't have, things I thought didn't matter to me.

Every day, I shoved those thoughts further back where I couldn't reach them. They had been gnawing at me, scraping the insides of my mind. Was this all there was to my life? Was I always meant to be a vessel for someone else's purpose, a means to an end?

"I—"

I couldn't answer the question and wouldn't confess to Aldridge that I didn't want any part of it, that I didn't want to be the chosen one. I wanted nothing to do with this prophecy, with the Dūshevs, or even with the Sāhers.

"You were never given a choice, and even now, the decisions are being made for you." He finished the thought for me. I felt his gaze landing on me. "If you keep biting your lips, you will eventually break through the skin."

It was one of those unconscious things I did when I was lost in my own mind. I had never actually bitten through the skin, but I had done it enough for him to notice in the short amount of time we had spent together.

Don't let him change the subject.

"I feel like I escaped Egypt too easily. How come they didn't torture the information out of me? I'm sure I would have folded like fresh laundry if they had been more insistent. I'm not that strong willed."

"You—they didn't torture the information out of you because if they did, your ancestors would interfere and give you access to powers beyond any of us. My father is a practitioner first and Dūshev second. He knows his limitations. He is a very calculated player, and he would rather torture everyone around you than risk the wrath of a thousand dead witches. He was confident he would get what he wanted from you in time."

"And what do you want from me?"

"Unfortunately, for you, I'm not much better than the rest of them."

I understood this was as far as I could push my luck. Eventually, he would tell me. Like any other villain with a manifesto, he would lecture his enemies.

١٦

SIXTEEN

Maya

Aldridge was very particular about where we ate. We ate the day-old sandwiches four hours ago. When I asked if we could stop by a fast-food place, he said he didn't make it a habit of eating rubbish. In some ways, he was very much a posh Brit.

By looking at him alone, I would never have guessed he was Adam's brother. They all resembled a bit of their father, but their looks mostly reflected their mothers. Seeing them next to each other, then yes, they were very much related. But individually, they were so different from each other. Aldridge was taller than most of his brothers, his skin golden brown like most of them, but his eyes were a specked amber, and his teeth sat in a flawless arch with pointy canines.

Gosh, he has a nice set of teeth.

We finally made a stop at a diner in the middle of nowhere. On the other side of the street was a closed gas station followed by a series of dilapidated structures.

It felt like we were in a simulation. The air wasn't moving, the scene so eerie quiet it gave me chills. The inside of the diner was nice and clean. Its staff knew Aldridge. The busboy winked at him before retreating to the kitchen. The waitress called him Tres, like the number. He was very comfortable with them, almost as if they were friends.

I couldn't tell if he was faking it or if my experience with him was the mask he put on for strangers.

Aldridge ordered for us when he went to talk to the red-haired waitress. She was mesmerized by him, giggling at the right moments. It was cute to watch because she was so endearing. We sat in a corner without speaking before the waitress brought us the food.

"Your usual, Tres." When she looked at me, she flashed the most sincere smile. "And for you, our eggplant sourdough." She winked at me.

The food looked so delicious I was afraid I wouldn't have enough room in my stomach to finish it. Toasted sourdough bread with eggplant spread, roasted goat cheese, walnuts, pomegranate seeds, drizzled with honey. The open-faced sandwich came with a side of burrata on a bed of savory balsamic tomatoes, topped with basil.

This was no ordinary diner. I couldn't believe it was located in the middle of nowhere. Every bite was so heavenly I wanted to cry. I ate and ate until I was about to burst at the seams. I finally pushed the plate away to stop myself from eating.

Aldridge got up and headed toward the door with the washed-out WC sign.

When he left, I caved and helped myself with the half-eaten pancake on his plate. He had ordered too much food anyway and didn't finish his sweet treat. These were probably the best fluffy pancakes I had ever had, and they even had the real kind of maple syrup, not the sugar-based ones.

I took the last bite drenched in syrup and let it melt on my tongue. Then I pushed my chair to reach the back wall. I wanted to rest my head against the wall, but the braid was getting in the way. So, I took the hair tie out and undid the plait, planning to braid it back in the car. It had been so tight, mulling at every strand I hadn't even realized it was giving me a headache. Letting my hair down was like taking off my bra at the end of a long day.

I closed my eyes to cherish the euphoric feeling of being perfectly content.

The lingering taste of maple syrup on my lips and the soft jazz playing in the background were moments I might never get to experience again.

I hated to take back my own words, but maybe I wasn't ready to let it all go. So what if I changed my mind and wanted to live a fulfilled life?

"Are you sleeping?" Aldridge asked.

"I'm having a moment," I said and closed my eyes again and crossed my arms.

The food coma was settling. I could take a nap on this floor if they let me.

"Please make it a habit of napping in the car and not while we're out, especially when I'm not there," he snapped for no reason.

"Of course! My mistake. What if I get kidnapped by a Dūshev. Oh no, wait . . ." I cocked my head and pressed my lips together.

The diner was basically empty. It was just us, three men at the bar, and the elderly couple who were barely able to hold their coffee mugs. I wasn't worried about anyone listening in on our conversation.

The redheaded waitress came to our table with an embarrassed expression. She was so gorgeous I couldn't help but gawk at her.

"Tres," she hesitated, biting her lips. It almost looked practiced. "Jimmy said—and I quote—'If he comes here again, making all these obscure requests without even sayin' hi, I'll spit in his food.'"

"Obscure requests! I always get pancakes," Aldridge scoffed and headed to the kitchen, while the redhead stayed behind with a twinkle of appreciation in her eyes.

"They're like an old married couple," she said, her eyes following Aldridge.

When she looked back at me, the waitress-tilt of her head was gone. Same with the smile I was so mesmerized by.

Without missing a beat, she asked, "Are you dating Tres?"

Clever girl.

"Absolutely not!" I spat. "I'm not into his species."

Anymore.

I left the rest to her imagination. I meant Dūshevs, but she probably thought I meant men.

When comprehension settled, she lost her composure. All color drained from her face as if she had seen a ghost— or a witch? It would at least explain her startled expression.

Hurriedly, she collected the empty plates and left without a word.

Maybe she thought I was hitting on her and got ashamed or knew about the Dūshevs.

Aldridge came back with a grin. "Go wait in the car. I'll be right out." He handed me the car keys and nodded toward the exit.

Being bossed around annoyed me but then a strange feeling settled in my stomach, and all I wanted was to leave that place.

I took his keys without any argument and headed for the door.

IV
SEVENTEEN

Adam

My father lost it when he found out Maya escaped, and I blamed myself for the mistakes that led us here. I would get on my father's good side again. I wouldn't let him shut me out.

My father was a very well-connected man, a "diplomat," some would say. He spent a great portion of his time with "Al Akhwan," an elite society for men of higher status. If three members vouched for you, you would be invited to interview for a membership. So far, only Edgar had been urged to join. Not that the rest of us were interested. It sounded like more work than anyone was interested in putting into it.

Being in Al Akhwan allowed you to influence events and make demands reserved for high profilers, like making people disappear. These favors obviously didn't come for free. My father had gone to great lengths to find her. When he had Maya's face planted on Interpol's site, I understood the level of obsession he had over this prophecy.

Besides government officials, my brothers were on this task as well. I stayed back with my father, hoping I wouldn't fuel his anger. Maya's cousin Sepideh proved to be more useful than expected, even though she only shared information with Fidel and never with my father directly.

Perhaps it made a difference in her heart that she wasn't directly working with my father, or maybe Fidel wasn't telling us the whole truth. Either way, with her help, we had caught three of their cousins and two older women from their coven. All unaware of Sepideh's involvement in their capture. Not that they were conscious enough to put two and two together. The majority of the time, they were kept under heavy doses of the sedative that Herman had reformulated.

Herman was a chemist, a medically trained doctor, a stem cell specialist and everything in between. He had the most diplomas and doctorates, and his knowledge was beyond comparison. My father relied on him for many things only shared among the elders.

Soon, I would be on that list too—an elder or not, they would have to include me.

The witches were brought in one at a time like cattle for sale. They were shown to us all in the evaluation room.

To determine if we'd met them before, my father wanted everyone to see the witches we were dealing with.

When the first one, Seema, was brought in, confliction lined Samuel's eyes. He hadn't been there when they caught her, and even if he had, there was nothing he could have done. Things were changing in this family, and there wasn't much we could do about it.

I gave him a sympathetic look, hoping it encouraged him to stand tall. I understood his pain, having had been in his shoes. I had loved one and been fooled like an idiot.

Shortly after, Roya was brought in, who Omar had dated years ago.

When the last cousin, Lara, was revealed, Amir had a meltdown. He seemed genuinely confused and kept repeating to himself what an idiot he had been.

Sepideh showed no remorse when she identified her aunts. She looked at them like they were complete strangers to her. It was my mission to find them, the entire coven if it was what it took to lure out Maya. She wasn't very close to her mother, but since we had tried locating her without any luck, my father deemed her mother a top priority.

"I have a few ideas on where some of them might be. As for Maya's mother, she hasn't practiced in decades. She left our coven and found God. It's more than likely she doesn't even know she has a daught—"

"Careful how you lie to me, child. Of course she knows her own daughter," my father said.

What he wasn't telling her was, you are only as important as the information you can provide.

"With all due respect, Father, I think she is telling the truth. It's the spell I told you about."

My father narrowed his eyes before looking back to Sepideh.

She nodded. "None of her human relatives or friends know her. It's genius if you think about it. She has no one to turn to except our coven."

Sepideh's only goal was to stop Maya and anyone in her way to fulfill the prophecy. I had yet to understand why, though. I refused to believe she didn't have an ulterior motive.

"The mother remains a priority until we are positive she knows nothing."

A lot of effort was going into finding the rest of the Sāhers.

My father was pleased enough with the meeting when he dismissed her.

"Stay," he commanded when I was about to leave with them. "Zaki and Amir, Adam will accompany you to Tehran. In fact, call for Henry and Malek as well. I need my strongest in the danger zones."

"*Hader*," Amir and Zaki said in unison.

They nodded obediently and searched for Malek and Henry. I stayed, knowing my father had more in store for me.

"This is your final chance before I pull you out of our ranks completely." He paused. "Have I made myself clear?"

I looked down, feeling content. "Yes, Father."

Tehran was much more polluted than I remembered. I had visited ages ago, but I didn't exactly know my way around. We were sent out to find their High Priestess Leyla. It seemed like a big deal, but Sepideh had warned us that the lead was weak.

I wasn't very hopeful. Even though we had found a handful, it had been a lot of effort on our part. We were given an address to check out, but the house looked abandoned.

The five of us teleported inside and slowly entered one room at a time.

All surfaces were covered in dust and appeared like it hadn't been touched in months. Every room reeked of sewage.

"Holy fuck, it stinks of death in here." Henry covered his face with his shirt.

The next room we entered had books scattered all over the floor.

"Let's just clear the rooms and get out." I picked up a book and shrieked, letting go of it.

The book burned the skin off of my fingers where I had touched it.

Amir and Zaki were instantly in front of me, examining the book. Zaki touched the book with the tip of his fingers and hissed.

"We need to take all these books with us," Zaki said and pushed them into the middle of the room with his foot. Then he picked up oven mittens and rearranged them into neat piles.

There were maybe eight or ten heavy leatherbound books in the middle of the room when Zaki started pushing furniture around and removing the corners of the rug under them. Amir helped him fold the ends of the rug over the books and wrapped them in like a burrito.

"I'm taking these home. Clear the rooms and come back home. I don't think there's anyone here," Zaki said and disappeared with the makeshift package.

We rummaged through the rest of the house and found nothing of interest. Amir was moving bookshelves around to see if he could find hidden passages. It didn't look like that kind of house, though. This place was not one of those lived-in spaces where generations had left marks of wear.

"Honestly, I can't think clearly in this horrid stench," Henry complained, moving toward the window to open it when Amir came into the room.

"Guys, I think there is a gas le—"

But it was too late. The explosion hit us before I realized what Amir was trying to say.

EIGHTEEN

SEPIDEH

All my guilt, the betrayal, all the anxiety I lived with was going fester, even deeper if I couldn't atone for what Leyla had set up for them. She was more prepared than I expected.

Leyla had predicted their moves and had planned accordingly. In Shirin's house, Leyla had left enough Easter eggs to pique their interest. Zaki left moments before the house exploded, but Adam, Henry, Malek, and Amir were still in the house when it happened.

She knew they could escape, but it was definitely not without causing damage. I was just grateful Fidel wasn't one. The four had teleported back with third-degree burns and open-flesh wounds. The elders, mostly Herman and Karam, did what they could to disinfect and close the sores until the right medical equipment was brought in.

They were going to be wary of me, probably blaming me for leading them into a deathtrap. Which was why Fidel confined me to my room until he had things under control.

I spent my solitude trying to figure out how to track Maya down with nothing to work with, having already tried all the simple tracking spells. I didn't have any of her blood, and the hair she had left on her bed and pillow didn't seem to work.

I was missing something. The hair should have helped, but somehow, all the forces were against me. Probably Leyla's handiwork. Her spells were extremely potent and full of intent. Her and her damn prophecy. How had she won the favor of our ancestors I would love to know. She wasn't working alone.

I was zoned out, gazing out of the window when Fidel came into the room.

"Any luck with the spells?"

"Not yet. Are you sure she didn't leave any shoes in her room?"

I knew the answer. It was the first thing I asked about. It would be the easiest way to find her if I had a pair of her shoes.

Fidel shook his head.

"Why was she even wearing shoes inside? Who does that!" I exclaimed.

She had lived there her entire life. Of course she would act like them and wear outdoor shoes inside. She probably sat with them on the bed as well.

"*Shibshib* don't count as shoes," he said, pointing to his feet before his eyes grew to saucers. "Do they?"

"What are you talking about!" I snapped.

I didn't mean to. I was just on edge.

"Slippers!" he said and disappeared on a whim.

I had stopped anchoring when I got here. Adding to their anxiety was unnecessary. If, suddenly, they weren't able to teleport because I was around, they would get creative and drug me too.

Within seconds, Fidel was back, clutching a pair of men's slippers. "Try with these!" He handed them to me. "They are the slippers from the bathroom. She was the last person to use that room. She would have used them in the bathroom. That should mean something, right?"

I couldn't help but smile at his beautiful, beaming face.

I had done object tracking before with a pendulum, but tracking people was considered the darker arts. Not that I was shy of that. If you had dealt with necromancy, all else felt like child's play. Still, there were no guarantees in *jadugari*. There were many ways to do a tracking spell with shoes. Unfortunately, I was only taught one—granted, a very effective one. I had one shot, so once the slippers were burned with the mark, they were useless for tracking.

He helped me clear the space, brought me a jar of salt, and stepped back as I created a circle and lit candles in the four corners. Fidel sat on the chair a good few feet away from me in case the whole thing went up in flames. He watched me carefully as I unsheathed the athame.

"Where thou step, the soil recalls. Where thou wander, shadow falls. Winds reveal thy path and guide me true. Lead me forth and grant my pursue."

I cut across my palm with the athame and let the droplets land on the soles of slippers. The blood slid and moved until a web of interconnected red lines covered both soles. With my blood, I traced sigils on the marble floors, covering the entire salt circle. When I finished the last of them, everything turned to nothing, and I ceased to exist. In my mind's eye, I saw it. I saw where she was or could be. Time wasn't linear but stacked, parallel and multidimensional. It was all the things and nothing all at once.

Gently, my senses returned, my body grounding as it settled into itself. My blood ran cold when my vision didn't return as my other senses, and I wondered if that was the price of betrayal. It wouldn't surprise me if the ancestors took my sight because of the prophecy.

I inhaled a relieved breath when my sight gradually came back to me.

Fidel walked up to me, worry etched in his eyes. "Don't hide from me, Sepideh. I can see what it does to you, and I don't think it's worth it if you have to drain yourself every time we need something." He cupped my cheeks. "My family is not worth it. We can just leave."

"She has to be stopped and so does your father. I just wish we had more people on our side."

"I can't risk it." He sighed, his forehead touching mine. "I can't risk you."

I kissed him without pressing the matter further. This was an argument we had had before. He didn't want to confide in anyone in case it backfired.

"I think I know where she might be," I said, changing the subject.

I described the area I had seen in great detail. We were looking for a gas station, a diner called Sussie Ann's, and a vacant building. Sussie Ann's turned out to be a chain, but he finally narrowed it down to two places. He pulled up a picture on his phone of the diner next to a gas station. It looked pretty accurate until he showed me another location that looked exactly the same. When he turned the arrow around to the building next to it, I was sure we had found it. On the side of the building, bold red graffiti spelled out the words *From the river to the sea*.

"This is it. This is where I saw her," I said.

"Dallas." He zoomed out on the map. "I just need to find a spot I recognize that is close enough."

"When you find her, don't hesitate and don't let her touch you!" I said and grabbed his arm to get his attention. "Fidel, listen to me. She is stronger now. She can take advantage of your powers just by proximity. Don't let your powers reach the surface. Shield yourself like I taught you and don't hesitate to kill her."

"Don't worry. I know what I'm doing."

One moment, he kissed me, the next, my hand was hanging in midair. It only occurred to me after he was gone that he went after her without so much as a vial of the sedative. He had to rely on catching her off guard. If she was on the road with her mother, there was nothing to worry about because *Khale* Hila didn't practice. If she was with Leyla, on the other hand, Fidel might be in a run for his money. Leyla was always ready to take a man by his throat.

١٩

NINETEEN

Maya

The parking lot was empty save for three cars and Aldridge's, which was in the far-right end slightly out of view from the diner.

When I reached his car about to unlock it, the reflection of a man behind me appeared.

Startled, I turned, registering he was swinging a steel pipe at my head. My reflexes were fast enough, and my forearm took the blow.

The shock went through my arm and into my body, but the adrenaline kept me from collapsing at his feet.

I know him! It's one of them.

Realization dawned on me, and I staggered back.

He swung again and hit my ribs this time. I stumbled, pushed up against Aldridge's car. The Dūshev kept swinging at me, aiming for my head, but bashed my shoulder instead.

I fell on my ass, crab walking sideways to get a peek of the diner, but his tall frame blocked my view.

I have power. I have power. I have power.

"I'm sorry, but I have to do this," he said. "The prophecy must end with you."

He needed to kill me, but he hadn't planned it very well.

I didn't move a hair, trying not to alert him.

I have power.

The need to survive grew tenfold, and all I saw was red.

Bleed! I commanded.

He took a deep breath, steeling himself for murder, and was about to swing for my head again when he stopped dead in his tracks.

Scarlet covered the whites of his eyes until it spilled over the rim.

He gripped the pipe harder, aimlessly swinging it around and grunting, while the other hand was rubbing the blood away from his eyes. When he realized nothing was helping, he slammed the pipe against the ground, aiming for whatever came closest to him. It slammed into my fingers and snapped me out of the trance.

I grounded myself and staggered back. If I wanted to come out of this alive, I had to do something. I had to anchor him, burn him where he stood so his soles would melt and fuse with the ground.

Burn!

With less than a thought, fire erupted around him. The steel pipe fell from his hand, clattering on the ground when he screamed at the top of his lungs, losing the voice in his throat, trying to make it stop. Blisters formed on his bare flesh, bubbling and bursting.

Enough! Stop it! Please, a voice screamed in my head.

I released the anchor on him just as I saw the front door of the diner open from the corner of my eye.

Aldridge.

The Dūshev was gone before I did something I couldn't take back.

I would have killed him without hesitation had it not been for the voice in my head.

Aldridge had teleported in front of me, not caring if anyone saw him.

To be fair, I had just put a man on fire with my thoughts, not caring about the consequences.

I wanted to survive. My life was tricked out of my grasp, and I wanted it back.

I want to live.

"What the hell was that?" he said and helped me up.

All he probably saw was the fire that vanished into thin air.

I got up, stiff. "Your brother, he attacked me," I said with a shuddering breath.

"We need to get out of here." He dragged me to the car, opened the door, and shoved me inside before speeding out of the lot.

"They found me," I said mostly to myself. "The braid. I took out the braid."

Idiot!

As if on cue, my hands started to shake when I desperately needed to braid my hair. Hastily, I took a small chunk of hair from the nape of my neck in between my fingers and started braiding. The words of the enchantment slurred on my tongue as I spoke them out loud, not caring what he heard. If I wasn't sitting already, I wasn't sure my legs could carry me.

I can't breathe. I can't breathe. I can't breathe.

I didn't want to cry in front of him, and I couldn't stop myself from hyperventilating. Images of his burning flesh flashed through my mind. I almost burned him alive.

"Breathe, for fuck's sake!" Aldridge said, his hand landing on my shoulder.

I jerked from his touch, which made him pull his hand back. My heart was hammering against my chest, my vision blurring and hands violently trembling.

"Breathe!"

"I am fucking breathing!" I snapped back.

It didn't deter him, though.

"Your body is going into shock, and I can't stop the car right now. If you don't breathe, you will pass out."

"Okay," I whispered, closing my eyes.

"Take deep breaths as you count to four and then exhale on four."

It helped slow my racing heart but not the shaking of my limbs. *I need to throw up.*

Gradually, I was beginning to feel the impact of the blows my body had taken.

I can't breathe. I can't breathe. I can't breathe.

Aldridge registered something in my face and rolled down both windows immediately, letting fresh air flow through. It was all it took for the bile to rise in my throat and for me to haul my upper body out of the window to throw up.

He didn't stop the car, didn't even slow down. By the time I was done, he was handing me a water bottle. Instinctually, I tried to grab it with my dominant hand, but as I tried to lift it, my eyes almost went to the back of my skull from the pain.

How did I not feel this before now?

My right arm was battered so badly it was probably fractured in multiple places. I couldn't move my fingers, especially the ring and pinky he had hit with the pipe. I left my right arm resting on my lap, took the bottle from him with my left, and put it between my thighs to unscrew the cap. I had no strength and struggled to even grip it.

Aldridge opened it for me, letting the cap fly under my seat. "Leave it," he said before I moved half an inch. "Drink."

I swished water in my mouth and spat it out of the window before drinking some. I still felt like shit, but I could finally breathe, relieved I had survived. He rolled up the windows when I leaned my head back and closed my eyes.

"I'm going to ask you this once—"

"Don't be ridiculous," he said, voice steady and low.

"You were conveniently not around when your brother found me and beat the shit out of me," I stated, needing to accuse him.

"If I wanted to kill you, I would've done so already. I don't need other people to do my job for me. And I'm inclined to believe that if you wanted me dead, you would've tried to kill me at that motel. And before you ask, yes, that was a test. Congratulations, you passed. I think we've established an ironic sense of trust between us."

I wanted to laugh at his ridiculous approach.

"I can still change my mind and kill you. Sleep with one eye open."

"Right now, you're the one with both eyes closed, so perhaps you do trust me even though you won't admit that to yourself."

I couldn't muster enough energy to look at him. He was right, there was a sense of safety with Aldridge. At least until he got what he wanted from me.

"Someone is on my tail."

I opened my eyes, confused by his statement. Aldridge had a phone pressed to his ear. I couldn't hear who he was talking to or what was said on the other end.

"I didn't see. She lit him on fire before he adhāred. That should be a clue."

Another quiet moment passed.

Aldridge hummed and disconnected the call shortly after.

I had been sloppy, not thinking ten steps ahead. The Dūshevs had been around long enough to know at least one witch willing to help them.

"It's my fault," I confessed, finally meeting his eyes. "I undid my braid at the diner."

"So you've said." He glanced over, his eyes landing on the haphazard braid peeking out through the layers of my hair.

I shouldn't have told him, but it was too late to deny it.

"You wouldn't have found me either had I been more careful. The veil would have kept you in the dark regardless of the witch helping you with tracking."

"The braid shadows you."

It wasn't posed as a question.

"Before you get any clever ideas about chopping my hair off, braiding is one way to do it. There are plenty of other methods."

I lied. There weren't any as bulletproof, and I couldn't trust him with that kind of information over my head.

"That's not what I—"

"It could also be the Firuzeh," I said under my breath, more to myself than to him. *Maybe if I take out the last piece of Firuzeh . . .* "I can be completely rid of them."

. . . Rid myself of all the things that tie me to the prophecy.

"What are you talking about?"

"I need to see a dentist," I exclaimed.

"Why?"

I wondered if lying was an option or not.

"I need to pull out a wisdom tooth as soon as possible."

"They are not tracking the stone, if that's what you're thinking. When I'm done with you, you can pull all your teeth out."

He knows!

"Is my cousin in tow with you guys?"

He could lie to me—he probably would, but I had to ask. It would either ease the guilt or bury me deeper.

"It seems like it," he said, revealing nothing with his words. "My father seems to think the stone carries the prophecy. What are your thoughts on that?"

"What is it you want from me! What is so wicked and secret that even your family can't know?"

I was tired and broken in so many ways, and I didn't care to change my tone with him. I didn't care if my sharp tongue would get me in more trouble. I was in so much pain I didn't know what to do with myself.

"I need you to help me retrieve a book."

"Are you giving me back after I've helped you, or are you going to kill me yourself?"

"I'm not handing you over to my father, but I might be tempted to kill you myself if you get on my nerves or get in my way."

His answer was so blatantly honest I didn't know what to do with it. Did he think we're friends, just casually making small talk?

"Don't be so smug. No matter where I go, how fast I run, the prophecy will dig its claws into me and drag me back. Whether I like it or not, I'm doomed to finish what has already begun." If he was going to instill fear in me, I would at least try to return the favor.

"You think you can scare me off with your prophecy, witch?"

"Don't you get it! You will all die if this prophecy is fulfilled." I waved my arms for emphasis and hissed from the pain, having forgotten about the shattered bones.

I settled it back in my lap and looked at him with the same intensity as before. In truth, the prophecy's fulfillment was a complete mystery to me. Perhaps they would die or turn human and old age would catch up to them.

"If you want me to kill you, just say that. I can burn the car down with you in it and still protect myself. What are you, thirty, in human years? I'd say you've lived a lo—"

He swerved the car on to the shoulder, stopped the car, and turned to face me fully. "Do it." He pinned me with his unwavering stare.

With the rage building inside me, I could light everything on fire. I couldn't save myself, though. Though his arrogance almost made me want to try. We both knew what leverage he had over me. I wasn't the collateral I worried about. My mother was, my brother, my father . . .

"Make sure you follow through the next time you threaten me," he said, rolling back onto the road. "Or I will make you wish you did."

I wanted to fire something back that would make him feel as helpless as I did.

"I don't know what kind of sugarcoating Adam had to do to convince you to fuck him, but there is no such thing as human years for us. I'm well past three hundred eighty, and that's all there is to it."

His words were like barbwire twisting, tightening, and drowning me in my own blood.

I can't breathe.

The pain of my physical body went to the back of my mind as fresh blood spilled from the place where my soul had been. Maybe I wasn't supposed to breathe anymore. Maybe he was right, and Adam was trying to make his supernatural side more digestible for me. But I did not need to be reminded of Adam, not even the good times.

I wanted to forget him all together.

Aldridge was different from his brother. He was calculated and unapologetic. From what it seemed, ever since he got his soul back, he didn't act on impulses. I couldn't rage-bait him into my preferred course of action. I needed to be nice to him and loosen his tongue before following him into a trap like a blind mouse.

Be nice. Show interest. Men like that.

"What's with the number three?"

"What do you mean?"

He looked confused.

"Why did she call you Tres?"

"It's—" He shook his head, grinning. "It's short for Andrés. I go by Andrés."

Hmm. Suits him better than Aldridge.

"My father named me Aldridge after one of his fellow tradesmen, John Aldridge in England."

"I always thought your name had such a Cream Crusader ring to it."

His head tilted back against the headrest, and he burst into a deep roar of laughter. His long neck exposed as his cheek dimpled and teeth glistened like they were meant to break barriers of skin.

"Back then, my father did a lot of business with the English. Many of us have English names because my father looked up to them. Ethnically, we are one thing, culturally another. With time, we morphed into something third, but I've grown up with the Cream Crusaders. I've seen all their facets and how their sharp edges can cut."

"You grew up in England?"

It was a stupid question, really. His accent was indistinguishable, but I had thought they all grew up in Egypt until a certain age.

"Yes, even after my father got bored with my mother and moved on to someone else. He always had multiple partners at the same time—of course, my mother didn't know that. She never talked about him after he left." He shook his head as if reliving the memory.

When the knowledge settled, I had to keep myself from gasping out loud. "Wait! You lived with your mother. I thought all your mothers died during childbirth."

"Not my mother. She was a practitioner."

"She was a witch!" I whispered to myself, dumbfounded, and turned to fully face him as he focused on the road ahead.

The movement almost brought tears to my eyes. My rib cage constricted my lungs, making my breath to hitch in my throat. I forced the tears back, hoping I hadn't lost momentum with him.

"Did your father know she was a witch?"

He nodded.

"She was English?"

I was pushing my luck.

"No, she was originally from Navarra, Spain—ironically famous for its witch trials."

It explained why *Andrés* was so well versed in spells and wards. Maybe he was even dating a witch. *Roya! No, probably not.*

My mind was drawing conclusions based on nothing, but it would be interesting to see what kind of person he was into. When I first met him, I thought Dissie was sleeping with him, but it was all a woven scheme made for my perception.

Dissie, Adam, Leyla, and even Sepideh played a hand in the deception of my reality, a game I could see no end to. At least Andrés was upfront with wanting to use me for his benefit. Andrés or Drés, I wasn't sure I could get used to that name. It sounded forced and didn't roll off the tongue easily. I would have to come up with something easier to call him before I killed him. Perhaps Andy or Ridge or Drés like his friends.

No! I'm not his friend.

Perhaps just Rés, then. My face is the last thing you will see before you die, Rés.

I made a promise to myself. No one would leverage anyone against me.

Eventually, silence coated us like a thin layer of oil, and the pain came rushing back.

The day's events were going in an endless loop in my head. Dirty motel. Yellow teeth. Flickering lamps. Beautiful redhead. Syrup coating my lips. *SLAM!* Arm. *SLAM!* Ribs. *SLAM!* Shoulder. *SLAM! SLAM! SLAM!* Fire erupting, engulfing. Smoke rising. The smell of burning flesh coating my skin.

Until I finally drifted off and woke up seven hours later. The hibernation state I had suddenly started entering was starting to freak me out. This was exactly what happened when Adam had taken my soul and my body was preparing to die.

Is it happening all over again? I can't double die, can I?

It was pitch black on the road apart from the cars coming from the opposite side of the median strip.

Out of pure habit, I was going to rub my eyes with the heel of my palm, but I couldn't even straighten my right arm. It was stuck at a ninety-degree angle, stiffened the way I had left it resting on my lap.

When I tried again, it took everything in me not to audibly squeal. The same applied to my fingers. They were all stiff. My hand was stuck in The Creation of Adam position. My pinky was swollen and definitely broken. I didn't dare pull up my sleeve to inspect the damage further up my arm. Not that I could see much in the darkness.

"How are you feeling?" He had watched me feeling out my hand for injuries.

"When will we be in New Orleans?" I asked, avoiding telling him I was on the brink of tears. "I need to stretch."

"In about thirty minutes."

He sounded tired and probably was from driving non-stop. Thirty minutes. I could deal with thirty more minutes.

٢٠

TWENTY

MAYA

We were in New Orleans, but I didn't pay much attention to the streets or the route he took. If I wanted to run away, I could, but I wouldn't do that. I was done running from them.

We drove into the driveway of a house shrouded in darkness. All of the lights were off, and heavy wards blanketed the entire property. It felt far more secure than any place I had been in, even Leyla's house. Aldridge, *no. Rés.* Rés carried our bags into the house. He led me down a hallway, opened a door to his left, and threw my bag in there.

"Please, do not make yourself too comfortable. You are not alone in this house, but no one will bother you in this room."

I had a lot of things I wanted to say to him. Instead, I decided to keep my mouth shut.

The room was definitely a guest bedroom. Nothing significant about it, no paintings, no trinkets, no character but not as prison-like as the one they gave me in Egypt. There was a bathroom attached to the room and towels on the bed. *Wow, Southern hospitality.* I even had my own bathtub, and it was so clean I considered drawing a full bath right then and there.

With grunting, hissing, and spilled tears, I undressed and went in to take a shower. A nasty bruise was blooming a few inches under my breast. In fact, my whole right side was bruised from the hip and up. My arm was still suspended in the air at an angle.

I kept my hair out of the spray of the water. I was too tired to start a detangling session. I left the braid untouched as well. I wasn't sure I could make another without my right hand. At least not before it had healed a bit.

When I finally found a position where I didn't feel like ripping my arm out, I lay down to rest on the bed. I had planned to get out of the shower, get dressed, and maybe wait an hour before snooping around in the house. But as soon as I put my head down, my brain shut off.

I woke up to sunlight streaming in through the cracks of the curtains heating up my face and the faint voice of a woman singing in Spanish.[2] I had heard the song before but not quite this a cappella version. When I finished brushing my teeth, it was all quiet again. I did everything with my left hand, and it was beginning to overwhelm me. I had no idea how people with disabilities managed basic tasks without their spirits breaking. A broken arm was all it took for me.

I left the room to go find *Al—Rés*. I refused to call him Aldridge. It was associated with everything that reminded me of Adam, and I just couldn't make myself say Drés. So, Rés it was.

The house seemed eerily quiet, like someone was holding their breath.

I went into the living room and found it empty. It was so full of light and color. A light catcher was dangling under a hanging plant above the window sill. And plants! Plants everywhere. The only curtain not drawn was the one with the light catcher. Because it was slightly spinning, it reflected these beautiful pastel colors all over the walls and the designer sofa. It couldn't be classified as a couch—

Al Margen de Ojalá - Andrés Iwasaki

it was far too pretty to fit under ordinary. An all-glass coffee table was set on top of a deep burgundy-and-navy-blue carpet. Just by stepping on it, I could tell it was a silk carpet, and I was sure it was a Persian one.

I lifted the corners until I found the sticker that had turned brown with age. It read Kashan and the size in meters.

This house didn't look like it belonged to Rés, and my suspicion was confirmed when I was crouching, scouring through the books stacked on the shelf under the TV. It was almost all romance novels, some of which I had read some on my wish list. A smile tugged at my lip because at least I could read on my way to hell.

"Are you done snooping around?" a female voice yelled from another room.

She startled me so much I dropped the book, and because I wasn't thinking, I tried to catch it with my broken hand before it thudded on the carpet. I picked up the book and put it back before following her voice.

I was mortified for being caught, but I wasn't going to let it deter me. Light was pouring through an open door at the end of the hall close to the front door. When I stepped into the doorway, I found myself in the kitchen.

The kitchen had a lot of character and was definitely being used for cooking and not just an extension of the house.

A gorgeous girl with long dark curly hair and hazel foxy eyes was sitting at the table, staring right at me with a mug pressed to her lips. She was wearing a yellow summer dress that was cinched at the waist, going up in thin straps. Her wrists were stacked with bangles softly clinking with every movement. Her fingers were adorned with a collection of gleaming rings—all real gold, I could tell. One in particular stood out, a rock of a diamond set in an engagement ring, but with all the other rings surrounding it, I couldn't be sure. Everything about it was complementing her golden bronze skin. She was so beautiful it hurt to look at her, a true vision.

Rés sat next to her.

"I'm sorry. I didn't realize anyone was here," I said, still standing in the doorway.

Rés glanced up from his phone but didn't seem alarmed.

So, I shouldn't be either.

She put the mug down, giving me a challenging look. "You're very careless for a witch," she said while twirling a thread between her fingers. "It was no effort trying to find a strand of your hair in his car."

Not a thread then. I knew where she was going, and it was starting to get interesting.

"Everie," Rés sighed, looking at her dryly.

She was unbothered and instead held up a finger to shut him up. *Hot!* She was in charge here, and she knew it.

"How easy it would be to hex you."

Her smile widened.

I walked up to the table amused and pulled out the chair with my good hand and sat in front of her.

"I would love to see you try," I said with the most sincere smile and reached for the mug she was drinking from.

I sipped from it, thinking it would be coffee, but to my pleasant surprise, it was tea. My eyes almost rolled back in my head as the hot beverage went down my throat.

"Are you consenting?" She was holding up the strand of hair between her fingers.

"Everie, cut it out," Rés warned.

I almost forgot he was there. *Rés.* The name was growing on me. It was starting to suit him.

"She wasn't asking you." I gave him a quick glance before looking back at her. "Go on."

She grinned, wicked and beautiful. I had no idea if my efforts to ward off hexes would work, but it was a solid spell I had spent weeks perfecting. It would be smart to test it out with someone who wasn't biased while still having the circumstances somewhat under control.

"Mmm . . . let's see, what shall I do to you." She wasn't going to truly hurt me, but she definitely wanted to prove a point. "How about hives? Or . . . what do you need air for?"

The hair slowly burned from one end like a dynamite fuse, while her unwavering gaze was on the hollow of my throat.

Doubt crossed her features, and I realized it was supposed to be happening to me.

I clutched my chest with my good hand, let my head fall back, and gasped for air.

"Enough, Everie," Rés demanded. When I didn't stop heaving, he raised his voice. "Ev!"

"I'm not the one doing that!" she exclaimed, sounding confused.

I couldn't tell if she was alarmed because she was scared of him or if they really couldn't lose me. As entertaining as it was, I couldn't keep it up and burst into laughter.

"Bitch!" she said under her breath when she realized I was acting.

I caught Rés holding back a smile before I met her eyes again.

"Great to know I'm valuable."

"How?"

Her eyes narrowed into slits.

"Sorry, I can't tell you. It's a closed practice." I took another sip of her tea, taunting her.

"Bullshit!" she snapped.

"I'll tell you what. You heal my arm, and I'll teach you how when I'm strong enough to slap him across the face." I hoisted my bad arm onto the table, pulled up at my sleeve, and showed her the swelling and the newly acquired bruises.

I hadn't trained in healing at all because it was Sepideh's expertise. I had expected her to be there with me, expected everything from her without actually asking if it was something she wanted.

"I'm not sure if it's broken or not. He did a number on me."

Everie craned her neck.

Rés stood. "Let me look at that," he said and reached for my wrist.

His fingers had barely touched me when I pulled back, forgetting how much sudden movements hurt. Seeing his hands about to close around my wrist triggered something.

I can't breathe. I can't breathe. I can't breathe.

My heart was suddenly picking up pace, hammering against my chest. He stepped back with both his hands up defensively.

Everie got up and approached me.

"I'll look at her," she said, her sassy expression swapped with something else.

When she reached for my hand, I didn't hesitate. Her guise had dropped, and she was suddenly so different, so gentle. Her fingers were soft as feathers around my wrist.

"I will press down gently, but it might still hurt like hell," she said, waiting for my permission to proceed.

I nodded, and she pressed with her fingers, feeling out my bones all the way from my wrist to the crook of my elbow. It didn't hurt as much as I expected it to. Then she twisted my palms upwards, and I hissed from the pain.

"It's most likely just a sprain." She inspected my fingers. "Can you make a fist?"

"Not at all. I have zero mobility in my fingers. Why are you so nice all of a sudden?" I flinched when she pressed further on each joint.

Rés was back in his seat, pretending to be very focused on something on his phone, but I could practically see his ears pointing in our direction.

"I was merely doing a professional assessment of you." She shrugged. "And as for your arm, I'm afraid we need to amputate it," she said with a decent poker face.

I couldn't help but huff out a chuckle.

I like her!

"I can't magically fix it, but I can make the healing go a bit faster with a salve," she said and went to pour herself another cup of tea.

She turned to Rés when she sat again.

"I'm not going to cancel, Drés. It's tradition! And, no, we cannot just move it somewhere else. You show up without notice and expect me to change all my plans."

"I texted you," he countered.

"Yesterday!" Her eyes darted to the clock on the wall. "Shouldn't you be leaving?"

Whatever it was they disagreed about she wasn't having it. She got up and went into her walk-in pantry and pulled out jars, shooting a string of Spanish words at him.

She was speaking so fast I couldn't make out anything. Not that I had learned any Spanish other than a few words.

He answered, "Probably tomorrow" in English and something that sounded like *key dollar* in Spanish, which I highly doubted meant "key" and "dollar." Then he was gone, and I was left alone in a house with a witch I couldn't completely trust.

Although she was quite cocky, she didn't give me serial-killer vibes.

A moment later, she placed a bowl of yogurt in front of me. She had topped it with oats, dried coconut shavings, nuts, and dried blueberries.

"Eat," she ordered. Like Rés, she was very assertive in her tone of speech. "I'll make the salve for your arm."

"Do you always give such delightful first impressions, or is it just for me?"

"Hmm," she said and pulled up a mortar and pestle and started mixing all sorts of things in it while humming to a song.

It was her I had heard singing earlier.

I took a spoonful of the yogurt and continued sipping from her tea. With literally no shame left in me, I couldn't be bothered to care.

If this was a Persian household, I wouldn't have dared to eat or drink unless it was offered to me at least three times. I didn't choose to come here, so she had to deal with a lack of manners.

She pulled out the chair next to me and set the mortar and gauze on the table. "Pull up your sleeve again."

I did, and she rubbed the paste all over my arm. She looked so benign, not the same person who tried to hex me two minutes ago. Her touch was delicate as she wrapped my arm in gauze while half humming half singing a French song she didn't know the lyrics to. [3]

"Hmmm . . . Hmmmm . . . *Parfois on croit entendre quelque chose . . .*"

She went on, and the song finally clicked for me.

"Something, something, *mais ce n'est pas vrai*," I finished for her. "No?"

She beamed. "Yes! I love that song. Do you speak French?"

Pas Vraiment - Stromae

"No—I mean, I had French in school, but I don't actually speak it. I used to listen to a lot of French music and remember the lyrics for some reason."

She wrapped my arm perfectly snug and put it in a makeshift sling around my neck. I didn't need it, but it was nice to have.

"And thank you. As soon as I can use my hand again, I'll show you how I shielded my hair against hexing. But it only works against intentions and verbal hexes. I still have to actively ward against direct attacks and tracking."

The healing time would also allow me to assess her before teaching her anything.

"Is that how you were found?" She poured me more tea and sat next to me.

"Well, yes. I have been careless, so it's my own stupidity that got me here." I gestured at myself and our surroundings.

Her head tilted, and pity flooded her eyes.

"Drés is not an evil person," she said.

"Maybe not, but it's all the same in the end. They all want something from me."

Her lips pressed together because she knew I was right.

"How did he even do this to you?" She nodded toward my arm.

"Steel pipe. He was aiming for my head, and I blocked it with my arm. From there, he just went to town." I got up and pulled up my shirt to show her my bruised ribs.

"Holy shit. You've really taken a good beating." She grimaced. "You know, the worst thing is, Fidel used to be trustworthy. Then he met that demon blood of a witch—no offense—and everything changed. I'll be the first to say that my brothers are brainless." She stuck her fingers into the mortar to scrape out the remaining salve.

"Wait, back up. Your brothers? Aldri—Drés is your brother? The Dūshevs! That's not possible!"

"Here, let me," she said and tried to turn me.

I reluctantly turned, giving her better access to my torso.

"Of course I understand it's hard to believe—I am so charming and beautiful and smart and sexy, but where do you think he got his looks from? Not from my father, that's for sure." She smiled. "Drés is my baby brother."

"That's not possible," I said again, still in shock.

"What! Because of the *only boys are Dūshev* propaganda? That's all a load of crap my father tells that to the boys to create a placebo effect or something, training them to believe they cannot have girls. I wasn't the first nor his last daughter, but we're all hush-hush—I can tell you that much." She finished smearing the salve on my ribs.

She was about to cut up a piece of gauze when I stopped her.

"There is no need."

She shrugged. "Alright. It doesn't look as bad as the arm anyway. Did you know gauze was first made in Gaza, Palestine. Hence the na—"

Three hard knocks sounded at the door, and I froze.

She rolled her eyes and seemed to be annoyed.

Everie went to open the door, and the voices returned tenfold.

Holy shit!

It was as if five people were shouting in my head at the same time. I hadn't heard any voices since the motel and had forgotten how invading they were.

Linda! Tell her! Tell her! He is cheating with—tell her now! Tell her! It's that harlot. Tell her! Linda! Tell her! It's Linda. Linda. Linda. Tell her!

"This is really not a good time, Ruth. I have a friend over." I couldn't see who she was talking to because she had only opened the door slightly, but the voices were still going at it in the background.

"Please, Everie. I haven't slept for days, and I know we have an appointment next week, but I can't go on like this." Everie looked at me.

I gave her an approving nod.

It was her home, and I was forced on her by Rés. There was no reason for her to be so considerate.

As soon as the lady entered, the voices intensified. They kept repeating the same sentences and wouldn't stop shouting in my ear. I thought they would go into the living room and talk, but the lady walked into the kitchen.

"I'll give you guys some privacy," I said, immediately getting up from the chair.

"No, please stay," the woman said and reached for my shoulder. She noticed the sling and didn't proceed touching me. "I don't want to be a bother. Please sit, I won't be long."

I didn't want to stay and at the same time I didn't want to be rude.

Everie shrugged, took the mortar to the sink, and washed her hands.

"I'm Ruth." The lady sat before me, looking at me expectantly, making me feel awkward and slow.

"Betty—short for Elizabeth."

Everie gave me a quick glance before reaching for a drawer.

Harlot. Tell her! Tell her! Tell her! Linda. Harlot. Tell her! Tell her!

While the voices kept coming and going, Everie had pulled out a tarot deck from a velvet pouch and shuffled. Ruth was telling her how she felt watched and always freezing in her bedroom.

Everyone had heard a story or two about the occult in New Orleans. It attracted a lot of tourists, but I hadn't thought this was how Everie made a living. Especially because she wasn't exactly a fraud like most readers. I had never considered this as a way of life. My *Khale* Hana never read for strangers. Although taboo, it was still normal to have your coffee or cards read in Iran, but my family didn't want that kind of attention on them. *Tell her! Tell her!*

The voices were still there but not as aggressively as before. *Tell her! Linda. Linda. Linda.* It felt like they were waiting to be released again. The question was, could

Everie hear them, too? And if so, was she the one holding them down to a minimum?

"I don't think a reading will help. I'm telling you, every time I go into that room, it's like a bucket of ice is being poured over my head. You've got to come to my house," she said.

Everie stopped shuffling. "You know I don't do house visits, Ruth."

Tell her! Linda. Linda. It's Linda. Tell her! Tell her! Tell her! Tell her! Linda. It was getting louder and louder again. *Tell her! Tell her!* And it was starting to suffocate me so much I had to walk out of that kitchen to keep from screaming.

"I have to excuse myself," I said, and when I got up, the voices died down to nothing.

Stay, please stay! Tell her!

I halted mid-step. The last one was a plea directed at me.

When I Finally welcomed the request, images flooded through me. Their sweaty bodies, his hairy back, and her red nails scraping against it. I heard their grunting and moaning and saw it all. They showed me all the ways they tried to connect with Ruth. All the omens and warning signs they sent her.

An avalanche of words were coming out of Ruth, but they didn't seem to register in my brain. I had to make her stop talking.

"I'm sorry if I am being presumptuous, but you are married, correct?" I said.

There was no sign of a wedding band, but I had seen all I needed to see.

"Yes?"

"I'm going to be very blunt with you because someone is begging me to tell you. I hope that's alright." I waited for her consent.

She nodded.

I avoided Everie's searing gaze, in case she wanted to kill me for interfering.

"He is sleeping with Linda in your bed while you're working night shifts at the hospital. That's why you can't sleep in that room."

Her hand went to her gaping mouth as she processed every word. Finally, it was quiet. All the shouting and pleading had stopped. I was about to leave when she grabbed my shirt.

"How can you be sure?" She released me when she saw my expression.

This delusional piece of work was still trying to convince herself it wasn't happening.

"Ask your husband what he thinks of Linda's blue heart tattoo, and he will give himself away by saying he doesn't like it."

The pelvic tattoo was old and blurred out, something Linda must have gotten when she was very young.

I didn't bother to bid her goodbye or even explain myself. She came for a reading, and she got one. All I wanted to do was to wash this invisible grime off of me.

It wasn't long before Everie came and knocked on my bedroom door. Well, her guest room, technically.

"In here," I shouted from the bathroom.

I had filled the tub with steaming hot water to the brim, added soap, and submerged myself in it, except for my right arm, which was dangling from the side of the tub. Might as well enjoy the Southern hospitality as long as I was there.

Everie opened the door and took in the steam.

"I know I was out of line, but it was the only way I could make them shut up," I said before she could scold me like Rés.

"How long have you been communicating with spirits?"

"It started recently. I think I need to close a portal or something. It's very overwhelming."

"Hmmm . . ." She sat at the lip of the tub and dipped her finger into the water, whirling it around as if she was mixing sugar in a hot cup of tea. "You should veil with ointment on your third eye."

"Could you not hear them shouting?"

"No, I'm fully veiled. I only let them communicate through the cards. Otherwise, I would go insane, but next time, stay out of my readings. I don't want to be dragged into hospital staff drama." She got up.

"Wait!" I reached for her with my sprained arm by mistake and hissed. "Can we go back to you being a Dūshev?" I couldn't help but ask. "Do you then, like, live forever, like the rest of them? And have powers and teleport?"

"I do have powers, but we are not the same. My father spends a lot of resources on his sons—it's a long story. I'll tell you another time. I have things to do now," she said and started toward the door.

I lingered in the bath, intending to leave when the water cooled, but it never did. Maybe Everie enchanted the water to stay burning hot just the way I liked it, or it could be that no time had passed. Or . . . maybe that's what she wanted me to think.

Music was playing from the living room, and if I listened closely, maybe I even heard muffled voices. There could be a chance she wanted me to stay in the hot bath while she had people over. It piqued my interest enough for me to get out of the water and pat myself dry.

I changed and ventured out to where I heard Everie speaking to someone in Spanish. I thought she was on the phone until I heard another girl say, "*De verdad.*" Even though I had heard that phrase before, I couldn't remember what it meant.

"Shoot! I completely forgot you were here," Everie said when I was only a few steps from the living room.

I hadn't even appeared in the doorway yet. The bitch could see through walls or something.

"Come say hi, Maya," Everie commanded, just like my mother would when she was on the phone with a relative she wanted me to greet.

I did the grown-up thing and walked into the living room with a polite smile on my face. Everie had welcomed me into her home, whether forced by Rés or not. She had been nice to me.

A girl was sitting on the sofa with one knee pulled up to her chest. She had her back to me, facing Everie but turned when I entered.

"This is Maria, one of my closest friends," Everie said.

"Nice to meet you," I said and pressed my lips together in a tight smile.

I just didn't know how not to be awkward meeting new people. The girl appeared innocently sweet with a wide smile, honey-streaked hair, and hazel eyes.

"*Mucho gusto*," she replied.

Which I figured was her being polite to me.

"Don't look so scared. She speaks English, too," Everie said to me before rising from the sofa.

I wanted to defend myself and let her know I wasn't being weird on purpose, but Everie had walked away.

She got to the door a hair before the doorbell rang.

I didn't know how she always knew. Either she felt energies vividly, or she was seeing into the future. I was still standing in the middle of the living room like a statue when Everie and two guys walked in.

Both guys had luscious, dirty-blonde hair with a flawless shine, falling in soft waves. Although that was where the similarities ended. One was athletically built, the other skinny and tall, with a handsome face.

"This is my b—fiancé, Luciano," Everie said, smiling at the broad shouldered one.

He had kind eyes, the kind of guy you would expect helping an old lady cross the street.

"Nice to meet you," Luciano said and reached for a handshake.

I offered my left hand. "Sorry, this one is out of order." I gestured to my arm.

"All good." He gave me a soft smile.

Everie smiled. "And thi—"

"Lorenzo. The smarter, more handsome brother," he said about himself, giving me the urge to puke.

I still shook his hand out of respect and caught Maria rolling her eyes. It reminded me I didn't shake her hand, and it would be too awkward to do so. What if she thought

I wasn't a girl's girl? Especially in front of Mr. Smart and Handsome?

"Will Lorenzo be joining us tonight?" I asked and pretended to look over his shoulder.

Everie broke out in laughter, showing off her perfect white teeth.

"*¿Que listo, no?*" she said to Maria.

Bingo! If they kept it up like this, I would end up learning Spanish by the end of the week.

Lorenzo looked like he had the devil dancing in his eyes, but he tried to appear unbothered.

Three more joined, then another three. Someone had brought empanadas and different antipasti: olives, artichokes, cheeses, and stuffed bell peppers. They obviously all knew each other and were speaking mostly in Spanish but switched to English whenever they caught my eye and realized I didn't understand. The brothers Luciano and Lorenzo were Argentinian. Carlos, Alba, Maria, Sofia, and Alberto were Mexican. And Armando, Valentina, and Adriana were from Honduras.

The wine glasses emptied, and we moved on to hard liquor. I hadn't planned on hanging out with them, but I was too curious to stay away. When I finally wanted to retire for the night, they wouldn't let me. For a bunch of non-Iranians, there was a lot of *tarof* going on. They each took their time to corner me, asking me questions about my age, where I was from, and what languages I spoke. No one seemed to care why I was there or who I was to Everie. I didn't mind, though. They were nice people, and I was drinking and having fun.

Later, a guitar was brought out, and some sang, including Everie, who was actually half decent. The alcohol worked its way through my system, and I became a part of their vibe.

Luckily, Lorenzo approached me last.

"So . . . demon blood—"

"Come on, no need to call me that. You can handle a little heat," I said.

He smirked. "Trust me, I can handle a lot more than heat."

"I'm sure you think you can," I said.

I was getting slightly tipsy, and maybe he was getting a little more interesting to talk to.

"Is that a challenge?" He arched a brow.

I shook my head, not wanting the conversation to go there because I truly wasn't interested in him that way.

"I like that you say the first thing that comes to your mind, especially to someone you have never met before. Kudos to you!" He clinked his glass to mine.

"You don't exactly look like the kind of guy who would get his feelings hurt by something like that. Also, I feel like, sometimes, men need to be put in their place," I said.

He chuckled and took a big swig of his drink.

"Have you been in New Orleans before, or is it your first time?"

"First time," I chirped, leaving out the parts that stung.

"Oh, you must go for beignets before you leave. Even if it's in the French Quarter. It's really that good!"

He was so enthusiastic about it I almost wanted him to take me. I had heard of the famous New Orleans beignets, though, not on my list of things to do.

"I can tell Ev to take you to my favorite place. It's a small hidden gem, not very touristy," he continued.

"Thanks. That's very sweet. I'm not sure how long I'm staying, though."

In reality, I wasn't sure if I was allowed to leave the premises. *I can do whatever the fuck I want.*

"That's a shame. I hope you get to see the French Quarter at least."

Maybe Lorenzo wasn't so shallow after all.

Luciano came up to us and put an arm over his shoulder. "If he is bothering you, don't hesitate to slap him across the face." He looked at his brother. "*Dejá de hacer chamuyo.*" Luciano gave him a gentle clap on the back.

Go make chamoy, maybe? Are we having mango with chamoy? I'm so confused.

"There's been times when I didn't mind sending you to the emergency room myself," Carlos said.

I nudged Lorenzo's arm. "I bet you hear that a lot."

He liked the attention, even if it was the bad kind.

"I would love to see you try, Carlos," he said and put a blunt between his lips. "Actually, I'm sure you can knock me out after this one." He gestured to the blunt.

"Keep me company outside?" Lorenzo asked and made a loop of his arm.

Since I only had one functioning arm, I slid it through his, with a drink in hand and all. My right hand didn't hurt at all, but if I used it carelessly, I would regret it in the morning. The alcohol was making me feel invincible. Instead, I kept it in the sling and moved it minimally.

Lorenzo looked back at his brother before we walked outside, but I didn't catch the interaction between them. He lit his blunt and took a long drag, then offered it to me.

I shook my head. "Let me see what happens to you before I accept to smoke whatever's in there."

He rolled his eyes. "Please, I only smoke greens." He didn't offer it again, and I was glad of it. "Drés brought you here?"

I nodded.

Of course they knew already, but what else did they know? And why was he not there himself?

"He can be a little rough around the edges. Only his agenda matters, and sometimes, it feels like you're just a chess piece being pushed around." He took another drag, then another, and seemed to forget what he was saying.

"Where is the but . . . ?"

Lorenzo smiled a boyish smile, then shrugged. The mask had dropped, and he let me see a side of him he hid from most people.

"Should I be careful?"

"Nah, it's not like that. I'm just saying don't expect him to take your ideas, thoughts, feelings, or well-being into consideration."

"It's the way of the Dūshevs," I said, hoping I wasn't stepping into deep shit.

Either Lorenzo wouldn't know what that meant—or worse, would run his mouth to the others. I didn't know how much they had shared with their friends.

"Drés only listens to himself . . ." He paused. "Sometimes, it's okay to say no."

There was no reaction to the mention of the Dūshevs. Either he expected me to know more than I did, or he didn't hear me right.

Did they all know? Were they connected to the Dūshevs somehow?

"Thanks, Lorenzo."

I already knew I couldn't trust Rés. No matter how much sanctuary he offered, he was still a Dūshev, and he still needed something from me. If I didn't pay what I owed to Rés, he would take it from somewhere else.

"Enzo."

"Okay, Enzo. What about you . . . Should I be careful around you?" I teased, knowing I was being foolish.

In the end, I wanted nothing from him. I was simply entertaining myself.

"Only if you're looking for a good time, then, yes. I'm known to get myself in trouble, and I'm terrifyingly compelling."

"What is a good time?" I asked, nursing my drink.

He smiled, his eyes glinting under the porch light. "Next Friday, sneak out after midnight, and I'll show you."

"Why do I need to sneak out? I'm allowed to leave."

"No, Ev would never let you leave the house with me."

"So, you are trouble?"

Is this flirting or boredom?

"*Claro que sí.*" He winked at me.

I understood that! I was so excited. I was learning Spanish one expression at a time. I liked to think I had a knack for languages, or at least I was good at pretending because I always got the accent right. I was especially good with lyrics.

٢١

TWENTY-ONE

Maya

I woke up with a massive headache, even though I drank plenty of water before bed and took two painkillers as a precaution.

My clothes were drenched in sweat—and not the normal kind, the kind where it feels like you're sweating the liquor out of your system.

I got up and took a quick shower before going to the kitchen. I was so parched I could drain the ocean plus a cup of tea, a cup of traditional Persian tea with cardamom and saffron.

Maybe Everie has cardamom with all the jars in her pantry.

If she let me, I would make my own tea.

Everie was sitting in the living room, reading a book, music playing on low volume in the background.

She peered up from her page. "Do you feel as bad as you look?"

Instinctively, I wanted to drag a hand over my face but stopped myself from moving too much.

"I made more paste for your swelling. It's in the kitchen. The tea is ready but probably cold now, but the fries are still good. I just ate a couple more."

"Fries and tea?" I asked.

"Best combo." She smiled and looked back down at her page.

I went into the kitchen and reheated the tea on the stove. While I was waiting, I took a fry and dipped it in mayo.

It was still crispy and so fucking perfect. She had put a ton of vinegar powder and salt on them, which was exactly how I liked my fries.

Before pouring myself tea, I took the paste and spread it on my arm.

The bruising had gotten worse, with various shades of purple and yellow. I couldn't tell if the swelling had gone down or worsened. It still hurt like hell—that's all I knew. I pulled my shirt up and tucked it between my teeth to get better access to my rib. I couldn't see what I was doing because the bad arm was in the way, and every time I tried to lift it, I brought myself to tears.

"Do you want me to help you with that?" Rés said, scaring the living shit out of me.

He didn't move. It looked like he was waiting for me to allow it before he approached, which was nice enough, considering everything else.

"Sure," I said and turned to give him access.

What am I doing?

He took a small glop of paste and spread it in a circular motion against my skin. Instantly, the sensation of his touch sizzled through me. The skin-to-skin contact gave me better access to him and his powers.

I could become dependent on the feeling, dependent on how much it made me feel alive. The touch of his cold fingers raised goose bumps not just from the chill but from something else I couldn't name.

He redirected me with a touch to my elbow, a touch he didn't let go of so easily.

Every touch sizzled through me like a shot of adrenaline. This feeling had to be what people were chasing when taking drugs. *This is what it feels like to be alive.*

His thumb grazed my skin in a caress before he let go.

"Thanks," I croaked, clearly losing it.

I poured myself a cup of tea and sat across from him.

"So, what's the plan, Dūshev?" I tried to sound as casual as possible.

"Well, first, we need to wait for you to completely heal, which is a waste of my time, frankly," he said and got up to pour himself tea. "Meanwhile, we can still work on your skills. It's not ideal with the arm, but here we are."

"My skills?" I arched my brow.

"Yes, we need to perfect your sloppy attempts at anchoring, grounding, harnessing, and of course, your special skills, demon blood."

"What's up with the demon blood thing? Is that a slur you guys use?"

I wasn't offended—I just didn't understand the connotation.

"Because you are . . . your blood is flammable."

"No, it's not!"

The rumors these people spread about us was beyond me.

"Yes, it is. I've seen it." Then he reached for a knife, offering me the blunt end. "Try poking your finger, and we'll test it." He plucked another knife and poked himself in the pad of his fingertip and let a drop drip on the table.

I would've said no, had he not poked himself. It seemed foolish, but I wanted to prove him wrong so bad, to rub it in his stupid face.

I offered my left hand so he could draw blood from my finger.

"Oh, of course, I forgot," he said and took the clean knife. "We just need a tiny drop."

I made sure my hand rested on the table so he didn't need to touch it to press the tip of the blade to my finger. I wasn't sure how I felt about touching him yet. It freaked me out. My subtle attempt didn't stop him from taking my hand in his. I braced myself, holding my breath for the sensation of his touch, hoping he couldn't tell the blood sizzling under my skin.

Don't fool yourself. The sensation is not real. Wake up!

Rés showed no sign of feeling anything when our hands touched. The sensation was all in my head. *He is just another Dūshev.*

The puncture wasn't deep, but I still flinched and accidentally pulled away from him. A tiny droplet grew on the tip of my finger and dripped onto the table.

He found a long candle lighter in a drawer, quickly pointed it at his own droplet, and ignited it with a flick. Then he did the same with mine, but when he pulled away from my droplet, a blue flame lingered before it died down.

"No fucking way!" I muttered.

How was this possible? It must have been a trick. What reason would he have to trick me? I was the one asking about demon blood.

"You're telling me you didn't know this?" His eyes narrowed as he leaned back in his chair.

Like he hadn't expected this reaction.

"I'm almost too scared to ask you what else you know about us that I don't."

"I don't know much. I've read the basics, the origins of your family and how far back they go. I know about the little strife between our families, and I've heard a couple of versions of the prophecy you're tangled in," he said, waiting for me to find the courage to ask the right questions.

"What do you know of the prophecy?"

It's just a conversation. We're having light conversation, nothing too deep.

"I found three versions that were similar. I believe they're rooted to the same script. I'm not sure which one is the original, but the message is clear, the prophecy will be fulfilled. What that entails, I don't know." Rés rose from his chair, heading out of the kitchen, clearly not willing to answer any more questions.

I sighed deeply and took a much needed sip of the tea.

Wake up! Wake up! Wake up!

Rés returned to the kitchen with a piece of worn down paper. "Have a crack at it. Maybe you can figure it out."

I took the paper from him and unfolded it. In what I assumed was his handwriting were three different variations of the same prophecy.

On the last day of Pisces, he is truly born, his soul full but not wholly his. Hand in hand, they share a soul and carry the Feyrouz into darkness so grim that all shadows pale in her steps.

At the peak of spring, when the last flower blooms, he must claim what is rightfully his, to make way for what's truly hers. She will drink from the vessel and erase generations of spite.

She who forcefully bears the soul of our enemy must release it to the thirteenth son on the thirty-third day of

Nowruz with the blessing of Goddess Ishtar. She will sacrifice our blood and flesh to retrieve what is rightfully ours and bring order to nature.

The words on the paper rang true. I had read at least ten other variations of the prophecy, and they always led me down the same route.

I peered up at him, bewildered. "Why are you giving me this? What's your stake in the prophecy?"

"If you stick around, you might find out what my stake is." He was daring me to run away. "Besides, I need you at your best. I need to train you and trust that you won't fuck it up when I send you into the lion's den. I need you willing, *bruja*."

I rolled my eyes, thinking of ways I could respond without incriminating myself. "I already told you I would get the book for you, and for your information, there is nothing willing about my existence. I'm a pawn in their game."

In your game! Because you're holding my family over my head.

"Whose game?"

Lie to him.

"My family's, my ancestor's, the universe's. Heck, even your father's game. I'm just a soulless vessel to be used."

He wanted me to do his bidding as well, so how was he any different?

"I don't believe that."

Perhaps he thought his words could make a difference, or maybe he pitied me, which was worse. I didn't want his or anyone else's pity. His attempts at being nice slipped through the cracks of my nonexistent soul. This was my fate and my problem to solve.

"Your beliefs don't change anything, Dūshev."

I tried saying his name, but I couldn't force it. I thought that if I called him by any of his names, it would make him too real. I couldn't have that when all I wanted was to take my rage out on him and his kind. The feelings were so intense I wanted to carve them out of my heart.

How did I still have thoughts, feelings, and free will, when I was supposed to be as empty and soulless as they claimed? Why did it hurt so much more to be alive?

I had never felt more alive, never thought leaving the Firuzeh behind would trigger an understanding of my mind. I was learning the difference between my thoughts and interjections. And while I knew my own words apart from others, I was almost in control of my feelings. I didn't feel as lost and disconnected as I had before. Like I was finally on the right path and nearing the finish line.

"There is something else."

I looked up from the paper still in my hand. I had been staring at it all this time without actually reading the words.

"This is just a theory, but it's only fair I share it with you."

"Go on," I said, waiting impatiently for him to get to the point.

"When my mother was alive, I never felt out of place or out of touch with reality. That all changed the night she died and passed on her soul to me." He paused, fog obscuring whatever his mind's eye tried to forget. "Perhaps we have been misunderstanding the prophecy." He was hesitating to share his thoughts, afraid I would use them against him.

"What are you trying to say?"

"I think I am the one who was truly born on the last day of Pisces because that's the day my mother died, and I received my soul."

"What!" I blurted out before I was able to process what he had said. "You think we—"

I wasn't sure what I was asking, but he seemed to understand my unspoken words.

"You must have felt it when we—"

"When we what?" I pressed.

I had to hear him say it first. I couldn't make assumptions or reveal anything.

"I don't know," he sighed. "Perhaps it's my body reacting to y—being used as a power source."

"What does it feel like?" I dared ask, treading on the eggshells he had left behind.

"Relief," he said without meeting my eyes. "It feels like I can finally breathe after an eternity of being in a chokehold. Like a heavy weight has been lifted off my chest."

For me, his touch brought strength and clarity, the energy filling my body with vitality I had never felt, not even when I had a soul. While he was trying to relieve himself from the burden of his own soul, I was thriving in the power it brought me.

"And you think this has something to do with your soul?" I asked, needing the confirmation.

Never had I thought him a vital part of the prophecy. Whether I did, I was grateful for the revelation. His theory was definitely something to take note of.

He shrugged.

I leaned back in my chair, nursing the cup of tea, unable to take my eyes off of him. "Do you think your soul—"

I couldn't complete the sentence. I simply couldn't ask him what I truly wanted to know.

"Is supposed to split between the two of us?" he finished for me.

I took a deep breath, collecting my thoughts. *Forbidden fruit. No! Shut it down! Not another Dūshev. Never again.*

No matter how he treated me or how things progressed, I couldn't let myself forget what the last one did to me.

Was his soul the reason I was drawn to Adam—if it was him all along? I recounted all the steps that had led me to Adam, all the choices that brought this curse on me.

"Regardless, we shouldn't test the theory."

The faintest smirk played on Rés's lips, distracting me from what I was about to say.

"Don't get ahead of yourself. I would rather tie a noose with dirty floss and hang myself with it than share a soul with you." He chuckled, playing games with me. I needed my head in the game if I wanted to be rid of the prophecy, but he didn't know that. For all he knew, I was still a very devout Sāher. "I don't get it. What is it you want? You're warning me about something I can potentially use against you. Do you want me to fulfill the prophecy?"

"I just thought it was worth mentioning in case you found yourself off track."

The glint of amusement never left his eyes.

"Don't let your three functioning brain cells worry too much about my prophecy," I said, wanting to smack the stupid grin off his face.

٢٢

TWENTY-TWO

Maya

We had spent the entire morning on meditation and grounding. Rés wanted to go over anchoring with me, a technique used by all practitioners. I had read a lot of theory on anchoring, but I didn't have much practice with it. His technique, on the other hand, was more of a ward. After grounding, he would create an orb, a dome that worked as an anchor to those inside and a ward against those outside.

After countless failed attempts, I was successful in holding up the dome long enough to see satisfaction in his eyes. I opened myself up and let the elements speak to me. The still wind under the dome begged to be commanded, and I would be a fool not to listen. It swirled in circles around us, lifting strands of my hair with it. I tried to channel more of it and quickly felt the dome slip.

"Focus!" he snapped for the thirtieth time.

"You just fucked it up, Dūshev! I almost had it."

"If you're trying to throw around Dūshev as a slur, it's not working. Do you, by any chance work better under pressure?"

"I don't know, why?"

"Just wondering. We'll test it out tomorrow. For now, try to focus on one skill at a time. You're not exactly a mul-titasker."

"Do you need me to take a personality test as well for this position?" I rolled my eyes.

"No need. I can already tell that you're going to be a pain in my a—"

"Oh, because you're such a picnic to be around?" I let out a breath and went back to grounding my energy.

Then, brick by brick, the dome took shape around us.

"I can still teleport," he announced, as if I had asked.

My lips parted about to ask for a clarification, but I stopped myself. He read the confusion on my face and responded accordingly.

"If I can teleport, you are not effectively holding up the enclosure."

"Wait, you can teleport while I'm near. You shouldn't be able to."

The ability to hold them in place had been out of my control, a subconscious matter, and whether it was anchoring or not, I had done it to Adam before.

"Please, my brothers might not be able to, but I can slip through the pathetic net you demon bloods cast around you."

Interesting. He could break through it, but his brothers could not. Rés was different. He was a man on a mission. Complying meant access to Dūshev powers and his father's wealth, yet he remained defiant, just as Adam had described. *What are you after, Dūshev?*

Suddenly, he snapped his fingers in my face, demanding my attention.

"What!"

I hadn't heard him say anything. I was supposed to get into a meditative state to ground and anchor, but my brain had wandered.

"I am not your friend, demon blood, and you are not on vacation. I need you for one thing and one thing only. If you are not useful to me, you are expendable."

Enzo's words echoed in my head. *Only his agenda matters, and sometimes, it feels like you're just a chess piece being pushed around.* Enzo was right. Rés was selfish and only cared about one thing. So much for "*I need you will-ing . . .*"

"What is this book that you can't get yourself?"

I had no doubt it was a book of forbidden knowledge or some closed practice he had no business meddling with.

"I thought you would never ask." His tone carried a hint of challenge. "It's the Grimoire of Harut and Marut, of course."

"The original grimoire?" I gaped at him, thinking he must have lost his mind. "You want me to find a three-thousand-year-old book that no one has seen?"

The Grimoire of Harut and Marut contained divinely granted knowledge. It was the first grimoire written by the hands of angels.

I will be in his debt forever . . . He sure wasn't lacking audacity, asking for the holy grail of books.

"Of course not. Don't be daft. It took me a lifetime to locate it. I already know where it is. You simply must retrieve it for me."

"Why don't you get it yourself. I'm sure you're more than capable." On top of being a Dūshev, he had his greedy fingers dabbling in magic, too.

"Believe me, darling, if I didn't find you useful, you wouldn't be here," he deadpanned. "Now, do it again, and focus this time. Show me the powers your kind gained from sharing blood with the devil."

Bastard!

Implying we didn't have the right to our powers was below the belt, even for him.

"Anything else I can provide you with? Would you like me to share the coven secrets with you, too!"

"How will I know what you are good for if you don't show me?"

Porru! He meant it! And even had the audacity to be annoyed.

"No, please, take a seat while I lay bare years of secret history and closed practices for you," I retorted with a sharp edge.

"You can skip the history lesson. Just show me what you are capable of."

"*Jadugari* isn't merely a thought and a blink!" I snapped.

"Sure it is. I've seen you put things on fire—and people."

"I've only done it twice, and both times . . ."

Adam's face came into view.

I can't breathe. Stop, please stop.

I took a deep breath, unable to fill my lungs, knowing it was all in my head.

Adam's hands gripped my wrists, pulling my arms above my head.

I can't breathe. I can't move. Please stop. Please stop. Please stop.

With another ragged breath, I willed my eyes to look at what was before me. I would not let him take my sanity with everything else he had taken.

"That was . . . circumstances."

"Prepare yourself for tomorrow." He glanced at his watch and left me with my demons.

I stayed behind in the living room until my hands stopped trembling and my skin stopped prickling. *Ghandet oftadeh.* I would have made myself Chai nabat to soothe my pain, but I didn't have any nabat.

I rose early, planning a secret shopping trip before my session with Rés, only to find Everie already awake and busy in the kitchen. She handed me a cup of tea the moment I stepped into the kitchen, always a step ahead.

"Do you need anything else?"

A knowing twinkle glinted in her eyes.

I shook my head, nursing the tea.

She had pulled out a bunch of ingredients for a cake, and I had the sudden urge to get up and help her or at least entertain her while she did her thing. *Perhaps in a different life . . .*

"I'm making my mother's brownies." She smiled at the bowl. "I woke up missing her awfully."

Her beautiful, sad expression brought tears to my eyes.

"Have you ever been able to . . ."

I didn't know how to ask, in fear of being disrespectful. I didn't know her thoughts and beliefs on the afterlife. Luckily, she understood and shook her head.

"I don't think I could bear it either." Her eyes glistened. "If I found out she hadn't crossed beyond the veil."

I nodded. I wouldn't be able to accept it either if I heard my grandmother's voice in my head.

Of all the shit I was going through these past few months, my time spent with Everie was peaceful. I enjoyed being around her. Getting to know her made me feel normal again, alive. Maybe in another world, we could have been friends.

"*Mierda*! I'm out of eggs," Ev said before shouting for Rés.

"Andrés!" she shouted again, even louder this time, before taking off her apron and grunting colorful words in Spanish when he didn't answer.

"Do you need anything from the store?"

"No, thank you."

She arched a brow. "Don't lie to me, demon blood."

I couldn't help but smile. There would be no keeping secrets from her.

"Don't worry about it. It's not something you can find in the supermarket."

She had been gone for less than a minute when the world went dark around me.

A plastic bag was pulled over my head as a hand closed on my mouth over the bag. I tried to scream for help, but no sound passed my lips. Fear coiled around me like a deadly cobra. He had found me when there was no one to witness my death. Breathing through the plastic bag proved impossible.

It's a Dūshev. Use his power, use him!

The ambush had paralyzed me, but I found my strength again and arched my back in defiance, resisting the impending death.

You have his power.

My good arm flailed in protest, attempting to pull his hands from my face before my vision blurred completely.

Feel the power at your fingertips.

I swung my head back and headbutted him. The impact was hard enough to loosen his grip on me.

"Good, now set the world on fire, *bruja*," Rés whispered into my ear.

It's Rés!

As soon as I heard his voice, the tension and fear left my body, and I let out a shaky breath, almost like a sigh. He was testing me! I knew the *pedar sag* wouldn't hurt me—not yet at least. *I'm going to fucking kill him!* Instead of fighting back, I let my body relax, so I became dead-weight in his arms.

"Oh, shit!" he said when I went limp.

I will show you, Dūshev. Adrenaline pumped in my veins when his arm circled my waist, trying to keep me upright. As soon as he pulled the bag over my head, I punched him in the face. My fist collided with his jaw instead of his nose like I intended. Had my right hand worked, I could have done much more damage.

"Fucking bastard!" I shouted and scrambled back from his hold.

It still caught him off guard. A stunned silence followed. Shock and disbelief etched across his face. I could tell it hurt because he instinctively brought a hand to his jaw.

"Play games with me again, and I will cut you open in your sleep!" I screamed, my voice scratching. I stormed out, slamming the door behind me, before the tears welling in my waterline spilled.

"We're not done here, *bruja*! You will try again." He teleported, appearing in front of me, blocking my way.

"Get out of my face or so help me god, I will burn this whole house down."

"Show me," he hissed, leaning over me.

The impact of the punch had finally caught up with him, and he was fuming from it.

"I fucking can't."

The tears ultimately spilled, and I wished I could turn away from his unbothered gaze. I didn't have the ability to summon fire like he assumed. It was uncontrolled and chaotic.

Even with his anchoring dome protecting our surroundings, it was a disaster waiting to happen. I could accidentally trap us both in a dome of fire and burn us alive.

Rés was selfish. He wanted a demonstration of controlled chaos, something he could potentially use in his personal arsenal, and I wouldn't let that happen.

I wouldn't become his weapon. I wouldn't let anyone use me for their own gain or let a fucking prophecy control my life, with or without a soul.

٢٣

TWENTY-THREE

Maya

Ever since Rés pulled that stunt on me, he hadn't attempted to "work on my skills" or do more of his meditation sessions. I didn't tell Ev about what happened during the thirty minutes she had gone to the store. This wasn't her fault. She couldn't help it that her brother was a sadistic asshole.

I had barely seen him the past couple of days, and it was exactly how I liked it. That way, I had more time with Ev. I was convinced she didn't just tolerate me. She was enjoying my company, having a good time and laughing with me.

"This book will give me an ulcer," she said and smacked the dark romance novel I still hadn't gotten around reading closed. "It's time for me to go anyway. I'll be back in the evening." She was going with Luciano to his parents' place, and I would have the house all to myself for the very first time.

The plan was to put my very honed skills in glamouring to use. I had spent a lot of time perfecting my glamour magic, thinking I would have to hide my appearance when looking for the Dūshevs and fulfilling my duties as a Sāher.

In case my clothes were being tracked, too, I went to Ev's closet and rummaged through her stuff. She had told me that if I ever needed anything, I could borrow from her.

We were almost the same size, although she was a lot taller and crafted to perfection like a goddess. Her closet would make any girl jealous, me included. It was full of linen mid-length dresses, colorful tops, and flowy skirts. Everything in her wardrobe was ironed, hanging perfectly straight. *Does this girl not have anything less than ethereal?*

After more rummaging, I found a pair of loose, ripped jeans and an old band T-shirt. I couldn't imagine her in something so casual. It looked like something from Maria's closet. The jeans had a loose fit, which was perfect.

I caught my reflection in the mirror. The T-shirt wasn't ironed, so I looked a little *shelakhte*.

I made sure the braid in the nape of my neck was still intact before chanting the glamour spell on myself, a spell

I had practiced a thousand times. Even if they found my location, they wouldn't recognize me in a crowd.

I seek aid to veil the eye, face shifting, features fading. Grant me now this blinding trance, a cloak of lies, a face unseen.

Ev's house served as the anchor for the spell, meaning it wouldn't work on anyone who lived there. The glamour would hold until I stepped back in and would have to be repeated if I wanted to go out again. There wouldn't be any need for that, though. I'd only be out for a couple of hours.

I was hoping to find a Middle Eastern market and pick up a few things. Other than that, I really wanted to see Bourbon Street, maybe be lucky enough to catch someone practicing on a saxophone.

Oh, and maybe I can get beignets.

I didn't get the name of the place Enzo talked about, but he did say there was a popular place in the French Quarter.

I grabbed one of Everie's slides and hurried out. When I got outside, I made sure to get a good look at the house, remembering what it looked like. Gray house, white col- umns, and black wrought-iron railings.

The houses on the street looked like something from a western movie. I had never actually seen anything like it. They were colorful and old in a colonial style, with balconies and carved details attached to the roofs.

A lady walked past me with her dog, and I decided to keep in step with her to ask for directions.

"Excuse me, do you know how I can get to Bourbon Street?" I asked, hoping it wasn't too far away, since I was on foot.

"You need to go the other direction, baby," she said with a soft smile. "You go all the way straight till you see a big yellow sign for burgers. After the burger place, you turn right. If you pass the mini mart, you've gone too far."

"Thank you."

I walked even faster than before until I saw the yellow sign for burgers.

Turn right. I looked up at the street sign. *This is Bourbon Street? That can't be right.*

It was very underwhelming. It was either the far end of Bourbon Street, or there was more than one Bourbon Street here. There were no stores, no bustling, no music, no nothing. It was just rows and rows of the same colorful houses with balconies. I started to wonder what was so great about it since it was the one mentioned in most movies.

I walked the narrow street at least seven or eight blocks before it started looking right. The bars, cafés, and restaurants started appearing, and I found myself getting excited. Purple, yellow, and green flags and bead necklaces were hanging from every balcony.

This place was probably even better at night. What was iconic was that, on almost every street corner was either a singer or a brass band. It was hard not to stop and listen to all of them. It made me sad to think this was my only opportunity to experience New Orleans. [4]

A man was singing a song in with a guitar slung around his neck. I understood nothing from his words, but he carried the lyrics on his sleeves and let us have a taste of his loving soul. A tiny bite of New Orleans was better than nothing at all. I smiled at my surroundings and couldn't remember the last time my heart felt so full.

I took a right on St. Peters Street and stopped by the corner of Royal Street where a girl with a bohemian vibe was singing the blues. I simply couldn't resist; her voice was so deep and hurt, it made me cry on the spot. How

Disfruto - Carla Morrison

was there so much talent in one place. After two songs, I tipped her and went down Royal Street instead.

That was where the gold was. Every other door was either the entrance to an art gallery, an antique jewelry store, vintage shop, or some other quirky thing. I mazed through the different stores and found myself in front of an occult shop. They had a wall full of tarot cards, shelves with Florida water, black salt, colorful candles, incense, and all sorts of occult books. At the back of the store was an altar for Marie Laveau and a bucket of colorful notes with people's wishes and manifestations.

I picked an empty pink one and contemplated what I would write. My first thought was love, but then I ended up crushing it, realizing I couldn't write with my left hand. I threw it in the bucket with all the wishes. *What will be will be.*

I browsed more until the guy behind the register caught my attention.

"Can I help you find anything?"

"Uhm. Yeah. Do you sell ashes?" I asked. "Not human remains."

I wasn't actually looking to buy, just curious about how obscure my request could get. If they had ashes, I would get ashes of a large frog. Ashes mixed with a binder, like cypress oil, could be made into a permanent hair removal pomade. Russian practitioners used walnut shell ashes for the same purpose, so it always made me wonder if all ashes worked the same, if the right intent was set.

"You need a more"—he paused and pressed his lips together—"authentic situation. We cater to, you know . . . Tourists." He gestured to a lady writing her wish on a piece of paper by the altar.

"Of course, thank you."

I walked all the way to Jackson Square where artists were setting up their paintings and handmade sculptures. Tarot readers were getting their tables ready while musicians played in the background. If I had the time, I would have gotten my cards read for fun. It would be interesting to see if any would tell me about my impending doom.

On the other side of the street was the longest line I had ever seen in my life. *Café Du Monde.* Passing horse carriages, I crossed the street, joined the queue, and wondered if I had enough time.

"It's worth the wait. Especially if you haven't had beignets before," the guys in front of me said.

The line moved surprisingly fast, and the beignets were truly amazing. They were sugary pillows of perfection; soft, warm, and sweet. I bought six and ate two while walking back. There was powdered sugar everywhere on my clothes when I was done.

Initially, I wanted to find a Middle Eastern store. Instead, I found a corner store run by an Indian uncle, and I decided it was good enough. They usually had the same things as us. I bought some tea, green cardamom, nabat, and rosewater since they didn't have the rose buds I liked to use. He had saffron, but it was baking in the sun on the shelf, which spoils it. I was just grateful he had green cardamom and good tea.

The walk back took almost an hour because I had to stop for a few essentials for my glamour work if I needed to sneak out again. The sun was starting to set, but I knew Ev wouldn't be home, and if I was really lucky, he wouldn't be there either. When I neared the house and saw the lights were on, my stomach twisted. I slowly pushed the handle down, trying not to make a noise. I had left it unlocked, knowing she had heavy wards in place. Besides, no one in New Orleans dared mess with a witch and something told me, she was well-established in the community.

As soon as I stepped in, Rés was marching toward me. "Where the fuck have you been?" His steps were charged, radiating anger.

"Out getting beignets," I said, putting down the bags and slid off the shoes.

"What if someone saw you?" he barked as he stepped closer, forcing me to back up against the front door.

The angrier he got, the more British he sounded. He wasn't going to like my reply—that, I was sure of.

"First of all, it's 'saw,' not 'sarr.' And secondly, I already—"

He smacked his hand on the door. "Are you takin' the piss?" I scoffed at him, but if I was honest with myself, then his attempt at scaring me into submission actually worked. "You do not leave this house without my knowledge."

His voice was dangerously low, barely above a whisper, sending shivers down my spine.

I wouldn't let him see me cowering in his presence.

I tilted my head, bringing my face mere inches from his, and placed my left hand on his chest. The gentle placement caught him off guard.

"You do not tell me what to do."

I had lowered my voice to match his. And then, with all the force I could summon, I shoved him back.

He chuckled, barely moving, as if he was rooted to the spot. My cheeks burned.

Perhaps my hand had lingered too long on his chest, perhaps wanted to feel something and used this as an excuse to get what I craved, his powers.

The power billowed between us when we touched, even through layers of clothes.

Something dangerous crossed his eyes, like this was the moment he would decide if I was worth keeping alive. It was so exhilarating knowing I put myself in this situation, that it had nothing to do with the prophecy. If he killed me because of my reckless behavior, it would be my own fault. Deciding when and how to die seemed to be the ultimate luxury, a way for me to claim agency over my life.

"Do not put me in a situation where I have to step out of character, demon blood, because I will show you Dūshev like you have never seen it before."

Fuck.

I gaped at him, unable to clear my head. If I was to drown drinking the blood of a Dūshev, I would decide whose hands I would allow crushing my windpipe before it happened. Something had snapped inside of me, and I was sure he saw it, too. We hadn't touched since my hand dropped from his chest, but fuck how desperately I wanted to feel his energy, to feel powerful again. I ached for it.

"If you jeopardize my plans one more time, I will tie you to the bed and let you starve."

His threat didn't match the nonchalance of his voice. Something had snapped in him, too. He craved relief just as much as I needed his power. He wanted to hate me but couldn't seem to convince himself.

His gaze drifted to my lips for a fraction of a second. The simple action was an aphrodisiac.

"You wish," I said, my own voice betraying me.

Fuck. Fuck. Fuck!

"Don't test me, *bruja*," he said and stepped back.

Fuck, I need to shut my mouth with a spell.

I went to my room and changed back into my own clothes aggressively.

I was angry with him for trying to tell me what to do and angry with myself for liking the way he wanted to control me, liking how he towered over me, how possessive his lingering gaze felt. I wasn't stupid. I knew what he wanted from me, knew it meant nothing of the sort. He wanted me for the sole purpose of bringing him the most valuable book known to witches. But, fuck, it felt nice to be at his command.

Wake up, for fuck's sake!

I wasn't sure if Rés left the house or just went into his room, and I didn't care. I wouldn't hide from him or be bothered by his existence.

I went into the kitchen and made myself a cup of tea, yet I decided I could enjoy it in the privacy of my bedroom.

I didn't see Rés for the rest of the evening. Everie came home but went straight to bed after checking on me with a raised brow, like she hadn't expected to find me in the bedroom with a book in my hand.

I was drifting in and out of sleep when I heard tapping from the window. At first, I thought I imagined it, but then it came again. I got up from bed and pushed the curtains to the side, only to find Enzo standing outside looking from left to right.

Very carefully, I opened the window. "What the hell are you doing here?" I whispered.

"I thought you wanted to go out?" he asked, seeming genuinely confused. "There's an Argentinian party . . ."

My first thought was Rés would have a field day. My second was to give him a reason to tie me to the bed.

You're such an idiot.

"Let me get dressed real quick."

I wore the same outfit as earlier because it didn't require thinking. Then I double-checked my braid and spoke the glamour spell into place. My gut twisted in anticipation, but I didn't let feeling keep me from climbing out of the window.

"Wow! That glamour is solid. I don't even—wow!" Enzo said, studying my face.

Of course he would see the glamour. He didn't live in Ev's house. I hadn't even thought about how I would explain myself. He wasn't scared, just surprised. *They are all in a coven.*

"If we get caught, we're both dead."

"That's why it'll be fun, *brujita*. But let's hope it doesn't get to that."

We walked a block down where Enzo had a cab take us to the other end of the city where this event was taking place. Argentinian flags were everywhere, and people were wearing striped soccer jerseys some even had their faces painted. You would think it was a celebration after a soccer match.

Enzo introduced me to some of his friends, and from there, it was shots after shots. The music was mostly reggaeton, and the energy was beyond anything I had ever tried. Everyone was speaking Spanish, and they all assumed I understood, too.

During the first hour, there were professional dancers on the stage. Afterward, around twenty people with white-and-blue umbrellas made their way onto the dance floor, bouncing to the music.

Most of the night, I was dancing with this girl called Roxy. Her energy felt right. She was brave and careless, and the stage was hers. She was making out with a girl that seemed completely obsessed with her. The other girl took molly openly on the dance floor, then offered us some.

"Are you sure?" she asked, looking only at Roxy. "The party will enhance in sooooo many ways for you, especially when they release the balloons." She pointed at the ceiling.

I looked up, and sure enough, there was a huge net with white and blue balloons.

Roxy declined. Moments later, the girl was making out with another stranger and disappeared into the crowd.

Roxy and I were having a blast. We were dancing, singing along—or technically screaming. I had always been good with lyrics but couldn't sing if my life depended on it, yet I remembered lyrics regardless of the language. Sometimes, the words even made sense.

I had lost Enzo long ago, and I couldn't find it in me to care. I was letting it all out, as if it was my last night alive, my last night of unrestricted fun and freedom.

I befriended another girl in the bathroom, and she told me a whole story in Spanish that I didn't understand anything of. She was just as drunk as I was and didn't notice I was answering her in English with, "No way," "Oh my god," and "Wow."

We danced some more, and I knew my feet should've been hurting, but I was blissfully unaware. My skin was burning, my fingers tingling.

What if I burn this whole place down? What if my powers suddenly explode out of me?

"Enzo, Enzo. I found her," one of Enzo's friends yelled over his shoulder and pulled me by my waist.

A moment later, Enzo was by my side.

"Shit! I forgot this was what you looked like," he said to himself. He pulled me by the arm and led me toward the exit.

"Ouch!" I yelped.

I had forgotten to be careful with my arm. I was slowly sobering up, and the pain was returning. When the alcohol wore off, I would surely feel the aftermath.

"We need to go home, *brujita*. Apparently, we're in deep shit."

"The balloons haven't been released yet!" I said, furrowing my brows.

"I told Ev that we're in the cab on our way home."

It was only when we sat in the cab I realized I hadn't spent time with Enzo whatsoever. We danced for a short while, but then Roxy came, and I forgot all about him. Maybe he didn't have an ulterior motive and was simply being genuinely welcoming. Or perhaps that was his strategy—getting me to trust him enough to lower my guard. He knew who I was or, at the very least, had a rough idea.

"What's your deal, Enzo?"

"I'm not thrilled either, but I don't want to lose my head to Ev."

"That's not what I'm asking. I'm talking about the Dūshevs and the prophecy," I whispered.

I didn't want to say too much in front of the driver. Although this was NOLA, and they either believed everything they heard or nothing at all.

"My obligations are to the coven only—everything else, I don't give a rat's ass about," he whispered.

I was right! They were all a part of her coven.

"Does the coven approve of the prophecy?"

"Ask Ev," he said blankly, ending the conversation there.

Even drunk, I couldn't get anything out of him.

After an eternity of silence, the car finally came to a halt. Ev stepped toward the cab as I was stepping out, but she wasn't looking at me.

"Get into the car," she said to Enzo, gesturing to a car on the street.

I had thought she would be mad at us, but she seemed more concerned about Enzo.

"Don't patronize me, Ev," Enzo said and walked past me. "If he has a problem, he can say it to my face."

So, Rés is the one with a problem. But then they switched to Spanish. We went inside, and I felt the glamour melt off my skin, the alcohol enhancing the sensation. I didn't see Rés anywhere, and I didn't want to.

"I'll just make myself comfortable until he gets here," Enzo said and went into the living room.

I needed to take a shower and cool down. I'd had such a great night and then he had to ruin it.

I went to the bedroom and was about to pull the T-shirt over my head when Rés's voice boomed across the house.

"Where is she?"

I'm so ready to fight you.

I yanked the bedroom door open but stiffened. My feet cemented to the floor when I found him on my doorstep.

I hadn't expected to find him in front of my door, and it completely subdued me.

He stared me up and down, taking inventory of my appearance. "I will deal with you later." He walked back to the others.

I followed him out, trying to think of something clever to say.

Who the hell do you think you are? No. Eat shit. No. I dare you to tie me to the bed. Fuck. No! I was not in the right headspace.

"If you ever fuck with me like that, I will crack your skull open on the pavement. Do you have any idea how stupid that was? They are actively looking for her," Rés said to Enzo.

His voice raised enough to give me goose bumps. I realized I liked seeing him seething.

"I was just taking good care of our guest, *tre' errores*," Enzo replied with barely an S in the end of his words.

His eyes sparkled with mischief. *Three errors? Mistakes? What mistakes?*

"I asked to go with him," I said calmly as I walked into the living room. "And I was under a glamour." Ev gave me an acknowledging nod.

I don't think she expected me to defend Enzo. I didn't want him to take all the blame for something I willingly did.

Rés didn't spare me a glance when he spoke again. "Get in my way again, and I will make you my third mistake."

"*Basta ya, Andrés,*" Ev said before looking at Luciano.

She didn't seem too concerned about them fighting. It probably wasn't the first time.

"I was only trying to show her a good time before you use and discard of her."

"Enzo!" Luciano warned. "We're leaving."

Rés had turned to leave when he stopped in his tracks and teleported in front of Enzo, standing only inches away from him.

"If you mess with my things, Lorenzo, I promise you it's the last bloody thing you do."

"I'm not a fucking object!" At that, Rés finally acknowledged me, narrowing his eyes.

"On your bike, Lorenzo," he said, his eyes still locked on mine.

What the fuck does that even mean?

Luciano led Enzo out and poked his head back through the doorway. "*Amor*?" he called, looking at Ev.

"Coming," she said and gave Rés a disapproving look.

Ev left with them, and only when the front door closed did Rés speak directly to me.

"You are my fucking thing until you have paid off your debt." He stepped closer, his scent surrounding me like a pack of wolves. "After that, you can hang yourself, for all I care. Or better yet, give my father a ring and let him know where you are."

Possessive . . . Stop it. Focus!

"I told you I was glamoured!"

"We don't know if your glamour works!" he snapped before stepping back. "I know you are looking for a fight, demon blood, but you can save it for tomorrow because right now I could rip your fucking head off. The risk you put us all in, just because you wanted to party for one night."

"Don't you think I thought of that! I might not live to see another year so excuse me if I don't follow all your ridiculous rules. I know I owe you my life, and I wouldn't have gotten out if it wasn't for you. I know that, and I'll pay you back. I will do anything not to be tangled with a Dūshev again, but I also just want to live a little before everything goes to hell!"

I was out of breath.

"Have you considered that you might not be all that powerful since my father took the stones from you. Just like Fidel found you once, he could again, and I'm not interested in handing you over to them. Not now nor ever!"

"Stop fucking lying to me. You can quit pretending that you care about anything but the grimoire. I'm just a chess piece you are moving around—and that's fine—but have the common decency to tell me straight up!"

Rés was on his way to his bedroom, but that didn't stop me from shouting at him.

I was looking for a fight—he was right about that. I was drunk, heated, and ready to claw into him.

I stormed after him and didn't stop when he tried to slam the door of his room in my face.

"I want to fucking strangle you!" I said through gritted teeth.

"Likewise." His eyes fixed on my neck and made me think of reasons I would allow it. "The saints know the restraint I have on myself."

It wasn't what he said, but the way he was saying it, the way his eyes bore into mine. *His hands around my neck, followed by a bite.*

What damage could his fangs do? What would he taste like? Bitter bourbon or honey? And—

Stop it!

I crossed the threshold and stepped into his room. A double bed with a dark wooden frame was pushed up against the wall with a nightstand on each side.

"I fucking dare you to try, Dūshev."

I meant it in more ways than I cared to admit, and before I knew it, it became my reality.

"I said don't fucking test me."

His hand wrapped around my throat, and he shoved me against the wall, lifting me off the ground.

Fuck!

He was getting to me without knowing it. This wasn't the reaction I was supposed to have. I was supposed to fight. *What is wrong with me? This isn't supposed to be so fucking . . .*

His hand tightened around my neck, and I was reminded of his powers. They were surging through me like a current, desperate to drag me under. There was so much of it, so much of him, it was enough to spill over. How could he even be in his own skin with so much energy pulsing, begging to be used.

"At least pretend like you followed me in here to fight, or I might actually think you want something else," he said, his fingers flexing slightly while still holding me in my place.

With a wicked grin, I looked up from beneath my lashes. "Wishful thinking," I croaked.

He was suddenly so close, his face inches away from mine.

"Yours or mine?" he whispered, and I could almost taste him. Then he stepped away, releasing the grip on my neck. Cold water washed over me when he broke the touch.

٢٤

TWENTY-FOUR

Maya

I had woken up to Rés slamming his fist against my door, shouting for me to wake up. The horrid hangover was my punishment. It didn't take a genius to figure out I would wake up with a massive headache from the copious amounts of alcohol I drank the night before. My eyes and feet were hurting—hell even my hair was hurting, but the worst pain came from my arm.

I had expected my arm to heal faster. It had been weeks, and I still couldn't grab things firmly, not even utensils while eating. I couldn't put my hair in a ponytail or a bun because it required both hands and, apparently, a lot of strength. The mental toll almost made me cry, since I couldn't do basic human tasks. It was one of those days when I wouldn't mind staying in bed all day.

Reluctantly, I went into the living room looking for the devil himself. He had said something about teleporting when he banged on my door. I didn't know what he expected from me, but if he thought I would dabble with that ever again, he was out of his mind. The few times I teleported I was in full prophecy mode. It was done out of necessity, not by choice. Clearly, I worked well under pressure—that didn't mean I was suddenly a skilled Dūshev.

"You look awful," he said as he sized me up.

He was holding a book. *The Silk Road.*

Of course he would read nonfiction. Pretentious asshole.

"I do have a massive headache, thank you very much. Now, what do you want from me?"

"Let's begin, shall we. Anchor me, so I won't be able to adʰār—teleport," he said and corrected himself right away. Then he vanished and reappeared again two steps to his left. "I thought I told you to focus."

"Can you give me a fucking second?"

He was so impatient it was getting on my nerves. It wasn't like anchoring a Dūshev would help me achieve anything.

"I'm starting to think you can't do anything without your little blue stones." He circled me. "Are you even capable of anything useful?"

He was so fucking smug I wanted to slap him. I couldn't wait to get his stupid book and be done with him. Maybe then I would go back and finish the prophecy so they all could go to hell.

All in due time. You will get to do it all. No, that's not what I want. I have free will.

He teleported and reappeared behind me, startling me. "Still not working." Then again, in front of me. "Short sleeved actions," he tsked, clicking his tongue against his teeth. "And easily distracted." He stepped forward, away from me. "What are you actually good for?"

I was burning from within, and I was sure he could tell. If only I could teach him a lesson without letting the whole house go up in flames. It wasn't Everie's fault her brother was an absolute pain in the ass. *Burn the book.* It certainly looked like a special edition. It was leatherbound with gilded edges, and there wasn't a bookmark in it, so he would lose his place. *Let the pages go up in flames . . .* He was too busy taunting me that he didn't pay much attention to the book. Only when the flames reached his hand did he react.

I did it!

"Are you absolutely mental!" he barked and dropped the book.

"Not on the silk rug, you idiot." I panicked and kicked it away.

The book stopped burning before it hit the carpet, but I still went down on my knees to see if I had damaged it. I would hate to be the one damaging Everie's things because the idiot got the best of me.

"It's an antique Kashan. Do you even know what they are worth?" I snapped.

"Yes. I bought it." Rés crouched, picked up the book, and flipped through the burned pages.

Pieces of charred paper flaked off and swayed through the air.

"Back to work." He turned to me. "Now anchor me."

It was easier to focus when I hated him. If he wanted me to use his technique, I would. I visualized the orb closing around him, trapping him in this room with me.

"Good," he said. "Now release me."

I didn't.

"Release yourself. You should know how to slip through my pathetic net, no?"

"I said release me." He stepped toward me.

I wondered if he regretted teaching me. He hadn't thought it through. The technique would give me power over him, and he was too arrogant to see it. Regardless of the satisfaction I felt, Rés still had leverage over me. He knew where my mother was and where my brother and father lived. Rés was always ahead, and I could never let myself forget that.

"Your wish is my command," I said mockingly and curtsied before him.

"I'm sure you find yourself very amusing, but I'm not training you out of the goodness of my heart or because I'm bored. I need you to be in complete control of your powers when we go for the grimoire. You will not mess this up for me. Do you understand?"

His words came out slow and commanding.

"Yeah, yeah, yeah. Otherwise, you will kill me. Blah, blah, blah." I rolled my eyes.

His threats were weightless, and everyone could see it.

"You assume the worst from me. Have you ever considered that I want the grimoire so I can stop this unnecessary war? That perhaps there is a way to end this without more bloodshed!"

"Please," I scoffed. "Says the guy who kidnapped and almost killed me because he had beef with his brother. If you wanted to stop an unnecessary war, you would have left me with your father. Eventually, I would have died, and this whole thing would be over. So, clearly, you want something else. I bet the Grimoire of Harut and Marut comes with a lot of forbidden knowledge."

"First of all—"

"Spare me! I don't care what your endgame is. You're all the same. You take and take without asking."

Even though I was curious about what he wanted to say, I needed him to understand how transactional this was. If he later decided it was important for me to know what his endgame was, he would tell me.

Rés took a menacing step toward me. "I had no intentions of taking anything from you or getting you killed back then, *bruja*." He spat the word like an insult, and it was getting old. "I was hanging on a thread, and my only objective was getting my soul back. For what it's worth, that moron paid for the artistic liberties he took."

Beating me up in a basement was artistic liberties? How poetic. Despite what he had done to me, it was water under the bridge, a forgotten lifetime. What Rés did back when he was Aldridge to me didn't even scratch the surface of my wounds. Betrayal cut so much deeper than physical pain.

Flashes of that night, of Adam, played in my head. The weight on top of me suddenly felt so real. The hatred in his eyes, his hand around my wrists.

I can't move. I can't move. I can't move.

I was flipping through the same horrid memory when Rés spoke, saving me from reliving everything all over again.

"My father is too blinded by fear to understand what's really going on. Those who run from a prophecy only draw its claws deeper to their wounds. Once in motion, a prophecy cannot be stopped. We can only hope to change its course."

"Right," I uttered hoarsely, almost unable to speak.

He composed himself. "Enough talk. Let me see how well you manage teleporting."

"Right," I said again without thinking. "Wait, what? You want me to teleport?"

"Yes. Adam said you could do it by touch." He moved closer and held out a hand for me.

My heart pounded violently and my breath hitched in my throat as I stumbled back, only for my legs to lock, refusing to move. A shudder ripped through me as my hands trembled.

I squeezed my eyes shut, every muscle bracing, terror flooding my veins. *Please. Please don't come closer.*

"Please don't touch me," I kept my eyes closed.

"Maya." His voice echoed like a shipwreck reaching the ocean bed. "Breathe, I'm not touching you." I opened my eyes and saw the cautious look glazing his eyes.

"I-I can't do it. I can't go back." I took a calming breath. "What if I touch you and end up in Egypt? They'll drug me into oblivion, and I will never see the light of day."

The thought of going back to that room constricted my throat. I was haunted by the images, of Adam on top of me and his hold around my wrists.

I can't move. I can't move. I can't move.

"That's not possible," Rés said, pulling me out of my head. "The facility is warded. The closest you can get is the courtyard."

As long as he kept talking, my mind stayed tethered, safe from the dark places I wanted to forget. His voice was a lifeline, steady and grounding, and I couldn't help but wonder if he knew how it helped.

"Take my hand now," he demanded. My eyes snapped up to him, ready to object. "Breathe. I'm asking you to take my hand because I'm anchored. You won't be able to teleport even if you tried."

I looked at the hand he was offering, hesitating to take it.

"We have touched before, and you haven't accidentally gone anywhere because I'm always anchored near you," he assured me.

Let's not pretend his touch doesn't ground you. Take what you need. I took his hand, and his powers enveloped me, expanding my chest, giving me room to breathe.

"It's my wrists," I confessed, my voice barely above a whisper. "When you reach for them, it—" I swallowed. "It sets me off. It's so pathetic, but I can't help it." A lingering stroke of his thumb sent warmth through my skin, and I forgot we were supposed to be mortal enemies. "I'm so much weaker now. I don't have the same fire as I used to. I barely have anything left. I am empty . . . less than. So, whatever high expectations you have of me, lower them because there is nothing left of me."

"I don't believe the oceans could put out your fire, demon blood. You are not your powers, they are an extension of you, like your hair, your scent, and the words you leave behind."

He could be all sorts of ways, if it meant getting what he wanted. *Nothing good can come from following a Dūshev into deep waters. You know this. Don't make the same mistake twice.*

٢٥

TWENTY-FIVE

Adam

I woke in the middle of the night, my throat raw and aching. My room was pitch black—just the way I liked it—but this time, the darkness felt absolute. I couldn't even make out the shapes of my furniture. Reaching for my water bottle, my fingers met nothing but empty space. Frowning, I pushed myself up on my elbows, feeling around for my phone on the nightstand—only to find it missing too.

"Fucking hell."

I rubbed my eyes and swung my legs off the bed, but the floor never came. Instead, I was weightless, suspended. Something cold clamped around my ankles and wrenched me downward. My body was ripped from the bed, plummeting, gravity twisting in ways that didn't make sense. Then—impact. A sickening crack as the back of my skull met the marble. Pain burst through me, sharp and electric but distant, like it belonged to someone else. Something was wrong. I was wrong. This body wasn't mine, this helpless, breathless thing that lay sprawled in the dark. It wasn't mine.

I tried to move, but the air itself coiled tight, thick and alive, pressing into my ribs, slipping between them like fingers searching for something to steal. A shadow loomed above, but it wasn't a shape—it was a void, and it was alive, shifting, watching, swallowing the air, swallowing me. I thrashed—or maybe I didn't. My limbs felt slow, disconnected, dragging behind me as I gasped for a breath that never came.

The blackness thickened, creeping into my mind, my consciousness until a deep hoarse voice spoke from all directions.

"I could keep you here for an eternity, torture you repeatedly and never bore of it, but frankly, this is all the time I have for now."

A pair of yellow animal eyes peered at me from a distance. Everything went black again, and I woke with a gasp, the sharp edge of reality slamming into me like a blade.

"Fuck!"

My breath came ragged, my pulse a frantic drum in my ears. The moon cast a cold glow across the room, just enough to catch the glint of my water bottle sitting untouched on the nightstand. I reached for it, then stopped, my fingers curling back when a biting chill crept over my skin. The room was too still, too silent, the kind of quiet that felt unnatural.

My body screamed that it wasn't real, that I was still tangled in the nightmare's grip, but my mind wasn't sure.

"I'll come back whenever I please with a newfound desire to break your spirit. Then bring you back to normal and do it all over again. All the while, your mind screams at you, begging you to move, to fight back, or even wake up from this dreadful nightmare. You won't be able to escape until I release you. You will beg for forgiveness, repent, and swear on your pathetic life that you will never do it again. And when I do release you, you will know, in the back of your mind, that I will come back and do it all over again. That you cannot ever sleep in peace. You will dread the nights because I will be there whenever you least expect it."

I woke again, back in my room. Sunlight bled through the curtains. My throat was raw, the air scraping against it like sandpaper.

I shifted, reaching to pull the covers off my damp skin, but I felt a tug. Cold metal bit into my wrists. I was cuffed to the bed, and no matter how hard I jerked against them, the chains wouldn't budge.

The door creaked open, and a person stepped inside, clad in scrubs—mask, cap, and gloves. His gaze locked onto mine and my stomach turned to ice. The same golden ones that had watched me from the dark, the wolf's eyes.

This is a nightmare. This is a nightmare. This is a nightmare.

A nightmare that seemed to continue in infinite layers.

"You know how they say, 'The pain is all inside your head'? Maybe you can use this opportunity to see if you can shut it off. If you can stop feeling altogether."

His voice pierced through my head like shards of glass. The words lingered, and with them, a razor-sharp pain gnawed at my skull. It twisted deeper, relentless, until I woke up truly this time. I was back in my room in Egypt. The familiar warmth of the air, the weight of reality settled around me. There was no strange, warped sensation of being trapped between worlds. No uncanny valley. It was always easier to recognize all the obscurities after waking up.

The same dreams plagued me every now and then, and without fail, I couldn't make myself snap out of them.

They locked me in, strapped me down, and forced me to suffer. I dragged a hand over my face, quickly got out of bed, and stepped into the shower. The cold spray of water helped steady my heart rate.

My father had asked me to join a meeting with the elders. Herman summoned me. He went as far as escorting me from the bedroom himself.

"Adam, we might not always see eye to eye, but I hope you believe me when I tell you that I only want the best for all of us. What he is about to offer you is a once-in-a-life-time opportunity, one none of your brothers has had the privilege to be a part of."

My eyes searched his face, trying to find something I could trust, but all I felt was doubt.

"Just promise me to think of your words," Herman said before leading me inside.

All elders were present, patiently waiting for us. It was like an intervention, but if Herman was telling the truth, it was something else entirely.

"Adam, I would like to ask you something." He paused, and I tried my best not to roll my eyes at his theatrics. "How devoted are you to this family?"

"As devoted as one can be," I answered, hoping it was the correct one.

My father was like a teacher, looking for a specific sentence that he wanted his students to repeat.

"Do you believe we are in alignment with our true purpose in this world? Do you believe in our legacy?"

"Yes, of course."

He nodded approvingly. "And you must have thought to yourself, what about the ones we leave for death to claim."

This was one of the first things I had brought up to him when I started taking souls. I had been broken, unable to understand the complexity of our purpose on earth.

"I understand what it takes, Father. I am well aware that there are a finite number of souls, and the population is growing at a rapid pace. If we stopped intervening, society would collapse within a couple of hundred years. The way humans treat their souls is not sustainable."

It was a practiced answer but also the truth. Because what else could we do, let them destroy the few million remaining souls?

"Then you will be thrilled to learn that even those we leave behind have a purpose," he said and smiled. I didn't follow. "What I am about to share with you, is meant only for the ears of my council. I realize now that I've imposed my dreams and aspirations on you because I desperately want to see you in my council. I've always known you would carry my legacy to greatness long after I'm gone. It's written in the stars and whispered in the wind, Adam. I understand that fatherhood isn't for everyone, which is why I'm relenting for you. Perhaps the next generation isn't meant to have sons."

I stared at him, my eyebrows raised in disbelief. He wanted me to become an elder without burdening me with fatherhood. But why . . . what was it he wanted me to do for him exactly.

"Do you accept my offer, son?"

"Father, I am truly honored but also taken aback by the sudden change of heart."

I had to be honest with him if I wanted him to open up and be honest with me.

"The truth is, I am not sure I will survive this prophecy. Each day Maya remains free, our legacy is at risk. I must make difficult choices to ensure that all my children are thriving before the day comes."

His words were a heavy blanket on my heart. *Perhaps he is changing.*

"What I want you to be a part of is the Dūshev legacy. It's something your brothers and I have been working on for a while now. We run a state-of-the-art medical facility leading the way in regenerative medicine. Herman has discovered a unique cellular transformation in the stem cells of the soulless that enhances vitality and overall well-being. We have been able to develop a revolutionary treatment that promotes health and rejuvenation like never seen before." My father went into further detail on how stem cell technology worked and how proud he was of Herman. "Of course, we do our utmost to maintain the highest standards of care, monitoring, and support for our participants. They receive the necessary medical attention to sustain their well-being throughout the process. That way, even the soulless ones have a purpose in this world."

"I have no background in medicine or science. How would I be able to help?" I asked, truly dumbstruck but tried to keep my face as neutral as possible while I could almost taste the bile rise in my throat.

Participants, he called them. *Participants!*

He spun his story well. *That way, even the soulless ones have a purpose . . .* but he was out of his mind if he thought I was on board with this. No way in hell would I be a part of his bloodstained scheme.

"There has been a few instances with break-ins, documents, and even patients gone missing, and we can no longer put our faith in the mortals to do the job. I need someone I can count on someone I can trust to be the head of security and logistics. I'm aware that it's a great responsibility, and it will take up most of your time, but you will be generously compensated."

I nodded, unable to form words.

All my life, I had idolized my father, believed in his vision, believed that what we did was for the greater good, that there was a divine purpose for the souls we took for the pain and exhaustion me and my brothers endured. At least a purpose beyond greed.

It turned out I had no grasp of the reality I was living in. If I thought my father was rich before, there wasn't a word for what he actually was. Greed had ruined the man

I knew, and I wondered what he saw in me that made me a fitting successor. Had I convinced him I was as rotten as he was. Me, more rotten than Aldridge.

He finally picked me. The family secrets were revealed to me at last, and what I learned completely changed how I viewed my brothers.

"It's something you need to carefully consider. You will most likely not have time for your writing and performing," my father said.

So, he was paying attention. Though he wasn't aware I had been dropped by my agent long ago and would probably never go back to writing again. Too much had happened for me to return to Mist Creek and pretend I was Adam Pave, the poet.

٢٦

TWENTY-SIX

Maya

Day in and day out, Rés forced me to work on my powers until I had a breakthrough and finally produced a controlled flame. I still didn't have any luck with moving objects like I used to, but it was something.

"I will enclose it if you could try a storm again," Rés said.

The last time I had tried bending air hadn't gone so well. I nearly broke an antique lamp.

"You want me to create another tornado inside the living room?" I asked. "Do you want your sister to kill us both?"

"Your mental incapacity is giving me a headache. Did I not just say I would enclose it?"

"You're giving yourself too much credit. It wouldn't be the first time the dome collapsed over our heads, and I don't want to be the one facing Ev's wrath."

"Let me worry about Ev, and get on with it, will you!"

I took a deep breath before grounding myself.

He was doing the same because an inexplicable calm always settled over him when he enclosed us in the dome. He'd taught me, helped me perfect the skill. I could successfully cast the circle and enclose us in the dome, but he was so much better at it. Mine would collapse within seconds if I tried wielding the elements simultaneously.

Rés could hold up an atomic bomb inside himself without breaking sweat. I had only seen his collapse once, and back then, he was doing it without his soul.

The air hummed beneath my fingertips, bending to my will and answering my needs. The weight of its movements satisfying, but I wanted more, wanted to call upon a storm.

I stepped forward, extending my hand for him to grasp. He accepted my touch, his fingers curling around mine, letting me cheat to reach into the bottomless well of his powers. The wind coiled, then erupted outward, spiraling into a furious cyclone. We were caught in the rising storm, our clothes lashing against us, my hair whipping in every direction, a wild thing caught in the wind's fury.

Rés almost lost his footing, his eyes wide with something between hunger and astonishment.

I released his hand and let the power die in the space between us. The flurry dissipated, and everything went still.

"That was fucking brilliant," he said, his eyes ablaze.

"How is this helping anyone?"

"It's not. I just enjoy the rush of adrenaline."

"You're joking?" I gaped at him, but he merely shrugged.

I turned around and went into the kitchen to make myself a cup of tea because if I stayed behind a second longer, I would rip him to shreds.

Sometimes, he made me do the stupidest things for his own amusement, making me use my reserve of energy for no apparent reason.

The tea had finished brewing when the front door unlocked and Everie walked in. She was in a weird mood. I offered to pour her a cup, but she refused and went into her room saying she was tired.

When Rés walked into the kitchen, I gestured to the cup that I had poured for him. I took my own and sat facing the window. This had become our routine. I would work on my powers, while he would come in late, practice with me a bit before coming up with a different way to test my abilities for his own amusement. Or he would criticize the most minuscule thing, and we would fight before I would go out and make tea. He always joined for tea.

"Did you do something to my cup?" he asked.

"I spat in it."

Idiot.

He shook his head and took a sip. It was piping hot, but he didn't seem to mind.

"Andrés!" Everie's voice came hushed and urgent. We both turned to her, and she looked horrified. "*Papá* is coming. You both need to get out of here. Now!"

All blood drained from my head.

I'm done!

The air was hot and suffocating. Cold sweat crawled down my back, clinging to my skin.

I tried to swallow, but my throat had closed up, my pulse hammering against the tight space.

Rés got up from his chair, approaching me.

"Listen to me, Maya. Before I touch you, you need to gather your thoughts. I need you to teleport back to the diner where Fidel attacked you. Try to focus on the parking lot."

I got up and took a step back, causing the chair to fall over.

"I can't," I said, tears welling in my eyes, my hands trembling.

I can't do this. I can't do this. I can't do this.

"He's not going back there again. It's the last place they will look," Rés said, trying to maintain eye contact.

I couldn't breathe. My blood buzzed under my skin. My head started spinning. I was going to faint.

I can't get caught again. I can't go back.

"Andrés, get her out of here!" Everie warned.

I wanted to try, I really did, but I couldn't. What if I teleported myself back to Egypt? Back in that room, that bed?

I can't move.

I looked at Rés, pleading, begging for a way out. "I can't do it, Rés! You don't understand. I-I can't."

I was terrified of going back to that prison, stuck under the same room and forced to lie in the same bed. The images had circled in my head enough times that I had convinced myself I would manage it if I tried teleporting. What if one mental image was all it took?

"It's too late!" Everie said. "Both of you, get into the pantry."

I'm going to faint.

Rés grabbed me by the arm and pulled me inside the pantry. *He's anchored. I can't go anywhere. It's not possible.* The door was left ajar, not enough to show anything, but was still insane to leave it open. I wanted to say something, but I couldn't. It was all I could focus on.

Rés grabbed my face with both his hands, and his power coursed through me again, grounding me.

"Are you listening?" he whispered. "If we're about to get caught. You must go! No matter where, you have to try to get away. Do you understand?" His gaze was so intense I didn't dare to say no. "I will find you before them."

I believed he would at least try, that his determination to find the grimoire was enough to save me from his father.

Three soft knocks sounded from the front door, and every part of me screamed for me to hold my breath. Rés turned my body, pressing my back against him, blocking the sliver of light seeping through the crack in the door.

Don't breathe, don't move, don't exist.

My breathing got hard, and my vision blurred.

This is too loud. I'm breathing too loud.

I was about to clap my right hand over my mouth but instead winced at the fast movement. Fuck! My arm had healed but sudden movements hurt, and I hadn't gotten full mobility in my fingers.

When Everie headed to the door and opened it, my body went rigid. Even the smallest shift could break the fragile silence and make it real.

"*Papá*," she said. "Come in." She sounded cheerful, and it somehow eased a tiny part of my fear.

"Hello, *baba*," he said.

It's him.

He stepped inside.

Rés shifted, and I remembered he was still there. His hand closed over my mouth, stifling any sound.

I curled tighter into myself, forcing my body to be small, nothing.

Tears were streaming down my face and on to Rés's hand. My legs were trembling beneath me, and I was afraid my knees would give and accidentally make me knock something off one of the shelves. The echo of their footsteps approaching sent my heart pounding in my chest.

Sensing my body's shift, Rés encircled my waist, pulling me near while his hand firmly covered my mouth to silence me.

I was completely flush against his body. Suddenly, I wasn't sure if my heart was beating because his father was one door away or because I was pressed against Rés.

We had never been that close or touched for that long. I felt all of him, the steady rhythm of his heartbeat, the calm rise and fall of his chest, the slow circles his thumb traced on my arm. I would gladly drown in it.

"Who were you drinking tea with, *baba*?" their father asked Everie, his voice dragging me back to reality.

Fuck! Fuck! Fuck! Those were ours!

I craned my neck to look at Rés, who looked like he couldn't care less.

Our eyes met, and he squeezed my arm gently.

Why do you feel so safe when you are everything but?

"Aldridge was here," she said.

This was the first time I had heard her say his real name, or at least the one his father had given him, one he didn't seem too thrilled with.

"Where did he go?"

"We were in the middle of a conversation, then his phone rang, and he left," Everie replied.

"I thought you were hiding Luciano from me. Tell me about him. Is he good to you, *baba*?"

When the conversation turned to Luciano, I could breathe again. He was there for his daughter and her love life, asking her questions like he really cared.

"*Sí, Papá*. I've never been more sure, and Aldridge loves him. And you know how difficult he can be. If my brother can be happy for me, bonding with the man I love, then you must, too."

"*Arwah yesa'duna*," he breathed in a foreign tongue. "I must meet him before any bonding ceremony takes place."

"*Por supuesto, Papá*."

She sounded genuinely happy. The subtle sound of a chair scraped against the floor and the click of the cabinet opening.

"Don't pour anything for me." Another chair slid across the floor, and panic gripped me. "Tell your brother to come find me."

I heard shuffling—and maybe a kiss? Then Rés's hold on me loosened slightly as if he sensed his father's absence because a second later Everie called out, "He's gone."

"You did good," Rés whispered, his breath hot against my ear. Then he stepped back, and his hands were off of me before I could turn around.

I wasn't sure if I was able to move just yet.

Everie spoke again, Rés already outside the pantry talking to her. For a moment, I couldn't do anything. I couldn't think clearly or wrap my head around what had happened.

I have to get out of here!

I took an uncertain step out of the pantry, making sure no one was there.

". . . At least now he won't come until the ceremony," Ev said.

Her words turned in my head even though my brain couldn't comprehend anything.

"I have to go to Maria's, but I'll be back soon."

Ev wasn't speaking to me, but I had a feeling she wanted me to hear her.

I have to get out. I can't breathe. No, stay. You must, you have no other choice. Wake up! Wake up! Wake up! Where will you go? How will you veil? Think!

Without a word, I went straight past them, headed to the bedroom, and started fiddling with my days' old braid.

It had matted in such a way that I needed both hands undoing it. I didn't care how much it hurt using my fingers. I just needed this braid remade and reinforced so I could veil properly.

"Maya," Rés called.

How many times had he called my name? Did he only use my name when he was serious? Had I done something wrong? He entered the room and stalked toward me, stopping only a few feet away.

"I know you are panicking right now, but he is not coming back. My father loves Ev and wanted to check up on her. He does that sometimes. He didn't come here looking for you."

"I'm fine," I said, trying to convince myself. "It just freaked me out."

I was still trying to braid my hair, and no matter how many deep breaths I took, I couldn't steady the trembling.

"Let me help you," Rés said, closing the distance between us. He gently wrapped his fingers around mine and eased my hand away from my hair.

Our eyes met, and a silent agreement passed between us. He then reached for the piece I had started on and began braiding with practiced ease. His fingers moved through the strands, creating a neat braid.

"Shit," I said. "I forgot to do the incantation."

I could only hope I appeared shaken and confused. I would let the earth swallow me whole before admitting his presence distracted me. Rés undid the braid without complaint and started braiding again as I recited my practiced words in a whisper.

"By shadows cast and unseen ties, cloak me now from their prying eyes. Cloud my presence, make me unseen, keep me safe from any harm. Guardian mothers, silent and wise, wrap me in your darkest skies. As moonlight weaves its silver thread through my hair, protect me now, from all despair."

I didn't care if he memorized them. He wasn't going to create a counterspell. If he wanted his father to have me, he wouldn't go through all this trouble. All he wanted was the grimoire.

Even though it was the only thing he wanted from me, I couldn't look away from him. In the shared space between us, time stood still.

What is wrong with you? He doesn't want you! He wants the grimoire. Get a hold of yourself. You are worthless to him.

"We will start practicing teleportation tomorrow," he said.

Unlike me, he didn't put meanings where meanings didn't belong. He wasn't affected by any of this.

٢٧

TWENTY-SEVEN

ALDRIDGE

She always found new ways to get under my skin. Like clockwork, every day brought a fresh argument—whether it was the way I pronounced my words, how I took my tea, or the fact that my breathing distracted her from securing a ward in place. Getting on my nerves was her favorite pastime.

"Do you call this tea?" she grimaced.

The way I make tea is perfectly fine, thank you very much. She, on the other hand, boiled the tea leaves to oblivion. It often turned murky because she had zero patience and wanted to extract the flavors fast, claiming this was the Persian way. It would've been if she had the patience to let the water boil before putting the leaves in and then let the tea simmer instead of violently burning it. Not that any of it mattered—I would eat Enzo's sweat-soaked *chanclas* if she asked me to.

"Honestly, I can't believe you brought me here, knowing your father visits his daughter unannounced," she said out of the blue. It had been a week since my father was here, but she seemed to have recovered. "Are you allergic?"

"Allergic to what?"

"To common sense because there must be a level beyond stupid reserved for you."

I couldn't help but grin. "Maybe I want to keep you on your toes."

It was a risk, yes. But where else could I have taken her where she was protected by wards around the clock?

"I mean, now I understand why you were so emotional when I snuck out of the house."

"Emotional?"

The wicked grin didn't reach her eyes, but I understood.

"Is it some kind of sport to you? To see how far you can take it . . ." I paused, leaning back in my chair. "Before I get riled up." I smiled, letting her interpret my words however she liked. Then I stretched my legs under the table until they brushed against hers.

She knew it as much as I did. The furtive touches had become an unspoken ritual between us. Neither one of us dared to address it, and I was probably the one most hungry for it, dependent on the relief it brought me.

"Anger is an emotion, is it not?"

"You're absolutely right. I was quite emotional." She smiled, sipping the tea she claimed she didn't like.

"Speaking of your father . . . You need to tell me what's going on if you want me to help you properly. I understand you don't trust me with all your grand schemes, but if I don't know the risks, I can't prepare for it. Had I known your father showed up unannounced, I wouldn't have been so careless going outside, and I probably would have been more cooperative during your lessons."

"You're right," I said. "I deemed it the best option to come here and never gave you a choice or an explanation."

She scoffed. "As if I ever had a choice."

"You do." *Now*, I wanted to add. "Would you believe me if I told you that you could walk out of this house and never look back?"

If she knew how much of a choice she actually had, would she still stay?

Her eye twitched when I offered her freedom.

"Hard to look back when you're dead." Her smile was strained. She thought we were still playing cat and mouse.

"You feed off the fear—the cold stares, the empty threats—because it gives people a reason to hate you, to keep their distance but truly you are not the skin you wear. So, tell me Andrés, why on earth would you let me out of the bargain we made? What you failed to ask yourself is why I haven't left already. You just assume I'm still scared of you."

There was a challenge in her words. It was a good question, a question I couldn't answer without letting the mask drop.

"Why haven't you left?"

"Perhaps this was my plan all along. To get my hands on the Grimoire of Harut and Marut."

Still wanting to play, I see. I'll bite.

"Or you finally realized that I'm your only chance at survival."

"Maybe I'm still deciding on ways to kill you."

"We already established that you won't do that, darling, but feel free to indulge in your fantasies about me."

She didn't respond yet her face flushed pink.

٢٨

TWENTY-EIGHT

Maya

I was tired of hiding, of running, of being at everyone else's mercy when I should have been making my own decisions all along. The honest truth was, I wasn't sure if I was capable of it, for all my life, I had let circumstances decide where I should go and what I should do.

I didn't look for a job—I was offered one by chance. I didn't decide to move out. I was forced to because of Dissie and my father. And for all my indecisiveness, I ended up in the middle of a prophecy where all my steps were predestined.

Was my life even my own if all I lived for was fulfilling a prophecy? I didn't even have a soul, so how much of my life was actually real? My thoughts and feelings felt real, and even though my decisions felt like my own, I couldn't be sure.

I had decided I trusted Rés and believed I could be free of the prophecy by helping him. If a way out of a prophecy existed, the answer would be written in the Grimoire of Harut and Marut. And if I wanted to get my hands on that book, I had to do as I was told.

I found Ev in the living room fiddling with some yarn and beads while swaying and humming. A song was always playing in her head. Oftentimes, I could guess the songs she was humming and speak them out loud, which really excited her.

"*Prends-moi dans tes bras* . . . Hmm-hmm-hmm-hmm," she hummed quietly.

"*Parce que je vis ma vie pour toi juste pour toi,*" I finished for her, though I wasn't sure if I got it a hundred percent right, but then she looked up with a big smile.

"Ding! Ding! Ding! You know, me and Maria always play this game where we take Spanish songs and translate them to English. Then the other has to guess what song it is."

"What's the prize?" I asked, wishing I spoke Spanish.

"What do you mean what's the prize?" She tsked. "It's a great honor to be a Grandmaster Champion." She tied three knots on the yarn and let another bead through.

"You know, Maria really likes you, and she's a hard one to crack."

"Honestly, all your friends have been so nice to me, even though I was dumped here, crashing your private parties. I know you didn't ask for this, but you've really made me feel welcome."

"Why are you saying friends like that? And what are you buttering me up for, demon blood?"

"Oh, I didn't realize I could say coven out loud." I winked at her.

"How did you guess?"

"See, I wish I could say, I'm just that smart, but Enzo, he runs his mouth a lot. Maybe he thought I already knew because of who I am and all that."

"Of course he did." Ev rolled her eyes and held out the loop end of the yarn. "Hold here please." Then she added more beads to the end.

I had no idea what she was making. It wasn't coming together in the slightest.

"I'm making a knotting spell."

She answered the question in my mind.

"The hexing ward I have on my hair is also a knotting spell," I offered.

"I knew it!" she exclaimed and plucked a hair out of her head. "Show me." She offered me the hair.

I shook my head. "Don't make hair offerings to a demon blood that could burn your house down to the ground."

"Look at you, lecturing a High Priestess. Besides, don't act too cocky. Drés told me you wouldn't even jeopardize the rug." She smiled triumphantly.

Asshole!

"You can't pluck it." I took my hair to the side and brushed it with my fingers to catch a loose strand.

Several came out. With curly or wavy hair, there was always loose strands of hair in between the ones still attached.

"You take one, make three knots. First one in the center, then one on each side." I demonstrated with my own hair.

"Then you will need one black and one white candle, both anointed and dressed. Tie the hair around each candle and form a bridge, then light the candles on a new moon while you read the incantation."

"What's the incantation?"

"Hair of mine, entwine with care, bind these knots, strong and rare. Strands of magic, bind so tight, guard me through the darkest night. Knot by knot, my safety sealed, from dark magic's reach. May these knots repel, without fail, those who seek to hex, bewitch, or assail. So, mote it be."

"You have to write that down for me."

"Are we friends now?" I grinned.

"Not even close." She took the yarn with beads and put it away in a basket.

"Come help me cook. I can't decide what to make. I wanted to make dumplings—I have some in the freezer, but then I remembered Drés brought home Oaxacan cheese, and I wanted to make quesadilla. You know what would be great, too?—*guacamole con totopos*. Maybe we should make all of it and eat a little bit of everything." Her eyes lit up. "You know I have a rule. If I'm eating, then so must everyone else, and whatever I cannot finish, you must finish for me."

"What am I, a garbage disposal?"

"Shame on you. I don't throw out food. Whatever is leftover Drés can have." She smiled, as if I was in on a secret, and he was not.

We decided to skip the dumpling and prepped lunch right away. At first, I thought she wouldn't like me to help. But then she put the stone mortar in front of me and left me in charge of finishing the guacamole while she heated up tortillas. She made a couple of quesadillas and brought a paper bag full of homemade tortilla chips and two jars of salsa.

"I like to put salsa on the side of guacamole. You should try it," she said and scooped a heap of guac with salsa.

I tried the same and instantly regretted the amount of salsa.

"Shit, it's spicy, but holy fuck, this is the best thing I've ever put in my mouth." I couldn't stop adding the salsa, even though my lips were burning.

We ate until we couldn't breathe, and if it wasn't because of my Persian instincts I would have lied down. Instead, I got up and cleaned the mess.

"Why do you always get up and clean right after food? You're literally excused from labor because of your arm.

You make me look bad!" Ev got up with me and emptied her plate.

"It's fine. I need to move it so it gets back to normal."

"You know, you don't owe me anything. Drés brought you here. You're a guest—"

"Guest?" I couldn't help but grin.

Of course, she didn't know about my last conversation with her brother. She didn't know I wanted to stay.

Ev returned the smile. "A prisoner, then. Act like it."

"Do I have yard time?"

She laughed at that.

Ev was just my type of girl. Her tongue was long, as the saying goes in Farsi, and she didn't take dire situations too seriously. I would have loved to be her friend, but she'd never believe my sincerity. She'd probably assume I was only trying to gain the upper hand over her brother. In reality, I didn't care what she was to Rés. She didn't have a say in the prophecy, and even if she did, I wouldn't ask her for help.

Her life was untainted by this, and I wanted it to remain that way.

Not long after, Rés came back with the phone I had asked from him. I told him I wouldn't even attempt to teleport without one, just in case I ended up lost somewhere. Rés placed the phone on the table and fixed himself a plate. His legs brushed up against mine under the table. I couldn't figure out whether he was doing it on purpose or his legs were so long that this was just the way he sat.

"I put the location on so I can always track you," he said before dipping his quesadilla in the salsa. "Now that you have it, will you practice going from here to the living room?" He offered me his hand as if our legs weren't touching under the table.

Perhaps I was imagining it. *No!* His powers were definitely there. I knew what it felt like, how his powers buzzed through my skin, and I hated to admit how much I loved the feeling. His hand was still hanging in the air, waiting to be accepted.

I wanted to say yes, wanted to get this thing over with no matter how scared I was. Of course, I wouldn't just disappear into thin air without a conscious thought. I knew what it required of my brain. Having an intrusive thought to punch someone wouldn't magically make it happen. You would have to decide to do it.

The same applied here. The thought wouldn't transform into action without a conscious decision.

I took a deep breath, put the phone in my pocket, and took his hand. *Another excuse for touching him.*

"You won't get lost, I promise. It's not that hard. You just need a bit of focus."

There it was again.

Focus, focus. Fucking always focus.

I closed my eyes and imagined myself in the nothingness, dissolving like I had seen Adam do it.

Adam. His hands.

I can't breathe. No, stop!

"I can't!" I burst out, letting go of Rés's hand before standing from the chair.

"I can't do it!"

"You almost had it," Rés said calmly. "Try again."

"What if Adam finds me?"

Rés's eyes darkened. "He will never put a hand on you again." It was like he knew what I was thinking and had lived through my deepest fears. "Sit," he said and pulled out a chair.

I sat, looking at my hands. There were no marks on my wrist, yet I felt the lingering pressure of his grip. *This feeling has to be dealt with. It has to go away.*

"How do I make it stop haunting me?" I breathed.

"Facing your demons is the only way."

"It was my own doing. I brought it upon myself. I let—"

"No."

I took a deep inhale before deciding that I actually did need to talk about it.

"You don't know what happened. I thought I could fool him again. I thought I was so fucking smart, but he wanted revenge and . . ."

It was well deserved. Finally, I admitted it to myself. I deserved what Adam did and what I was most afraid of, was if he wanted more, that he wasn't done with me. An eye for an eye.

"I actually do," Rés said. "I know what happened because I saw it. I assumed you had guessed as much—that you remembered your dreams."

"What?" I looked at him, my brows pulling together.

"To earn back my soul from my father, I had to trade my services. I am a dreamwalker—a form of astral projection. I don't just enter dreams. I shape them. I can appear in any form I wish and bend reality for the dreamer. I was assigned to you because I'm the only dreamwalker in the family."

"How many times?" I asked, remembering every instance I had dreamed of him while in Egypt.

Yet when I woke, his face was forgotten.

A knot formed in my stomach.

"Too many times, I'm afraid. It's not something I enjoy doing. I lose sense of reality when I roam the realms," Rés said.

I blinked but couldn't quite form an answer.

I couldn't expect anything from him. He was not my friend—that, he had told me enough times. I was nothing to him, and he owed me nothing. Still, it felt like betrayal.

"After Egypt?"

"No." His gaze, serious and unwavering, swore everything his words couldn't. "I saw what he did. I saw the way you relived it in your dreams," Rés confessed.

He thought he knew my pain because of what he saw in my dreams, not knowing I only had myself to blame.

"You saw a version of it. You saw what you wanted to see because you hate Adam for taking your soul, but you don't know what you saw. I wanted it, I initiated it, and I thought I could double cross him again, and I was wrong.

The fact that he took revenge is fair on his part," I said with more heat than intended.

"Why are you defending that bastard after what he did?"

Rés matched my tone, which made no sense. It wasn't about him.

"Because I deserved it!" I almost yelled, and a tear slipped down my cheek.

Rés seized my shoulders, ready to shake me.

He's not anchoring. You could disappear, run from the confrontation like you always do.

"No, you don't, Maya." His expression was dark with anger. I didn't want to hear it. *He's not anchoring. Just go.* "You dese—"

And I did. I made a conscious decision to teleport into the bedroom, and it worked.

"It fucking worked," I whispered to myself, wiping away another tear.

A few seconds passed before an alarm sounded from my pocket, and the door to my room burst open.

"Bloody hell!" Rés breathed as he walked into the bedroom.

The phone had stopped ringing.

I pulled it out of my pocket and saw he had saved himself in as Andrés.

Remember to put the phone on silent.

"Don't you dare do that again without warning. How do you feel?"

"I, uhm. Let me try that again." I reached for his hand, and he hesitated for a second before offering me his hand. "Living room."

It happened again, but this time, I was out of breath. Rés walked into the living room, watching me with a smile.

"Why am I so tired?"

"It should feel like the first time you're running. You have no practice, but I think you should push yourself and try one more time back to your bedroom."

This time, I took his hand and let myself savor it. His energy was something else, something so rich and vivid, a high without the bad trip. His powers poured down my throat like honey, and I wasn't sure if I could ever have enough. I teleported to the bedroom and dropped to my knees. I had to shift and sit on my ass, or I would face-plant on the floor.

Rés came into the bedroom to make sure I had arrived in one piece. "Get some rest. We will practice again tomorrow."

Stay, I wanted to say. Instead, I nodded and dragged myself to the bed.

۲۹

TWENTY-NINE

MAYA

The days blended together as we worked on the same things over and over.

Rés was right. Teleporting was like running, equivalent to a marathon. In the beginning, I was exhausted after just three times. After nearly practicing every single day for a week, I could go ten times before I was completely drained.

I still couldn't do it without the help of his powers. I needed the whole Firuzeh for that. I had perfected my landings over short distances, but long-distance teleportation was a different challenge. I still hadn't tried venturing outside the house. I would eventually, but Rés wanted that "eventually" to be sooner rather than later.

"How long does your glamour spell hold up?"

"Until I am back at the anchoring point."

"Good. We're going outside." He left no room for argument. "You will aim for the diner. It's secluded, easy to remember, and I'm hungry."

"The diner where I nearly got killed?"

He must be out of his mind.

"No one will go back looking for you there. Besides, your glamour spell works perfectly fine, right?" His brow raised.

"Yes," I forced out.

I didn't like the way he implied that my spellwork wasn't as good as I said it was. *I'll show you glamour.*

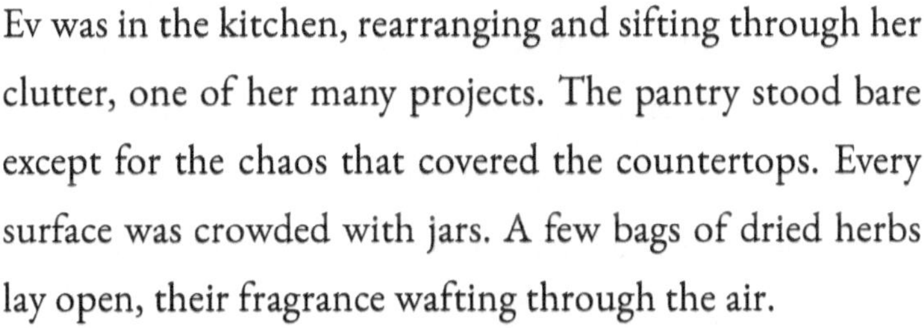

Ev was in the kitchen, rearranging and sifting through her clutter, one of her many projects. The pantry stood bare except for the chaos that covered the countertops. Every surface was crowded with jars. A few bags of dried herbs lay open, their fragrance wafting through the air.

With Everie, the kitchen felt like a living thing.

"How's your arm, by the way. Better?" she asked, looking at my arm.

I hadn't been wearing the make shift sling for a while.

"Yeah, much better, actually. I have full mobility. It's still sore, but I can grab and lift things now."

"Brilliant! Nicking the grimoire shouldn't be a problem, then," Rés said as he walked into the kitchen.

His eyes widened when the chaos of the kitchen unfolded before him.

"For the love of God, Everie."

"*Cállate*," she said. *Hah! I know what that means.* "I was looking for rosebuds and couldn't find them because there is no system here!"

"You better finish this today," Rés warned.

"Be grateful I let you step foot in my mother's house, Andrés."

"I'm grateful for Luciano—that's what I'm grateful for," he said, looking at me. "Let's go."

He only extended his hand to me once we were out of Everie's line of sight, and I couldn't help but wonder why.

"Where do you want me to land, exactly?" My arms hung limply at my sides.

"Try aiming for the far side of the parking lot. We need to avoid being spotted."

"I could still be seen." He stepped closer, towering over me, his scent blanketing the air I breathed.

It took everything in me not to close my eyes and revel in his presence when he slid his hand into mine, his fingers wrapping around it. I was terrified, and he was aware of it because he was still anchored in place. What if Adam was waiting for me?

You're glamoured!

I couldn't second guess myself because I had to do it, had to face my fears if I wanted to find the grimoire and be done with this prophecy.

"Drop the barrier," I said.

A breath later, I found myself under the baking sun in what looked like the back of a tall building.

Where am I? Is this the right place?

My vision blurred, and a dizzying sense of urgency took over. I had made it out somewhere, but where that somewhere was, I had no idea.

I had managed just fine teleporting inside the house, excellent even. So, why the hell was this any different? The open space, the air—everything should've been easier, but instead, it felt like I was lost and the world was pressing in on me. The phone in my pocket rang, obnoxiously loud, cutting through the tense air. I cursed under my breath, silenced it quickly, and answered the call, trying to steady my breathing.

"Where are you? Your location says you are here," Rés asked.

Thank god. I exhaled sharply. "Hang on." I walked all the way around the building, my mind racing until I ended up at the spot where Fidel had found me.

I'm okay. It's fine. I'm fine. I don't look like me.

Rés appeared around the corner. *It's safe now. I'm safe.*

"Good job, demon blood." Because his words were a double-edged sword, I couldn't decide whether to feel relieved or trapped. "They're not going to come here." He assured me. He was probably right—there was nothing to fear. Yet I was shrouded in uncertainty. *Your veil is strong. Your glamour is solid. My glamour!* A spark flickered inside me when I remembered my glamour and the things I had planned for Rés.

"I'm fine. Let's get something to eat," I said, forcing my voice to sound casual, masking the shift in my mood.

Rés walked ahead of me, my steps steady and deliberate behind him. I spotted the redhead as he pushed open the door, the doorbell chiming above us. *Showtime.*

"Drés!" she said with a bright smile before I took a step beside him and caught her eye.

"Blimey! We *dew* look *similah*," I said in the thickest British accent I could force. "He *tolks* about *chew oll* the time."

Rés's head snapped in my direction, giving me a look as if I'd lost my mind.

I had glamoured myself to look exactly like her. To everyone but Rés, I was her spitting image or as close to it as I could get.

"You do?" she asked Rés.

It was all she heard from what I had said.

"This is Rosa." Rés gestured to me, stifling his surprise. "Everie thinks you two look alike, but I don't see it."

Bravo, Rés. Catching on quickly.

"You're also from London?" she asked, grabbing a menu from the table, then led us through the restaurant. Rés put a light hand on the small of my back, guiding me. She caught the gesture before I could step out of his reach.

"No, *techniclaay*, I'm *eye-rish*, which explains the red *hare*, but I grew up in Oxford."

Rés stared at me, dumbfounded, clearly not expecting a full backstory for my character.

"The college?" She shot me a quick, confused glance.

"Yes, I grew up at uni. My *faather* is a professor in the *daark aarts,*" I said, making sure to drag my A's and leave out the R's.

She smiled halfheartedly, as if she hadn't asked me the question herself.

I looked at Rés from the corner of my eye, unable to hide my smirk.

"Let me just wipe down the table before you sit, Drés," she said, her hand already reaching for the cloth behind the bar.

"Sharp as a marble, that one," I whispered, just loud enough for him to hear, never breaking character.

He scoffed, and a laugh caught in his throat.

That snagged her attention.

"Jimmy isn't here today, but the new guy is pretty good. He makes the best apple pie, but don't tell Jimmy I said that." She disregarded me completely when gesturing for us to sit. "Are you having your usual, Drés?"

"Yes, please." He gave her one of his most devastating smiles.

She then turned to me, waiting expectantly. I was about to say "Me too" when I realized I wasn't supposed to know what his usual was.

"*Ji* know *whot*, I would *luv* to try the apple pie you mentioned." She nodded, scribbling on her notepad. "*Fank yew*," I said in the most obnoxious British accent.

"Do you want to share?" Rés asked me, catching me off guard.

I nodded, chewing on my bottom lip to suppress the sigh.

He's asking about the food, nothing else.

He grabbed the menu from in front of me and handed it to her. "Then we'll have the aubergine sandwich as well and a sweet tea for Rosa."

"A plate of pancakes, one eggplant sourdough, apple pie, coffee, and sweet tea," she repeated, her smile genuine when meeting his eyes.

"Yes, thank you, darling." He waited till she was out of earshot before he spoke again. "That was the worst British accent I've ever heard in my life."

"That's what you sound like to the rest of us. It's actually really hard to force it. How do you do it every day? My whole jaw hurts."

"I don't force it. It's just the way I speak."

"Who's Rosa?" I asked, my curiosity slipping through despite my best efforts to hide it.

"It's short for *mentirosa*."

I was about to ask what it meant when the redhead returned with our drinks. I didn't have the energy to force more than a smile at her.

Suddenly, I felt an overwhelming wave of exhaustion wash over me, my vision beginning to blur. My blood sugar must've been dropping.

I leaned back in the booth, resting my head against the wall, trying to steady myself as everything around me seemed to drift in and out of focus.

"Drink the sweet tea. Low blood sugar is common when you're traveling long distances for the first time."

Then he stretched out his legs under the table, leaning one of them against mine.

"Does it help if we touch?" he asked.

For the very first time, he acknowledged what had always been left unsaid. The more time we spent together, the more it became apparent that our proximity was a sticky, sugary poison.

The first taste was sweet and unassuming, the second, thrilling—never losing its effect. But after that, it was addictive, a craving woven into my very existence. The need for physical touch had become an undeniable necessity. Without it, I was surviving on whatever was left from the Firuzeh, existing solely on the bare minimum.

The same seemed to happen to him. Though he never said it outright, I could see it—the way tension coiled beneath his skin. He was restless, aching for relief. There was no need for explanations or excuses because there was a silent agreement between us. We indulged in whatever this was.

"Yes." I closed my eyes and exhaled deeply.

This couldn't be right. It simply couldn't be the only way I felt like I was truly alive.

Am I nothing on my own? Is his touch a curse?

The food arrived, and I straightened in my seat, breaking our touch. I immediately regretted it, but I wasn't going to depend on him. I couldn't live my life through him. Soon enough, I would be on my own, and I needed to remember what that felt like.

The apple pie was very average, but the pancakes were just as delicious as I remembered. They were served with fresh figs, raspberries, blackberries, and maple syrup. I had planned to eat the sandwich, but I was full and didn't want to spoil my bliss.

I leaned back again, closing my eyes.

"If you need it, why do you deny yourself my energy? It doesn't drain me."

"Don't worry, I couldn't give two fucks about draining you dry. I'm cherishing the moment." I closed my eyes again. "Give me two minutes, and I'll be ready to go."

I needed a moment to recover from the food coma and the taste of maple syrup on my lips.

"Stop biting your lips."

My eyes snapped open and found him studying me. It wasn't what I had expected to hear from him.

I leaned over the table closer to him and lowered my voice. "Or—hear me out—you could stop staring at me." I held his gaze.

His eyes dropped to my lips for a second before it was pulled away by the redhead, who called his name and waved him over.

He put on a perfect smile and walked over to her.

She beamed, thinking she was in competition with me for his attention.

Little did she know, all she had to do was to lose her soul and Rés would be all over her, too. That she, too, could be a means to an end if only she had been stupid enough to lose her soul to a Dūshev.

Rés was still chatting to her when I headed out of the door for fresh air. There was no reason for me to sit and wait for him as if I had nothing better to do. Not that I did. And I couldn't go anywhere without his help.

"Is it so bloody hard to wait!" Rés snapped when he finally caught up with me.

"I was just giving you privacy, you blind brick. The girl likes you."

"I didn't ask for privacy," he said, taking a threatening step toward me.

"Well, technically, you didn't tell me to stay either."

Rés inched closer. "Every day, you find new ways to get on my nerves," he said through gritted teeth. "Is this what you do? Wake up every morning, thinking, *How can I piss off Drés today?*"

"I usually wake up thinking of ways to kill you, but then I feel bad for Ev because she is actually nice."

"How honorable of you not acting on your demon blood impulses. Is the Feyrooz in your tooth not doing its magic?"

I had completely forgotten he knew about it. The fucking bastard had walked in my dreams, taken whatever information he wanted from my head.

"If it wasn't for the lack of Firuzeh, I would have killed you long ago."

Would I? I didn't know if I would. Had I ever been in control?

Was I in control when I betrayed Adam, when I pretended to give up my powers to be with him, or was I just doing my ancestors' bidding? In that bedroom, I fed him lies that turned sour in his heart. *I deserved it.* Before Rés noticed the movement, I took his hand and teleported, aiming to land at Everie's. The problem was, it wasn't where my mind had wandered. *If you don't face your demons, you will never forgive yourself.* Only, I hadn't expected to face my demons right that second.

When I opened my eyes, I wasn't in New Orleans like I had expected. *This can't be right.* I felt my throat tightening, my lungs unable to work at full capacity. Panic crawled up my chest as I took in my surroundings. The sudden absence of sunlight heavy in a way that made every breath a struggle. *This can't be. Please. I can't breathe.*

I was standing in the very place where I had betrayed Adam, the cabin in Scotland. The bed was undone, curtains drawn, and dust had collected on the windowsill. The sun was rising, its rays bathing the room in a soft gold, casting long shadows on the cursed space.

The room smelled of him.

It smells of him! He is here!

My hands shook as I fumbled, looking for my phone. Thank God I had put it on silent because, when I touched it, it vibrated. Rés was calling, but I couldn't risk answering. I had to hang up right away. The vibration was too loud.

It's too fucking loud. If Adam was truly there . . . Fuck, fuck, fuck!

I can burn this whole house down—with myself in it. He is not here. Why would he be here, of all places? He is not here. He is not here. He is not here.

There was a dresser next to the window and nothing else, no closet, no nothing. I couldn't remember if there was a hiding place beyond this bedroom, and I wasn't sure I dared to risk it.

The bedroom door was ajar. My phone buzzed again, and my heart dropped. I hung up again by reflex and had forgotten it was clutched in my hand. Surely, if he was there, he would have heard it by now.

My heart was racing and my palms sweating, but I still crept closer to the door in slow steps to avoid making any sound. I had to make sure I was alone, so I poked my head out of the room looking to both sides of the long hall. I could see most of the living room and kitchen, but there was no one.

I'm okay. He is not here. I'm okay.

Relieved, I decided I wasn't brave enough to venture out of the bedroom. Less movement meant less exposure.

Is there a pantry here? I can hide in the pantry!

My phone buzzed again. This time, I had received text messages. First one was from the carrier.

> Welcome to Scotland.
>
> Great news, calling & texting here are included in your plan at no additional cost. You can add data roaming credit to your plan on our mobile app or on our website under My Services. The international roaming rate for data is $0.20/MB . . .

There was more to it, but I quickly went to the next text message that was from Rés:

> Why tge fuck did you turn off your location.
>
> If you want to run away be my fuxking guest.
>
> I am not playing games with you.you can rot
>
> un hell

It was clear by his typos that he was furious.

Instead of responding, I called him right away, turning down the volume. It beeped once before he picked up.

"What!" he snapped.

"Rés."

His name was the first thing that came out of my mouth. My whimpering voice betrayed me more than I had anticipated.

"Where are you?"

His tone immediately changed.

"I'm in Adam's cabin in Scotland," I whispered.

"What cabin?"

"He's not here right now, but please, I'm—" I swallowed the lump in my throat and felt the tears trickling down my face. "I don't know if he'll be back."

What if Rés decided he wasn't coming? What if he decided this would be the time he would punish me for doing whatever I wanted? I didn't come here on purpose—he had to know that.

"Maya, listen to me. Find yourself a place to hide. Behind a door, in a cupboard—just hide. It will take me a few minutes, but I will find you. Are you listening?" I nodded as if he could see me before I croaked a delayed yes.

I didn't know how I managed to, but a few seconds later, I ventured out of the bedroom and into the open kitchen where there was a walk-in pantry the size of a shoebox. There were cans of baked beans, tomato paste, and a few cans of something called Irn-Bru.

Everything went black as I closed the door. The only sliver of light came from the keyhole. I counted my breaths and lost count so many times I had to start over. What felt like an eternity passed by before my breathing had calmed down.

I peeped through the keyhole and could see most of the kitchen, the edge of the couch and the hallway leading to the bedroom and front door.

No one is here. I'm fine.

At least, inside the pantry, I was safe. I looked through the keyhole, and there was still no one there. *Breathe. It's fine. You're fine.*

Something changed in the air, an eerie quiet that wasn't there before. It didn't sit right with me. I kept looking, waiting for something to change before my eyes. And as if the prediction wanted to come true, a person appeared in the kitchen, standing by the stove. I was sure my heart stopped for a second.

This is the end of me. The phone! If he calls, I'm done.

I tried to figure out how to turn off vibration but ended up turning the phone off completely out of sheer panic. There was no doubt about it.

Adam is here.

I knew him. I had obsessed over him enough to know every atom of his being. I knew how he carried himself, how he stood, how he moved.

He is here. He is really here.

I nearly fainted at the realization.

Don't breathe. Don't move a hair. Don't blink.

He didn't move either, not until another one appeared. It was one of the elders; not someone I could fool or buy time with. I was too afraid to break eye contact, certain he would feel my stare if I held it long enough. My energy would give me away. Tears started to blur my vision when

I heard Adam speak. I was prepared to stop breathing if it saved me from being discovered.

"You can have a look yourself. I searched everywhere. It's not here."

He sounded both exhausted and annoyed.

The brother walked around, half inspecting the space. "Show me the bedroom."

"I've turned every leaf, but please, don't take my word for it."

Adam's words came with a bitter taste. The brother followed Adam through the long hall, but before he was in my blind spot, he looked back at the pantry door—no, at me. For a second, his brother glared me in the eye through the key hole. Then he disappeared into the hallway.

You're imagining it. He hasn't seen you. You're fine! You're glamoured! I took a deep breath. *I'm fine. I'm fine. I'm fine. What if the glamour stopped working?*

My whole body trembled. I was sure they could feel the tremor through the floorboards. I wanted to cover the keyhole with my hand, but I was afraid the door would give and make a sound. Slowly, I rose and covered my mouth with my shaking hands.

I can't go back. I can't go back. I can't go back.

Even with my eyes closed, the tears wouldn't stop streaming down my face. The rush of the blood in my ears had drowned out all sounds outside of that pantry. I had no idea how long I had been standing there. Only when I could hear the creaking of the floorboard nearing closer did I snap my eyes open. The suspense numbed me, and I couldn't make myself snap out of it.

I thought I was stronger, thought I had more control over my mind, thought my consciousness was mine. Even though I convinced myself I had grown, that I had become strong and resilient, all I did was freeze when the doorknob turned.

This is it.

Everything turned black, and all blood drained from my head.

When the door fully opened, and I finally looked up to meet his eyes, a sob escaped me. Rés was standing in front of me, his chest rising and falling visibly.

Relief washed over me like never before. I could finally breathe again.

I let myself collide with him, fall into his chest. My arms wrapped around him like he was the only thing keeping my heart beating.

I'm safe now. I'm safe. I'm safe.

"Breathe," he whispered against my ear and rested his chin on the top of my head.

I made an involuntary choking sound as I burst into tears, my face buried in his chest. He pulled me closer, his arms tightening around me, and it was like a dam broke. I cried like I was a child again. A child who had been taken from her parents, a child who was never hugged, a child who made herself breakfast and lunch, a child who was always alone.

"Deep inhale."

His hand moved up and down my back, smoothing the fabric of my shirt.

Why does it hurt so much? Why am I so broken?

Rés didn't let go, didn't try to make me stop. He was just there. Held me until there were no tears left and the pain had moved to the back of my broken heart.

"You're good. Breathe. You did good."

I'm good, I tried convincing myself. *I'm good.*

Reluctantly, I pulled away, not fully letting go of him. If I had an ounce of dignity before, it was gone now.

"Ad-Adam was here, with someone else."

He had to know I was crying for a reason, that I wasn't just a pathetic excuse of a girl, scared of her own shadow.

"I know." He stepped back, cataloging me from head to toe like he was looking for something.

I had to look at my trembling fingers, pulling at the cuticles, or he would see the effect he had on me. He tilted up my chin to scan my face. Meeting his gaze hurt in places I never knew existed because I saw all the things we could have been. *I wish I had never met you Rés because I don't think I can survive you.* He was so easy to rely on, to trust.

"We have a lot of places in Scotland. I didn't know which one you were in, so I had Edgar help me find you," he said, his expression shifting back to neutral.

"Edgar knows?" I asked instead of pouring my heart out.

"Yes, of course. You didn't think we were all bad, did you?" The corner of his lips curled into a sad smile.

I don't think any of you are bad. I only think I am. [5]

Rés led me out of the cabin without explanation, and I didn't ask for one either. The truth of the matter was, I trusted him with my life. I wasn't going to pretend anymore. He stopped in front of me, placing his hands on my

Paeez - Shadmehr Aghili

shoulders and turned me to face the cabin. It was sitting on a clearing, surrounded by a sparse forest. Yet all I could see was the pain I had caused, the blood I had sacrificed, the mistakes I had made.

"I need you to burn the cabin down to the ground. An exercise if you will."

Of course, he was thinking strategically. His empathy for me had probably passed as fast as it had arrived. *He wants to use this opportunity where you feel your weakest to practice and become a weapon because his mission is still his top priority.*

"Now," he demanded, stepping back from me.

I did as I was told. I didn't argue, didn't roll my eyes. There was no wind left in me. The fire manifested easily this time. A controlled chaos, fueled by self-hate. I could make the flames reach the sky or dull them down to tiny embers. It didn't need oxygen to spread. It needed me.

I let it all burn until only the charred skeleton of the cabin remained. The flames disappeared as if they had never been in the first place. If it wasn't for the heat of the flames that flushed my cheeks and the cloud of smoke in the sky, I would have thought I had made it all up.

Immobile, I stood, looking at another result of my destruction, the result of my ignorance, my fear, and my desperate need to belong and realized I was the problem. I always blamed everyone else for the bad things in my life. Instead of focusing on my choices, I zeroed in on my circumstances. The destruction I left in my path was all my own doing.

Blinded by the illusion of being the chosen one, I created a false identity for myself, convincing myself that my existence meant something. My lineage, the prophecy, and magic created a deceptive sense of acceptance, whereas I should have been killed once my soul was taken. It wasn't my soul to begin with, anyway.

Adam wasn't the villain. I was. I ripped Adam's feelings to shreds when I left him, when I played games with him from beyond the grave.

I killed his brothers one by one with no remorse and had gone too far. There was no going back from it. Being the one who ruined everything, I was one who wasn't strong enough to resist the influence of the ancestors who helped push me on this path. There was no one else to blame but myself for my weaknesses. Every malicious, vengeful action was my own, and every cruel step I had taken had brought me here.

The shame of it would follow me the rest of my life.

I wasn't looking for forgiveness from Adam. I didn't deserve that. I was looking for justice, and perhaps I could still give him that. Perhaps I could still make things right.

٣٠

THIRTY

ALDRIDGE

When I realized my mistake, it was already too late. I should've gone with my gut feeling and chipped her instead. She had asked for a mobile phone, and I obliged.

When her phone died, I nearly lost it. I imagined it all too vividly—my brothers capturing her once again, her unconscious body limp in one of their arms.

The image was unbearable, a cruel vision I couldn't shake. I wouldn't just stop them from touching her—I wouldn't let anyone so much as lay eyes on her. *I'm afraid she belongs to me only.*

When Maya was first caught, Adam had been the one to call our father, giving away their location. My father had sent my brothers Zaki and Fidel—neither of whom I could trust nor turn to for help. Their loyalty was to my father alone. None of us had thought to ask where Adam had been when Maya went after him, and there was still a chance he was using the safe house. If not for Edgar, I would have wasted even more time chasing her, going from one cabin to another.

Edgar, quick-witted as ever, played his part flawlessly. He summoned Adam, pressing him about the day Maya had found him, probing for clues about the missing stone Adam was accused of hiding.

Adam grew defensive, unable to understand why the accusations kept coming. He was desperate to prove his innocence, determined to show he wasn't hiding anything, and offered to show Edgar the cabin himself. Once they were out of the way, Edgar messaged me, and I could finally go get her.

My heart shattered when she collapsed into my arms, her sobs unraveling me completely. Every ounce of restraint I had on myself crumbled to dust. I rested my chin on top of her head, closing my eyes to steady my breath. Refusing to accept the truth wasn't going to make it go away. Her well-being was all that mattered.

How could I make her pain my own, take away the hurt and sorrow, and give her everything I had? All I could think of was becoming one with her, binding myself to her in every possible way. She held claim to half of my soul. I was convinced of it more than anything else, but I prayed, pleaded to every god and deity I could think of that I was wrong about the prophecy—that I wasn't the one destined to share a soul with her. If I let myself be selfish for a fraction of a second, I would have a hard time finding reasons why I couldn't run away and have her for myself.

What was to happen to me after the war was over? Was I supposed to carry on as if nothing had changed? Was I meant to pretend I could survive a single day without her proximity? At every touch, I was reminded of how still the ocean could be if I just let it happen. If I just gave in and let the universe decide what would happen next.

It was a selfish thought. I was selfish for wanting her, selfish for ignoring all the things that could go wrong. I had to pull myself together before she noticed the shift in my behavior. She needed to be able to trust me, especially while I had her running around doing my bidding.

"I'm done here," she said, looking up at me with tear-trickled cheeks.

I wanted to wipe them away, to hold her, to let her find comfort in my touch like I did in hers. If I looked at her long enough, I would convince myself she longed for me, too.

"Are you ready to go home?" I asked her instead and offered her my hand.

"I'm ready to get you the grimoire," she said, steeling her features, locking away whatever she was feeling.

The grimoire.

I had lost sight of my purpose in all of this, of why she was there in the first place. As we got closer to the finish line, the grimoire faded further into insignificance. It became nothing more than an afterthought, overshadowed by her. She wasn't merely a pawn for me to use, and I didn't want her to be. I was afraid of letting her go in the off chance she wouldn't come back. And frankly, my fears had nothing to do with her running away with the grimoire.

The moment I sent her into that convent, I would lose access to her. She would be all on her own, relying on her wit and skill to get out.

Infiltrating a demon blood convent turned to be the stupidest idea I had ever come up with, and not trying it could have detrimental consequences for all of us.

۳۱

THIRTY-ONE

ALDRIDGE

He had slaughtered them all. In a blind, savage frenzy, my father wiped out every single one of the Sāhers he had imprisoned, Sepideh included. Edgar had entered the great hall and found the remains of their bodies scattered and torn apart. Blood coated every surface, spattering across the walls, dripping from the paintings. My father had decapitated them and arranged their severed heads in a circle, in the center of the room, with a ring of salt surrounding them. If it was for ritualistic purposes, we didn't know because my father had disappeared after that. I had witnessed a lot but never had I seen my father do so much damage. How much more were we going to allow before drawing the line?

Edgar called for an emergency meeting to inform everyone, even the youngest ones. His practiced and polished words didn't reveal his contempt of our father.

"Is no one going to say anything?" Fidel asked, his spirit not only broken but out of reach. "How much longer will we pretend that he isn't the devil reincarnated?" He looked at the elders, expecting justification for the cruel reality.

This was the way our father broke us, the way he so foolishly created distance between himself and his children. Had he paid attention, he would have known how much Fidel loved Sepideh.

"We do not take profanity lightly, Fidel. And as for our father, I have no doubt that he had his reasons. Every decision he makes is deliberate, every action with purpose. He has never acted without careful consideration. Do you truly believe he would betray our legacy now?" Herman said, my father's ever-loyal soldier.

"Enough with the manipulation!" Adam raised his voice. "Fidel is right. We can't excuse his behavior. How much more will you stand by and watch before you finally open your eyes? Before you see what we have become?"

Interesting. It turned out Adam had grown a pair. His perception of our father finally changed after the truth had been revealed to him. *It took you long enough.*

"We don't have time for your ego trip." Herman dismissed Adam with a flick of his wrist.

"You simply can't all be this brainwashed. I refuse to believe it!" Adam continued.

Samuel gave him an approving nod that both Edgar and Karam caught.

No one else intervened because everyone knew the time and place for opinions.

"Adam," Herman warned, unaware of just how alone he truly was in this crowd.

Yes, there were a few who truly shared our father's beliefs, but only a scarce few.

"No! This is wrong!" Adam shouted. "First, he convinced us we were doing God's work by taking souls, then the obsession with procreation, and now he's on a murder spree because of a rock. Maybe they were right to want to restore the balance of nature. Maybe we deserve to be eliminated from the face of the earth. And let's not forget the clinical trials on innocent fucking children!"

Bravo, Adam. You're finally getting it.

A few quick glances were exchanged between the ones who had no idea what was being discussed. Edgar rose from his seat, followed by Darius and Karam. Herman moved to stand as well, but Edgar placed a hand on his shoulder. "You and Fazel stay with the rest, while we have a word with Adam and Fidel in private."

Herman sank back into his seat, his lips curling into a smirk as he met Adam's eyes.

"Follow along, please," Edgar said.

I knew it was the moment the rebellion would be revealed to Adam. Though I had whispered it in Fidel's ear before, this was the first time he would hear it from an elder.

"Of course!" Adam exclaimed as he got up. "Take away the troublemakers so the rest can be indoctrinated."

He didn't resist and neither did Fidel. If they were nervous, they hid it well. I was surprised by the shift in Adam's attitude. Perhaps there was hope for him after all. Not that it could ever erase the pain he had caused. *For that, you will pay tenfold.*

"Where do you suppose Father is?" I asked Herman when they left the room.

"I'm assuming he is looking for the rest of them," he answered, his voice flat, as if there were no other possible explanation. "I believe our father has grown impatient with these witches."

My heart sank when her mother crossed my mind.

"Great, why are we here, exactly?" Skandar asked, knowing I couldn't rush out of there like I wanted to.

"Gee, I don't know, Skandar, maybe we need to discuss the six severed heads in the great hall," Omar deadpanned.

"While that sounds delightful, I have more interesting endeavors to occupy myself with," I said and pushed my chair back.

"Sit, Aldridge," Herman commanded.

I smiled, unable to keep a neutral expression. "Please, brother, let's not pretend. If father is not here to enforce his rules, I'm nothing but a forgotten memory to this family. Try not to think of me too often, as I tend to get nightmares from your face." I winked at him and left the room.

He had far more important matters to deal with and couldn't afford to be distracted by someone like me.

I didn't have time to sit around and look at Herman dig for gold in his ass. I had to find Maya's mother before my father did. I really needed to talk to Edgar, but he was in over his head, stuck dealing with those two morons while Herman breathed down his neck.

"Hold on." Skandar caught up with me in the hallway, grabbing my arm before I could decide what to do next. "Let me help you."

I nodded, appreciating his ability to read the room. Regardless of the rebellion's existence, only a handful of my brothers knew about Everie, and even fewer knew I had Maya. Skandar was one of the selected few I trusted with everything.

"Go to Mist Creek. I'll meet you there after I've talked to Ev."

I needed all the help I could get, but first, I had to talk to Everie. Only she could create wards powerful enough to keep our father out.

I was home in an instant, careful not to cause a stir and wake Maya. I could only imagine how she would react to her entire family being slaughtered. If I had to stay behind to prevent her from doing something stupid, I couldn't go make wards for her parents.

I explained everything to Everie, every gory detail of how our father killed them to then cast a circle with their heads. Ev was certain our father had performed a sacrificial ritual to a powerhouse of a jinn, one that demanded far more than pickled gherkins and cloudy lemonades. Their souls had been the offering, but what he had gained from it we had yet to discover.

Ev wasted no time, giving me detailed instructions. She handed me four labeled glass jars for fistfuls of soil from each corner of the property. Then she gave me two small linen pouches for hair from each, strands plucked from the root. Ev and Maria would cast the ward when I'd return the soil and hair.

I exhaled slowly, checking my watch—6:00 a.m. Mist Creek was two hours behind, which meant they were likely still asleep. Her father and brother were my first priority. After securing them, I would go looking for Maya's mother. Her mother was still a demon blood. She would be smart enough to ward on her own. Though the thought offered no comfort. There was no time for hesitation.

By the time it was noon, I had gone back and forth seven times between Mist Creek and Maria's house where Ev was. Ev wanted us to take other measures, just in case casting the ward from a distance didn't work. Meanwhile, Skandar had been keeping watch outside their house. Luckily, my father hadn't shown up. With Skandar leading a small group, we took turns watching the house while awaiting news from Edgar, which came faster than expected.

Edgar called us back for the second time in the span of twenty-four hours. The evaluation room was charged with tension. I caught Adam's eyes tracking me from the moment I entered the room till I sat down. Our father walked in looking extremely worn out. Considering what he had done within the last twenty-four hours, it didn't come as a surprise.

"If you're wondering why the tide has shifted, it's because I've seen the full scope of what we're up against. The odds were always against us, but thanks to Fidel's little informant, we know the High Priestess has betrayed her entire coven to seal the fate of all Dūshevs. Win or lose, she would see us destroyed. Which is why there was no other option for me than to take their lives. Their souls are the only sacrifice that can put an end to the prophecy. Only with their blood can we buy our freedom. Anything less is surrender—and we do not surrender."

"What does that mean exactly, Father? Will you have us wipe out entire bloodlines?" Adam asked, his shock plain as day.

That boy couldn't bluff to save his life.

My father cast him a scornful look. "I am not a monster. The mortal men in those families are guilty of nothing except choosing poorly. I am only protecting my family. War demands sacrifices. The Sāhers chose to challenge forces beyond their grasp, and they paid the price. With the sacrifice of their souls, I was offered the whereabouts of every coven member, active and dormant. Except for three, the High Priestess Leyla, her daughter Shirin, and your beloved Maya."

Nonchalantly, our father admitted to killing a whole lineage of demon blood witches, including Maya's mother. I was too late. My only consolation was that at least her brother and father were safe from harm.

"The three of them seem to be above all law and order of the universe. That means we must use unconventional methods to locate and eliminate them—by any means," he addressed all of us.

Adam's chair screeched against the floor as he shoved it back, the legs catching for a second before jerking free. He stood abruptly like he was holding back the urge to punch a wall.

"Adam, if you cannot sit down and receive a message leave the room," our father said.

Adam hesitated, frozen by the look on our father's face, the quiet, unforgiving expression of a man who had finally run out of patience. Seeing that, Adam lowered his gaze and dragged his chair back without another word. He sank into it, accepting defeat, his shoulders folding inward. Adam stayed silent for the remainder of the meeting.

I was drained, barely holding myself together, too tired to fight the guilt of putting Maya in that position. I could barely bring myself to go home, knowing I had to face her and confess the horrible truth of my father's actions. No matter how awful it was, she needed to hear it from me. Hiding the truth from her would only make it worse.

I found her lounging in the living room with a book in her hand. As soon as she met my eyes, she straightened, settling into a more composed position on the sofa.

"There is something you need to know."

"What's wrong?" she asked, pushing herself up from the cushion as if bracing for the bad news.

When the words finally left my mouth and the horror of my father's actions hit her, she froze, silent and unblinking. Her stillness was unnerving, her eyes empty as if the weight of the revelation had paralyzed her.

"Maya."

I was ashamed, lost in how to approach her, knowing no words could undo the damage my father had done.

She let out a shaky breath. "My mother—" Her voice cracked. "She was Muslim . . . She wasn't one of them."

Silent tears streaked her cheeks, tears that weren't meant to be shed. There was nothing I could do or say to mend her broken heart. She gazed at her trembling hands before grabbing my arm. Her nails sank into my skin, biting deep enough to draw blood. I didn't pull away. She needed an outlet for the raw pain she was holding back, and I was more than willing to bear it. The sting was nothing compared to what she was going through. I'd let her stab me with a dagger if it meant she didn't have to suffer alone.

"Stop anchoring, Rés," she said quietly, her voice steady, her eyes burning with unwavering determination. "I need to go."

"I can't," I said, my words thick with the weight of how hard it was to let her go. "Not like this. You will get yourself killed."

She stepped closer, her chest rising with fury. "My brother is probably home alone and fucking defenseless. If you don't let me go to him, I promise you, my survival will be the least of your problems."

"Your brother is fine, your father, too. I have the house warded and watched."

Her face crumpled as if she couldn't hold herself together any longer, a choked sob escaping her lips.

"I have to see him, Rés," she whispered, her plea unraveling me.

The raw desperation in her voice hit me like a wave, crushing me in ways I hadn't prepared for—the kind of pain that could swallow a person whole. It was too much.

This time, I couldn't help but cradle her face in my hand, my thumb brushing away an escaping tear, as if trying to erase a hurt I couldn't heal. I let my hand drift from her cheek, down the curve of her neck and shoulder, skimming along her arm before softly drawing her into a hug.

She collapsed into me then, her body giving in to the overwhelming weight of her sorrow. In that instant, everything she had been holding back poured out.

Her sobs were raw and uncontrollable, her chest heaving against mine.

I held her tighter, feeling the weight of her pain seep into me, knowing I could do nothing to make it stop.

When her cries softened into sniffles, she gently eased away, looking at me through her wet lashes. "I will kill your father, Rés, if it's the last thing I'll do." I nodded, accepting my father's fate and let out a heavy breath. "I want to go to Mist Creek. I need to see them, at least from a distance."

I couldn't deny her. Letting her aďhār was a risk, and I could only pray she wasn't planning to run away to unleash her wrath on my father before she had the power to stand against him.

"Ground your energy and cast a glamour. Then we'll go together."

I kept my words free from any emotion—afraid if there was a hint of affection in my delivery, she would take it the wrong way. I had already crossed the line by pulling her into an embrace when I saw the hurt in her eyes. I was the one to initiate the first touch, something she never asked for. I was scrambling to prove that we weren't all cold-blooded killers, that I had a heart, and it bled for her.

Before leaving, I ensured the facility grounds were secure, just in case she chose to flee to Egypt. To my relief, she kept her word and went only to her father's house.

We stayed and watched until she finally glimpsed her brother through the window of his bedroom. Tears silently welled in her eyes before falling freely.

I couldn't stop myself from stepping up behind her, wrapping my arms around her trembling form. In that moment, nothing in the world could have stopped me from holding her.

There could never be anything tangible between us, and we both knew it, but that didn't mean I couldn't offer her my power and steady her through touch. The least I could do was let her tap into my magic, a form of reparation toward her endless well of suffering.

She didn't speak, but she accepted what little I had to offer. She reached up, her hand finding mine, and for the first time, she held my hand, a quiet gesture that echoed louder than any spoken words. It wasn't supposed to mean anything, but it was two people accepting they couldn't pretend to be enemies.

"Do you mind if we go visit my grandmother's grave?" she asked quietly into the wind.

"Where is it?"

"Behesht Zahra, in Tehran. No one is there at night."

Ask for my heart, and it's yours, Maya. [6] I released the anchor and squeezed her hand once. She disappeared shortly after.

I hadn't been to that cemetery, never had a reason to until right then. Stories were told about the one in Najaf. Stories about the ones who never crossed, about curses that plagued families who stepped over graves, and tales of the ones who went mad when staying after sunset. I could only assume the same was whispered about Behesht Zahra.

It wasn't difficult to find her, since I had learned from my mistake the first time around and changed her plan to one with international roaming. I wasn't losing her again.

The sun had dipped below the horizon, yet the sky clung to the last traces of dusky blue, casting a dim, ghostly glow over the sprawling cemetery. Endless rows of graves stretched into the distance. Not a whisper of wind stirred, only the weight of an eerie stillness pressing against my skin. My phone's screen glowed faintly in my palm, guiding me through the maze of the dead. I followed the tracker and found her kneeling next to a grave, her fingers

Yar - Faramarz Aslani, Babak Amini

resting lightly against the marble. As I stalked closer, she lifted her gaze, eyes locking onto mine as she finished reciting the final words of Al-Fatiha.

"*Ameen*," I said.

She scoffed, with a slight shake of her head. "Two heathens, letting the word of God pass their lips."

"The Quran brings solace to a lot of people, Muslim or not."

"It's the only prayer I know. My grandma taught me to recite it whenever I felt lost." She crossed her arms, her gaze still fixed on the grave, as if searching for answers in the engravings. "Have you ever been so lost you thought you could never get out?"

I drew in a slow, measured breath, feeling the weight of the past settle over me.

"The night I got my soul. I was oblivious when it happened," I breathed. "I was jolted awake from my sleep with a violent surge of energy that tore through my core like it was trying to break free. I swung my leg over the edge of the bed, my body moving before my mind could catch up, my instincts pulling me toward my mother's bedroom. I walked in to find her stiff and silent, lips tinged blue." I paused again, having a hard time reliving the memory.

"I touched her hand, delusionally expecting warmth, only to be met with the unyielding chill of death. My mind refused to process what my eyes were seeing, as if waiting for her to move, to prove me wrong. I stumbled forward, shaking her, screaming her name, begging, pleading for a response. Something changed that night. The world tilted. It felt like I had been poisoned, like something inside me had been ripped apart and stitched back together wrong. My skin was too tight, my body foreign. The days that followed were a blur of sickness and silence.

"I let my father and Ev believe it was grief, that my body was breaking under the weight of what I had seen. Those were lies. The reaction came from my mother's soul finally taking root inside me, leaving no room in my core. I was drowning in it, suffocating, and that feeling never stopped."

Until the moment your touch shattered every belief I had.

She turned, studying my face, curiosity flickering behind the warmth of her eyes. "Do you feel guilty? For having it," she asked, as if she could see straight through me and still choose to care.

"I used to, but I have learned to accept it. Thanks to Everie. In those dark years, she was a mother to me in every way that mattered."

"I love Ev," she said.

There was no hesitation, no doubt. She meant it.

٣٢

THIRTY-TWO

Maya

As the weeks passed, I became more and more detached from life. I was numb to all my feelings. I felt nothing, not pain, not happiness, not even anger. Why would I? I was soulless.

Soulless people didn't feel anything. I didn't care whether the prophecy was fulfilled. No one was forcing me to do anything. Rés had no leverage over me, not after I learned that he was keeping my brother and father under wards.

Yet I still chose to stay. Perhaps out of gratitude, perhaps because I felt indebted to him—or maybe because I had nowhere else to go. I had no purpose in life. I was back to square one, even further behind.

I doubted the grimoire held any answers, but I would help him, if that put his heart at ease or gave him a sense of autonomy over the situation. Maybe, in doing so, I could right all the wrongs I had made. The Grimoire of Harut and Marut probably came with a hefty price. I couldn't imagine it wasn't cursed to harm or kill anyone who dared steal it. If helping Rés steal one of the most important books known to all practitioners meant redemption for all I had done, I would do it in a heartbeat and pay my debt to the universe.

According to legend, the Grimoire of Harut and Marut could not be touched by a soul, a gray area I found myself in, one that seemed almost too convenient. I was soulless and yet still bound by oath as a Sāher. I could cross the threshold and roam the sanctuary, searching for the book, with nothing standing in my way.

The fact that I was ready to get the grimoire didn't matter to Rés. He was on his own schedule and adamant about doing things his way; he was pulling strings and calling in favors from people who had no purpose to be involved. He knew a former matron who would help me get admitted as a stray without raising suspicion. The sanctuary had a reputation for its rigid rules and its notorious matrons. Rés was certain it was a place where girls were sent to be broken and molded, their wills stripped away through discipline and control. And of course he would think that. God forbid they were merely dedicated to studying the old scripts and passing down the knowledge to younger generations.

I was meant to be admitted and partake in their initiation ceremony. Luckily for Rés, the one thing that I had been good at was reading. In my first few months as a Sāher, I did nothing but endlessly read, study, and memorize every book my family had collected. If there was one thing I was prepared for, it was this. I knew my wards, spells, hexes, and curses.

Until it was time, I had to stay in the shadows, but I treated matters with the seriousness they deserved. Even though Ev assured me the glass was spellbound and no one could peek in, I never passed the windows. I was constantly glamoured in case I had to leave the house in a rush.

Amidst all of this, there was the matter of Everie's upcoming wedding—which I had no place in, nor was I in any position to attend, given the circumstances.

Ev had told me countless times how much she wished I could attend her wedding. I could tell she truly meant it, but we both knew it was something that could never be. She was planning an intimate wedding at her father's vineyard.

He was obviously attending and more than happy to pay for it all after he had met Luciano. Apparently, they had met several times over dinner, like normal people.

I wondered how much Luciano knew about the Dūshevs. I, for one, couldn't believe how many times their father had been in New Orleans without my knowledge. I bet they both expected me to have another full-blown panic attack and spared me the trouble. What they didn't realize was how little it mattered to me; how insignificant life had become. Even the thought of going back to Egypt and being locked away forever couldn't stir any fear in me. *What will happen will happen.*

Ev's friends were invited to come over later in the evening for another one of their Friday catch-ups. These people really loved each other and used every opportunity and excuse to be together and enjoy life. Even though I was there with them and felt so welcomed by all of them, I couldn't help but feel a twinge of jealousy over their bond, their closeness, and the pure love they shared. Everie always cooked the main dish, while the rest of them would bring sides, snacks, or booze. [7]

"I'm craving Indian today. I want to make Roghan Gosht with rice and yogurt," Ev Said.

"Is that a lamb stew?"

I wasn't sure, but in my head, I translated it to *oil meat* because many words in Farsi were similar or the same in Urdu, Kashmiri, and Hindi.

"Yeah, what's the name of that yogurt salad with chick-peas, potatoes, onions, and what more? I have to look it up." She got up and pulled out jars of herbs, spices, and a big bag of rice.

"I think it's called Chaat. Do you mind if I make the rice?"

If there was one thing I had taught myself to make, it was Persian rice. Persian rice was unmatched, and it is a hill I am willing to die on. The Afghans knew how to make rice, too, and I had to give the Indians credit for the rice they made with cinnamon, bay leaves, and pieces of meat but rice with *Tahdik* was something else.

"Sure, how long do you think you need? So I can plan my own time."

Baddi Doub - Elissa

"At least forty-five minutes."

I washed the rice right away until the water ran clear, then I left it to soak till evening. My mom would have said it wasn't enough time, since she always left them overnight. Being in the kitchen, helping Ev, gave me a sense of belonging, like I was part of something, part of a family. I quickly pushed the thought away and tried my best focusing on the task in front of me.

"Is everything okay?" Ev asked.

Gun to my head, I couldn't lie to her, even though I tried.

"Yes, why do you ask?"

She posed that question a lot lately, and I wondered what I had looked like.

"Because you are constantly sighing."

"I am? I haven't noticed."

I played it off. My problems weren't hers. If I needed to numb myself more than I already was, I could drink my brains out at the party. I didn't see myself as the self-destructive type just because I wanted to turn it off. Of course, it would be what people saw if they knew the deepest corners of my mind.

I was simply tired, tired of playing a game in an avatar I didn't pick. Tired of not knowing what was real and what was not, tired of thinking I was going crazy and thinking I needed to wake up from this nightmare. Tired of only feeling alive when I got the energy surge from Rés. My problems weren't his problems either.

٣٣

THIRTY-THREE

Aldridge

I came in late and changed before greeting them. Ev had invited them over, as she did every week. Most Fridays, we sat playing cards, drinking. On the rare Fridays when a new or full moon would fall, participation was expected without exception because we would gather for certain rituals. The same applied when the seasons shifted and during pagan holidays.

"*Che, tre' errores. ¿Cómo andá?*" Lorenzo said when he saw me.

The joke was getting old, and it carried no weight anymore. He was faffing around for no reason. Tres was just my name now, especially since she had made her own adaptation of it.

Lorenzo was standing by Maya, Sofia, and Carlos. Maya had no clue what was being said in Spanish. It was Carlos who, without realizing it, threw me under the bus.

"Maya, has anyone told you why we call him *Tres*?" Carlos asked her.

Bloody hell. I wasn't even sure why I lied about it in the first place. *How vain of me.*

"I was under the impression you called him Drés because of his last name but tell me more." She glanced at me sideways, then looked back at Carlos.

"Please, don't hold back on my account," I said, trying to lick my own wounds.

Enzo didn't miss a beat. "You see, we used to call him Andrés, so you're not far off, but we soon learned that he had to make the same mistake three times before he truly learned from them."

Sofia cut in. "The name stuck when his car was towed in front of the Three Legged Dog for the third time."

"Don't remind me, Sofia! They were so good! I could eat crawfish every day," Enzo said and then looked at Maya enthusiastically. "If you ever come back during spring, you have to try it!"

The conversation luckily shifted, and I excused myself to get a drink. Under other circumstances, she could have been a part of this coven. With the eye rolling, the snarky remarks, the sarcasm, she fit in perfectly—she was perfect.

In another universe, she would have been friends with them, friends with Everie, and a part of this family, but we were not in a different universe.

The coven were Everie's chosen family, her people. Nothing was more honorable than asking your family to perform a bonding ceremony. She wanted the coven to bond her and Luciano. She had decided this. I had no say in her decision, and neither did my father.

I wouldn't take away her opportunity to live her dream even if it meant letting her age naturally. I didn't want to be selfish about it, and surprisingly, neither did my father. This was the first time she had proposed the idea of a bonding ceremony.

A bonding ceremony was stronger than any oath or contract. It was where the phrase *"Till death do us part"* came from. Accepting a bond as a practitioner was very rare and very sacred. It tied you to the lifespan of your partner. She would grow old and grey with him and, eventually, die next to him. It wasn't an easy thing to accept, but I knew how much she wanted a child she wouldn't outlive. It was the reason she never had kids to begin with.

I wanted to see Ev live happily with Luciano. He was the definition of patience and empathy and would listen to Ev's endless blabbering. He would help her start a new hobby, only to abandon it two weeks later. He wouldn't be bothered if she started singing in the middle of a conversation because he had said a word that reminded her of a song. He could follow her train of thought when she picked up a discussion from the day before. He was perfect for her in so many ways.

"Are you listening!" Ev smacked my arm.

"Jesus! Yes, I am!"

I wasn't.

"I would love to have the ceremony done outside. I'm just not sure if it's too much. Do you think we can get a tent made of linen instead of that horrendous plastic material? The frequency needs to be in tune with the earth. On the other hand, I don't want to spend too much money on it. Oh! And I want lemons everywhere. The spirits love lemons. Maybe indoor is better," Ev said.

"The jinns love lemons, too. First, you wanted eucalyptus and candles only, now lemons and linens, tomorrow, who knows, maybe pomegranate?"

From the corner of my eye, I saw Maya leaving with Lorenzo. She had grown comfortable with him—a little too comfortable for my liking. Lorenzo wasn't a bad person. He just happened to end up in terrible situations because he acted on impulse.

"Close your eyes, Tres," Ev said, circling the ice cube in my drink with her finger. "Your heart is showing."

"What was that for!" I pulled my glass away from her and made a show of ignoring her comment.

She shrugged. "To help you relax a bit. There is nothing to worry about."

"*No estoy preocupado.*" I took a sip, hiding behind my glass, aware of how much satisfaction she had in being right.

"I know you are intellectually malnourished, but for the love of god, *usa tu cabeza.*"

"Anyway, since your father loves to spoil you, I think you should go with what you actually want. He can afford it," I said, circling back.

She had a tendency to get off track.

"It's not about the money. And I know what you are doing. We are talking about you!"

"We were actually talking about your wedding," I countered. Maria came up to us with a bowl of crisps in her hands. "The gardens are better. It's not too accessible, which is what we need, and it literally looks like something from a fairy tale. If you ask me, having it indoor would ruin your linen vision."

"I agree," Maria said. "*Esta no es una boda común*, Ev. I love you, but you also need to think about all the wards that need to be put in place. It's not just about how it looks. Although the aesthetics are immaculate."

Maria didn't know our father would have the place warded like a fortress, but there was so much excitement in Maria's eyes, so I didn't comment on it.

"*Es mejor, ¿no?*" Ev asked.

Adriana joined the conversation, and I saw an opportunity to escape. The front door had opened and closed, and I went to see if Maya and Lorenzo had come back inside.

٣٤

THIRTY-FOUR

Maya

Enzo and I went outside so he could smoke. Since he had told Ev he'd quit for good, he had to sneak out to do it. I didn't mind keeping him company. Once Enzo opened up to me, he was surprisingly kind and very likable.

I followed him down the porch steps and almost lost my footing, twisting my ankle.

"Shit!"

"Are you drunk?" he asked, grabbing my elbow.

"No."

I was swaying a bit, but the good kind of swaying, not the seasick kind.

My gaze drifted over the quiet street. I was glamoured, of course, and not too worried about being outside. The evening air carried a crisp wind that slipped through the gap in my T-shirt at the small of my back.

"At least I won't have to carry your drunk ass far if you pass out."

I couldn't help but giggle. After the night when we snuck out together and were yelled at, a friendship formed. It became clear Enzo wasn't interested in me in that way, and I found so much comfort in that.

We rounded the corner and settled onto the bench beneath my bedroom window, the quiet of the night wrapping around us.

"You know what drives me crazy? One minute, she's letting me see the most vulnerable parts of her, and the next, she's speaking to me like I'm the last person she wants to see."

He probably felt Maria was giving him a hard time, but it was more than just that—messing with each other was part of their friendship. The difference was that Enzo was stepping out of the friendzone and outside of that space where words carried more weight. He wasn't saying it, and he didn't have to for me to know he had feelings for her.

"It's like she is always out to humiliate me."

"Please, you're asking for it. You are so obnoxious sometimes. It's like you want people to roast you."

Enzo grinned. "Come on now."

"You are picking fights with a Leo woman, and you love it, so stop complaining. If you want a different reaction, maybe you should try a different approach. You're not . . . un-nice."

"Un-nice is not a word," he said and took a long drag, embarrassed to ask the question we both knew he wanted the answer to.

"Do something nice for her. What does she like? What is she into?" I asked, leading him in the right direction.

I was sure he had memorized every freckle on her cheeks.

"She likes reading. She has wall to wall shelves with all these colorful books. She is always talking about this book boyfriend to Ev. *Gus would never do that. I wouldn't mind if Gus . . .*"

"This is your way in, you idiot. Gus is the blueprint. Be Gus!" I said exasperated.

Lucky for Enzo, I knew exactly what book boyfriend it was. Everyone deserved a Gus—I just hadn't thought Maria was the Gus type, she looked more like a dark-romance type.

"What more?" I asked, giddy at the thought of them on a date.

"She used to go to this French restaurant and get a burnt sponge cake, the sticky ones, but they stopped making them, and she hasn't had them ever since."

"Burnt sponge cake?" I frowned. "You mean Canalé?"

"Yes! Exactly. And she loves oysters, and once, she said she really wanted to try a pottery class."

He was so excited when he talked about her it almost made him adorable.

"Someone has been paying attention," I teased.

He tried to hide a smile. He pressed the burning end of the blunt into the ground, twisting it until the ember fizzled out, leaving behind a faint wisp of smoke.

As we made our way back around the house, I stumbled on something, my foot catching just enough to throw me off balance. I reached out blindly, my hand shooting out to grab the first thing I could find, which was a rough wooden post. I grabbed it just in time to stop myself from crashing face-first into the dirt.

"How drunk are you?" Enzo asked.

I corrected myself and noticed blood trickling down my wrist. "Shit, I'm bleeding!"

Enzo took my hand to inspect it in the dark. "You need to get that cleaned."

When we got back inside, I saw the shallow cut across my palm. There was no pain, but blood was dripping down, as if I'd been stabbed.

Enzo pulled me into the kitchen, running cold water over my hand, making sure no dirt or debris was left in the wound. "We should've went to the bathroom. Blood in the kitchen sink is disgusting."

"I'll clean it later. Get me a Band-Aid, will you?" I said, keeping my hand under the tap.

"Ev has so much shit I don't even know where to look," he said, going through the drawers.

Rés walked into the kitchen, startling us both. "What are you looking for?" he asked, looking at Enzo.

"Band-Aid. She cut herself," Enzo said.

Rés put his glass on the counter. "I'll help her with the plaster. Go back to the others."

Rés wasn't asking. Enzo knew that because the next thing he did was look at me and roll his eyes.

"Find me when you're done here." Enzo winked at me before leaving, thinking I needed a way out.

Rés's eyes tracked Enzo out of the kitchen before he turned to face me. "Let me have a look." He walked closer, reaching for my hand.

"Enzo was helping look through the drawers."

"I don't want him touching what belongs to me," he muttered.

I wasn't sure if I audibly gasped or if my lungs contracted.

"You mean what belongs to Ev." I was pulling threads because I was simply too tipsy to assume. "It's her house, her kitchen, her stuff."

"Right," he agreed, examining my palm, his thumb moving along the side of my hand.

His touch was molten lava against my skin. When he let go of my hand, a chill crashed over me, sharp and jarring like ice water pouring down my spine. I couldn't lie to myself anymore. I needed his touch, needed his proximity.

"What is it you don't like him touching?" Maybe it was the liquid courage in my veins, or maybe the act had been slipping away between us for a while now.

"You," he said, his expression unreadable. "Can you sit on the counter for me, please? I can't work like this."

I was too stunned to move. Were the last few words not exchanged between us? Before I could say anything, he lifted me up and placed me on the counter. For the briefest moment, his hands were on my thighs, and I couldn't think of anything I wanted more than his hands on my skin.

"Perfect," he said, taking my hand to put the ointment on the wound.

Things moved fast, then slow, and then time disappeared and reappeared again. He was standing between my legs, putting a thin strip of gauze on the wound before sealing it with medical tape. One hand held my wrist, the other traveling to my elbow, up my arm. I didn't let myself move. If I did, I would either break the spell or lean further into his touch.

"Tell me to stop," he said.

His voice was just above a whisper, his hand still roaming, traveling over my shoulders, and to my nape. *Fuck!* His thumb was grazing my jaw, slowly tilting my head back while he moved closer.

I was under a spell and enchantment because, fuck, I couldn't help myself. My eyes rolled back.

He was so close now, his lips grazing my ear.

"Tell me to fuck off," he whispered.

My mouth went dry. I wanted nothing more than the taste of him on my lips.

"Fuck," I let out by accident.

"Fuck what?" he pressed, still not letting his lips come close enough.

If I was to die, I could at least indulge. Couldn't I?

"Tres!" Ev shouted from the hall, and all blood drained from my head.

I pushed him away and jumped down from the counter.

Rés was calmly putting away the ointment and gauze by the time Ev walked into the kitchen.

"Did you get the—" Ev was about to say something when she noticed my hand. "What happened to you?"

"Nothing, a tiny cut."

I wanted to bolt out of that kitchen before any signs of Rés's touch showed on me. I was sure he had left a trail on my skin. Sure that if Ev looked at me long enough, she would know. I was sure she could see right through me.

Instead, she looked at me warily.

Rés had left by the time she spoke again.

"Can I ask you something? But you must promise me either you answer honestly, or you don't answer at all."

I couldn't tell if she was disappointed or worried.

"Wouldn't my silence be the answer in itself?" Whatever I said would give me away.

"It's not a yes-or-no question."

"I'm all ears."

"If it was up to you, what would you do about the prophecy? I mean, do you believe it must be done? Do you want to? Do you feel forced?"

I was taken aback by her question. It came out of nowhere. Of course, she was worried about her brother and father. Perhaps these things mattered even more since she was going to get married.

I took a glass, poured myself water, contemplating how to answer. "To be honest with you, I'm not sure I understand the prophecy. I don't know what the endgame is. I don't know who's right or wrong—hell, I don't even know if I am meant to survive it. In my family, it is said to be unchangeable, that even if I had known back then, I wouldn't have been able to change its course. My only option is running; either alongside the prophecy or away from it. There is no standing still for me. But to answer your question, no, I don't want to fulfill the prophecy." I paused, seeing the relief in her eyes. "But I don't agree with what they do, either. I mean, is soul-taking really necessary?"

"No!" She sat across from me. "I agree. It's greedy and does not align with our values."

"With whose values, exactly?" I challenged.

"With mine, with my coven's." She leaned over the table, forcing me to look her in the eye. "I promise you they are not all bad, but this whole business goes far deeper than any of us had imagined. We are trying to—"

"Don't tell me. Don't tell me anything. I don't want to know."

She leaned back in her chair again, accepting that it was where I drew the line. I had seen and heard enough about them, both good and bad. I didn't care for more information because I already knew how I felt. If that meant I was to stay delusionally ignorant forever, then so be it.

٣٥

THIRTY-FIVE

MAYA

For the next couple of days, Rés avoided my existence. He only spoke to me when it was strictly necessary, and only about the things he wanted me to work on while he was away.

It had gone too far between us, and he clearly regretted his drunken mistake, *tres errores*. What seemed like a line we would never cross dissolved below our feet. Either way, I couldn't put much thought into it because it was time to seek out the matron, whose endorsement would help secure my place in the sanctuary. I cast a glamour, keeping my features close to my own. Rés wouldn't see the illusion, but I would, and since this was the face I'd wear for weeks to come, I needed to be comfortable with my reflection.

It was evening when Rés finally appeared at the door, car keys in hand, his gaze drifting everywhere except to me.

"We're leaving. Are you ready?"

"By car?"

I had assumed she lived in Scotland.

"No, with my private jet," he deadpanned. "Yes, by car! She lives somewhere remote near Pipe Creek. It's a nine-hour drive, so bring a change of clothes."

"Nine hours! I am not made for the road. I will literally die!"

"You will not *literally* die. We'll stop for food."

"Where? The diner where that hard-boiled shrimp works?" it came out snappier than I had intended it to.

Rés finally peered at me, his carefully placed mask cracked as he shook his head, smiling.

"Are we feeling a type of way, Maya?"

"Please, Andrés, don't flatter yourself. I was just reminding you of your type. We all make mistakes. No need to dwell on them." His jaw clenched, but he didn't counter back.

In the car, I was again met with silence, and because I knew Rés would fold into his own thoughts while driving, I brought a book with me from Ev's shelves.

The streetlights, streaming through the window, cast moving lights and shadows across the pages, making it almost impossible to concentrate. Not that I could focus with him by my side. I read the same page for the third time before pulling my feet up onto the seat, drawing my knees closer to my chest to rest the book on them.

Rés groaned and flicked on the light for me.

"It's perfectly legal to drive with the lights on," he said.

"I know that, Andrés!" I said and turned it back off. "I feel observed when it's on!"

"I like it better when you call me Rés."

I closed the book and fully looked at him. I hadn't realized I had called him Rés out loud—at least I couldn't remember I had. "It doesn't have to be weird. I'm perfectly fine being your friend. The lines don't need to blur."

I probably wouldn't have been so blunt with him if Ev was there. I would've been too shy or self-conscious. Not that anything had happened, but it was definitely a gray area. If I had the courage, I would be honest with her, and if it wasn't her brother, I would ask her opinion.

"Friends," he said, his eyes revealing nothing.

I used the opportunity as an excuse to extend my hand, needing the physical touch more than he did.

His hesitation stung, but he finally took my hand, giving it a gentle squeeze before releasing it to interlace our fingers.

It means nothing. It means nothing. It means nothing to him.

Our silent agreement didn't include the impact all of it had on my mental health or feelings. No matter how much I tried turning my brain off, I couldn't see past the small gestures. I couldn't ignore the way he always caressed me when we touched. The movement was subtle, enough to go unnoticed. I couldn't claim it as anything but a mindless habit on his part. My logical brain was aware of that fact, but my heart wouldn't listen.

Warmth spread through me without permission, making my heart swell until it lodged in my throat. I welcomed the pain because at least it wasn't the mourning that plagued me.

"There are no lines," Rés said under his breath long after our conversation had ended.

I was halfway asleep with my hand still in his. When I woke up again, the sun was rising on the horizon, and a jacket was covering me as a makeshift blanket. The radio was playing soft blues, low enough to fall back asleep to.

"How long have I been asleep?" I asked, shifting in my seat.

My ass had gone numb.

"Just a couple of hours. Go back to sleep. I'll wake you when we arrive."

"We need to make a stop. Don't you need to rest. You haven't slept at all."

"I'll be fine. We're almost in Houston. I'm not stopping," he responded, his voice coming out hoarse.

"I wasn't asking, Rés. I'm tired. My whole body is aching." I undid the seatbelt and turned in my seat to stretch my legs over his lap.

He lifted a brow before gently placing his hand on my shin, his fingers curling around my leg and finding the curve of my knee.

It was a risky move, a pathetic excuse for wanting to touch him, wanting him to touch me. I desperately and shamelessly needed to break every barrier between us.

"*Vale*," he said with a soft v.

The rising sun cast shadows across his striking face, giving his skin a flawless glow.

I couldn't help but drink him in, committing every detail of him to memory. I wanted to hold on to this moment, to remember everything about him as if I could keep it forever.

"In Farsi, *Bale* is the formal word for yes. So, I'm just going to assume you are agreeing with me." I leaned the back of my head against the window, enjoying the view and the way his power gave me comfort.

His thumb made soothing circular motions on my knee, as if it was the most natural thing between us.

"*Como debe ser,*" he said, as if I understood.

"*Pendejo,*" I said confidently, having heard it being tossed around enough times.

He smiled wide enough for his canines to show, and I wondered if it was possible to pick your own core memories. Because, if I could, I would beg the universe to store this for me.

"*Kashke kasane dige boodim,*" I sighed to myself, hoping we were different people.

Dreaming of a different reality.

٣٦

THIRTY-SIX

ALDRIDGE

I went from walking on eggshells around her to slipping back into the same old habits within hours. It wasn't healthy, and it wasn't good for either of us. *Friends*, she had said, extending her hand. I turned the word in my mouth, feeling it sour on my tongue. This was going to be a boundary I would struggle to keep. It took everything in me not to lift her hand to my lips and press a kiss against her knuckles, the ink on her fingers. In the end, I was just a man, and she was becoming my greatest weakness.

I hadn't slept properly for days and had lost all sense of time from traveling back and forth between my father, Mist Creek, and home. I actually really needed to rest, or I would get us both into a car accident. I was just trying to avoid being confined to a room with her because it was hard enough as it was.

After the third place with zero vacancies, we finally found a musty motel that accepted cash and didn't ask for ID.

"Wow, I actually expected a roach infested room," she said. "This is surprisingly clean."

"Mmm," I agreed, still checking for bedbugs before touching anything.

The beds were far enough apart that, even if I stretched, I couldn't reach and touch her. *Just an observation.*

I was so tired I turned off the lights while she was still in the bathroom, my body sinking deeper into the mattress as sleep tugged at me. My eyelids grew heavier with each slow blink, the world around me softening at the edges.

I could hear her moving around, quietly but not quiet enough. The rustle of fabric, the faint creak of the floorboards, the soft clatter of something being set down. I tried to tune it out, let the sounds fade into the background, but each shuffle pulled me back from the edge of sleep. Another quiet movement, a sigh, then stillness.

After a while, I heard her move again and shuffle out of the bed. She stood between our beds, hovering over me like a ghost. I was suddenly fully awake, keeping my eyes closed as her hand slowly but surely neared my face. The heat radiating from her skin was a stark contrast to the air-conditioned room. When her knuckles almost grazed my brow, a switch flipped in my brain; she was going to be the death of me. Before she got a chance to draw back, I grabbed her wrist and opened my eyes.

"I—" She gasped and stumbled on her words. "I wasn't."

I kept a firm grip on her wrist until I was standing upright looking down at her, studying the movement of her eyes, the beat of her pulse, the bob of her throat. My thumb moved from the pulse on her wrist, and to the middle of her palm, rubbing gently up and down like a worry stone.

I don't know what came over me, but I brought her hand to my mouth and placed a gentle kiss in the center of her palm before releasing her. "Trying to kill me, bruja?" Her lips parted in shock or perhaps in an attempt to respond. "Or was there something else you wanted?" I said, trying to maintain the façade of my alter ego. The villain who isn't afraid to get his hands dirty, who disregards everyone's feelings, and who might just take a bite of the red apple.

"No," she rasped, taking a step back, collecting herself. "I was just feeling drained and wanted to—" She chewed on her lip, trying to come up with a reasonable answer.

I cupped her jaw in my hand and with my thumb plopped her bottom lip free from her teeth.

Her lips were glistening in the dim moonlight, and all I could think about was how it would feel to sink my own teeth into them.

I swallowed, trying to find any semblance of restraint. My backbone and discipline were nowhere to be found.

I leaned closer, so we were only a breath apart. "Tell me what you want."

All she had to do was ask, and I would throw it all away. I would let the whole world burn for her.

"I—" She leaned slightly into my touch before pulling away. "This was a mistake."

Whatever you want, bruja.

I let my hand fall to my side and stepped back. An awkward pause followed as she glanced at me, then looked away. When she propped herself onto the bed, I went around my own and pushed it forward with my knees, so it was flush against hers. She was staring up at me, but I couldn't return her gaze.

"Don't worry," I assured her. "It's so I can hold your hand while you sleep. I won't cross the line again. I promise."

"I'm sorry," she said when I was on my back again.

In the darkness, I took her hand, ignoring the aching hole in my chest.

"Don't apologize. You did nothing wrong."

I wanted to kiss her hand again, but I didn't.

٣٧

THIRTY-SEVEN

MAYA

I didn't wake up to touch him out of mischief or desire. I simply couldn't stay still any longer. Sleep had abandoned me, and the restless energy in my limbs demanded movement. I rose from the bed, to pace around the room, but then my eyes found him, bathed in the soft glow of the night.

He looked so peaceful, so utterly unguarded that I couldn't help but drink him in, an indulgence I had never been afforded before. My gaze traced the quiet rise and fall of his chest, the way the shadows played across his features and the way moonlight caught the planes of his face.

I had the impulse to place my palm against his cheek, to trace the shape of his brows. Without thinking, my hand lifted, hovering just above his skin before my mind could catch up. And then, his eyes fluttered open.

He grabbed my wrist and got up in that instant.

My breath caught and heart plummeted. I was frozen, caught like a deer in headlights, exposed in a moment I hadn't meant to be seen.

Then he kissed my hand, *I think?* Obviously, I had thought of it, thought of him in that way, but I promised myself I wasn't going to make the same mistake twice. I had to learn from them, and no matter how much I wanted to, I wouldn't let my feelings get in the way.

The problem was, even if I took my feelings out of the equation, there was an agonizing need between us. Whether it was sexual tension or the energy exchange, it was present and dangerous.

The night before was the second time he slipped. Just for a moment, just long enough for me to see what lay beneath the carefully crafted facade. There was no hesitation, no retreat. Just the weight of his gaze, heavy with unapologetic desire, searing into me like a brand. It was the most beautiful thing I had ever seen. There was a thunderous current between us, but I would not bring death and sorrow, and I would not ruin another man.

Farnazeh lived in a house surrounded by a wrought-iron gate at the entrance. The entire plot of land screamed *Visitors Unwelcome!*

We drove further down the street, parked the car, and made our way back to her house.

The gate was unlocked and although heavily warded we easily passed the threshold. The moment we walked through the wards, my glamour slid off me like a second skin.

Shit!

"Her wards just neutralized my glamour," I whispered to Rés.

It was like stepping through a veil spun from honey and venom. A tempting invitation bound to come with a cost.

The moment we neared the porch, the front door swung open. When it clicked in my brain, my breath hitched and goose bumps prickled my skin. Farnazeh looked pleased with herself.

"Aldridge," she said as a way of greeting.

Rés put a hand on my back. "This is—"

"You've got to be kidding me," I said, unable to process the fact that the sand-tray lady was standing before me.

"I told you. You'll be back when you need me again," she said.

Rés turned to me confused. "Do you know each other?"

He tried to communicate something else with his eyes, but I was too distracted.

"It was only possible because of your divination." I looked at Rés, wondering if he understood where he had brought me. "She showed me how the prophecy would play out."

"Follow me," Farnazeh said, ignoring what I had said.

How did that vision end? Whose side was she on? We still followed her to where she had a patio with a table, several chairs, and a large umbrella providing shade. Her patio was filled by well-maintained pots of plants and shrubs. She gestured us to sit, and once she settled herself on one of the chairs, she gave me a once-over. It made me self-conscious about Rés's hand that had never left the small of my back. Having him in my orbit at all times was reassuring and intoxicating, and I wouldn't want it any other way.

"*Paa tu tale gozashti,*" she said to me, implying I was setting myself up for trouble.

"And what's your holy role in this?"

Did she think I was oblivious to the mistakes I had made, how far I had gone?

Rés immediately turned to me with a warning look that said don't fuck this up!

When she continued in Farsi, I started wondering what she had promised him, what lies she had fed him.

"*Beman begu dokhtar, ta che hadi hazeri barash talash koni?*" *Tell me, girl, how much are you willing to struggle for it?*

"*Rahe hale dige nist.*" *There is no other solution.*

"I was asking about him," Farnazeh said, gesturing to Rés.

In Farsi, there are no pronouns. People and objects are the same. So, when she asked me how much I was willing to struggle for *it*, she meant *him*. She thought I was doing it for him . . .

"I would love to help brainstorming ideas if you would put on the subtitles for me, please," Rés said, having no idea what we were talking about.

"No need. She will stay with me, and I will instruct her on how to act and, most importantly, speak. You can come collect her tomorrow," Farnazeh said.

Rés's politeness crumbled, and I could tell he wasn't going to let two witches be alone without overseeing everything himself. Under the table, I rested my hand on his knee, a silent reassurance, hoping he would trust my judgment of her. He went completely still under my touch.

"I guess I'm just wondering why you're helping us," I said.

Farnazeh had caught it. Her eyes flicked up from the movement of my hand.

"*Alaghemandi.* I'm curious to see how you will manage such a task. The grimoire that has been left untouched for millennia."

There was challenge woven into her words.

"I'm assuming you want something?" I asked.

"I have already negotiated with your—well, *nimet.*" *Your other half.*

She smiled with her eyes focusing solely on Rés, like she had already solved the puzzle.

"Yes," he confirmed. "We have agreed that Farnazeh will get access to the grimoire after it has been in my possession for thirty-three days."

I wasn't going to lecture him on how long it could take to potentially read and understand a grimoire that ancient. It was not the time nor place for it. And it was already too late for that.

"Access to the grimoire and the only Sāher able to read it."

I didn't turn to look at him. I was so disgusted I wanted to knock his teeth out.

Rés and I didn't speak until we were all the way out of her property and on the street. As I got the bag out of the car, turning to leave, Rés stepped in front of me.

I put my hand up. "No need to give me a speech. I'll shut the fuck up and behave," I said, reminding myself that I was only there to fulfill a task for another fucking bastard.

"It's not what you think," he started. "I made that deal long bef—"

"It's not? Oh my! What a surprise, Aldridge. Is there something you haven't told me?" He twitched when I used his real name. "I should've known you'd lie through your teeth to get what you want. To be fair, I would have, too, if I had to rely on the bitch who double-crossed Adam. No wonder you've been leading me on. I invented th—"

He clamped his hand around my jaw, shoving me back against the car.

The metal was hard against my back, a sharp contrast to the press of his body caging me in. His grip was firm, possessive, fingers pressing into my cheeks as he leaned in.

"It's unbelievable that you have the brass neck to be standing here accusing me of leading you on when you've been doing exactly that for the past twenty-four hours," he hissed, his breath ghosting over my lips.

He had no idea how much he affected me. *For the love of god, get a grip!* I scolded myself.

"Me!? Are you mental!" I wrenched my face free from his grasp to regain power over me.

He grinned, pleased with himself for getting a rise out of me. "Mental? Am I rubbing off on you?"

I had started mimicking him and his stupid accent without realizing it, but I wasn't going to admit to it.

"Get off me, Rés," I said calmly.

"Sure," he stepped back. "But you're not going in there alone. I don't trust her."

"I'm sorry! Did I dream all of this? Did you forget why you kidnapped me to begin with? Why the fuck am I here?"

I was back to shouting at him again, but he had gone still.

"What if I'm wrong?" he whispered, seeming genuinely apprehensive.

The moment I met his pleading eyes, my next argument died on my lips.

"Do you actually believe you will find answers in the Grimoire of Harut and Marut?" I asked instead.

"It's our only hope."

He did not clarify who *our* was supposed to be. His family? Both our families? The two of us?

"Then we won't know until we try, Rés," I said and took the bag I had dropped on the ground. "I have my phone with me. I'll call you if I need anything." His hand twitched, but he didn't stop me.

I walked toward Farnazeh's house without looking back because I had no idea how to part from Rés without all my feelings showing on my face. I stepped through the gates, and to the entrance of Farnazeh's house and still I didn't hear his car door open or engine start as I had expected to.

A moment later, the door opened, and she beckoned me inside.

"Your training starts immediately. We don't have much time because, on Tuesday, you will leave for Scotland."

"What?!"

"Follow me," she said and turned on her heels without waiting for a response.

I dropped my bag in the foyer and hurried after her, stepping into a room thick with the scent of incense. Stacks of taped-up boxes lined the walls some sagging at the corners as if they'd been sitting there for years. Papers, books, and trinkets were scattered across every available surface, a chaotic mix of forgotten and half-remembered things. The dim light filtered through heavy curtains, casting long shadows over the clutter, making the space feel even smaller than it was.

"What do you mean this Tuesday?"

She was rummaging through the drawer.

"For the initiation, of course." She turned back toward the dresser, her fingers trailing over the cluttered surface of half-burned candles, scattered rings, and a tiny vial of something dark, before she yanked open another drawer. "Now, where did I put it . . . Ah! There you are."

From the bottom drawer of the dresser, she pulled out neatly folded red fabric. It smelled a bit musty and looked the part, too. I sniffed it one more time and grimaced.

"Vintage sheets," I muttered under my breath, thinking she didn't hear me.

She snapped upright and all but snatched the fabric from my hands, shaking it out with a dramatic flourish, narrowly missing my face. "Cloak, not sheets," she snapped sharply. "And show some respect. This is a sacred garment, passed down through generations of demon blood Sāhers. Without it, you cannot pass through the portal or the wards of the castle." With that, she strode toward the door, her tone shifting to pure irritation. "Pick up your bag from the floor! Have you learned nothing from your mother!"

I stiffened at the mention of my mother. I'd heard enough insults about her parenting over the years, too many to count. She was gone, dead because of her futile efforts to keep me away from them, from the magic, the rituals, the people who'd never see her as anything but a misguided fool.

There I was, swallowing the insult without a word. I couldn't even defend the woman who'd tried so hard to protect me from all of it. *Swallow your pride, girl.*

"Witches in red cloaks hidden away in a castle. What is this, a cult?" I dragged my feet as I followed her up the flight of stairs.

"What a disgrace you are to our community. Maybe you will fit in perfectly in Chinkāri, after all," she said as we reached the landing. "This is your bedroom for the night. Put the bag on the chair and turn off your phone before coming down to me."

I checked the phone for a message. There was none. Rather than turning it off, I set it to silent, no vibrations. Before heading downstairs, I glanced out the window. All I could see was thick fog.

When did that happen?

For a second, it freaked me out, and I wondered if I was walking into some kind of trap. In the end, I decided against it and pushed the thought aside, heading downstairs. The creaky steps groaned under my weight as I descended, the air cooler here, carrying a faint smell of old wood and humidity. I found Farnazeh in the dining room, hunched over a pile of books scattered across the table.

"Before I can send you there, you need to learn how to walk without stomping. You need to learn how to curtsey, and if you want to minimize your punishment, there are words you need to familiarize yourself with."

Punishment!

My brows may as well have reached my hairline. I was about to ask her what she meant by punishment when she spoke again.

"Whenever you are summoned by a matron, you must remember to curtsy and respond with, *dar khedmatetun.* When they offer you a meal, you lower your gaze and say, *mamnun.* When they—do you need to write this down?"

"No. I got it. Please continue."

I knew the phrases—I just never remembered to use them. I wasn't exactly raised in a traditional Persian household, so the mannerisms and common courtesies were never really engrained in me. Sometimes, they were poetic, other times a bit too much, like *"dar khedmatetun."* which meant, *at your service.*

She nodded. "When they dismiss you for the night, you say *lotf kardin*. Now, on to the way you carry yourself."

She went off on a tangent, lecturing me about walking silently, curtseying properly, keeping my head lowered, always hiding behind the hood of my cloak and never meeting a matron's gaze unless I was explicitly told to.

If I dared to do any of those things, she warned, punishment was certain. It varied depending on who caught us, ranging from something as mundane as cleaning the fireplace or scrubbing toilets to something far more brutal.

A girl was said to have lost her tongue for talking back. They'd actually cut it out! Rés wasn't that far off, after all.

After hours of walking straight, curtsying on command, and practicing the meticulous ritual of cleansing the cloak, my body had grown stiff and my mind sluggish with boredom. Each movement felt more like a blur, the repetition endless.

I barely noticed the time pass until, at last, she finally fed me Fesenjoon. Tasting the stew with rice and tahdig almost made me cry; not because I was hungry but because I hadn't realized how much I had missed having a family, a family I could never have. I missed my brother so much it hurt.

You can't think of him now. It will break you. He's safe. That's all that matters.

I swallowed the knot in my throat and with it the last spoon of rice.

"*Dastet dard nakoneh, zahmat keshidi.*" I thanked her for her efforts. "It was delicious."

"You're learning. Very good. Take those three books with you to your room and do not come out before you have finished them." She gestured to the books at the end of the dining table.

I was about to argue it was impossible to finish all three books on such short notice. Then I remembered how I had rushed through the books back in Iran when I was first learning about our ways. If I couldn't read them in full, I would just skim.

Once in my room, I washed and changed into pajamas and put the books on the nightstand by the bed. Before going to sleep, I checked my phone and saw twenty-eight missed calls from Rés, all from the past hour. Shit! Besides the missed calls, there was one text message from him.

I released a breath, relieved to see it was just one of his many threats and quickly typed out a message to him.

He called again, and I was about to hang up when I thought better of it.

"D'you know how many times I've called!" he spat through the phone, fuming on the other end.

"Mm-hmm," I said, trying to be as quiet as possible.

"Maya, I need to hear your bloody voice right this minute. D'you understand!"

"What is it!" I whispered, not wanting Farnazeh to listen in on our conversation.

He heaved a sigh before speaking again. "I tried going through the gates when you didn't pick up, but she's warded the house against me, and I started to think it was a trap." He paused. "I—I just need to know if everything is okay. Are you unharmed?"

"I'm fine. Why are you so riled up?" I asked because I desperately wanted him to voice it out so the truth could pull me out of my delusion.

"Why do you think, demon blood? Is it so strange that I worry about you?"

"Yes." I sighed faintly.

"Regardless of what you may think of me or my family, we're not all evil. I don't have ill intentions, and I will not let you pay the price of my misjudgment or this prophecy."

His words hit me like a wave, drowning me in guilt.

I don't think you are evil, Rés. I have yet to find myself worthy.

٣٨

THIRTY-EIGHT

MAYA

I had filled the tub halfway with scorching hot water and soap, steam rising in thick curls, filling the room with a fragrant warmth.

Eager to sink into the heat, I tried to get in immediately but recoiled as the water seared my skin. I adjusted the temperature, letting the cold water run for a few moments until the burn subsided. Still, I wasn't patient enough to fill the tub all the way because I was determined to make the most of the little time I had.

I had brought a book, a glass of wine and lit a scented candle. The sweet vanilla aroma mingled with the steam, promising a quiet evening of relaxation. I took a long gulp of the wine, its tartness instantly puckering my mouth, the rich warmth spreading through me as it slid down my throat. I set the glass on the footstool next to the tub and finally sank into the water.

It was still hot, a lingering burn against my skin but enjoyable. I closed my eyes, letting the soft Latin music drift from the living room and into my daydream. [8] The rhythm, the warmth, and the enveloping scent almost felt like I was on vacation in Mexico. The illusion shattered with the harsh slam of the front door, the sharp bang pulling me back to the present, back to reality.

"Everie!" Rés shouted a couple of times.

"She is not home you idiot," I muttered before he started shouting for me.

"*Bruja*!" He opened and closed doors, looking for me. *What the fuck have I done!*

"What!" I yelled back, hoping he would understand I was taking a bath.

That did not deter him until it was too late.

"Why is no one—"

He stopped short when he saw me in the tub.

Not that I was the least bit concerned, but from where he stood, all he could see were the foaming bubbles.

"What do you want?" I asked, reaching for the glass of wine, knowing damn well the movement would shift me

Viente años - Buena Vista Social Club

just enough to reveal my nipples. I took a sip, noticing how his jaw clenched.

"Do you know where Ev went?" He tilted his head to the side, his neck shifting with a sharp crack as the tension in his muscles released with the motion.

"You don't care where she went, as long as she's not back within the next . . ." I cocked my head. "Ten minutes?"

I was doing the most, and I didn't care. I was aware of my actions, and I would stand by them.

"Is that so?" He stepped closer, took the glass from my hand, drank the remaining wine and then set it down.

"Maybe a hot bath will relief the tension in your neck."

One moment, he was fully clothed, standing over me. The next, he was in the water, naked, devouring me like I was his last meal, his last breath.

My body instantly responded to his touch, giving in to all his unspoken commands. The taste of iron coated my tongue, and I realized I was biting him, too. One hand was around my throat, tightening and releasing in intervals allowing me to breathe, the other was exploring every inch of my body.

I tried to focus, tried to let my hands wander, but all I could do was get a hold around his neck and let my nails dig into his skin. He was biting me, kissing me, and pinching my nipples sore, leaving bruises on my skin, making me writher from both pain and pleasure. His hand moved down my stomach, and in one swift motion, two of his fingers were inside me.

I had to grab the lip of the tub for purchase as a moan escaped me, and I gasped for the air he barely let me have.

The sensation had me lost out of my mind, begging to be dragged into places where everything was forbidden.

He left peppered kisses along my jaw until he reached the shell of my ear.

"Softer?" he asked as he pulled away and loosened the grip around my neck. His two fingers traced away from me, while his hand made its way up my side, reaching my breast where his thumb traced my perked nipple before his tongue took over. I pulled his face to mine and licked the blood from his bottom lip where my teeth had sunk in. "I want to drown, Rés," I breathed into his mouth.

He kissed me softly once, then twice.

"Then, hold your breath, *bruja*." His lips crashed into mine before he submerged us both under water, spread my knees apart, and pushed into me.

I jolted awake, gasping for air, my heart racing as the cold sweat clung to my skin and drenched the sheets, in a bed that wasn't mine, in Farnazeh's house. It was a dream. Just a dream. None of it was real.

I had been free of all the intrusive thoughts and dreams for so long that I had completely forgotten how real they felt. If it hadn't been for Farnazeh's wards, I would have accused Rés of walking into my dream like he told me he did in Egypt. Yet this was all me. The choking, biting, pinching, and drowning were all my fantasies. If he ever found out, I would be mortified.

I tried going to bed after that but couldn't. By the time I looked at the clock on the wall again, it was six in the morning. Instead, I decided to power through the last two books Farnazeh had given me.

There was a lot about the origin of demon blood Sāhers, and their purpose at the Chinkāri sanctuary. It started out innocent enough, a place for the girls in need of guidance, girls who had nowhere else to go.

Regardless of how many times it was mentioned that the girls asked to be sent to the sanctuary, I had a hard time believing the words. The more I read, the more it became apparent that no matter how much they carved and decorated the apple, it was still rotten inside. It was a boarding school for ill-behaved girls.

The girls who were admitted were under conservatorship. Their "guardian" would decide the length of their stay and any attempt at escape before their "term" ended was met with the highest form of punishment, their infamous "isolation therapy," where the victims were held in a magical state of limbo. They weren't physically harmed, but their minds were relentlessly torn apart, stripped of sanity, and left to rot in silence.

It was never clear what some of the girls experienced during these punishments, as they were either too traumatized to speak about it or had been left lobotomized by the ordeal. Their minds gone quiet.

There was even an incident of suicide after they had kept a girl in that state for two weeks, her mind finally cracking under the relentless torment. After Fereshte killed herself, they decided three days was more than enough to get the message across. The story of Fereshte was a hand-written warning in the margins.

Whether it was Farnazeh's way of scaring me or someone's actual notes, I wasn't going to ignore them.

It took me all morning and afternoon to finish the books. When I did, the scent of food wafted through the cracks in the door, as if she had expected me to finish at that exact time.

I washed, changed, and packed my bag before heading downstairs. I found Farnazeh in the kitchen, preparing dinner—Tahchin, to be exact.

I never liked that. It was a texture issue for me. The rice sticky on the inside but crispy on the outside and worse of all, the chicken was too chicken-y. Of course I wouldn't tell her that.

"Good, you've finished. *Kashke Bademjoon bokhor ta daghe.*" She turned and motioned me to sit.

I hadn't even noticed the Kashke Bademjoon on the table. That, on the other hand, was my favorite appetizer, a dish made of mashed eggplants, sautéed onions, dried mint, and most importantly kashk, which gave it the tangy taste I loved so much. A bread basket with nun Barbari sat next to it.

My mouth was salivating, but I couldn't, for the life of me, let go of what was hardwired in me and start eating without her. Shortly after, Farnazeh sat opposite me, serving me a plate of the dip with a piece of bread before taking some for herself.

"*Merci*," I said before tearing a piece of the Barbari and dipping it into the Kashke Bademjoon. "Who's going to be my guardian?" I finally asked after eating another mouthful.

"I am."

"And how long will you tell them to keep me?"

"I have signed you for the minimum, eleven days. If you need more time to acquire the grimoire, you will have to tell me. Most don't stay beyond the thirty-three-day mark."

"Will you accompany me for the initiation ceremony?" I took my third bite, trying not to appear too hungry or greedy.

"Admission to Chinkāri is never forced on anyone!" Farnazeh snapped. For some reason, she was very offended by the question. "It's a choice they face. Either they accept it or give up their powers and live peacefully outside the community." They faced being stripped of their powers and excommunicated or doing as they were told. It wasn't fair. Farnazeh seemed set in her stance, and there was no point in arguing with her. "I have packed the cloak for you in a velvet bag. It's hanging by the door. Only wear it as you are about to pass through the portal and not a day before."

"And how will I get there?"

"Aldridge knows where to take you."

My mouth dried at the mention of his name and the images from last night's dream.

"You can leave after we've eaten. He is waiting outside," Farnazeh said casually, as if it wasn't the rudest thing to have him wait outside like a mutt while we ate.

"He is outside right now?" I asked, already getting up to wash my hands.

Farnazeh had a puzzled look on her face, as if I was stupid. "He has been parked on the street since last night," she clarified.

Since last night!

He had just waited outside.

Reluctantly, I thanked Farnazeh for her hospitality, took my things, the velvet bag, and hurried out of the door. Good thing I didn't get more than a few bites in, or I would have felt so bad.

٣٩

THIRTY-NINE

ALDRIDGE

The moment she stepped through the gates, the knot in my chest loosened. I got out of the car, not to greet her nor to embrace her—that wasn't our norm. Still, I went around the car and opened the door for her.

"I learned everything I need to know. I'm ready." She beamed like she needed me to be proud of her.

"Good job, *bruja*." I closed the door behind her.

We could technically leave the car and aďhār home from here, but I needed the extra time to ground myself around her. I sat behind the wheel and turned the key before reaching for her hand without hesitation. When her fingers curled around mine, I released a heavy breath. The way I had nearly cracked a molar from the tension of her absence was absurd.

At this point, who fucking cares if I have convinced myself that she is mine! The dream I had while I dozed off in this bin of a car destroyed me. It altered my brain chemistry in ways I never thought possible. Good or bad, it wouldn't change anything between the two of us, which was the most frustrating part. I was angry at the world, angry with myself, my life, and everything in it. Except her.

I stroked the back of her hand with my thumb, trying to remind myself this was not permanent, that her presence was temporary.

We had been driving for an hour without the exchange of words. She didn't ask where we were going or complain like she used to. Perhaps she was as tired as I was. I hadn't slept and could barely keep my eyes open.

"I have to get some rest," I said as I pulled up to the same motel from the day before.

Maya said nothing when we got out of the car, and it was starting to unnerve me.

I stopped in front of her, halting her steps. "What's wrong?"

"We don't have all the time in the world, Rés," she said, hesitating. "The initiation ceremony is on Tuesday."

"What initiation ceremony?"

"The initiation ceremony at the sanctuary in Scotland. She told me you knew where to take me."

"This Tuesday? Absolutely not! We can wait for the next initiation."

She shook her head, peering up at me through her lashes. "This is it."

What she didn't understand was I wasn't ready to let go. *Tuesday is two days away.*

"It's not realistic. We haven't gone over everything and then there is the wedding."

I would make up excuses if I had to.

"I'm not going to the wedding, remember? And our practice is closed, just like yours. There is nothing you can prepare me for."

"No!" I snapped louder than I intended to. Doubt flashed across her eyes before she wiped it away.

"If you have me on a wild goose chase, Aldridge, just tell me. I have no fight left in me. If this is another ploy against your father—"

"Maya, stop." I breathed, pinching the bridge of my nose, offended by the mere suggestion. "I just don't know how to let you—" *Go.*

The last word was left unspoken. What was fair to say out loud? What wouldn't be selfish and still not a lie?

"Let me what? Was this not the whole plan? To get the grimoire and find a way around this prophecy? Or was that just to keep me docile?" she bit out.

Something ticked in my brain, and pure anger boiled up inside me. I stepped into her space and forced her to back up against the car again. "Can you shut the fuck up for a second!"

A flash of surprise crossed her face.

I cornered her like prey, and she seemed to enjoy playing cat and mouse. For a second, I wondered if the dream I had of her was one we both shared memories of.

"Never!"

The corner of her lip curved.

I was so fucked. Her defiance was all it took for me to break and lose all control. *To hell with it!* I grabbed her neck with one hand and yanked her upwards before crashing my lips against hers in a kiss so hungry and desperate, even the gods held their breaths.

I pulled away to look at her, to truly see her. Her cheeks were flushed and her lips parted. I leaned in and kissed her again, this time, more tenderly, intentional. She kissed me back, standing on her tiptoes, letting me cradle her neck and deepen the kiss a second longer than I deserved.

"*Besarte es como ver las estrellas.*" I let out a deep breath and let my arms slack at my sides.

When I released her, reality crashed over me. I was in such a moral dilemma so starved and parched I could deprave a nation. If this was another dream, I could have forgiven myself for my selfishness, but it wasn't, and I shouldn't have done it. I shouldn't have let my impulses control me. I would've gone blind if I went another day wondering what she tasted like. I simply couldn't exist without knowing, and it was as devastating as I had anticipated.

What I wouldn't give to have you all for myself.

"What?" she rasped, looking at me confused.

"I'm sorry I broke my promise to you." I stepped back from her. "I haven't slept," I mumbled, trying to justify my terrible mistake. "I need to get some sleep before we go anywhere."

٤٠

FORTY

Maya

The moment he fell asleep, I got up, locked myself in the bathroom, and broke down in silence. I was muffling sobs, my breath hitching as my body shook from the pain. What the hell was I doing. Why was I so pathetic?

He doesn't want you! You're making up a connection that is not there.

I was just another inconvenience in his great scheme. *You're all alone.*

Those who loved me had forgotten I ever existed, and those who hadn't were all dead.

"Maya," Rés said from the other side of the door.

Shit! I can't let him see me like this.

"What!"

My voice trembled more than I wanted it to.

Rés tried turning the doorknob once. "Open the door, Maya."

I had no energy to keep fighting everyone around me. There was no reason for me to pretend. What was the worst he could do? I was already broken.

I wiped my face with my sleeves and opened the door. At the sight of him, new tears formed, threatening to spill. I looked away and tried to push past him, but he pulled me into a hug and placed his chin on top of my head. I tried to fight it, to break free from his hold, but his arms only tightened around me. I would be lying if I said being embraced by Rés wasn't the safest I had ever felt. It felt like the only place I truly belonged.

"I'm sorry. I'm a fucking idiot. I—" He inhaled. "I don't know what I'm doing. I don't know if I'm making the right or wrong choices. I don't know whether the prophecy has an effect on me or if I'm moving on my own volition. I just know that you mean everything to me."

He breathed out heavily when I finally managed to push away from him. No matter how it felt, I was done being manipulated with.

"Maya, I—"

"Please, Rés." He sighed at my plea and brushed a tear off my cheek. "Don't." I stepped back. "I'm already here. I'm already doing your bidding. There is no fucking reason for you to mess with my head, too. I'm just a fucking girl. Soul or not, I have feelings, real human feelings and—"

"Do you think I planned this. I don't know what I'm doing!" He raised his voice, his eyes blazing with fire. "I'm fucking trying." He nearly shouted.

"Then stop fucking trying!"

He stepped closer, grabbing my face with one hand, squeezing hard enough to prevent me from speaking. "Listen to me for a second!"

"Spare me!" I shouted back and yanked my face free.

"I've fallen in love with you, demon blood!" he shouted in my face.

His confession pulled the rug under my feet. I could say or do nothing but stare at him. His scent enveloped me as if it was the first time we met. Then he rested his forehead against mine, and his hand slid to my nape.

"I can't take it anymore, Maya. Tell me to fuck off. Tell me that I've lost my mind, that I'm delusional for feeling this way." His words came out in a whisper. He tucked a lock of hair behind my ear and trailed his thumb along my jaw. His eyes bore into mine, his lips inches away. "Only you can convince me that it isn't really happening, that all of this is the result of the prophecy altering my perception."

"Is that so terrible?" I whispered, looking at my feet. He tilted my chin up, his thumb grazing my bottom lip, his eyes lingering like a starved man.

"It's devastating . . ." he said, his breath was mixing with mine. "To yearn for someone, you can't have. *No buscaba nada, pero en ti lo encontré todo.*"

I didn't dare ask what that meant because his first words were enough to destroy me. His other hand traveled up my arm, brushing over my shoulder before gently cradling my face.

His lips ghosted over mine. I could almost taste him. "I'm losing my bearings, Maya. Tell me to stop because . . . Because if you don't, I'm not sure I can stop myself from kissing you."

My thoughts scattered, my pulse quickening. The world around me blurred, leaving just raw intensity of the moment.

Even though I could've said something, anything, I didn't want to.

When I didn't respond, his lips finally brushed against mine, gentle at first but with a hunger that burned beneath the surface. My lips parted for him, letting his tongue sweep against mine, possessive and eager, like he was claiming me with every stroke.

His hand tangled in my hair, pulling me closer, tilting my head back, and I couldn't suppress the soft moan that slipped from my lips. My grip tightened on his shirt, fingers twisting in the fabric, needing something to ground me. But there was no grounding.

Rés was all-consuming. His touch, his scent, his kiss, the raw heat of him pressed against me. The world around me fell off its axis.

The kiss deepened. His hands roamed, exploring, memorizing every curve, sending waves of heat rolling through my body, unraveling me piece by piece. My fingers trailed up his back, nails scraping lightly over his skin. His muscles tensed beneath my touch, and he groaned, low and primal, pressing his body against mine, making me feel exactly how much he wanted me.

The pull between us was unbearable, each movement and every touch pushing us further over the edge, tearing at the line between control and surrender. If I let him continue, he would have given me an orgasm where I stood.

"The line between wanting to strangle you"—his hand wrapped around my throat, his thumb pressing lightly against my pulse—"and fuck you has blurred ever since I first touched you." His words were spoken into my mouth before he bit down on my lip, hard enough to leave a taste of copper behind. "I must find another way to please you while restraining myself." With a swift motion, he lifted me off the ground with one hand, his fingers devastatingly close to touching my most sensitive parts.

My legs wrapped around his waist, pressing against him in hopes of whatever friction I could get. He responded accordingly, his touch teasing.

I gasped when his fingers grazed me between my legs. Even through the fabric of my night shorts, the slightest touch sent a shudder through me.

"Jesus Christ, you're soaked," he groaned against my ear.

Heat flared across my cheeks, shame flickering through the haze of lust. But his fingers never stopped their slow, torturous teasing. I forgot all about who he was and why he was forbidden fruit. My head fell back as his name left my lips in a breathless whimper.

He walked us to the bedroom, then lowered me onto the edge of the bed.

You're a whore, giving yourself to another one of them.

Then he touched me again, and the words drowned out in the sensation of him. *Damn the prophecy.* I had to have him at least once before everything went to hell.

"Look at me." He nudged my chin up, forcing my gaze to meet his golden eyes. They burned with something almost feral. So beautiful. "You can never moan another man's name."

"No?" I arched a brow, smirking, despite the way my body trembled under his touch.

His hand wrapped around my neck again, squeezing just enough to make me gasp.

"Do you understand?"

His voice was a quiet command.

Pure possessiveness flooded his eyes. Then his lips replaced his hand, pressing a kiss to the hollow of my throat, his tongue flicking against my skin. I moaned a barely audible *yes*. I would do and say anything to make this feeling last forever. I needed more, and soon, I would be begging him for it.

His hands skimmed down my sides, fingers hooking into the waistband of my shorts.

"I need you to use your words before I make you go blind from the orgasm, demon blood." One hand traced an agonizingly slow line above my entrance, his touch featherlight over the drenched fabric.

I grabbed him by the back of his neck, arching into his touch, my lips grazing his ear.

"Rés," I breathed. His name fell from my lips like a prayer.

"I need your consent, Maya. I need you to tell me without any hesitation before I can go any further."

My eyes locked with his, unflinching. "You can do to me what you want, Rés. I'm yours! In this universe and the next."

His pupils dilated, his canines flashing as he exhaled sharply, like he was barely holding himself back. Then, with one swift motion, he pulled my T-shirt over my head, leaving me bare before him. His gaze raked over my body, heated, possessive.

"You're beautiful beyond measure."

His hands found my breasts, thumbs grazing over hardened peaks before his mouth replaced them. A shudder racked through me at the sharp sting of his teeth, followed by the soothing warmth of his tongue.

"If I could do to you whatever I wanted," he murmured against my skin, "I would fuck you so hard you'd forget your own name." His fingers dipped lower, peeling my shorts down my thighs, spreading my legs wider. He pinned me to the mattress, his weight pressing me down. "But perhaps I can still make you scream my name until you lose all sanity."

He bit down on my neck, dragging his teeth and tongue down my body, leaving a scorching path from my breasts to my stomach, lower and lower, until his mouth hovered between my legs. His tongue flicked the bundle of nerves, making my eyes roll back into my head.

"Andrés!" I gasped, arching off the bed, the pleasure blinding.

His hand wrapped around my throat again, his grip firm, squeezing in rhythm with the flick of his tongue. "That's not what you call me," he murmured against my skin, pulling back just enough to leave me aching, desperate.

I was about to push up on my elbows when he pressed me back down.

"Beg," he commanded, a wicked grin playing on his lips, trailing a lazy finger down my center.

"Please," I gasped, trembling beneath him, from the need to be touched.

"Please what?"

His voice was pure sin.

"Please, Rés!" I pleaded arching into his touch.

He smiled, dark and satisfied. "Good girl."

A pleased grumble vibrated in his throat as his tongue found me again, moving with devastating precision, pierced me, slowly sending me over the edge. But he didn't stop. He held me tighter, his grip unrelenting.

"One more, *bruja*."

My body obeyed him, unraveling, surrendering completely. The pleasure built higher, tighter until I shattered apart beneath him, crying his name, and letting the orgasm ripple through me all over again.

٤١

FORTY-ONE

Aldridge

She was still panting when I settled next to her, her body trembling from the pleasure I had wrung from her. I licked the remnants of her orgasm from my lips, savoring the taste, intoxicating and addictive.

What ecstasy you taste like.

There was no going back now. I had come to terms with the fact that I would never deny myself her touch again. She belonged to me, in every way that mattered—mind, body, and soul.

Maya propped herself up on one elbow, meeting my gaze, her skin flushed, her lips swollen and bruised from my kisses. My hand traced lazy patterns over the peaks of her nipples, watching as goose bumps rippled across her skin and getting harder just by watching her. I could never get enough of her.

"Why are you still dressed?" she murmured, fingers slipping under the hem of my shirt before pulling it over my head.

Her hands roamed across my chest, nails grazing over my skin, making my muscles tighten. She tried to straddle me, and I caught her hips, stopping her.

"I won't be able to control myself if you place your perfect cunt on top of me," I warned.

She leaned in, her hardened nipples grazing against my chest, making my cock twitch.

"You think the gods will spare us because of a technicality?" she scoffed, taking my face in her hands. "All this . . ." She bit my lip, licked into my mouth, then dragged her tongue along the roof of it, making me shudder. "Counts as our sins."

"I won't risk it for the sake of my own pleasure," I said, slipping two fingers between her legs, teasing her soaked entrance.

Her hand slipped beneath the waistband of my shorts and wrapped around my cock.

My breath hitched as she freed me, stroking the length of me with slow, torturous precision.

Her lips brushed against my jaw, a whisper of heat. "I will not be satisfied until you're dripping from my mouth, Rés."

The image alone nearly undid me, but nothing could have prepared me for the way she took me into her mouth. Hot, wet, and unrelenting, her tongue massaging every ridge and vein as she hollowed her cheeks around me. Saliva dripped down her chin, her eyes glassy with tears as she let me in deeper, choking on me.

I lost it. My fingers curled into the sheets, ripping holes into the fabric as her tongue worked me over, slow and deliberate. Her pace quickening, teasing me closer to the edge before pulling back. She let my cock slide from her mouth, licking the tip with a devilish grin.

"You're killing me," I rasped, barely holding onto my sanity. Her eyes flickered with mischief. "Shove it down my throat. Make me s—"

I fisted her hair and thrust into her mouth so deep she gagged, tears slipping from the corners of her eyes. It was enough to send me over. I came with a strangled groan, the pleasure so intense it blacked out my vision. She swallowed some but let the rest spill from her lips, dripping down her chin and onto her chest. Then, she dipped her fingers into it, smearing my release over her breasts before sliding her hand between her legs. Something primal and vicious snapped inside me.

"You're unreal," I growled, shaking my head as I felt myself harden again. "I will not have peace until I have fucked some sense into you."

"Exactly," she breathed, positioning herself over me.

I should have stopped her. I had the opportunity. But the second she sank onto me, hot and tight and clenching, I was undone.

For a moment, I thought I had gone blind. Her walls pulsed around me and nothing else existed. I gripped her hips, driving her down harder.

She collapsed on top of me, skin to skin, breathless and moaning and begged for more.

"How hard do you want it, love?" I murmured against her ear, teeth grazing her skin.

"I want to forget my name," she replied, biting my neck.

I let out a low chuckle. "Paying attention, are we? Such a good girl." I bit her lips, then her throat, then down to her hardened nipples, rolling them between my teeth before flipping her onto her back.

One hand wrapped around her throat as I thrust into her again, harder, deeper, relentless.

She had no voice left to scream by the time she shattered around me, dragging me over the edge with her.

I slid out, my cum dripping from her.

Gathering her, I positioned her on top of me, her head resting against my chest, her skin flushed with the evidence of what I had done to her. There was no doubt she would have bruises all over her body the next day. Bruises that marked her, branding her as mine. [9]

Our naked bodies were tangled together, the heat of our skin still lingering between us. I held her close, pressing a slow, lingering kiss to the top of her head. My fingers traced gentle patterns along her back, over the soft curve of her shoulder, down her arm, memorizing her, grounding myself in her presence.

Then I felt it. The dampness against my skin.

I shifted, letting my hand glide up to cup her cheek. Wet, silent tears streaked down her face. A sharp pang shot through my chest. I tilted her face toward me, searching her expression, and my stomach twisted at the raw emo-

Nimeye Janam - Hamid Hiraad

tion in her gaze. My throat tightened with the sudden, brutal realization.

"Do you regret it?" I asked.

My voice was barely above a whisper when I kissed the tears from her cheeks, each one a fresh reminder of my own stupidity.

I had done this. I had pushed her too far. *I'm an idiot. A fucking prime example of an idiot.*

Her breath hitched, and for a moment, I braced myself for the answer that would gut me. But then she shook her head, the smallest movement easing the tightness in my chest.

"No," she rasped, her hands cradling my face as if she could hold me together. I kissed another tear as it slipped free. "I don't know how to convince you that none of this had anything to do with the prophecy. That—that I wanted this. I just can't help feeling like a whore who seduced two brothers into her bed."

"Shut up, Maya." My grip tightened around her, feeling the tension under her skin. "Nothing will change my mind about you, not even if you decided to fulfill the prophecy and killed me with it." I kissed her, needing to erase the very thought and lingering doubt in her mind.

She deserved to have a choice, even at the expense of my life.

I woke up to the absence of her touch. The space beside me was empty, the sheets cool where her body had been.

My chest tightened. For a second, I thought she had left, that she'd slipped out in the early hours, her regret so heavy she couldn't even bring herself to say goodbye. Though relief settled over me with the sound of running water from the bathroom.

Letting out a slow breath, I stared at the ceiling. I hadn't realized how the idea of losing her could pain me and feel so real.

I checked my phone and saw a string of messages from Edgar, one summoning me to another meeting, the next asking about my whereabouts. I called him back right away, knowing he wouldn't have asked where I was unless it was important.

By the first ring, Edgar picked up.

"Did I miss anything exciting from the meeting?"

"Depends if you think the end of an era is exciting."

Edgar's tone was nonchalant.

"*Kollu dah?*"

"Stick to Shami or Spanish your *Masri* is a disgrace to us." I visualized the grin spreading on his face. I hadn't been brought up in Egypt, so my Masri was rusty to say the least. "But yes, we are planning to shut down the labs within the week, and I need you to help with that."

"I can't," I sighed, apprehension weighing me down. "I need to get the grimoire first."

"But you don't need the grimoire anymore. Our efforts have paid off, our brothers finally all united, all in agreement. We can stop him and his whole practice without it. The conflict will resolve itself the moment we stop taking souls."

"I need two weeks, Edgar," I said, hoping he would understand.

A moment of silence followed before he responded. "Because the prophecy remains tied to her, regardless of Father's downfall." It was more a statement than a question. "She could get rid of the stone and cut the connection to the prophecy. Of course, if Maya is interested in a truce."

"Being without a soul, I'm not sure she can survive without the Feyrouz."

"And that's not a risk you are willing to take," Edgar hummed. "Very well, then. It seems I will have to be the one to impress them with my anchoring skills." He let out a soft chuckle.

Finally, a change in the weather. We weren't going to stay as a dormant rebellion. As much as he liked to downplay his hand in it, Edgar had planned it all. He had every step mapped out. From winning over the last few loyalists still clinging to Father's ideologies to finding a way to strip us of our soul-taking abilities and finally to coordinate how to anchor our father and Herman. Our father knew how to anchor, yes, but his meditation technique was flawed and nothing compared to Ev's technique. Besides, he wouldn't see it coming from his favorite son, the ever-loyal Edgar. What would happen to them had yet to be decided.

With Herman and our father locked up, my brothers plotted to shut down the labs and dismantle everything we were forced to be part of—every experiment, every lie we'd been forced to live under. They would end the pain and suffering for generations to come.

It was dangerous, nearly impossible, but if it worked, it would change everything. Whether it would restore the balance of nature, we wouldn't know. But the world would be a better place without our involvement.

٤٢

FORTY-TWO

Maya

Our stolen night had ended and reality came crashing back, cold and merciless. The weight of it settled over me like a lead blanket. We left the car at the motel, teleporting back to New Orleans so I could cast a glamour with a solid anchor before going to Scotland.

Time had slipped away beneath us, taking my best memories with it. In the blink of an eye, the warmth of the past few hours was gone. The touch of his hands, the way he whispered my name like it was something sacred, all vanished.

I found myself in an alley in Glasgow, the same one near the bar where I'd met his brother, Kristian. The brother I had seduced. The brother I had almost slept with for the sake of the prophecy. *I'm sure he's aware of all those details as well.*

I sat in the passenger seat of a rented car, driving on the wrong side of the road. Rés had one hand on the wheel and the other on my thigh. My fingers covered his, holding him like I could hold on to something already slipping away.

"Where is this portal, exactly?" I asked, my voice quieter than I intended.

"Fort William," Rés said.

I blinked, a flicker of excitement cutting through the heaviness in my chest. "Really?" I turned to him, grasping onto the distraction like a lifeline. "Maybe we can see the fort before I—"

"We will, *habibi*," Rés murmured, squeezing my thigh. "But there is nothing left of the structure in Fort William."

The endearment sent a shiver down my spine. I wondered how many had heard it before me, if there was a world where the word belonged to me alone. His voice dipped lower.

"Undo your seatbelt for me and climb onto my lap."

I hesitated. "While you're driving?"

He huffed a soft laugh. "Although I wouldn't mind it, I'm not asking you to get undressed. I just need your body to be flush with mine." He unbuckled his own seatbelt, waiting for me to do the same.

I did as he asked, maneuvering myself onto his lap, sitting sideways, my head resting in the crook of his neck. The world outside blurred past, but here, in his arms, time stilled for just a moment longer.

I inhaled deeply, breathing him in, the scent of him grounding me, intoxicating me. Without thinking, I pressed my lips to the space behind his ear, leaving a kiss behind. "I'm obsessed with the way you smell," I admitted, my voice barely above a whisper. "Ever since the moment we first met."

His grip on me tightened, his right hand sliding up my thigh, pulling me closer into him as if it was physically possible.

Chinkāri Castle lay nestled near the Scottish Borders, sitting on the southern bank of a river. But no roads led to it, no maps marked its location. The only way in was through the portal. The forgotten archway in Fort William was its threshold, but without the red cloak, the archway led nowhere.

Because of the red cloak, the Sāhers who stayed at Chinkāri Castle were often confused with the Redcaps from Scottish folklore, mistaken for creatures of legend. Cruel, fae-like beings with glaring black eyes, skeletal fingers tipped with curved red nails and crimson hoods soaked in the blood of their victims. Redcaps supposedly lurked in ruined castles, watching from the shadows, preying on the unwary.

But the Sāhers had migrated to Scotland for a different reason. They had settled south of Edinburgh and had come into possession of Chinkāri Castle. Within its ancient stone walls, they had opened their sanctuary, a place for witches who had violated oaths, doctrine, ethics, or coven law. Some whispered it was a prison. Others claimed it was a school for the wayward, a place of reform. But no one truly knew. What was certain was that the land Chinkāri Castle stood on had become sacred, a place so steeped in magic it welcomed only Persian practitioners through its gates.

I clung to hope that, somewhere within the grimoire, hidden beneath layers of ink and incantation, lay the answer to my prayers, the key undoing the prophecy, the curse, all of it. Some kind of loophole, a pardon from the gods, anything that would set us free.

There were the religious references to the grimoire of Harut & Marut and then there were the stories passed down through whispered conversations and ancient scrolls, the kind that made their way into legend.

Harut and Marut were not angels, they were the first practitioner to roam the earth. Their state of existence seemed beyond comprehension, and because of that, many referred to them as angels sent down to Babylon serving as a test from God. Harut and Marut taught magic at its purest form, whether it be dark or light, all of it had a purpose. They left behind the very first written grimoire. It became the symbol of all magical knowledge.

This knowledge spread like wildfire between continents. Covens all over the world started forming, secret communities where you could practice without judgment.

The grimoire had been lost for millennia, swallowed by time until whispers resurfaced, whispers that spoke of spells cast by Solomon himself, sealing the grimoire away in the library of Chinkāri Castle. Not locked away, not warded nor under guard. Because legend claimed that only a witch born without a soul could touch it.

It was late when we arrived in Fort William. When Rés said there was nothing left of the fort, he meant it. Calling the place Fort William was a ploy, a tourist trap built on the remnants of something long gone. All that remained was a weathered stone archway and the last trace of the old fort's foundation.

Rés's hand brushed the back of my arm, pulling me from my thoughts.

"Maya, look at me."

I couldn't. I already knew what I'd see in his eyes, and I couldn't bear it. The weight of his concern, his unspoken plea—it would shatter me.

"I'll be careful. I won't get caught."

"Will you look at me," he said again, softer this time. One hand traced the length of my spine, the other tilting my chin up. *Stop looking at me like that, or I will break.* "You will come back to me."

I merely nodded because the words were stuck, trapped behind the ache in my chest. He leaned in, pressing his forehead to mine. I closed my eyes, burning this moment into my memory. Maybe I had done something unforgivable in a past life. Maybe I was being punished for a sin so great I had to atone for it a thousand times over. And because of it, I couldn't be loved. I wasn't worthy of it, and every time I got close, it was ripped away. The gods didn't believe I was deserving of love.

"Maya, I—"

"I have to go," I said.

I couldn't bear it, wouldn't let myself dwell on the what-ifs. Nothing good ever came from being around me. If I let myself linger a moment longer, I wouldn't be able to let go. I wouldn't kiss him goodbye. It would mean too much and break my heart.

I backed up, but he pulled me back in for a devastating kiss before letting go.

"You will come back to me," he repeated.

Only then did I walk through the archway. When I turned back to have a final look at him, he wasn't there, and I wasn't in Fort William anymore.

Before me stood a pair of red iron gates, their bars twisting like veins of molten iron, separating the outside world from the castle grounds. Beyond them, a cemetery stretched out in eerie silence, tombstones half-buried in ivy, names eroded by time. Mist curled around the gravestones, licking at my ankles as I stepped forward.

I pulled the red hood of my cloak over my head and moved through the graveyard until I reached the stone stairs embedded in the side of Chinkāri Castle. I hurried up the steps, the cape flapping behind me.

When I reached the landing, the heavy doors creaked open before I could knock. A tall woman stood in the doorway, her face unreadable. She wore the same red cloak as me with a floor length white tunic and leather slippers. She stepped aside without a word and let me walk inside.

"*Mamnun*," I thanked her. *Remember your manners.*

She closed the door behind me and led me through the halls.

"This is the common room." She gestured toward a set of towering French doors, their glass panels veiled in layers of dust and shadow.

She didn't stop, and I barely caught a glimpse inside, figures draped in crimson cloaks moving like ghosts through the dimly lit space. We ascended a spiraling stone staircase, each step worn with age.

The sconces lining the walls burned with blue fire, casting an eerie glow over the arched ceilings. The higher we climbed, the quieter it became. The castle seemed to swallow sound, absorbing every footstep, every breath.

At the second floor, we veered into the east wing, the corridor narrowing as we walked. The windows were tall but thin, allowing only slivers of moonlight to spill across the cold stone floor.

She stopped at a heavy wooden door reinforced with iron.

"This is your room." She stepped aside, waiting for me to enter. "You are expected in the common room at midnight for the ritual. There is charged water in the tub for you to wash yourself in. Unbraid your hair, remove all your amulets, and only wear the linen chemise under your cloak."

She seemed like the type that didn't like stupid questions, so I refrained from asking where this linen chemise would be and whether I was to wash my hair, too.

The bedroom felt lived in, as if someone had just stepped out and might return at any moment. A massive wooden desk sat against the far wall, cluttered with stacks of books leaning precariously, their spines cracked. Among them, at least twenty candlesticks burned, dripping wax onto the covers below. The flickering flames cast restless shadows across the stone walls. Curious, I ran my fingers along the spines of the books. Encyclopedias of plants, guides to Scottish landmarks, dense volumes on meditation and astral projection—but nothing truly occult or of interest. No grimoires, no forbidden texts.

In the adjoining bathroom, a vanity was neatly arranged with cotton balls, soaps, and witch hazel.

As requested, I cleansed my face and unbraided my hair, watching the waves fall loose around my shoulders. Shedding my clothes, I stepped under the shower first, letting the warm water wash away the grime of travel. I scrubbed my skin, washed my hair, and brushed through the tangles before I went to the tub with charged water.

I hovered over it, dreading the plunge, but there was no way around it. I whispered the purification charm, watching as my breath curled white in the cold air, then stepped in. The shock stole the air from my lungs.

I was sure my heart would stop. I forced myself under, plunging completely beneath the freezing surface. I resurfaced with a sharp inhale, gripping the tub, my entire body shuddering from the cold.

Back in the bedroom, the chemise conveniently appeared, neatly folded beside the red cloak. Slipping into the garment and fastening the cloak at my throat, I snuffed out the candles one by one, watching as darkness swallowed the room. Then, without another thought, I ventured downstairs.

The same woman stood before me, wearing a black cape, the hood pulled so low her eyes disappeared into shadow.

Without a word, she stepped aside, revealing a vast, empty room.

The room was bare except for a massive salt circle in the center. The far wall flickered with the glow of hundreds of candles, placed in perfect orderly rows. Their flames cast long, dancing shadows stretching across the smooth stone floor. No chairs, no tapestries, no markings on the walls, just an eerie emptiness that made the air feel heavy.

I stepped inside, and the door slammed shut behind me. Before I could react, my body rose from the ground as an invisible force yanked me forward, dragging me to the center of the circle. I gasped as my limbs locked into place, my body going rigid.

And then I felt it—my magic, my very essence, being drained from me. It poured out like water slipping through my fingers, vanishing into the air. The loss was immediate, like a vital organ being ripped from my chest. Suddenly, I was just human. The absence of power left me hollow, exposed. I had forgotten what it was like to exist without it, without the constant hum of energy coursing through my veins.

Movement stirred in the shadows. One by one, figures emerged from the darkness, forming a slow, deliberate circle around me. Women, cloaked in black velvet, had their hoods pulled low, obscuring their faces. Their capes trailed behind them, whispering against the floor as they moved. My pulse pounded in my ears.

"Masireto gom kardi." You lost your way.

It sounded more like an echo than an actual voice.

"Umadam jobran konam," I replied, remembering I was playing a character, a Sāher here to make amends, to correct her wrongs.

This is a part of it. This is a part of it. This is a part of it.

One woman in front of me scoffed, which seemed out of place. She stepped into the circle of salt. The flickering lights bounced off the right side of her face, making the lines on her features seem sharper. She stepped closer while reaching for her hood, slowly revealing herself. I gasped when I realized.

"Zahmat keshidi," Leyla said sarcastically. *You shouldn't have.*

It was a trap, one I did not see coming. *Did you really believe you could waltz in here, steal an ancient grimoire, and walk out unscratched.*

"You veered too far from your roots, but I can't say I'm surprised with the mother who raised you." She shook her head in disappointment. "Ever the naïve little girl thinking she could outsmart everyone around her, let alone the oldest coven in Pars history."

Leyla snapped her fingers, and all the girls, none of whom I recognized, removed their hoods. Another snap, and I was lying horizontally, hovering mid-air. The room turned black, and all I could hear was the echo of the women circling me, chanting the same spell over and over again.

Through the veil of space, across realms untold, by threads of fate, let paths unfold.

In the blink of an eye, the world around me disappeared, and another unfolded. Even with the scattered stars, the vast expanse surrounding me was blanketed in darkness.

I was no longer hovering mid-air. No, I was walking barefoot in the sand. My steps were my own, yet the motion was not. The night wind of the desert greeted me, and I knew exactly where I was. My eyes adjusted, and I realized I was walking a path lined with palm trees and into a courtyard with a massive marble fountain. My body carried me to the fountain and one foot after the other I stepped into the water.

I remember faintly thinking how odd it was that I was perhaps a few yards away from the most powerful men in the universe, and no one bothered to guard The Holy Grail, The Fountain of Youth, The Chalice of Blood. No one was there to witness my sacrifice.

It's time you wake up.

I sank beneath the water, closing my eyes as my fingers brushed together in silent ritual, surrendering to what was required of me. The water darkened, thickening into blood, and I drank and drank and drank until I drowned . . . [10]

Khosara - Abdel Halim Hafez

EPILOGUE

Maya

Two years after waking up

In the real world, my parents never divorced. In the real world, both my parents were Iranian. In the real world, my brother was living with his girlfriend and would ask her to marry him in a week. In the real world, most of my family lived in the states. In the real world, I lived with my cousin Roya in a two-bedroom apartment in New York. In the real world, I was thirty years old, had a good job and should have been content with my life. One lucid dream shouldn't have made such an impact on my life. One lucid dream shouldn't have been able to alter my perception on life. *This is my real life, and everything else was a dream, a lie.*

That day, I had woken up unsure of my surroundings for a moment. Then realization hit me, and my true memories washed over me. I knew the layout of the apartment I had lived in for the past seven years. I knew the names of my colleagues. I knew the neighborhood cat, Lucy. I knew I couldn't do a correct downward facing dog even after a year of yoga. I knew I liked my food salty. I knew all the facts about me. *Because when you actually wake up from a dream, you have no doubt what's real and what's not.*

Two years later, I was still on antidepressant, anxiety, and ADHD medication. The ADHD was always there, but the tightness in my chest was new and never seemed to ease.

Before being diagnosed, I knew nothing about anxiety. I thought people who had anxiety were walking around scared of life. I thought anxiety meant your body responded with a panic attack to big crowds.

In my own case, I couldn't make sense of it; my body reacted like there was this impending danger creeping up on me, following me like a shadow. I still went to therapy for the side effects the dream had left me with. In fact, I paid for the best psychologists in the city, and still, I was nowhere near cured. That dream—the life I lived and everything in it haunted me like a true memory I couldn't let go of.

I saw him sometimes—or imagined him, I should call it. I was almost convinced I could will him into existence if I tried hard enough. When I looked through a big crowd, my eyes always landed on someone who looked like him until I closed my eyes and opened them again, and he was replaced with whoever was actually there.

In the beginning, it triggered panic attacks, but I had learned a technique to make the hallucinations go away. It didn't take away the hurt and pain, though. It didn't take away my feelings and memories of that life.

Stop it! It wasn't real. It wasn't real. It wasn't real.

It was just a dream. A dream I woke up from, two years ago. It was all in my head. If I had paid close enough attention, I would have picked up on the subtle clues, would have noticed all the things that didn't make sense. Parts of it was inspired by my real life, and the rest was all made up, a figment of my imagination.

Magic wasn't real. I wasn't a witch. Dūshevs didn't exist. My parents, Milad, my cousins, and Dissie, were in my dream, but the rest of the characters were all fictional. I couldn't remember any of their faces, as I had completely blocked out how they looked, even Leyla. There had never been a Leyla in my family. Not any of the Dūshevs, even

Adam wasn't real. He was such a huge part of the dream, a huge part of everything that happened in that life and still, I couldn't remember what he looked like.

They were all extras in my dream, except for Rés. I couldn't forget Rés. Every line and shadow on his face, the touch of his skin under my fingertips, the smell of his cologne that coated my hands, the rasp of his voice and his stupid accent. If I closed my eyes, I could still hear his whispers in my ear.

I love you Rés, real or not, I will always love you.

I never said it out loud, never dared to. I was scared— ashamed, even—for being so utterly delusional and out of my mind that I was in love with someone who didn't exist.

11

I took another deep breath.

I will get better. This is my year.

My chest tightened at the thought, and suddenly, my pulse quickened while I was sitting in Bryant park trying to read a book.

I tried the tapping method for a couple of seconds before putting the book away to look at the crowd of people before me. Then I took a few deep breaths, and

Konna Netlaka - Fairuz

as always, the air never filled my lungs entirely. I was constantly depraved of a full breath.

My eyes landed on a figure waving, and I waved back when I realized it was Dissie. She had already warned me she was going to be an hour late because of work. I didn't mind. I liked to sit and read by myself in Bryant park. With proximity to the library and my favorite sandwich spot, it was the perfect place.

She settled in the chair next to me. "Sorry! It got hectic at work. Have you eaten?" She looked at the paper bag from Lauren's Deli.

"No, I waited for you." I pulled the two sandwiches out and handed her one.

"What did you get us?"

"*Bademjoon.*"

She started unwrapping the sandwich. "Good. I'm cutting down on meat this year. Anyway, how did that date go—" She took a bite, groaning and rolling her eyes. "I'm so hungry. What was his name?" Her mouth was still full as she took the next bite.

"Sam, and it wasn't a date. We were at Susan's place for a small get-together, and she told me she would invite him too, so that we could meet organically." I unwrapped my own sandwich, took the first bite, and covered my mouth. "Supposedly, she didn't tell him anything. She was convinced we would get along, since we're apparently so similar. Turns out he has raging ADHD."

Dissie rolled her eyes, laughing. "Of course. Then, you must be soulmates."

The word triggered me. *Soulmates are not real.* None of it was real.

"He was very polite, actually. We got to talking—"

"Is he hot? Do you have a picture? I need to visualize," Dissie said, covering her mouth as she spoke, while still chewing.

"I don't have a picture, and, yes, he's cute."

"But?" she asked with a raised brow.

"No buts. He asked me out, and I agreed. He's going back home to Minnesota or something. I don't remember what he said, but when he's back, he's taking me to dinner at some hidden gem restaurant. He won't tell me which one, so I can't look up their menu, but he swears it's good."

"But you're not into him . . ."

I smiled. "No, but I'm stepping out of my comfort zone, remember?"

"*Afarin, dokhtare khub.* You know what? This is exactly how you get back out there."

We finished our sandwiches, then strolled through some of the stores on fifth before we headed our separate ways.

It didn't require much to hang out with Dissie, and she was nothing like the character I had made her to be in my dream. She was genuine, easy going, compassionate, and most importantly, she hadn't slept with my father.

I shared everything with her, even the dream. I had called her the day of, in total panic mode, needing to see my best friend. When she came over, I told her everything. First, she listened, then she asked questions as if they were true events, and she told me she believed me. It was all I needed, my best friend to tell me I wasn't having a mental breakdown. She didn't think I was crazy, didn't ridicule me for feeling the pain I felt. She simply listened.

After rotting in bed, feeling sorry for myself, I found a psychologist and psychiatrist started going to therapy with both.

The psychiatrist diagnosed me within a couple of sessions and prescribed me medication.

But the psychologist was much more demanding. He wanted everything in detail, always asked me to elaborate. It was hard sharing it all over again with a stranger, seeing him scribbling god-knows-what in his little notebook. He taught me the tapping method for my anxiety, said a bunch of things over the two years I saw him. And then he gave me homework, asked me to journal, to write everything in great detail. He wanted every minuscule detail of that dream. Things like what I ate, what clothes I would wear, what color wallpaper my bedroom had and then he would ask for more information. It was never enough for him, and I couldn't always answer the questions.

At the end, I was bored out of my mind because I had written the most important bits down, and it still hadn't helped with how I felt, how I sometimes saw glimpses of him before he disappeared, how I knew he wasn't real but still missed him. The therapy never helped me forget.

ALDRIDGE

I had heard good things about the events thrown by Under Those Publishing. Normally, this was the kind of thing I'd find exciting. But after the week I'd had, all I wanted was to order takeout and melt into the couch until I passed out in front of the telly. Once again, I had committed to plans during an extroverted high, only to regret it when the day arrived.

Enzo worked in publishing—finance, nothing creative—but he always got an invitation to these events, with a plus-one.

Enzo was a lady's man. He loved entertaining girls, making them laugh, and most importantly, making them yell at him—he liked that a bit too much. That night was no different: him charming every woman in sight until one was mean enough to spark his interest.

When I stepped outside, I found him already waiting in the passenger seat of his own car.

"You're driving," he announced, making himself comfortable.

Traffic into London on a Friday night could stretch the drive to two and a half hours. Hopefully, most people were heading out, not in.

"We're stopping for food first," I warned, taking the turn toward my favorite spot.

I had already placed the order ahead for pickup.

"You read my mind. I'm starving," Enzo said, stretching dramatically.

I parked the car, jumped out, and sprinted inside. The place was packed, but our order was ready, waiting at the counter.

Back in the car, I shoved the bag into his hands. "Hold this." I handed him his drink and tossed mine into the cup holder. "Now, open one up and feed me like one of those mean girls you love so much."

He snorted, sipping from his straw. "Of course, baby girl. I saw the way your toes curled the last time I fed you."

That, in turn, made me burst out laughing.

"What flavors did you get?" Enzo asked, clearly pleased with himself.

"I got us both the same. Louisiana rub, Korean, and Brazilian. Now hand me a box before I drive you and your car into oncoming traffic."

We were in a rush if we wanted to make it by seven.

"Double Louisiana for sharing?"

"Uhmm."

"I'm in love with you, mate!" He handed me a box, grinning. "I don't even need a girl in the yard as long as I have you."

"Don't get hard for me." I took a bite, instantly in heaven. "Besides, you sling your dick around too much for my liking."

"And I'll be doing just that tonight."

"What kind of people actually go to these things? Is it all industry people? Maybe I can butter up the CEO."

"If you're into old white men, then by all means. I don't judge." He smirked, throwing up his hands in mock defense. "But, yeah, more or less book people. A lot of celebrities are invited but don't expect any to actually show. Then there's the in-house authors, a bunch of book bloggers, illustrators, critics. It's a big deal. You should count yourself lucky."

"What would I even be doing on a Friday night if I hadn't met you?"

"Rule of thumb if anyone asks, I'm loyal, emotionally intelligent, incredibly smart, trilingual—"

"Your Spanish doesn't count. No one understands you."

"You understand me!"

"Because I've spent a decade suffering under Argentinian rule with you and your whole family."

"And don't you love it?" He flashed a smug grin.

I did. He was my best friend. His brother was like a brother to me. His mother, my mother. We were family in every way that mattered.

"Lucky to be in your vicinity," I said, shaking my head.

He winked, stuffing another fry in his mouth.

We arrived just in time for one of their award-winning authors doing her opening remarks for the event. Enzo had downplayed the magnitude of this party. A bunch of famous authors were attending, doing panels, signing books, and generally mingling with the guests. A makeshift bookstore allowed book influencers to fill bags with free books. Books by BIPOC authors were especially highlighted during the event. There were arcade games, a short film screening, an open bar, and lots of snacks throughout the night.

I was introduced to some of Enzo's coworkers and their plus-ones. One in particular was stuck to me like a bug on a glue strip.

"You would get along with my daughter. She is also studying to become a teacher," she said.

"Isn't your daughter sixteen?" Enzo asked.

"Yes, Mia is sixteen, but you haven't met my oldest," the lady said, pulling up her phone. "Let me show you a picture. She is gorgeous."

While she was scrolling through her phone, Enzo leaned over, trying to get a peek. "Are you hiding her from me, Carrie?"

"Yes, I am Lorenzo—ah, here she is. This is Millie," Carrie said and turned her phone to me.

"Millie," I repeated after her. "She is lovely," I said, unsure of what else to say. I looked at the girl again. Millie was beautiful, but she had those crazy eyes, exactly the type of girl Enzo would go for.

"Carrie, love, why are you keeping this gem from me?"

"Oh, have a day off, will you." She smacked the back of her hand against his shoulder. "You know exactly why."

The small talk continued and my brain automatically turned itself off until Enzo dragged me to the bar, and the party took a turn.

The morning after, my head was pounding, which made me want to throw myself out of the nearest window just to make it stop. The blackout curtains keeping out any indication of what time it was. My mouth felt like sandpaper, my body sore like I had gone ten rounds in a boxing ring.

With a groan, I shifted under the covers, opened my eyes, and saw Enzo on the other bed, shirtless, one leg dangling off, face pressed into the pillow as if trying to smother himself. Even in his half-dead state, I could see the remnants of last night's cocky smirk. The party had been . . . a lot. Champagne, whiskey—something neon blue that probably shaved years off my life. We had stayed too late, drank too much, and by the time we realized it, driving wasn't an option.

I dragged myself out of bed, shuffling toward the tiny hotel bathroom for a quick shower before The International Conference on Psychology and Mental Health.

MAYA

I could find no good reason to put so much effort into my appearance when I wasn't interested in Sam to begin with.

It's good practice to go on dates, I kept telling myself.

That way, I would get used to the idea when it actually mattered.

I had to distract myself, distract my mind from wandering back, distract my mind from the cavity in my heart. It was a life that never existed.

I was determined to get my mental state back to normal, and dating gave me a sense of normalcy. I picked a black miniskirt and decided to pair it with a black turtleneck and black nylons. I hadn't picked out the shoes, but if Roya wasn't going to wear her knee-high boots, I would borrow them. It was cute enough for a casual night out and not too dressy.

The doorbell rang a couple of times before Roya got it, who was going out, too.

"Maya, your date is here!" she yelled.

What the hell! How the fuck is he here?

I had given Sam our address but not the unit number, which was why it surprised me. He was supposed to text me before he went out, so I had at least twenty minutes to get ready.

Roya peeked her head into my room. "What do I do with him?" she asked, her brows rising to her hairline. "You're not even ready yet! I have to go. I can't keep him company."

"He wasn't supposed to be here until eight. Let him wait in the living room and tell him I'll be there in a minute."

"You're wearing those under?" She gave my panties a look before I slipped on the skirt.

"I'm not hooking up with him. It's just a date."

"Whatever. Call me if you need anything."

Damn this guy, I hated rushing. Then my tights ripped, and I had to replace them. I hurriedly shoved my things into a purse and rushed out to greet him.

"I didn't know you'd be here so soon." I was still trying to zip my purse shut. "Sorry for keeping you waiting," I said and finally looked up at him.

My vision blurred, and my throat closed in on itself.

No. No. No. This is not real. He is not real.

I closed my eyes and counted.

One . . . two . . . three . . . four . . . Breathe out. This is not real. He's not real. He's not real. He's not real.

When I opened my eyes again, he was still standing there, saying something I couldn't make out. Of course I couldn't hear him.

He wasn't fucking real.

I can't breathe. This is not real. This is not real. This is not real.

With shaking hands, I covered my eyes, trying to make the hallucination go away. Yet he stood there, as alive and beautiful as anything on God's green Earth. A gust of wind carried his scent to me.

I can't do this again. He's not real. He's not real. He's not real.

I was supposed to be normal. The hallucinations were supposed to stop. I was supposed to do better. I was supposed to be normal.

ALDRIDGE

When I heard that Dr. Albert Peters was coming from America to present a case study on the intersection of dreams and reality, I knew I had to attend the conference. Perhaps it would give me the resolution I had been looking for the past two years.

"Good evening, everyone and thank you for joining me. What an event! Huh. Today, I'll be exploring a fascinating and complex case study that pushes the boundaries between dreams and waking life. This case presents a rare opportunity to examine how vivid dream phenomena intersect with psychological exploration. Let's dive in, shall we?" he paused and clicked to his next slide that read *Theories and Frameworks*.

"Our patient came to therapy, exhibiting symptoms that blurred the line between reality and dreams. She struggled to distinguish between the two, but more notably, she developed a profound emotional attachment to the dream world—one that lingered long after waking. The dream itself was a one-time occurrence, yet its aftermath altered her reality. Dream-like elements seeped into her waking consciousness, distorting her perception and memory in ways that defied conventional understanding."

The next slide appeared. *Neurological Hypnosis and Links to Stress and Trauma.*

"Irregular temporal lobe activity or disrupted REM sleep might explain vivid dream phenomena. Exploring these neurological factors could provide insight into the biological underpinnings of such experiences."

He launched into a long tangent about sleep disorders, unprocessed trauma, and subconscious coping mecha-nisms—nothing I hadn't already ruled out myself. But then something caught my attention.

A brain scan flashed onto the screen. The date stamped on it was two years old. Worse yet, he had forgotten to redact the personal data.

Tsk, tsk, tsk, GDPR.

I did a double take on the patient's name before my reality crashed and coiled around me like a cobra.

My name is Aldridge Andrés. I'm thirty-five years old. I live in Reading, and I'm a psychology teacher by trade.

I tried to steady myself while Dr. Albert Peters went on and on about therapeutic approaches until finally wrapping up.

"I'd love to hear your thoughts if you have encountered similar phenomena in your practice, studies, or personal life," he said.

The room had started emptying out. Only two stood with him, asking questions. He was very passionate about the case study and would gladly stand there talking about it for another hour. When the last two left and he started collecting his things from the desk, I took my chance.

"Doctor Peters, I was wondering if you would let me pick your brain for a couple of minutes. I have a similar patient that I'd like to discuss. You seem to have done a lot of research on the matter."

"Why, yes, of course."

"With my patient, the memories of these dreams are very sophisticated. He recalls events and places he has never been in great detail."

"Same with my patient. It was striking. The way she described her life in a dream had this—this almost cinematic quality to it. I remember thinking how surreal it all sounded, how the dream spanned over years before she woke up. Jung's archetypes came to mind, of course." He smiled.

"And what of family dynamics, friendships, career? Were those similar to her real life?"

"Yes, funny you should mention that. That was one of the main reasons why she had such a hard time differentiating between the two realities. Actually"—he took out a folder from his bag—"I wanted to give everyone a sample of my last observations with the patient but then I realized I hadn't redacted the personal information." He took out a sheet of paper from the folder and handed it to me. "It wouldn't have looked good on my part if I handed this out to seventy people, but one won't hurt. Just promise me not to leave it lying around in public. Not that I think immigrants are the suing kind, if you know what I mean." He patted me on the shoulder and chuckled.

Not the time to bite back.

"Thanks. That's very kind of you." I forced a smile.

I quickly glanced at the top where her personal information was registered. There was her name, age at the time and address, no phone number or email. The blatant disregard of breach of confidentiality and professional ethics was astonishing. Of course, I said nothing. All my own ethics went straight out of the window the moment I saw her name.

My name is Aldridge Andrés. I'm thirty-five years old. I live in Reading, and I'm a psychology teacher by trade.

One day, I had let her walk through a stone archway in Fort William. The next, I woke up in a different world.

I wasn't confusing reality with dreams.

My name is Aldridge Andrés. I'm thirty-five years old. I live in Reading, and I'm a psychology teacher by trade.

The irony wasn't lost on me. Given my deep psychological knowledge, I should have been able to describe my delirium, delusional diagnoses, existential OCD, or confusion. The options were endless, but when you had to put yourself in a box, it was far more difficult than doing it to others.

My name is Aldridge Andrés. I'm thirty-five years old. I live in Reading, and I'm a psychology teacher by trade.

I remembered living places I had never set foot in. I knew my way in and out of multiple cities, including New Orleans, even though this version of me had never been to the US. I had witnessed historical events you only hear about from the past four hundred years. Those memories weren't from my imagination or read in books—they were real, and I refused to accept anything else.

It was real for me.

My name is Aldridge Andrés. I'm thirty-five years old. I live in Reading, and I'm a psychology teacher by trade.

Only when I arrived home did I actually dare to read the notes. I looked over the page a thousand times, sobbing like a child.

I found her.

Patient Information:

Name: [Maya Salehi] Age: [28] Gender: [Female] Address: [700 Lenox Av. 21F, New York, NY 10039, USA]

Presentation: The patient appears at ease. Emotional state is calm. Some lingering confusion and anxiety remain evident when recounting the dream that brought along doubts of existentialism.

Key Topics Discussed: Patient recounts key points of dream:

A life fully lived from birth to death (drowning). Uncanny valley. Patient describes a life like she currently knows it but with magical elements:

An order of soul takers

A coven of witches

A prophecy

Soul ties and shared souls

Patient describes deep lingering emotional ties to an individual from a dream (Rés) and the guilt that follows. Nocturnal experience described as intensely vivid and immersive, leaving patient with emotional residues that had influenced the waking mood. Patient reports being unable to leave feelings behind of said individual whom she was emotionally tied to. Patient describe it as a 'soul contract'. There seems to be an ongoing inability to accept actual memories and said dream. This includes fleeting moments where dream-like elements appear during conscious activities (brief hallucinations).

Mild somatic symptoms: occasional headaches and fatigue, potentially linked to disrupted sleep patterns. The patient is convinced their brain is "defected."

Observations: Patient's narrative reflects elements of derealization but stops short of full dissociation; possibly existential OCD. The blending of dreams and reality could point to heightened stress or a neurological factor affecting perception. Reflections during recounting suggests a deep-seated need to understand and contextualize these experiences rather than immediate fear.

Hypotheses and Considerations: Sleep-Related Disorders. Potential REM sleep behavior disorder or other parasomnias. Possible sleep deprivation exacerbating vivid dreaming and cognitive confusion.

Stress and Trauma: Underlying stress or unprocessed trauma may be contributing to heightened dream activity and emotional residue.

Neurological Factors: Consider exploring the possibility of minor temporal lobe activity irregularities if symptoms persist or intensify.

I had made a decision, and it would either make or break me. My heart was hammering, and I was sure I had lost the ability to breathe. The feeling was worse than anything else I had ever experienced. The anticipation would kill me.

I knocked on 21F, and a random girl opened the door. Of course, it wasn't Maya, at least not my Maya.

So, you are Maya Salehi. Good for you.

I stood, numb in my spot.

I had traveled all the way to New York to find her, to prove to myself that it wasn't just a dream, that I wasn't crazy.

"Are you—does Maya l-live here?" I asked in a last attempt at killing my curiosity and closing a chapter.

I wasn't even sure if she heard me because it took her a while to respond.

"Oh, you're Sam! Of course. Hang on," she said, shouting in the other direction before I was able to correct her. "Maya, your date is here!"

This wasn't Maya, but she thought I was there to take her on a date.

Maya is going on a date. My Maya?

"Give me a sec, and I'll get her," she said and disappeared into the flat.

The door closed in my face with a soft click.

I didn't dare move. *Please, God, I will ask of nothing else.* I prayed. What I wouldn't do to just hold her and let oblivion take me.

The girl returned and opened the door, beckoning me inside. "She is not ready yet. You can wait for her inside."

Her smile was polite and didn't seem forced or like an act.

I was led into their living room, and she gestured for me to sit down. Without a word, she grabbed her coat from the back of the chair, slipped on her shoes, and walked out the front door, leaving me alone in the flat, potentially alone with Maya. The door clicked shut, and her footsteps receded.

My heart was caving in on itself. The room suddenly seemed too small, too cold. Its air thickened, pressing down on me, drowning me.

I closed my eyes and tried to steady my breath, but nothing worked. Everything was fragile, like the world might crack open any second. A Persian song hummed in the background—soft, melancholic, like a ghost trailing through the walls.

Five minutes later, a handle turned, and a door creaked open, slicing through the tension. I froze. The moment I had been waiting for was finally here. I rose from the couch, the room spinning as adrenaline flooded my system. She stepped into the hall, and everything stood still.

"I didn't know you'd be here so soon," she said, her voice too tight, too practiced. My heart dropped into my stomach. She was rummaging through her purse. "I'm sorry for keeping you waiting," she added, finally lifting her eyes to meet mine, but she wasn't looking at me. She was looking through me, like I was a shadow in her space someone she was only just now realizing she had to reckon with.

Her eyes widened with terror. An expression I wasn't prepared for. It wasn't just surprise, it was fear.

I swallowed hard. "I'm s-sorry," I said, my voice low and shaky. "I know you're expecting someone else. I promise, I'm not here to harm you . . . or cause any trouble."

The words were hollow, useless. Panic twisted her expression, and a sickening knot formed in my stomach.

I tried to hold it together, but when I saw her trembling, her body screaming to retreat, I couldn't stop myself. I took a step forward. Just one.

Her breath quickened, chest rising and falling in sharp gasps. It was like she was fighting something inside her, seemingly on the verge of breaking.

"This is a dream. He's not real. He's not real. He's not real," she whispered to herself.

Her words hit me like a punch to the gut.

"Maya, please." I took another cautious step.

When she opened her eyes again, she truly took me in.

"Can—do you remember?" *Me*, I wanted to add. "Maya . . ." I breathed, taking another step toward her. "Maya, please . . . look at me," I said, my voice barely a whisper.

She shook her head, tears streaming down her cheeks. "If only you were really here, Rés." She sobbed and put her face in her hands.

Rés! She called me Rés.

"It wasn't a dream. It was real for me."

I could barely get the words out, my own tears threatening to spill.

When she finally looked at me, I couldn't help but take her hand and place a kiss in the center of her palm. The moment our hands touched, she gasped.

Instinctively, I pulled her into my arms, unwilling to let go of her.

Never again.

I closed my eyes. "I can't believe you're finally in my arms," I breathed into her hair, my hold tightening around her.

"Your heart . . . I can feel it beating," she said, her hands trembling as they found their way to my face, fingers brushing lightly against my skin before sliding around my neck.

Within the warmth of her touch was an edge of urgency, as if she was trying to ground herself, to tether herself to something real. Her nails grazed the back of my head, the slight sting sending a shiver down my spine

"Everything about you, it feels so real. How is this possible?"

I wanted to give her the answer she was looking for, but I was at a loss for words and found myself frozen under her touch. I could only pull away enough to see her face, her tearstained cheeks. One by one, I kissed her tears, then finally, I placed one on her lips.

When she pulled away, I was afraid I had overstepped, but she just gazed at me.

"I don't care if this is another dream." Her words came out throaty. "I made a mistake, and I realized too late." She paused, cradling my cheek. "I love you, Rés. I love you so much, it hurts. It left me scarred." She buried her face in my chest. "I never told you and then I woke up regretting it every single day for the past two years."

I wasn't sure how I was still standing upright, but I cupped her face and pressed my lips to hers. "I love you." My words came out choked together with my tears. Three simple words that meant everything to me. "I'd go through it all again, every second of it, if it was the only way to have you. I would sacrifice my soul and still it would never be enough because I more than love you, demon blood." When I kissed her again, a smile crept up on her lips.

"Nosotros desde hoy y para siempre."

PLAYLIST

Gole Yakh – Kourosh Yaghmaei

Al Margen de Ojalá - Andrés Iwasaki

Pas Vraiment - Stromae

Disfruto - Carla Morrison

Paeez - Shadmehr Aghili

Yar - Faramarz Aslani, Babak Amini

Baddi Doub - Elissa

Viente años - Buena Vista Social Club

Nimeye Janam - Hamid Hiraad

Khosara - Abdel Halim Hafez

Konna Netlaka - Fairuz